EARTHCARE

A TALE OF ECOTERRORISM

BOOK 3 IN THE FIREBIRD SERIES

IAN DOLBY

DISCLAIMER:

This is a work of fiction. While names, characters, businesses, events and incidents are the products of the author's warped imagination, places and locales are as correct as possible, but are used in an entirely fictitious manner. Some characters are a composite of several personalities the author has encountered in his travels across Australia as such richness of true-life character could not be ignored. However, any resemblance to actual persons, living or dead, or actual events is unintended, accidental and purely coincidental.

The opinions expressed by the various characters in this story are deemed appropriate for their role and should not be assumed to be those of the author. I ride bikes and embrace the right to freedom of the open road on two wheels for everybody.

Published in Australia by Silverbird Publishing

First published in Australia 2019

This edition published 2021

Copyright © Ian Dolby 2019

Cover design, typesetting: WorkingType (www.workingtype.com.au)

The right of Ian Dolby to be identified as the Author of the Work has been asserted in accordance with the Copyright, Designs and Patents Act 1988.

Dolby, Ian

EarthCare — Book 3 of the Firebird Series

ISBN: 978-0-6487179-0-4

pp442

ABOUT THE AUTHOR

I was born and raised on the Gold Coast, Queensland where my extended family always had boats. My love of sailing came from this background and developed through a series of racing catamarans that in turn led to the purchase of an old 47-foot wooden, engineless, monohull yacht that had been built in Ireland in 1905 and had taken part in the Dunkirk evacuation. I lived on this boat at a marina in Rushcutters Bay, Sydney Harbour for several years and my engine-free adventures on this wonderful old boat may one day appear in writing.

The love of flying dragged me away from the boating scene, and after 38 years of Commercial glider, aeroplane and helicopter flying, I have retired to live in country New South Wales with my partner, who is my Chief Editor, and our two cats. While my writing has evolved from a part-time hobby to become a full-time occupation, it is no less enjoyable.

Thanks to Jenny who has given up on trying to feed me at designated times and now just goes with the flow, be it up or downhill.

Thanks to my beta readers for wanting more and making constructive comments.

Thank you Lyn, for taking on the sub-editor role. When we are too deep in the forest......sometimes we need a tree-spotter

The Bandit has left us — too soon.
11/17 to 06/19. RIP our furry friend. You came to us on a mission...Mission accomplished, but never forgotten!

CONTENTS

PROLOGUE

It was a time when the world was being shaken and stirred politically by mass refugee migrations in the Northern Hemisphere, and the US of A decided to elect an arrogant, wealthy businessman to run the country, instead of one of the 'good ole boys' and then wondered if it'd done the right thing. To add to this interesting mix of events, the world was being forced to become more environmentally conscious by a series of extreme weather events. The 'Lunatic Fringe' had a wonderful time getting attention like never before, by claiming 'I told you so', and the weather anomalies were solely caused by the hand of mankind, while totally ignoring records which proved beyond doubt that global temperature change was very much a cyclic event in which the hand of man, this time around, had a relatively small part to play.

Although geographically insulated from the worst of the political insanity taking place in the northern half of the globe, Australia proved it was perfectly capable of churning out a few of its own 'Lunatic Fringe-dwellers'; one of whom was a wealthy, smooth-talking and charismatic character called Terry Williams. It was Mr Williams who decided it was time for him to take his first step onto the 'Whacko's World Stage' by starting, of all things, an Eco-Terrorist movement although it certainly wasn't called that at the time. History doesn't record whether he truly believed the stuff he sprouted in a series of expensive nation-wide advertisements, but it probably doesn't matter since he was having such a wonderful time being the focus of an unhealthy amount of media attention.

He was so encouraged by the result of a few well-placed advertisements, he promptly engaged the services of a well-known and highly effective public relations consultant named Paula Henderson. She happened to be a striking-looking redhead with a reputation for fast living; leaving a growing string of bankrupt and mentally shattered, formerly-wealthy husbands in her wake, while her personal net worth rose like a fart in a bathtub!

In blissful ignorance of this facet of Miss Henderson's personality, the pussy-struck Mr Williams had her assemble a small team to handle and massage his public image, leaving Paula to massage the rest of him in private. Following his success at gaining attention with his rants about Climate Change, he decided the time was right to put the next stage of his plan into action – to make Australia and the world take notice of the almost irreversible damage to the fragile earth which he insisted was caused by mankind's endless thirst for fossil fuels.

He made his start with the dual help of his highly-paid PR crew, and a political party with both a warped and unrealistic view of environmental issues, and an un-stated desire to overthrow the freely-elected government.

They saw the wacky, but charismatic Mr Williams as a figurehead to their devious plans, and promised him a ready supply of virtually unlimited funding.

From this, odd political alliances were forged and personnel recruitment commenced, at the same time as construction work started on what was now privately called the EarthCare Movement headquarters. This was established on 450 remote hectares of scrubby forest no one wanted, right in the middle of a large tract of scrub to the southwest of Brisbane, where the nearest neighbour was five kilometres away. Despite the 'Green' connections, all concerned conveniently overlooked the environmentally irresponsible fact that bulldozers were allowed to level fully half of the tree and scrub covered property.

A small and highly competent office staff, complete with a financial section under the control of an accountant, handled the funding which poured in from a variety of highly questionable, but discrete sources. The office staff were supplied with the latest and most secure computers money could buy and were protected by the best security people available. These two sections were the paid, core group of the fledgling EarthCare Movement which took up residence in the so-called Bush Retreat in very comfortable, almost palatial quarters. To broaden the appeal of the movement and give it some mass-appeal legitimacy, the builders moved next to erect long, barrack-style huts meant to house the hordes of hopefully devoted, but largely un-washed and un-paid followers of the latest EarthCare Messiah.

The Retreat was also carefully set up so the PR, Security and Administrative staff were kept totally away from all contact with the recruits.

In a stroke of genius by the PR crew, the Retreat was initially promoted country-wide as a no-frills, bare-bones retreat for alcoholic and drug-dependant cop-outs, as well as a Meditation Retreat for those who believed they'd simply lost their way in the world and needed someone to push their 'factory reset' button.

The bare-bones section was in barrack-style buildings, complete with basic facilities and strict discipline, while the Meditation Retreat was in the main building complex, where inmates were cossetted in the lap of luxury at ridiculous amounts of money per day.

Miss Henderson, showing an undiscovered talent for radical rehabilitation, worked out the procedures, and supervised a growing band of young and very attractive male and female Personal Trainers for the meditation inmates, while a group of ex-military drill sergeants looked after the bare-bones, rehab crowd.

The families of the alcoholics and druggies were charged a fortune for their dearly-beloveds to be half-starved, harangued and physically abused by the ex-military guys and girls, and then exercised by the PTs until they dropped in their tracks.

That's when the massage therapists and dieticians took over and re-built the shattered husks into functional men and women again. Surprisingly, the cure rate soared under the harsh regime and as the word spread, requests for vacancies routinely exceeded the number of staff on hand to apply the strict regime (known to staff as the 'beat the shit out of them' treatment) to the little darlings. In consequence, the staff numbers grew rapidly, with quite a few also succumbing to the brain-washing bullshit of Terry's Save-the-Earth mantras.

Personally, Terry was totally dominated by Paula's forceful personality and quickly became utterly besotted with her lush, compliant body, as well as his own ego-fuelled image as the figurehead Messiah the PR crew had promoted so effectively. Being under Paula's control, and her body most nights, he allowed her to effectively run the operation as she saw fit, while his former dreams of requiring every attractive female recruit to submit to his barely-adequate sexual attentions faded like the morning mist.

This setback to his Cult Leader/Sex God dream, as Paula carefully explained one evening as they sat up in bed sipping NV pink champagne in after-sex bliss, was necessary because selected volunteers for EarthCare, were being quietly extracted from the stream of Rehabilitation and Lost Soul Meditation clients and sequested in their own barracks, well removed from the paying clients. It would be disruptive to their training and discipline to have a parade of nubile young things attending his bedroom every evening. Besides, he had Paula to look after his every need, including quite a few he didn't know he had, didn't he?

The ones selected to join EarthCare, had generally revealed during their treatment that they considered their usual environment to be shallow and worthless. So several times a week, with the aim of attracting a few more recruits across to the 'Dark Side', Terry was trotted out to give a rousing propaganda speech to the assembled paying clients. While most of them thought Terry was a whacko of the highest order, a steady percentage defected to the new Earth-Care Movement.

It was during their nightly bed sessions, that Paula revealed her hidden love of S&M, something Terry discovered he quite enjoyed as well, once he became used to being beaten with whips and straps, and it was perhaps because he was so quick to embrace the pleasure offered by her darker side, which led her to suggest they should ramp up the aims of the EarthCare movement while still on a roll.

'Besides,' she pointed out one evening, distractingly massaging his limpness back into some sort of usefulness again, 'it's no good having all these bright-eyed young things at our beck and call unless we actually *do* something with them! From a PR perspective, we need to give them a focal point to work towards, one that will create the personal signature of EarthCare on the world stage.'

Terry thought it was marvellous idea, but didn't have a clue what would constitute the most effective demonstration of the power of their new organisation. Coincidentally, the answer to that question was displayed in 30-point type as the headlines of a national newspaper next morning, which described a multi billion-dollar contract for selling natural gas to China from a new gas field discovery offshore of the Pilbara region of Western Australia. The plan popped into his mind during breakfast as they sat on the balcony of their luxurious penthouse perched above the sprawling mass of buildings that comprised the commercial part of the Retreat and off to one side, the separate collection of barracks-type buildings which were slowly filling up with EarthCare devotees.

Over the next few weeks, planning sessions with a few of the brightest and most dedicated staff members, along with a few recruits, carefully selected for their particular talents, developed a rough plan to seize and hold for ransom a natural gas processing and loading plant near Onslow in Western Australia. Due to the extreme remoteness of the area, it became obvious that a small, well-equipped strike base would have to be established close to the target to enable proper reconnaissance to be made and to launch the strike force at the appropriate time.

While the need for secrecy was paramount, human nature prevailed and pillow talk amongst the planning staff led to hints of the grand plan being overheard by a couple of paying rehab customers, one of whom happened to mention the vague notions to his wife on return to civilisation. In turn, while she was bragging to her latte-set friends, with many lewd and crude gestures, about the effectiveness of the cure on her previously alcoholic and impotent husband, she mentioned the organisation seemed to have another 'Dark Side' and whispered that everything to do with it was segregated and very much off-limits to the paying guests. That information drew gasps of delicious delight from her pea-brained friends.

Except for one who went to some lengths to conceal the fact that she had a very sharp mind indeed and who promptly made a call to a friend in an anonymous office building in Canberra.

That friend in turn passed the tip up her command chain until a senior staff meeting was called and the suggestion was made that an undercover team be placed on standby while details were worked out. After the meeting finished, the co-ordinator looked up an inter-departmental memo dated a few months ago, and placed a call to South East Queensland.

SOUTHPORT YACHT BASIN, TUESDAY

I was sitting in my favourite waterside pub at Mariners Cove having lunch, a couple of lovely beers and a general chat with my very dear friends, Corrine and Dave. Ellie, the bar manager wandered over to see if we wanted anything else and hung about for a minute or two to have a bit of a chinwag while the bar was quiet.

After she went back to serve a rowdy table of ladies who looked like they were celebrating someone's birthday and preparing to dig in for the afternoon, Corrine asked casually, 'What are you doing on Thursday, Harry?'

I should have been alerted by the glint in her eye, but replied, 'Well...since Sandy's working, I'll probably be here having another feed and a couple of beers. Why? What've you guys got cooked up?'

'Well, remember some time back we talked about maybe upgrading *Seeker* to a bigger model?'

I thought, 'Yeah. Vaguely, but bloody hell, that was eight or nine months ago. Not long after the last job. I didn't hear you talk about it again and presumed you'd dropped the idea. So, are you still thinking about it?'

She grinned excitedly, 'Yeah well, a bit more than think. We've actually gone ahead and done it! The new boat arrived in Brisbane last Friday shrink-wrapped in plastic and has been at the Smith & Sons Boatyard beside the Gateway Bridge, getting checked over and detailed ready for delivery. The Aussie agent is supervising the work, but Smith & Sons know what they're doing and delivery is all set for Thursday. How about you come to Brisbane and help us bring it back?'

She and Dave wore matching excited grins. 'I'm honoured, but you might have said something months ago.'

'What, and spoil the surprise! No way! It's much more fun watching your face!'

'Very droll Mouse, very droll! So you'd better tell me all about it before I poke you in the ribs or somewhere more tender! What is it?'

'We stayed with the AB Yachts brand and went with the 100-footer. We spoke to the Aussie agent at first, but he seemed like a real goose, so we ended up talking direct to the factory. The 100-footer is a new model to the line-up. They'd already started on a new hull for a customer, but he went broke suddenly and had to cancel. He lost his deposit, of course. They were in a bit of a mess because he'd specified some changes to normal specs which required them to change the construction a bit.'

'What'd they change?' I had to know.

'Mainly the engines. The standard fit out is three MAN V12s of 1900 horsepower each, the same engine which we have in the AB68. Anyway, this customer wanted more power so he asked for three MTU V-16s with 2600 horsepower each. It meant the engine bearers had to be strengthened and once that was done and the engines fitted, the order was cancelled and they were stuck with this hull nobody wanted.

Except when we said we'd take it, but only at a substantial discount, they left the forfeited deposit in the pot and we tipped money in from there. The other change we wanted was to remove the centre diesel and replace it with another TF50 gas turbine, the same as in the AB68.

That saved 3000kg immediately since the turbine is only 1000kg in weight, but outputs 5600 horsepower, more than twice the power of the diesel at 25% the weight. Before they started fitting the internals, we had them design and fit extra fuel tankage to look after the needs of the bigger engines, but we asked for even more, so they fitted tanks into empty places that would normally be flotation space. The tanks are Kevlar®-lined and built-in using the boat structure so they don't add much weight. When it's all added up, fuel capacity has been increased by 25%.'

'That's very handy, but what about the layout? There should be heaps more room on the thing, seeing it's 22 feet longer.'

'Yeah, there is a lot more room. We liked the standard layout and went with that since it gives us two extra cabins with twin bunks up for'rard as a second crew cabin and a second twin-bed guest cabin. The second guest queen cabin is bigger than the one on the 68. That makes two queens, one of which is for guests, two guest twins and two crew twin bunk set-ups in the forepeak, making 12 beds altogether. Then if the weather is good, there are six daybeds up topside on the sundeck and another two behind the cockpit.

There's normally a large foredeck lounge, but we asked them to scrap it, reasoning that if you want to catch some rays, there's the stern daybeds and the upper sundeck daybeds. That should be enough.'

'I suppose that saved some weight as well?'

'Yep, it did. And the factory put in a bunch of extra storage lockers, which is really handy. They were puzzled when we asked for a 6m^2 flat section to be moulded in with a fitted marine carpet surface, but we didn't say it was for our favourite UAV.'

'Sounds great! So what's the go for Thursday?'

'We've traded the 68 in with the Aussie agent and because of the enhancements we added, we got a really good price. He's taken a deposit on it already, so we took a lot of stuff, including the perimeter security system, ashore to a storage shed. We'll take the 68 to Brisbane on Thursday swap the safety gear across and bring the 100 back.'

'Have all the systems been tested?'

'Yep! The agent says that everything has been checked and is working perfectly. The factory has already run the engines for twenty hours without problem, just to bed them in a bit.

They also fitted all those hidden lockers for the guns and valuables and being Italian, they love the performance potential of the boat. Once the diesels have been bedded in a bit more, the factory asked us to do a series of performance tests. They want to send a couple of their tech guys out with a bunch of recording gear to see how the boat performs with this power set up.

They were talking about offering this power arrangement as a performance option only on this model because it handles the extra grunt so well.'

'Sounds brilliant and very exciting. Roll on Thursday!'

Which it did and at 06:30 on Thursday, Dave laid *Seeker's* sleek, pointy bow carefully up beside *Firebird's* cockpit so I could step across. I carried a small bag with a few essentials just in case. At that hour the wind was calm, so once clear of the 6-knot zone, the boat rode flat and smooth at 60-knots.

In just over an hour after leaving the Yacht Basin, we were directed by UHF radio into a vacant berth at the extensive facility on the south bank of the Brisbane River, almost in the shadow of the Gateway Bridge.

There was no mistaking the new *Seeker*. It towered over nearly all the other boats at the facility. With its royal blue hull, white boot topping and a white stripe just under the gunnel, it looked fantastic.

'Wow!' was my only comment, while Dave and Corrine were almost speechless. The AB Yachts agent was a fussy little fellow who fluffed around getting underfoot until a well-built fellow with a deep tan and a competent air about him strode down the wharf to greet the new owners.

The rest of the morning was a constant round of inspection, checking, testing and demonstrations of equipment. Safety gear was transferred from the old boat, as well as personal stuff. The RIB dinghy came as well and fairly rattled around inside the storage garage in the transom which was big enough to hold a couple of jet-skis as well. The accommodation deck was like a labyrinth with cabins tucked in everywhere, although inside each they were spacious and with tasteful furnishings.

The engine room had standing headroom and was a showpiece of spotless, white-painted engines and other machinery. It was hard to believe the engines had already been run for 20-hours; the floor was spotless. The 5600-horsepower turbine squatted between the two massive V16 diesels looking like a small generator rather than a power plant that had more power than both diesels combined. With the bulk of the centre diesel missing, the entire space looked light and airy, with everything within easy reach.

The second-last piece of business was to take the boat out for a test run before handing over the final payment. The yard manager did the honours of taking the boat out, handling it with casual competence. Every system was tried several times and everything worked perfectly, right down to the five water-jet toilets and the semi-automatic anchoring system which used an Australian designed and made anchor, weighing in at 130 kilos.

Then papers were signed, obscenely large bank transfers made and the keys symbolically handed over. The old boat was patted goodbye before we climbed aboard the new spanking new *Seeker*, fired up the engines and pulled in the mooring lines.

The day was mild, so Dave elected to drive from the open sun-deck steering station that made close-in manoeuvring so much easier by virtue of its height and lack of obstructions. He kept the speed down and the boat off the plane for the run down the river since there was a lot of traffic, but once we turned the corner of the massive container terminal, he eased the throttles open. It was almost effortless the way the big boat lifted half of it's hull out of the water and onto the plane as the speed rose to stabilise at 35 knots. Dave experimented with the steering and was delighted with the responsiveness and lack of any sort of sensitivity. It just went where he pointed it, sitting level and slicing easily through the small swell. We all commented on the total lack of vibration that made the ride quite eerie, particularly sitting on the top sundeck where there was very little engine noise.

We took turns steering and playing with the throttles and I found it a pleasure and quite effortless to drive. So much so, that it was with a feeling of regret when we entered the 6-knot zone approaching the Yacht Club basin and *Seeker's* new home. Being larger, the new boat required an outside berth, but the shallow draft at 1.3 metres allowed a greater choice, although the new berth had been arranged months earlier.

By the time Sandy came home from work, Dave and Corrine had moved most of the stuff that had been temporarily stored ashore back aboard, and were serving celebratory cocktails on the upper sundeck.

It must have been a good party because our path back to *Firebird* in the dinghy later that night wasn't straight, although we managed to have a delightful romp before falling asleep.

CHAPTER 2

At 09:00 sharp on a very pleasant July morning, the taxi deposited me outside a beautiful old Queenslander house set in the middle of a street of old houses, most of them resting quietly in the shade of several huge Moreton Bay fig trees. Although the trees cost the homeowners a lot each year in extra maintenance, everybody was secretly very proud of their ancient trees, most of which were planted in the 19th Century.

I was due for my bi-annual investment review with my accountant, Mike Adams, a very switched-on and charming fellow who operated out of a couple of rooms at the front of his house which was complete with wide verandas on all sides, creaky polished floorboards and high ceilings. It was divided into four by two hallways that ran front-to-rear and side-to-side to make the most of any cooling breeze. He'd had air-conditioning discretely fitted to cope with the few months when the Gold Coast rivals the tropics in uncomfortably high humidity levels, but he avoided using it whenever possible. He and his lovely girlfriend Eva, who was also the receptionist, lived a life of quiet comfort in the old Queenslander and there wasn't much of a traffic problem getting to work.

His standard office uniform of board shorts, sandals and a Jimmy Buffett parrot shirt, might have turned some customers away, but that was just a front for a razor-sharp mind which effortlessly negotiated the minefield of Australian Taxation laws and helped to legally save his clients un-necessary tax payouts. In my case, he also dispensed invaluable investment advice and had become a close friend. I'd often taken him and Eva sailing on my 60-foot sailing catamaran, *Firebird*, which is my floating home.

Business concluded, I was sitting out on the wide front veranda waiting for the much-delayed taxi Eva had called for me, when my mobile phone rang and I grinned when I saw the caller's name.

'Hi Greg. Long time no hear. How's things going with Southport's finest this lovely day?'

'Gidday Harry. Things have been going pretty well until a call from the Commissioner this morning really stirred the pot, and has led to the boss and me needing to have a chat with you fairly urgently. Are you able to come over here? Sandy will be in on the conference as well.'

'Yeah, sure old mate. I'm on-shore at the moment and just finished with my accountant, so as soon as the taxi arrives, if it ever does, I'll come straight there. Will that do?'

'We can do better than that. Cancel the cab, give me the address and I'll have a patrol car there shortly.'

'Oh. It's like that, is it?'

'Yeah, it could be, so if you can oblige, that'd be great.'

'OK, mate. Send the car, but I won't be dressed up for the occasion.'

'So long as your dick isn't hanging out in the breeze, you'll be fine! See you shortly.'

By the time I'd dug out my mobile and cancelled the cab, it was only a couple of minutes before a marked police car with lights flashing pulled up out front. I could almost hear the little old ladies sitting in their front parlours pulling the lace curtains aside to peer out, 'tut-tutting' over the shame of having a business enterprise in their street attracting such a vulgar display of officialdom. The female driver, a neat, trim and attractive Senior Constable got out as I approached and came around to greet me.

'Commander Stevens? I'm Tracy Manning. I delivered Inspector Thomson and two Constables to Brisbane Airport a few months ago in connection with the bikie operation you were on and your name came up several times. It's a pleasure to finally meet you after hearing some of the details of the operation.'

I blinked at the torrent of information as I shook hands,

appreciating her firm grip and noting her amused appraisal of my clean, but paint-stained shorts, T-shirt and hastily slipped on boat shoes, sans socks.

'Very good to meet you too, Senior. Inspector Thomson mentioned you were very keen to get in on that case.'

Senior Manning smiled as she opened the front door for me, 'I did and still do Sir. I'm keen to be involved in some real action and from what I hear, trouble seems to follow you around. No offence intended, Sir. And please forgive me if I seem a bit pushy.'

I chuckled at her discomfort. 'No problem Senior, I appreciate honesty so I'll keep your offer in mind.'

'Thank you Sir, but now we'd better get moving. The whole Station is in turmoil this morning and Superintendent Casey would have liked you there an hour ago!'

So move we did, although it wasn't far to the Southport Station in a marked police car with the light bar flashing out its familiar pattern—thankfully the siren was left off.

Senior Manning stayed with the car, but wished me well and reminded me again that she was ready, willing and very able to take on any task. I smiled to myself, thinking that only in the Police Service would there be so many young men and women falling over themselves trying to get involved in the sort of mayhem which seemed to land in my lap on such a regular basis. Still, I hadn't lost anyone under my command since returning from the Middle East desert and that was a real blessing.

The Sergeant on the front desk knew me, so he just buzzed the internal door open with a cheery wave, but I was soon bailed up by a pair of young constables who weren't about to let a scruffy-looking bloke dressed like a boat-bum go wandering around the halls of power unchallenged.

'May we help you, Sir?' one asked.

'Yeah, you can,' I replied with a lop-sided grin. 'I'm just looking for Bob Casey's office.'

'Yessir. Is Superintendent Casey expecting you?'

'Yeah, he is. He called me in, so if you wouldn't mind pointing the way, I'll join him.'

'Follow me Sir; I'll show you the way.'

So I dutifully followed his tall frame along corridors and up the broad staircase that led to the Senior Officer's area and Conference Rooms. He knocked at the door of a corner office and announced, 'A gentleman to see you Sir.'

'Harry! Great to see you again! Please come in, come on in.' Bob Casey cried out with pleasure, jumping up from behind his desk and charging around it to pump my hand enthusiastically. 'Thank you Constable, but Commander Stevens is an old friend and is expected.'

The Constable's eyes widened at that mention of my rank, which I rarely use, but which sometimes comes in handy, and with a wry smile he disappeared back downstairs.

Bob smiled a little apologetically. 'The boys can get a bit over protective at times. Especially when they see disreputable-looking characters lurking in the corridors.'

I grinned back, as Bob rarely comes up with a joke, 'Here! Steady on with the 'lurking' tag. It's my job to look disreputable, but I definitely don't do the 'lurk' bit!'

He chuckled and ushered me through a door into an adjoining conference room with a large table in the centre, six chairs around it and a tray of tea and coffee makings and a large plate of gooey Danish pastries waiting. Going to the outside door, he stuck his head out and as was his habit, used his voice instead of the phone system to summon persons.

'Greg! Get your arse in the conference room. Harry is here. And bring Sandy too, please.'

There was a unintelligible yell from somewhere nearby before a medium height, brown-haired man in a grey suit minus the jacket appeared, moving as though his muscles and joints were very stiff. A tall, well-built and very attractive woman with glorious, glowing shoulder-length auburn hair closely followed him. She was dressed more casually with her shirt pulled delightfully tight across her ample chest but hanging loose outside her equally tight jeans. The fact that she was my live-aboard girlfriend and had shared two previous operations unscathed didn't stop me giving her a second look.

Greg shook my hand as he headed for the coffee pot while Sandy trailed her hand across my bum in passing as she headed for the table and took a chair. Bob and I joined them and he immediately kicked the meeting into gear.

'Thanks for coming in, Harry. This is what started things happening this morning.' He floated a sheet of paper across to me, so I had a quick read.

'Bloody hell!' I exclaimed. 'That's quite a target if the tip is correct. Taking over an oil and gas processing plant isn't messing around. But who or what the hell is EarthCare?'

Bob replied, 'They seem to have started as a retreat for alcoholic and drug dependant folks to dry out, as well as a place for the meditation bunch to go commune with nature and polish their aura or some other part of their anatomy. They've got 450-hectares of scrubby bush out past Beaudesert. Nice area from what we can see, and nothing underhand so far except that the bloke in charge, Terry Williams, seems to have a lot more money at his disposal than he could ever have accumulated as a minor industrialist with his own engineering business.

The financing behind him has raised some interest, especially now that this EarthCare mob may be flexing their muscles. There's been some very slick advertising and PR work done to promote both the retreat and Mr Williams personally as the guiding light for EarthCare, and that seems to be the work of a high-profile PR consultant, Paula Henderson.'

'So this email seems to have come from our own homegrown spooks that picked it up from some idle gossip. I wonder why my mob hasn't been involved.'

'You'd probably better ask them mate, since this other email came in shortly after.'

He slid another piece of paper across the table for Sandy and me to read.

'Bloody hell! No wonder the Commissioner's got his panties in a wad. His little scheme of creating the Special Marine Strike Force has paid off big time. I didn't think we'd hear any more about it. So, as of now, our little group has been officially re-activated!'

'Yes, you have been and what's more, ASIO, us and the Western Australian Police Force all want the SMSF to officially, but covertly handle the operation.'

I looked sceptical, 'what operation Bob? We've got nothing to operate on or with.'

He positively beamed, 'Ah, but that's not quite right. The Commissioner spoke to me at length this morning and to say he's excited would be an understatement. Anyway, he's tasked us initially to simply find out more about what this mob's up to, and what's behind the hint of a threat ASIO picked up. You're to answer straight back to Greg and me and I'll dial the Commissioner in from there. He wants this kept deep undercover with the fewest persons possible in the loop.'

I sat back and pasted my trademark cheesy smart-arse grin on my face, despite an elbow to my ribs from Sandy. 'Oh well, if that's all we have to do, we can wrap this by lunch-time and go have a few beers at the Yacht Club.'

Naturally, that earned me a glare from Bob, who's generally a bit strait-laced and doesn't take my peculiar brand of sarcasm very well.

Greg chipped in with, 'You're being a smart-arse Harry and as Operation Co-ordinator, I'm ordering lunch in for all of us. We'll be here until we come up with a plan to kick-start the first stage of this operation. We need to get a handle on what these people are up to before we can decide what to do about it.'

I nodded ruefully at him and Bob. 'Yeah. Sorry guys. It's just that people like the Commissioner love to fire off all these bright ideas, in the hope we'll stick our fool heads above the trench line yet again, to see if some bad guys are going to shoot back! Sounds more like my mob should be handling the whole thing.'

Greg stood, 'I can't disagree with you, old mate, except this has to stay deep undercover, so that's why the small and low profile SMSF got poll position. Anyway, for now, let's take a pee break, have some tea or coffee, then get our minds working to churn out a plan. That's your strong point as I remember Harry. So let's do it again please. We've been given all the resources we could want; money, equipment, anything we think we need, even up to full co-operation from the Australian Military if we want; so we have to be able to do something positive with all that!'

We all stood, and I nodded absently, my mind already working on the problem. Sandy knew the pre-occupied look on my dial as she pushed me toward the door.

'Go have a pee and take some pressure off your brain.'

'Nah, don't need to yet. You go and I'll just think a bit more.'

She shrugged and sat down again, while I stared out the window at the Broadwater glittering in the distance over the rooftops of downtown Southport, my mind churning over possibilities.

When I turned around with the basis of a plan in mind, I was surprised to see that not only had the others returned, but going by the half-empty plates of sandwiches and empty cups of tea and coffee, had been back for some time. I took my seat as Sandy pushed a plate of my favourite sandwiches in front of me along with a mug of tea.

'Here. Eat and drink, then tell us the plan,' she said with a twinkle in her eye.

So I ate and drank, letting that little kernel of a plan slowly take on some more substance.

Finally my silence got to Greg. 'OK Harry, that's enough feeding your face for a few moments. Can you give us some idea of what you're thinking?'

I finished chewing, washed it down with a sip of hot, sweet tea and said, 'Sorry about that, I just had a train of thought and needed to follow it. So, let's break the problem down and look at solutions for each step.'

I stood up since I seem to think much clearer on my feet; must be the ex-military Major thing, and with the white board in front of me, started the planning session.

'We need intelligence before we can make any further plans, so I suggest we focus all our efforts for now on getting that intelligence as quickly as possible.'

I looked at Bob and Greg, 'Do we have anybody on the inside with this mob?'

Both shook their heads, although Bob volunteered an answer of sorts. 'No real idea on that one. ASIO might, but it's very doubtful since EarthCare is so new and hasn't stirred trouble yet, there's not been any need to try an infiltration.'

I nodded, 'OK. But with this rather vague tip off, that's what we must do first up. Get someone inside.' I looked at Bob and Greg again. 'Do we know how they're recruiting for EarthCare?'

Bob nodded, 'Yeah. That came through this morning, verbally, after the emails. It seems they take volunteers from the paying customers at the Retreat for the EarthCare side of the setup. It means they've already been vetted to an extent, then they find out through normal conversation and at therapy sessions, which ones don't like the way the earth is being treated, or any other tree-hugger type sentiments. That's when Miss PR, Paula Henderson, gets a few together and rolls out Terry 'The Guru' Williams to charm them into thinking the best thing they could do in order to fix the world, is join EarthCare as a volunteer where they'll be fed, housed and get to take part in some revolutionary, earth-protecting activities.'

I gave an excited grin, 'Excellent! That's what I was hoping to hear. We need to choose someone to be a plausibly tormented soul and enrol in the meditation program. That would be the fastest way to get into the system, then make the appropriate comments about planet abuse and wait to be indoctrinated.'

That earned nods of agreement from the other three, so I went on, 'So, who's going to be the lucky boy or girl to earn a free holiday in Club Eco?'

Sandy spoke up, as it seemed that neither Bob not Greg were going to.

'I think it should be a female. She might have a bit of an edge in a mostly male domain, and I'll suggest Melissa. She's got the lowest profile of any of the team, although thinking it through a bit more, I suppose Corrine might be even better since she's got a genuine skill-set which would really appeal to a fledgling eco-terrorist organisation. If she has a strong whinge about pollution, then another about being an 'un-appreciated Afghanistan veteran', it might be enough for them to swing her across to the 'Dark Side'.'

She looked around expectantly to gauge our reactions.

I thought about it for a moment, couldn't see any downside apart from putting Corrine in harm's way yet again. 'Yeah. You're right. She would be the best for the job. And when it's time to launch a strike at them, she'd be the one I'd want on the inside quietly taking out the leaders.'

There was general agreement between the other three, so we decided to call in Corrine and Dave, two of the other members of the Special Marine Strike Force.

Greg called the radio room and had Senior Constable Tracy Manning diverted from patrol duties again to head for the Yacht Club tasked to pick up two civilians, male and female; ID required.

I pricked my ears up when I heard her name mentioned.

'I was quite impressed by her attitude when she picked me up this morning,' I commented to Greg when he hung up, 'and I remembered Sandy was too, during the last operation. She seems very keen to get into some action.'

Greg looked at me carefully, 'Yeah, she is keen. She's not long off the SERT course too, although as with several other officers, including those two you pinched off me last operation, we don't have any emergencies for them to get some real action training. But just get rid of that gleam in your eye, Harry. You're not going to pinch yet another of my best-trained officers to go swanning around on the high seas in that floating harem of yours. No way! Uh uh! Forget it!'

I laughed at his indignation, knowing if I really decided I needed Senior Manning, or anybody else for that matter, I would get my way.

Sandy made the call to Dave and Corrine, and found them just getting ready to go out to a late lunch, so she suggested they might like to visit the Southport Police Station instead, and if they were lucky, I would have left them some sandwiches.

'I might add,' she finished up, 'there should be a Police car out front in about two minutes to pick you up. The driver will be Senior Constable Tracy Manning and she'll want to check your ID.'

'*This sounds like official work to me,*' Corrine said, suddenly excited.

'Yeah it is,' was Sandy's short reply. 'See you soon.'

CHAPTER 3

So Corrine and Dave hustled and as promised, a marked police car was waiting out front of the yacht club with the engine running but thankfully, lights off. The Club Secretary, a fussy, but highly competent little man, was flapping around in the foyer, trying not to show how agitated he was about such a display of officialdom but concerned for the well-being of two of his best paying customers.

'Everything's OK, Mr Gentry. The police want our help with a minor crime we witnessed yesterday. Nothing important.'

Slightly mollified, Mr Gentry stopped flapping and just stared mournfully at the brightly decorated police car and the uniformed female Senior Constable who climbed out to greet her passengers. After the ID checks, they were on their way to the Southport Police Station.

'I don't suppose you know what this is all about?' Corrine asked the driver.

'No Ma'am I don't, except the station has been in a bit of an uproar since the Boss got in early this morning.' That reply ensured that the rest of the short ride was in silence.

When Dave and Corrine were escorted into the conference room by Senior Manning, Bob and Greg stood, Bob welcoming them effusively, since he does like to carry on a bit with the ladies.

'Great to see you again and looking so well after the last operation! That must have been quite harrowing for you.'

Corrine grinned at him, knowing what the old bugger was like. 'Oh, I don't know sir. We only had to kill five bad guys close up. Harry had most of the dirty work.'

Then she brightened up considerably, 'But we did get to blow that boat up; the one with all the bad guys in it. That was great fun!'

Bob visibly winced at her enthusiasm, but gamely came back with, 'Excellent my dear, excellent. And a very good job it was too. Now, please be seated and have some tea or coffee. I notice Inspector Thomson has managed to steal some sandwiches for you from the clutches of Commander Stevens.'

They smiled in appreciation and took two seats, Bob staying on his feet. He looked seriously at Corrine and said, 'The SMSF has been activated as of now, and we have a mission which will be explained fully in just a few moments, but we are going to need you to volunteer to go undercover and infiltrate an organisation. I'll stop there and let Greg brief you on the general situation that has caused the Commissioner to activate the SMSF, then Harry will explain his plan and your part in it.'

Dave and Corrine nodded without comment and then got stuck into the sandwiches and coffee, while Greg made a brief summary of what they knew so far and how the info had been picked up.

I then outlined my simple plan to infiltrate EarthCare via the Meditation Retreat.

I grinned at the girl I'd once rescued under fire and my dear friend, 'Your mission, should you choose to accept it, will be to phone the Meditation Retreat and try to get a booking for a one or two week stay, saying you desperately feel the need to get back in touch with the Earth and Nature and cleanse your inner self from too much bad karma or some such shit.

Don't go overboard with too much up front – let them ask. The good part is that you don't have to do much pretending in this role, in fact, you can virtually be yourself. Naturally leave out all mention of what you've done since the end of the Victorian operation but you should hint strongly at doing all manner of dark and dirty deeds while in the employ of a currently-locked-up bad guy. As much as possible, play up your SAS background and being such an unappreciated veteran.

If they are as efficient as I suspect, they'll do a background check and find everything is straight and you could be just the sort of lethal weapon who would suit the dark side of their operations.'

I stopped to let that information sink in, until Corrine looked at Dave briefly and nodded thoughtfully.

'Yep. That's not a bad plan and cover story. I must say it's so close to the truth they'll not find anything suspicious and if they ask what I've been doing lately, I'll tell the truth and say that after Xavier got locked up, we bought the boat and lived on it, did some charters before deciding to move to the Gold Coast for the winter and maybe permanently.'

'What if they ask about your financial background?' Sandy asked, playing Devil's advocate. 'Buying, then living on a large, flash boat at the Yacht Club Marina isn't low-rent existence.'

Corrine smiled, 'No problem. I just refer back to my previous employment and suggest certain aspects of it were extremely lucrative, especially the more illegal they were. That should convince them I'm totally immoral, deadly and therefore vital to their enterprise.'

That earned a general laugh around the table, although I noticed Bob winced again as he realised that Corrine was underselling the truth. She was far more capable, deadly and ruthless than anybody that he, or I for that matter, had ever met.

Bob took the floor again. 'So, you're happy to take on the role?'

Corrine grinned, 'Oh, sure. It sounds like fun. Loafing around in the sun being a millionairess can get boring at times, you know Bob.'

Bob pulled a face; being just a working stiff with the usual large mortgage which kept him watching his finances very carefully, he wasn't used to the carefree attitudes toward money that the truly, excessively financially secure so often unconsciously display.

'Unfortunately, Miss Johns, I don't have that knowledge, so I'll take your word for it and thank you for accepting the mission. Greg will be the Operation Co-ordinator, but Harry will be the first point of contact, so make all reports through him. I'll leave it up to Greg, Harry and yourself to work out the finer details, but we'd like you infiltrated ASAP.'

She nodded seriously, 'Understood, Sir. We'll get on it right away.'

'Very good. I'll leave you to it then and thank you for taking this on.' He headed back into his office, leaving Greg to take over the meeting.

'Righto Harry, what's your plan?'

'Pretty much like I said to Bob. Mouse should make immediate application to the Meditation Centre for a two-week stay as they'll get to know you better.'

I smiled at her, 'You'll need to play a lot of this by ear; just take every opportunity to let the right people know that you really hate what's being done to the planet and wish there was some way to stop it. Criticise the petroleum industry in particular for being money-hungry opportunists. That always starts an argument!'

Corrine laughed as I went on. 'I don't know what sort of approach will be made, or what else you might have to do to either earn their trust or get on the right side of whoever's doing the recruiting, but that's what you're there for. To do whatever is necessary to find out what's really going on, what's planned and who's behind it! Oh, and try really hard not to get caught out of character. I have the feeling these turkeys could be very dangerous.'

Everybody nodded seriously at that one, but just as we were about to break up to go do our various things, Sandy piped up.

'I'm sorry! I forgot to tell you all that I just received an email from our old mate Ian, the UAV designer who made *Dragonfly*, which we used on the last operation. He received so many good comments and requests from various Agencies who all want their own *Dragonfly*, he's decided to go into limited production. But first, he's made a few modifications based on the feedback we gave him after the bikie op and wants us to test it again before he locks the design in. He's sent one to us and hopefully, it should be downstairs in the Armoury. I'll check when I'm back in my office, but if we have to go anywhere, a *Dragonfly* will be a real asset!'

I grinned at her enthusiasm; for both the designer and his amazingly effective product, a fully autonomous, hybrid VTOL UAV with 8-hour endurance, real-time stabilised HD video links, two-way satellite feed and stealthy characteristics.

We broke up soon after; Corrine and Dave heading back to the boat for Corrine to pack and try to get a booking at the Meditation Centre; Sandy to contact the other members of the team, Sergeant Amanda Burke, Senior Constable Melissa Briggs, Senior Constable Alf Story and Senior Constable Charlie Jakes, appraise them of the developing situation and prepare them for action if needed.

I waited until the others had left so I could tackle Greg on what was a sensitive subject for him.

Without wasting time, I got to the point. 'Mate, I'm going to be a crewmember down if Corrine gets integrated into EarthCare and we're too small a group to soak that up, so I need a replacement for Corrine.'

He started to burr up, but then took a deep breath and calmed down. 'Yeah, you're right. I can't argue with you, except I'll bet you want to pinch Tracy Manning, don't you?'

I nodded ruefully, 'Yep. She's the one. She's keen and from what I've seen so far, I reckon she'll fit right in. Also, in case we have to move quickly on this operation, I'll need her immediately for training and familiarisation with our methods and for being on boats in general. If you could arrange her temporary re-assignment to the SMSF, I'd appreciate it, my friend.'

Greg shook his head in disgust. 'Bloody shame! Another good senior constable corrupted. At this rate, you'll have worked your way through the entire station by the end of the year!'

I grinned at his theatrical performance. 'It's not my fault you and Bob staff this place with the best of the brightest young graduates coming through the Academy each year.'

He threw his hands up in surrender. 'OK Harry, she's yours, but please let me have her back afterwards and preferably in the same mint condition she's in now.'

'Thanks mate. I'll leave you to get on with stuff and I'll try to chase her down.'

Greg grinned for a change. 'You're right about her being keen, so I think you'll find she's somewhere downstairs, hanging around in case you need a lift somewhere. Try the lunchroom.'

Before heading down, I stuck my head around the doorframe of Sandy's office, interrupting her as she ploughed through a pile of reports which were the constant nuisance to all senior officers.

'Hey, my lovely lady!'

She looked up and grinned, 'Hey yourself, big fella.'

'I've been thinking that since we're going to need another crew member to fill in for Mouse while she's gone, I was going to ask Tracy Manning to join us. What do you think, and do you know much about her?'

Sandy thought a moment. 'She's a good choice from the little I know of her. She's got a reputation for being a hard worker and is very driven to succeed. That's pissed a lot of people off, but it doesn't seem to worry her. She recently completed the SERT qualification course and even graduated which is almost unheard of for a female!'

As I nodded, Sandy grinned, 'Are you sure you don't want another guy? We wouldn't want to be too top heavy with females.'

I grinned back, 'No. I think the mix is pretty good with Dave, Alf and Charlie on *Seeker*.'

Sandy nodded resignedly; 'OK, but where's she going to stay? The word from that eternal font of wisdom and truth, the Girl's Room, is that off-duty, she enjoys playing up quite a bit, but she's very discreet. Definitely no drugs and she's a non-smoker, but likes a few drinks.'

I grinned back, 'Sounds like she'll fit in with us just fine. But on the official side, she can be in your chain of command and I've asked Greg to transfer her to us immediately for on-the-spot training and boat familiarisation.

But to answer your question, I thought she would take the port aft cabin. When Amanda and Melissa join, Melissa can go bunk on

Seeker with Charlie in the queen cabin. That is if she and Charlie are still an item? Then Alf can have one of the twin cabins. With the size of those palatial suites on that overgrown Italian phallic symbol, nobody will be cramped for space and the crews will be balanced in numbers. Tracy needs a bit of time to get up to speed on shipboard routine on *Firebird*, but that'll happen in due course.'

Sandy smiled at my obvious enthusiasm as she cryptically replied, 'Well, she should make an interesting addition!'

As she made no other objections or suggestions, I nodded and left her to the stack of reports, while I went to chat up, or otherwise officially brief, what I hoped would be our newest crewmember.

CHAPTER 4

It took a bit of searching, but when I finally found the lunchroom, Greg was right; Tracy was there, wading into a large salad roll with a mug of tea to wash it down.

She jumped to her feet as I wandered in, to the surprise of several other Officers having a late lunch, who wondered who the hell this scruffy-looking individual in paint-stained shorts, sock-less slip-on's and oil-stained shirt was, so I hastily waved her down.

'No need for that, thanks senior. But if you wouldn't mind, I'd like a private chat, so if you'd come with me and please bring your lunch.'

'Certainly Commander,' she said, licking a tiny smear of mayo off the corner of her mouth with the tip of her tongue, before hastily gathering up her half-eaten roll and mug of tea. I noted that her use of my unusual rank killed the conversation and attracted more attention from the other occupants than did my scruffy clothes, while several backs subtly stiffened. I led her back upstairs to the conference room we'd just vacated, the remnants of our working lunch still on the table.

'Get comfortable, please senior and resume your lunch. I have a bit of a tale to tell.'

Although I'd met her that morning, I took the opportunity to study her afresh while she settled, calmly meeting my scrutiny with her frank, open gaze. She had strong, attractive features and was tall, about Sandy's height. Her dark blonde hair was quite a bit longer than regulation length and she'd moved like a gymnast when I'd followed her into the room, with a slim, toned body and small breasts.

Her return scrutiny was just as penetrating and I was

uncomfortably aware that I didn't present a very professional image to a new work colleague.

In short order, I laid out the developing situation and my plan to gain some vital intelligence, before trying to plan further action. Senior Manning took all my briefing in, considered it for a few moments then, getting straight to the bottom line said, 'That sounds fascinating Sir and should be a very interesting operation, but I have to ask, what's this to do with me? I mean, why are you telling me all this?'

I gave her one of my looks, not the 'pissed-off Commander' one, but one not far short of it. At least she was perceptive enough to look a bit abashed and resumed an attack on the remnants of her roll.

'The reason you're being briefed in on this, Senior Manning, is that I'm offering you the opportunity to join the SMSF as a volunteer, since we'll be one crewmember short with Miss Johns playing undercover agent among the rich and witless and you have already expressed a strong interest in joining us.'

Finally, that grabbed her attention, as her eyes snapped wide open and she seemed at a loss for words for a moment.

'Ahh...that's absolutely fantastic Sir. I'm not sure what I've done to deserve this opportunity, but I'll accept immediately, even though I don't know what I'm joining. I mean, what's the SMSF? I've heard the acronym mentioned unofficially, but don't know what it stands for.'

I smiled at her re-kindled enthusiasm, but berated myself for delivering an incomplete briefing, something that in my former life would have earned the offending officer a severe tongue-lashing.

'Thanks for volunteering senior, and you are officially accepted into the unit, but I must apologise for not briefing you fully, since you don't have any background to our previous operations.'

I had a quiet chuckle while she looked on impassively, 'I guess our security has been better than I expected if the 'Ladies Room' grapevine hasn't spread the word about the SMSF.'

She raised an eyebrow, a neat trick I'd yet to learn, 'Oh, I didn't say that there weren't any rumours floating around, Sir. It's just that no one has a clue what SMSF means.'

'OK. My bad. SMSF is the Commissioner's pet project, and one that has been kept under very tight security, until now. It stands for the Special Marine Strike Force and came into being due to the success of the last two operations with which I've been involved. It's tasked with undercover operations where, for political reasons, the police are unable to act in a pro-active official manner, even with SERT. When handed a case, SMSF gathers intelligence on bad-guy activities and attempts to stop those activities from developing any further. That's where the pro-active, get-our-hands-dirty bit kicks in.'

I paused to see how she was taking this in and was rewarded by her rapt attention, so I took a sip from my mug of fresh Earl Grey before resuming.

'It's a small group of eight which includes two civilians, although one of those is ex-SAS and would be the match of any two regular officers. All five current Queensland Police Officers are volunteers and four have done the SERT training, as you have I believe.'

Senior Manning nodded. 'Yessir, I completed the course just a fortnight ago.'

'Excellent. And your firearms qualifications?'

'As I gained during SERT training sir. I believe that rates me expert in all forms of the Service's normal and special weapons.'

I nodded, my mind scrambling to remember the arduous training that candidates had to go through, and that of just five females who had been through the course, one was now in SMSF.

'May I ask about the nature of the past two operations that brought about the formation of SMSF?' she asked.

'Oh yeah, sure. Now you've volunteered, you're entitled to know just how much trouble you can get into by being in our little group.'

She laughed, but I answered her expectant look by saying, 'But as there's a lot to do right now, I'll have to postpone that discussion, although I promise to tell you briefly about them later today.

Orders transferring you to the SMSF are in your intra-mail box as we speak and you'll be reporting to Inspector Thomson in the first instance. One of the first things you'll find is that within the unit, we don't stand on ceremony at all and since we've been activated and are undercover as of now, it is to be first names only from here on, with absolutely none of the usual formalities which you've been used to. I believe this will be your first time going undercover?'

'Yessir. Buggerit! I mean...what do I call you?'

I chuckled at her momentary discomfort. 'Try using my name. It's Harry; Harry Stevens, and when you meet the rest of the crew, just use their first names as well. You're part of the team now and while the operation is running, you've got to put your old life aside. That means there can be no contact with friends or family, since you'll have a hard time trying to explain your altered status without giving the whole game away.

Do you have a significant other in your life that might cause a problem?'

She shook her pretty head. 'No, ah...Harry. Nobody like that, just a cat I share with my flatmate, a legal secretary who works at the courthouse.'

'Well, it's good you like cats, because I've got two and you can play with them all you want. They'll love it! But in a few minutes, you're going to go home and pack casual clothes and personal supplies for six to eight weeks in a couple of soft bags. While you're there, I'd like you to leave your flatmate a note saying that you've been suddenly sent on relieving duties out in the bush; please pick someplace so remote nobody can or will even want to visit you, and tell her you'll be in touch in due course. Don't bring too much stuff since space is limited and we need to be very mobile. A decent water and windproof jacket would be useful as well.

Also, no uniform, but please bring your ID and all your Service hardware, including your Glock 22. See the Armourer on the way out to get four more magazines and maybe an extra two or three hundred rounds of that .40 calibre stuff it shoots. Also, while you're there, I'd like you to try on a few different holsters to find one that is most comfortable for you to wear under loose shirts or tops. There's a belt clip version that fits your waistband, and some of the girls find it quite good. Try that and any other ones you might like. The Armourer will be expecting you as soon as we've finished here.'

She was starting to look a bit bemused by all these instructions, but suddenly asked, 'This is all very good Harry, but just where is it that I'm going with two months of gear, wearing loose shirts, my pistol and a heap of ammunition?'

I laughed at my forgetfulness. 'Oh dear, I'm sorry Tracy. I really am cocking up this briefing, because I clean forgot to tell you that bit. You're coming to live on my boat with Inspector Sandy Thomson, my two cats, Jasper and Krazy and me; Sergeant Amanda Burke will join us in a few days as well. The other boat that's part of the Strike Force is owned by Corrine Johns, ex-SAS and Dave Robson, a civilian, with Senior Constables Alf Story, Charlie Jakes and Melissa Briggs as crew.'

She looked a bit stunned. 'Oh, I know Amanda, Melissa, Alf and Charlie and I've seen Inspector Thomson, but living on your boat? I thought you lived in that lovely old house where I picked you up this morning. Is that why you're wearing...very casual clothes? I thought you were just some sort of eccentric beachcomber dude.'

I laughed. 'Well, in a way that's exactly what I am! I'm permanently undercover, so it's all part of my legend I've been carefully cultivating for the last few years. Being undercover is like wearing a body stocking where you have to adopt your new legend as completely as possible. It's also why I said you had to cut all contact with your old life, for now. Slipups have a nasty habit of causing good persons to get hurt by bad ones.'

'But aren't we going to be a bit crowded? That seems a lot of bodies on two little boats.'

I grinned at her concerns and misconception about what she perceived as 'little boats'.

'You'll see. I'm guessing you don't have a boating background, so there's a lot to cover for you to be useful on-board, which is why we'll be heading there just as soon as you've seen the Armourer, gone home and packed, left that note for your flatmate and got yourself back here. Dressed in casual gear, of course! Oh, and please don't stop for a chat with anyone on the way out. Just grab your personal stuff from your desk and get going. There's a constable already waiting outside the back door in your old patrol car to run you home; he'll wait for you to pack and then bring you back. Don't discuss this operation with him and he won't ask any pointed questions, so please hustle and I promise to answer any of your questions as we go.'

With a faintly bemused look back on her face, she pushed her chair back, rose and left the room. I gave her a few moments to head downstairs then went to Sandy's office.

'I think our new recruit is in for a big culture shock.'

In response to Sandy's raised eyebrows, I added, 'Just wait until you get back to the boat. I may need some help sorting her out! I presume you'll be heading out as soon as you've got things tidied up here?'

'Yeah. I'm just waiting on a call back from Alf and Charlie. They're out serving warrants, so they shouldn't be long. I've already seen Amanda and Melissa; they're downstairs doing paperwork for now.'

She pointed at a large oblong box like a small coffin leaning up against one wall with two shiny alloy Pelikan cases beside it.

'There's *Dragonfly*, the Ground Control Station and battery. Do you want to take it, seeing as there'll be two to handle it?'

'No,' I answered, 'I've got the dinghy down at Southport beach, so with Tracy and her gear we'll be bit full, but when you organise a lift to the Yacht Club, get help loading it onto *Seeker*, it's still the best platform to launch from.

And while I think of it, there's not really any hurry for the others to deploy to the boats, so they could probably stay on General Duties for a few more days if you like. So long as they pack their go-bag and are ready to move immediately.'

'OK, I'll tell them that and it will be a help here for a few more days to give Bob time to find a few temporary replacements. Taking six staff at once is a big hit for a station this size.'

'Yeah, I appreciate that, but we don't even know if Corrine found a vacancy at the Meditation Centre.'

'Oh sorry, actually we do know and she did get in,' Sandy confirmed. 'She just called me to say the Meditation Centre was delighted to have her come and stay at $2,000 per day. They even offered to pick her up since one of their vehicles is in town collecting supplies; so she's probably on her way there by now.'

'That's really good! Sounds like a nice business if you can get it! So is the tracking device working?'

Sandy tapped on a few keys on her Mac laptop then spun it around to face me. A detailed map of the Gold Coast was displayed, with a blinking, bright blue cursor marking our dear girl's progress out of town to the west.

'Good work! I'll leave you to get on with your delightful paperwork while I go wait for Tracy, then we'll head for *Firebird* and I'll start getting her indoctrinated.'

Sandy grinned. 'That'll be fun, Jasper and Krazy will have a new playmate.'

I poked a face. 'I fair cocked up her briefing earlier, so I'll have to make sure I do this one a bit better. Anyway, I'll see you when you're done with stuff and have briefed Alf and Charlie.'

She sketched a wave, her attention already back on the stack of reports she had to plough through before she could bail out for the day. I filled in time while I waited for Tracy by going down to visit the Armourer to see if he had anything interesting. Which he did in the shape of several different shotgun rounds he'd acquired and while I poked and prodded the different rounds, he told me Tracy had taken two holsters she liked, four magazines and a pile of cartons of .40 S&W ammo.

I was interested in the shotgun rounds and talked him into letting me have a few boxes of the so-called 'Dragon's Breath', an incendiary round which was supposed to set fire to the target out to about 30 metres or so, by spraying out a cloud of magnesium particles that burn at around 3100°C.

I also snagged a few boxes each of a new Armour-Piercing Incendiary round and a Thunder Flash round that was supposed to be similar to the 'Flash-Bang' grenades by producing a blinding flash and a 182db thunderclap that would incapacitate any unprotected ears with 15 metres, but didn't fire a solid projectile.

I'd just left the Armoury with a shopping bag full of new toys to play with, when I spotted our newest recruit coming in through the rear staff entrance.

'Well done Tracy. You've made good time.'

To her credit, she'd made the round trip in just thirty-five minutes and had one large backpack slung over her shoulder and was carrying a smaller, but heavy airline carry-on bag. My choice of clothing must have influenced her, since she wore a pair of delightfully tight shorts, a casual polo shirt that draped very nicely over her smallish breasts, and a pair of sockless runners on her feet. I had to admit that her version of boat gear looked a hell of a lot better on her than mine did on me.

She shrugged, much of her earlier enthusiasm apparently having evaporated. 'There wasn't much to pack, really. So I threw in some books and my laptop, not really knowing much about my new home. All the heavy stuff is in the backpack'

It seemed that the uncertainty of her immediate future was the cause of her mild gloominess, but she'd have to wait until we were aboard until I could fulfil my promise to tell all. 'Ah...yes. Well, if you can bear with me for a short time more, all will be made clear. Ah, here he is.' I pointed to the door she'd just come in, where the young constable who'd taken her home and back had appeared, his face lighting up when he saw me.

'Good afternoon Sir. I'm ready when you are. I parked the patrol car and have my PV waiting as requested.'

'Good work, Constable. There's just Senior Manning and myself to go down to the Broadwater Park south of the end of the main street. If you can drop us near the archway that marks the park, that'll be terrific.'

He looked like he was about to ask a question, but had second thoughts, directing his attention instead to Tracy's long and mostly bare legs.

'In that case sir, I'm parked just outside the door.' He seemed to think about helping with her load, but one look at her face had him leading us to the door, although he did hold it open for her.

His choice of PV was a neat little Subaru WRX in plain white instead of the electric blue colour the boy racers fancy.

'Nice ride Constable,' I commented.

'Thank you Sir. It's a really good thing; especially since I had it re-chipped and opened the exhaust up a bit.'

I chuckled as we climbed in, with Tracy in the back with her gear. 'You must get a few challenges from the local petrol-heads.'

He smiled, 'Being a petrol-head myself I certainly used to, but they all know the car and me by now, so I fit in with the crowd pretty well. They know how far they can push me before I have to turn official.'

We shared a laugh as he neatly negotiated the traffic and a few minutes later, delivered us to the designated spot.

'Will that be all, Commander?' he asked, staying in the car as we got out.

I stuck my head back in and shook his hand as Tracy dragged her gear out. 'That's all for me, thanks Constable, but you can expect a request to run Inspector Thomson over to the Yacht Club some-time in the next couple of hours. You'd better use the Patrol car for that run since there'll be some bulky gear she'll need a hand with. This PV run was for us to stay a little more low-profile.'

He delivered a beaming smile, 'No problem Commander, I'll look after all that. Call on me anytime.'

With a cheery wave he was off and I led Tracy on the walk through the park to the small beach. I was tempted to challenge her attitude, since grumpy or un-willing crew members are unsettling and can be dangerous, but decided to let the novelty of the surroundings work their usual magic.

However, now we were away from the station, she was the one to raise the subject.

She stopped beside a public bench seat and put her bags down on the grass, turning to face me with a serious expression on her face. 'You might have noticed Harry, that I'm not as happy with this situation as I was earlier. I was initially excited to be asked to join a group that seemed to have done some amazing things, but then I realised everybody around me appears to know what's happening, but I don't and I'm not comfortable with that. I like to know what I'm facing.'

I thought a few moments, recognising a person who was normally fully in control of at least her own life and was used to a more ordered existence.

'Look Tracy, if it's any consolation, this whole deal was lobbed in my lap just three hours ago, so I really don't know much more than you do at the moment.'

She made an angry gesture, 'Oh, it's not really the operation that bothers me all that much. It's more this boat and the undercover thing; having to ignore my friends for an unknown duration, and then there's everybody else on the crew who's worked together and done this stuff before. I know I wanted to get involved in some action, but I thought I'd at least know what I was doing!' She seemed to be fighting to hold back tears as she slumped to the bench, shoulders hunched in misery. 'I'm sorry for making a fuss.'

I sat down beside her and tried to come up with something to pick her up, but talking sense and giving guidance to distraught females isn't one of my strong points.

'If you really are that uncomfortable, we can go back to the station right now, you can go home, unpack and change back into uniform and nothing more will be said. But I think you're much stronger than that and I'm certain once you see your new home and meet the rest of the crew, you'll love it as much as the others do.

I've never had a D & M with Alf and Charlie, because they just adapted and got on with the job, but I know Amanda and Melissa had some misgivings and very quickly got over them. They'll help you sort yourself out. And I did say I'd tell you the full story as soon as we were aboard and settled. My weak excuse is that there's been too much happening too quickly to take the time to discuss everything fully with you. For the moment, I need you to trust me. I believe seeing your new environment will answer a lot of questions and the rest of the crew will support you.'

Tracy sat quietly, staring at the grass at her feet for a while, before she lifted her head and met my concerned look. She gave a wan smile, but that was better than before.

'I'm sorry to be such a sook, Harry, and I won't let anyone down. It's all been a bit sudden. If you're willing to help me learn, I'll do the very best job I can. I promise!'

That was good enough for me so I got to my feet and held out my hand to help her up. To my surprise, she took it, leaning in against me for a few moments, nuzzling my chest rather pleasantly, before stepping back, so I took the chance and gave her a strong hug that she responded to just as fiercely. After a few moments, she gave a little chuckle, before stepping back and picked up her gear.

'So much for the big, tough SERT Officer,' she said with a rueful smile. 'I'll be the butt of a heap of jokes once this gets around.'

I grasped her finely muscled shoulder firmly with one hand and looked her in the eye. 'We all have misgivings at times; me as much as anybody when it's my plan putting others in harm's way, but we roll with it and keep going. And what happens away from the station, stays away from the station. Our crew never tell tales!'

Finally, she gave a genuine smile and to my surprise, leant forward and kissed my cheek. 'Thanks Harry, I needed that. I'll be fine now, but if I need a hug or two at times, will Sandy mind?'

I laughed and spoke without engaging my brain, 'Mind? Hell, no! She won't mind in the least. She'll probably give you one too.'

Tracy raised an eyebrow at that comment, but said no more as I led the way to the dinghy.

41

CHAPTER 5

On impulse, I steered the RIB past the outer arm of the yacht club's marina and spotted Dave hosing down the black-tinted windows of the new *Seeker's* sleek, raked wheelhouse. On the run over from Southport, Tracy had settled down a lot, almost as if the act of leaving one shore and crossing the water had let her cross a mental barrier where she left her old life temporarily behind and was starting her new one.

She had been looking ahead as I aimed for the glittering, white glare of the multi-million-dollar collection of boat-building expertise bobbing gently in their marina berths.

'Wow!' she exclaimed, pointing ahead to the closest arm of the marina. 'Look at that long, low blue one. It looks fantastic!'

I chuckled to myself and held our course. 'You like that one, do you?'

She looked much more animated as she glanced back at me briefly, grinning with her longish hair blowing freely back in the wind of our passage, 'Of course I do. It's beautiful and looks like it can't wait to get going somewhere. Fast! It looks much better than most of those other great big multi-storied things wrapped in plastic!'

I laughed at her description which so closely matched my own feelings about 'plastic-wrapped gin-palaces'. Speaking up over the muted purr of the outboard motor, I said casually, 'Well in that case, since you like it so much and just displayed such excellent taste in boat choice, let's go say 'hi' to the owner.'

She looked back at me again. 'Really? Do you know him?'

I grinned, 'Yeah. You could say that. That's Dave washing the windows, and he's part of our crew.'

'Oh, wow...neat! But where's your boat then and is it like this one?'

'Nah. Mine's a bit smaller than that great lump of Italian plastic, and is a sailing catamaran.' She laughed at that, commenting, 'you can be a shit-stirring bastard at times. I'll have to talk to Sandy about you.'

'That'll be an interesting conversation,' I commented cryptically, 'especially the way the last conversation about me she had with another female turned out.'

I was saved having to explain my careless comment, by swinging around to neatly park the dinghy against *Seeker's* wide stern board.

'Bloody hell!' Tracy exclaimed. 'This thing's fuckin' huge! I didn't realise just how big it was until we got close.'

I hopped out, quickly tied up and held out a hand for Tracy, which she gladly took, not being used to the unsteady motion of the small RIB. We'd just climbed up to the broad expanse of the cockpit when Dave swung down from the side deck walkway, wearing just a pair of loose boat shorts, his tanned, heavily-muscled and bare upper body glistening with sweat. With a broad smile on his face, he greeted Tracy as if she was an old friend and I noticed the appreciative looks she was openly giving his toned body.

'Meet our newest crewmember, Dave. This is Tracy Manning; yet another copper.'

I dodged an elbow aimed at my ribs as Dave laughed, 'don't mind him Tracy. He's a bit of a crass bugger at the best of times, so when you can't stand his weird sense of humour any longer, just come on over here. You'll always be welcome.'

His easy manner and casual banter put her at ease immediately, as did the offer of tea or coffee. She chose coffee as we followed Dave inside and down to the lower galley, where we took a seat at the small dining table at one end of the galley on beautifully soft Italian grey-leather seats. Tracy's eyes were agog at the sheer opulence on display everywhere she looked.

Dave set about fixing coffee for Tracy, tea for him and me and when we'd been served, he invited Tracy on a quick tour of the boat to her delight and I could see that her pre-conceived ideas about 'cramped living on small boats' was being rapidly and dramatically revised.

We took our hot drinks up to the cockpit after the tour and when Tracy had run out of superlatives about what she'd seen, Dave looked at me. 'I suppose you've dragged this lovely, unsuspecting young lady here to fill in for Corrine while she's gone undercover?'

I glanced at Tracy before replying, 'Yeah, I have I'm afraid. And sorry about sending Mouse, but she really was the best one for the job. Not being a copper is a big help, since that background would be more difficult to explain away.

Her qualifications should appeal to the Dark Side of their operation, and with her cover being about 95% true, it's simple to remember. And if things do go tits-up, she knows how to handle herself so well, that I fear for the safety of anyone who tries to stop or hurt her.'

Dave grinned, 'I was mainly pulling your chain, Harry. But even though you're right about her abilities, I still worry about her. She's as gung-ho as you are and that's not always a good thing.'

I laughed, noting that Tracy was following our exchange very closely and seemed to be absorbing a lot of new information. I mentally shuddered to think of the Q & A session that would follow later.

'What's the program from here, now you've got a few things happening?' Dave asked.

I nodded, 'I discussed it with Sandy and we thought we'll leave Alf, Charlie, Amanda and Melissa at work for now, since there's no need to bring everyone aboard immediately. However, I wanted to get Tracy up to speed on the boats and how we function, then we'll wait until Corrine reports in and feeds us some intel before we decide what move to make.'

He nodded, 'Fair enough. I'm already stocked up with extra food and all fuel tanks are full, so if we need to move quickly, I'm ready.

But this talk of seizing a West Aussie gas plant is pretty radical. When I heard we were activated, I was trying to think how we as a 'Marine' unit could be useful, but now I understand.'

'Yes, that's a big worry, but I have a bit of a plan. I think we still need to wait for Corrine's first SitRep, but if the gas plant seizure is likely to happen, then we need to get ourselves and the boats over there as soon as possible since we don't know the bad guy's timetable.'

Dave blinked, but had obviously been thinking the same, and the logistics of the operation; otherwise, why would the authorities call in an undercover marine crew if they didn't want us to use the boats?

'I was thinking about that earlier and I've made a rough check of the distance and it's almost exactly on the opposite side of Australia, which means that to go north-about is around 3100 nautical miles, while to go south via The Bight would be around 3300 nautical miles.'

I thought a moment then said, 'Bugger it. Just when I need a calculator...'

Tracy dug interestingly in the front of her shorts, producing from somewhere a small mobile phone, giggling at the looks Dave and I gave her.

'Feed me the figures Harry and stop fucking around. There's a reason these things are called 'smart' phones'.

I grinned, then thought a moment. 'That sounds like a hell of a long way to go on one trip, but north-about is really the only way to go with much better weather and smoother seas, although *Firebird* would still be the delaying factor, but if we planned on an average speed of 14 knots...'

'That's 221 hours or just over nine days continuous travelling,' Tracy quickly supplied.

I grinned at her expertise, 'OK. If we allow stops to refuel, that might add another two or three days, so let's say 12 days to get into the area. That's not too bad. But we'll have to run a watch system to cover the constant travelling.'

Dave picked up on my thoughts immediately, 'I'll only have three watch-keepers, although it shouldn't be too much of a problem.'

I disagreed, 'Well it would be for that length of time with an inexperienced crew old mate, but not if I send Melissa over to you as well. I think she and Charlie are still an item and are sharing Charlie's flat. So that's four crew each; much safer and less tiring.'

Dave nodded agreement. 'That'll be excellent, Harry. But can you maintain a steady 14 knots?'

'Sure, better than that if there are good winds, but 14 knots is possible if there's no wind, although that'll be working the engines pretty hard. If the breeze is light, then we just run one engine to supplement the sails. It's going to be relatively heavy on fuel usage, but it'll get the job done. With no wind, the engines will use around 12 litres per hour each, but there shouldn't be too many windless days this time of year which will need both of them running hard. The tanks hold 250 litres of fuel for each engine, so even if the winds are very light, we could probably get...'

'Worst case, about 35 to 40 hours of motor-sailing per tank fill,' was my new secretary's reply.

'That's not a lot if we're trying to make time and distance. How about fitting a supplementary bladder tank or two?' was Dave's sensible reply.

I thought a moment, 'That's not a bad idea. In fact, it's a bloody good one. Perhaps a couple of 500-litre tanks down below on the balance point so the trim isn't upset and that could extend our endurance another 70-odd hours if conditions aren't too light. So that's a total of about 110 hours without re-fuelling. Not bad.'

Dave took a turn at thinking, before saying, '*Seeker* has got a lot of extra fuel tanks already and can easily carry more bladders, so if we're going to hit our employers up for bladder tanks, how about if we get another three 1000 litre tanks and mount them where we can. It won't upset the trim to any noticeable degree and that should extend endurances considerably. We'll be idling along on one engine staying with you, burning about 65 litres per hour, so my endurance with 12,000 litres in the internal tanks will be... '

'184 hours,' Tracy supplied with a cheeky grin, 'and 230 hours if you use all the three flex-tanks, or 200 hours using just one and Harry gets another 70 hours for a total of 180 hours.'

'Excellent! Thanks Tracy, I like that idea,' I said, 'nothing like too much fuel. That means we can easily make the run with only one stop for refuelling, perhaps in Darwin. It's about 1090 nautical miles from Darwin to Onslow, so the first leg to Darwin will be a bit over 2000 nautical miles or 143 hrs run time, worst case. Great stuff, both of you.'

Tracy was deep into our discussion and showed she had a very quick mind. 'Excuse my ignorance, but as an alternative, couldn't you put both boats on a freighter and just ship them around there?'

I smiled at her. 'That's good thinking and we could do that; but the problem is finding a ship going from here to somewhere near where we want to go and sailing when we want it to, which means maybe in the next couple of days. The cost to charter one would be ridiculous, so motoring on our own bottoms is quite reasonable. That's why even though there seems to be a lot of motoring and sailing, it'll be much quicker in the long run.'

She nodded understanding, but I was pleased she'd dialled into the discussion. It's not always necessary to be an expert on a particular subject to be able to offer some useful insight.

FIREBIRD, WEDNESDAY AFTERNOON & EVENING, SOUTHPORT YACHT BASIN

We kicked a few more details around but without word from Corrine, we didn't really know where we stood or what the bad guys were really planning. All we could do was get approval to buy the extender tanks and get them fitted. I made the call to Bob Casey and got immediate approval to get whatever we needed and he'd pass the invoices on to the Commissioner's office, marked for his personal attention.

If we kept this up, it would probably be the Water Police budget that was going to take a hit by using a lot of diesel fuel and receiving some extended range flexible fuel tanks.

I invited Dave over to *Firebird* for a drink and a feed, which he gladly accepted, so he followed Tracy and me back to *Firebird*.

I don't know what Tracy was expecting, but the big catamaran blew her away. Although 40-feet shorter than *Seeker*, *Firebird* was nearly twice as wide, which made for a vast increase in space. Fortunately Tracy was a cat person, so that meant Jasper was a big hit, once he went through his embarrassing female greeting routine of firmly nuzzling her crotch, much to Dave's amusement. She giggled and wasn't even slightly offended, but she really loved Jasper and little Krazy kitten. He took to her with his usual equanimity, but little Krazy knew she'd found a new human playmate and seemed determined to make the most of the situation.

So with a loudly purring, furry black scarf draped around her neck, I took Tracy on a tour of the boat, getting her settled into her aft cabin first of all then explaining the ship-board routines, do and don'ts and where to find essential supplies like tea, coffee and booze. She loved the huge refrigerated esky in the cockpit, and approved my choice of wines, beers and rum.

She noted without comment but with a big grin, the few items of personal stuff Sandy had left lying around in my cabin and was quite happy with her cabin. She loved the rest of the boat, especially topsides with the huge aft day bed and the twin trampolines and the bow seats up for'rard.

I promised to go through the various sail and engine handling routines once she had settled in.

After the tour, Tracy was sitting in the cockpit scratching Jasper's head, setting him purring like a small generator starting up, when she asked, 'Tell me how you came by Jasper? I mean, he's not exactly the average sort of reject you find in the local animal shelter.'

I took a seat myself and organised my thoughts. 'It's quite a story, but I'll give you the very brief version. Soon after I'd been recruited into the ACP, I was on a small operation that involved little more than to shadow a Korean freighter suspected of smuggling as it entered Moreton Bay, then allow a bunch of SWAT guys to do their gung-ho routine by swarming up the side of the freighter to take control and search it before stuff got lost overboard.

After they got it stopped, I was wandering around the ship seeing what the SWAT dudes were up to when I found the galley and must have looked hungry, because the Korean cook fed me something odd-looking but very tasty. While I was eating, he started giving me some very strange looks, to the extent that I started thinking I should have stayed near the big burly SWAT guys!

Then from out of the pantry, he hauled out this large, black kitten and gently presented it to me. Luckily, it was very docile and even seemed to like me.

Then it got a bit weird. This cook didn't have much English, but he managed to say, 'You interesting man...you very lucky man. Gods watch over you. This one cat...him very lucky cat too. He meant for you...him look after you...always. You look after him too...him very special, Chausie-cross...very unusual, grow very big. Very special'.'

I poked a face in remembrance of my feelings at the time.

'I'd wanted a cat like another hole in the head, but the old fella was so terribly insistent and the kitten did seem happy draping himself around my neck, just like Krazy's doing to you right now, so I ended up with a ship's cat, which at the time was simply another nautical tradition to follow. I had no idea about just how special Jasper was to become, although I did wonder when he grew so quickly. When he hit the 25-kilogram mark he looked just like a 2/3 scale black panther, with a narrow head like a cougar and a very long thick tail. Even as a kitten, he was fiercely protective of the boat and me and seems to understand when I ask him to extend that protection to friends. And he's still here now and still looking after us!'

Tracy clapped her hands softly and gave Jasper a long, hard look, and I could almost imagine her thoughts:

'Terrific cat, but Harry's delusional if he thinks Jasper understands

English. Harry talks to the beast as if it does understand which is eccentric but charming. Good watch cat though, with those huge fangs and claws. Much rather have him on our side.'

Before I'd finished the tale, Dave opened three beers, so I paused to wet my parched throat.

'I know what I've said about Jasper's spooky abilities sounds crazy, but Dave has seen what he can do, although I hope you'll be spared some of the more violent stuff.'

Dave nodded and hoisted his beer in salute. 'Hear! Hear! Brother! And here's to Jasper who has saved our collective bums on several occasions!'

Tracy still looked dubious, but nevertheless enjoyed petting Jasper while we waited for Sandy to make an appearance, but then she had another question which showed how much I'd forgotten to tell her.

'Just what is this Special Marine Strike Force that I've apparently just been seconded to?'

I groaned in embarrassment for not briefing her on that either, while Dave had a chuckle. 'The Commissioner had a brain-fart after the last operation.'

'That was the bikie-gang thing?' Tracy interjected.

I nodded. 'Yep. But backing up slightly to give you a better picture, the last two operations were much more involved and dangerous, exposed as we were, first hand, to some serious bad guys who were trying very hard to kill us. The first operation led, via a very peculiar set of circumstances, to me becoming re-acquainted with an SAS Trooper who I'd saved in Afghanistan. That person is Dave's lady Corrine, who has just gone undercover and at the end of that operation, she and Dave ended up with a 68-foot Italian speedboat named *Seeker,* which became their home.

Also, because of the success of those operations, the Commissioner allocated our whole crew from the bikie operation to a new undercover unit he created. The new unit was tasked with covertly investigating and hopefully quietly shutting down any unusual problems associated with marine activities that needed a more discreet touch than the Special Emergency Response Team. Unfortunately, we've not had any work since being formed just two months ago, so the team has lost much of its edge and we'll need to work together to get that back.'

Tracy nodded thoughtfully, showing a bit more enthusiasm than earlier, 'I understand the need for secrecy a lot better now, thanks Harry and I apologise for my earlier outburst.'

I waved the apology aside, 'No problem, but you'll be brought up to speed alongside the rest of us. Two months and no special work has left us all a bit dull.'

Just a few minutes later, Sandy called from the Yacht Club and Dave offered to fetch her. I watched them cart the *Dragonfly* boxes down below on *Seeker* then they boarded Dave's dinghy for the short run back out to *Firebird*. When she trotted up the stern steps, she had a beaming smile for Tracy and me and we both got a huge hug.

'Hi Tracy,' she said, slipping her jacket off and dumping her utility handbag, 'and welcome aboard. I hope these two clowns have been looking after you?'

Tracy hoisted her beer in reply, but added. 'Yep. They sure have. I've had the full tour of both boats and another information and planning session, so my mind is buzzing with new stuff.'

Sandy accepted a beer from Dave and took a long swig. 'Damn, that's nice after a busy day.' She had no further news and joined us at the table, while she and Tracy assessed each other. Tracy's check-out was open and speculative, since to her, Sandy was very much an unknown factor, especially holding the rank of Inspector. Nobody at the station knew what she was like away from work, especially because her reputation had grown hugely since the last two operations and she rarely associated with work colleagues on a social level.

On her side, Sandy knows what I'm like around pretty ladies and fortunately isn't possessive or jealous when a new one comes along in the line of work, as was the case with Tracy. As I fondly remembered, with a pleasant tickle in my groin, she was also not averse to cuddling up to the right lady if one took her fancy. So the hug she gave a surprised Tracy was Sandy's way of letting Tracy know that all was well.

So while their silent assessment of each other continued, I brought Sandy up-to-date on what we'd planned in her absence.

She approved the ideas, just as Dave's phone made a sound that was reminiscent of two cane toads mating.

He shrugged apologetically. 'It's a message notification.' But when he looked at the sender ID he got excited, 'It's from Corrine. We thought that while she's at the Retreat, it'd be normal for clients to let their family know they were alright.'

Sandy nodded impatiently. 'Yeah, Dave. Stop fussing and tell us what she says.'

He grinned at her. 'In case her communications were being intercepted, we tried to work out a simple code, but there wasn't time, so she's just saying what would be expected between a resident and her family, but with hidden meaning.'

I nodded. 'Yeah. We did something like that in the desert. So what's the message?' That comment brought a sharp look from Tracy who obviously didn't know my background.

Dave woke up the phone screen again. 'She says, '*Hi Hon. Arrived OK. Lovely people, lovely place. No expense spared so I am very comfortable. Met the boss, Terry Williams on arrival. Very impressive man. He has a lovely partner, Paula, who looks after PR and advertising and she was very chatty and friendly. We got along very well! Just like old friends. I spent quite a lot of time with both and had more forms to fill out about my past, but I guess it's what they need to know if they're going to try to cure what's been causing me to become so disenchanted with the way the whole planet is being treated, but I won't start on that again.*

Give my love to your Mum and Dad and tell them not to worry if they don't hear from me directly for a while. Terry says that we, (there's a few more like me just arrived) will have to go into seclusion for a while so the therapists can work on us without distractions. Sounds like fun as there are six or eight lovely big men looking after us; and you know what I'm like around good-looking, muscled up men! I'll not be able to send a message by phone, since I have to turn it in–no distractions remember, but I'll talk when I can afterwards. Terry and Paula are very optimistic they'll be able to treat my problem and make me very happy with myself again. Won't that be wonderful!

Anyway, I gotta go now. Dinner is served and at least I'm not on a diet like the ones here to dry out or on a weight-loss program. The food looks fantastic but there seems to be a lot of staff for just a few customers. No matter. I guess it just means we have the best of care and attention. I already have the attention of several of those big men therapists I mentioned before. Yum oh!

Bye darling and don't be too good, 'cause I won't be.'

'And that's it.' Dave finished with a sigh. 'It really doesn't sound like the girl I waved goodbye to this morning.'

I clapped my hands, 'No it doesn't and that's really good. She hasn't forgotten what to do when being covert.'

Dave looked puzzled, 'But she hasn't told us anything, and my parents died years ago. She knows that.'

I laughed, 'Yes, you and Mouse know it but the bad guys don't, since they aren't investigating you. 'Mum and Dad' would be Sandy and me and she's told us that she and a few others are going into lock-down for a while and have to hand over their mobiles. She also told us she's under close watch, that there are up to eight well-trained guards watching them and there are a lot more people there who aren't clients, so they could be the ones that have already been recruited and are hanging around to get further training. She also said she's had to give up a lot more information about her past, which means that they're still recruiting. I'd love to be a fly on the wall; they're going to love her once they get her full history.'

Dave looked worried, 'But she'll be all right, won't she? I mean... they won't hurt her or anything?'

'Nah. They'll look after her like she's royalty. I'll bet they start

the 'come and join us, it's the best way to cleanse your psyche' routine almost straight away. She'll fit in like a natural. She also said
that she's going to go along with them and their plans for a while,
but that she'll be looking for any opportunity to create mayhem
without being sprung. That's what she's really a natural at!'

54

CHAPTER 6

Corrine finished her beautiful meal, to the delight of the serving staff, with a double helping of Pavlova, extra cream and ice cream, but to the rather false dismay of one of the so-called therapists.

'My goodness, Miss Corrine, if you keep eating like that, you'll be as fat as a pig in no time!'

She shook her head. 'Nope. Won't ever happen. I never put on weight, although if I don't eat, I'll lose heaps. It's something to do with my metabolism or something like that.'

She knew exactly what caused her enormous appetite, but wasn't going to share that knowledge with anybody in this place.

She'd just finished her second cup of excellent coffee, when one of her minders who been a lot less than solicitous toward her, said 'OK, girlie. That's enough for tonight. The kitchen's closing and you need to be in your quarters.'

Fighting the urge to drop him on the spot for the insulting 'girlie' word and tone, she smiled sweetly and allowed him to almost drag her out of her chair and whilst still holding her arm, roughly propel her down one of the long corridors leading away from the central Admin and communal dining and recreation areas.

Twisting her head to read his nametag, she asked. 'So what's the go, Dwayne? I thought for $2,000 per day, I didn't have to cop verbal and physical abuse. Or is this part of the therapy? As in, is this the 'good guy, bad guy' routine? Like, everybody's been so nice up until now, until you turn up with an attitude. What's your problem?'

He growled at her. 'I don't like you spoiled little brats with too much money who get into trouble then expect hard-working normal people to grovel at your feet trying to fix you up!'

She looked sideways at him with a cheeky grin. 'Apart from the fact that I'm not in any trouble, are you sure that's your problem, or do you just want to get into my panties? You might have done a lot better if you'd just asked nicely!'

That comment must have struck much too close to home, for Dwayne went white and snarled at her. 'You little prick-teaser! If I want to get into your pants, I'll just do it and there'll be none of this 'asking nicely' bullshit! You lot make me sick! There's a few more like you here at the moment and you all just need a bloody good fucking! My mates and I know how to sort out your dainty little heads all right! Except we'll start at the other end!'

Corrine grinned at him again, 'Oh I love it when a big, strong man like you talks dirty to a little girl like me. I get quite hot all over and particularly damp between my little leggies! Whatever am I going to do?'

He stopped, jerked her arm painfully again and growled at her again, raising one huge, meaty paw to cuff her about the head, when a strident voice echoed down the hallway behind them.

'Good evening, Mr Dwayne, I trust that you're not having any problems with that young lady who also happens to be a highly valued client?'

Dwayne instantly dropped his hand, letting go of Corrine's arm, although livid marks showed the extent of his feelings.

'No Miss Paula,' he replied to the tall, strikingly beautiful red-head who strode briskly down the corridor toward them. 'We were just...'

'I can imagine what sort of discussion you might have been having, Mr Dwayne. I'd be obliged if you'd mind returning to the Admin area and wait there for me. I'll see Miss Corrine to her quarters, thank you.'

Dwayne glared at both of them, before marching stiffly back up the corridor without a further word.

'I do apologise for your treatment Miss Corrine,' she said, gently taking Corrine's bruised and aching arm and examining it under one of the many soft lights lining the long corridor. 'We haven't been operating very long and unfortunately, our Personnel Director hasn't quite worked out the right sort of people we need, so we occasionally end up with a 'Dwayne' type. Still, I can assure you that you won't have to worry about him again. Now we might detour via the doctor's office before we continue to your quarters.'

'Your doctor is on duty at this time of night?' Corrine asked politely.

Paula gave a small chuckle, 'Oh, yes. He's paid extremely well to be available 24/7 and ready to treat everything from a bruised arm to appendicitis. We have a lot of other people here and some are doing rather, shall I say, rigorous training, which sometimes leads to injuries, while others are recovering from narcotic or alcohol dependence, so the medical team is always ready.'

Paula looked annoyed with herself, as if she maybe shouldn't have revealed all of that information, but by then they'd arrived at a set of wide doors which opened automatically, admitting them into what appeared to be a full surgery with examining rooms. A very pretty receptionist who was familiar with patients with odd injuries turning up at all times of the day or night, lead them into an examining room where Paula handed her over to a young and good-looking doctor who was waiting for them.

'Call me when you've finished please Doctor, I've just got some disciplining to do!' Paula commanded sternly, before she swept out of the surgery.

'Certainly Miss Paula, I'll do that.'

Corrine thought her bruised arm would hardly be a test of his skills, but despite the superficial, but painful nature of the injury, he made a careful examination, asked how it occurred, (manually, third-party he was told briefly), he then applied a small amount of a strange, nicely pungent-smelling, dark green paste to the area of now quite extensive bruising which Corrine admitted to herself, did hurt quite a lot.

Within seconds, the pain faded, leaving Corrine with a calm and floaty feeling that was most pleasant. 'Wow! What is that stuff?' she asked, leaning back in her chair.

He seemed to be quite happy to talk about a safe subject and said, 'It's a herbal concoction made by natives on an island in the western section of the Indonesian Archipelago. Jill, my nurse and I, were travelling through some of the more remote Indonesian islands on a yacht, when we came across this girl, or young woman to be more precise, who had the most amazing story of getting separated from her archaeological party. She was captured by pirates, then briefly escaped from them only to be captured by some primitive local tribesmen who took her to their camp where the self-appointed king was a grossly-fat white man who held her safe, but still a captive on the island. She had to take part in some slightly bizarre sexual happenings, but from what Anna said; sorry, I meant to say her name was Anna, her participation was at least semi-voluntary, and so she wasn't hurt.

In fact, as a result of those happenings, she was treated rather well, except the boss guy wasn't about to let her off the island.

However, to cut a long story short, Anna escaped by stealing a canoe and paddling south until she ran out of food and water which was about when we tripped across her.

And that was the first time we heard about the green paste.

Originally, the islanders used to just make enough for their own purposes, but a few years back, when the white dude boss found out about it's properties, he got them organised to make larger batches of it and brought in small cosmetic jars and cartons so they could package it for export. Since they were supplying a very limited market to only the wealthy Chinese in Hong Kong and Shanghai, and charged heaps for it, the money has poured in, with the boss keeping most of it, but giving enough to the natives to make their lives safer and more comfortable. They were happy, so it seems a good arrangement for both sides.

The paste has the most amazing healing properties, some of

which you're currently experiencing, and seems to be useful on almost any injury, even open wounds.'

'But how did you get hold of it?' Corrine asked, grinning stupidly, her head buzzing very pleasantly and oddly enough, even a familiar and very nice sensation tickling her groin.

'When we picked Anna up, she had a box of the jars with her and talked me into taking most of her stock in exchange for some cash and a ride out of the area. I ration this stuff carefully, since a chemist friend says he can't seem to quite duplicate the chemicals involved as it's all herbal and the bushes it's derived from only grow on that island.'

'Sounds like it would be very lucrative to make a trip to the island and set up a steady supply.'

He got a cunning look on his face. 'I had thought of that, seeing as I know where it is, but I've got some loose ends to straighten out first. But you're right, it's on the agenda as soon as I'm able and have built up or acquired the funds to get a boat.'

'I've got a boat,' Corrine said quietly, 'although it might not be good to advertise that around here.'

He looked carefully at her. 'Is this the drug talking, or you?'

Corrine laughed, 'Probably a bit of both, but I'm not bombed out enough to realise that things aren't entirely kosher around here. That gorilla who did the job on my arm is a good example of what's a bit fishy, so my suggestion of a deal isn't just talk.'

He walked casually over to the half-open door and looked out at the receptionist still sitting at her desk on the other side of the room, then came back to the chair where Corrine sat. 'You have to be ultra careful around here. It's said that some walls do have ears, although most staff are paid very well to just do their job and ignore anything odd that they might see or hear. The only other person I trust is my theatre nurse so be careful what you say and to whom you say it.'

'OK, 'Corrine said quietly, 'but think about the boat idea. I can help and my partner and I like different and interesting schemes.'

'What is it, sail or power?'

'It's a 100-foot powerboat. An Italian AB100, which is very fast with very long endurance and sea going. But since I've just arrived, can you tell me what's going on so I don't run foul of more clowns like the one who did this to my arm?'

'OK. I like the boat idea and I'll discuss a deal with my partner. If you're here for the Meditation Retreat cure, you may be assessed as suitable to be approached to join the rather more radical Earth-Squad movement as a volunteer.'

All attention now that some good info was starting to flow Corrine asked, 'What's that entail?'

'If accepted, you'll terminate your paid program and move out of your luxury quarters that Madame Lash will be escorting you to shortly, to move into dormitories for the EarthSquad Volunteers where you'll be trained in various ways of getting revenge on those organisations our esteemed leader Terry Williams and his partner in crime, our dear Paula, deem as suitable targets.'

'Why do you call her 'Madam Lash'?'

He gave a mirthless chuckle. 'This is where you'll have to tread carefully. She has a nasty habit of selecting new recruits for some sessions of S&M; whether they want to or not. Unfortunately, she seems to have taken a bit of a personal interest in you already, so there must be something in your history that marks you as a strong potential recruit. Is that assessment correct?'

Corrine nodded, deciding to trust this unlikely ally. 'Yes. There could be stuff there that would interest them. I'm ex-SAS with training in sniping, all weapons, demolition and close-quarters assassination.'

The doctor blinked, 'Bugger me! I hope we can stay very good friends. And you're right that your CV would interest them greatly, so you can expect an approach very much sooner rather than later. I'll be involved since I have to do the full medical workup on every recruit, so I expect to see you back here in a few days, although I'd like to look at that arm again tomorrow anyway. I'll tell Paula you need to take things easy for a couple of days until the bruising settles, although this ointment promotes very fast healing, but I don't let on to them about it.'

'So the next big question is—what does this EarthSquad do that's so radical?'

He held his finger to his lips and said softly. 'That can wait until I see you tomorrow for more treatment on your arm. If I don't call Paula to say you're ready, she'll be getting concerned. And a concerned Paula is not a good thing. OK?'

Corrine nodded, 'OK, Doctor. But what do I call you? Doctor seems a bit formal if we're going to be co-conspirators and partners in an ointment enterprise.'

He let loose with a beautiful smile that lit up his whole handsome face and held out his hand, 'Roger Jacobs.'

'I'm Corrine Johns, Roger. Pleased to meet a friendly face in what seems like a very hostile environment and thanks for the info. I'll be looking forward to hearing more tomorrow.'

'That's no problem, Corrine. I'll arrange for you to be brought here before lunch. And now I'd better call Paula. Take it easy with that arm; it will get sore later on tonight when the ointment wears off.'

The last had been said more loudly as Roger moved to the door and asked the receptionist to call Paula to escort Miss Corrine to her quarters. She did and mere minutes later, the lady herself swept through the door, a high flush to her cheeks and a feral glint in her eye.

'How's our patient, Doctor?'

'Extensive soft tissue damage to her upper right arm, to which I've applied a topical analgesic which will reduce the pain and swelling, but it will re-occur throughout the night, so I'm giving her some pain-killers to be taken when needed. And they will be needed,' he turned to me, speaking in a severe tone, 'I don't want any heroics, young lady. Take them and get some sleep. That injury will keep you from doing very much at all for several days.'

He looked back at Paula, 'I hope there won't not be any recurrence of this sort of thing, Miss Paula. It's potentially quite dangerous the damage your strong-arm people can inflict.'

Paula waved her hand in dismissal of what must have been an oft-repeated complaint, 'Yeah, yeah! I hear you Doctor. This particular problem has been taken care of and I can assure you that it cannot happen again. Anyway, I must get Miss Corrine to her quarters so she can get that rest you've prescribed.'

'Very well Miss Paula, but here are some tablets for Miss Corrine for tonight when the pain kicks back in, and I'll need to see her tomorrow, say, just before lunch if that will suit?'

Paula thought a moment, 'Yes. That should be suitable. I'll make a note on her schedule. Now, come along dear girl. I fear you've had a very poor introduction to the Meditation Centre but hopefully we can redress that bad start very quickly.'

With that, she escorted Corrine out of the room and along yet another long corridor, although this one was considerably more upmarket than the utilitarian ones she just left. There were no sounds and numbered rooms were to the left and right. Paula stopped at Room 38.

'Here we are my dear. I do hope that you'll be comfortable. We've gone to considerable expense to make the rooms as upmarket and relaxing as possible. There is also 24-hour room service, so if there is absolutely anything you need, just pick up the phone and dial 1.'

By now, she'd opened the door with a coded swipe card which she handed to Corrine and ushered her inside a palatial suite of three rooms. The expansive living room had floor to ceiling glass windows that gave a restful view across a manicured grass lawn to a small lake where graceful black swans paddled serenely in the last of the light. Beyond the lake, virgin bush ran toward a series of modest hills which had turned a soft, purple shade in the dying light of the well-set sun. There were no fences to spoil the peaceful scene of the careful blend of man's influence with nature.

Closer at hand, the living room sported a well-equipped bar, a small dining table and writing desk. Comfortable chairs and lounges abounded. A door to the left led to a large bedroom, complete with king-size bed and an en-suite bathroom with a double shower stall with multiple showerheads to form what was promoted in the handouts as a 'stand up spa'.

Corrine turned to Paula after her inspection. 'This looks extremely comfortable thanks Paula, but I'm afraid my arm is starting to cause me some pain as the good doctor suggested, so I might take a couple of those pills and try to get some sleep.'

'Of course, dear girl and my sincere apologies for what has happened to you.' A strange, hungry gleam seemed to come into her eyes as she added, 'If it's any consolation, Dwayne has been severely dealt with and his employment terminated immediately. Unfortunately for him, he won't be able to compete in any more body-building events, or even be seen in public for a very long time.'

Corrine suppressed a shudder, although she felt no compassion for the brutish Dwayne, and casually said, 'Sounds like a suitable punishment for stupidly acting like a Nazi prison camp guard.'

Paula beamed approval at that response. 'I'm so glad you approve, my dear. Now I'll leave you to settle in and please, do try to get some rest. As you indicated on your application, full breakfast will be served here at 07:30 and your first meditation class will be at 09:00. One of our guides will collect you at 08:55. Good night for now Corrine.'

With that, she turned and silently left her.

While making preparations for bed, Corrine mentally took stock of what she'd learned since she'd sent the first text to Dave.

1. *Although painful, the rough up she'd received from Dwayne had allowed her to meet the Doctor who seemed to be an ally, but the morning would prove whether he'd dobbed her in to Paula, or would continue to disclose more secrets that would let her get to the heart of things faster than expected.*

2. *Roger had disclosed the connection between the Organisation's benign front of the Meditation Retreat, and the radical action*

group EarthCare and, ultimately the 'military' side of the so-called retreat, EarthSquad.

3. *Roger also had a potentially very lucrative product to sell, the all-curing ointment that would require a boat trip to setup a supply line and,*

4. *She still had her mobile phone.*

After taking two of Roger's tablets, she composed a lengthy message to Dave and sent it before crawling into bed and slipping into a dreamless slumber.

CHAPTER 7

While Corrine was slowly wakening in her palatial suite in the south-east Queensland bush with a very stiff and sore arm, on the opposite side of the vast, largely uninhabited continent, a lean young stockman sat comfortably slouched in his saddle and allowed his horse to take an easy pace along the dry, red rocky plain. His packhorse who followed, laden with water, supplies and camping gear, was also grateful for the easy pace. It was his second day on patrol of the southwestern sector of the extensive 225,000-hectare Maude Station, right in the middle of the Pilbara iron-ore area of Western Australia.

The boundary and water bore patrols were normally done by helicopter in the station's little Robinson R-22, but since the pilot had recently resigned to move on to bigger and better helicopters in the nearby oil and gas fields, and as the tiny, fragile little thing always seemed to need something to be fixed on it, the manager was quite happy to send out horse patrols instead.

Apart from the usual checking of the bore water pumps, troughs and windmills, the stockman had been asked by the Station Manager to see if he could find any trace of a small herd of valuable cattle. They normally liked to hang around this barren, southwestern corner of the station where the low escarpment sloped down to the mass of marshy, mangrove-lined small creeks which drained the higher ground. At the last head-count, done with the helicopter six months ago, they seemed to be missing from their usual feeding grounds.

He'd just skirted a dry, shallow lake bed which was nearly nine kilometres long and gently nudged his horse in the direction of several large patches of slightly raised ground that remained covered in sparse, tough grass and low bushes year-round. It was the area where the small herd of cattle usually liked to graze and hang out, with fifteen or so females under the control and protection of one old, but still feisty bull. Both horses were more than happy to head toward the fresh feed and picked up the pace a bit. A rough track marking the property boundary fence ran west to east along the southern side of the largest, grass-covered piece of raised ground. The track and fence then dropped off the low escarpment and stopped at the edge of one of many small creeks meandering down to the ocean, which was just five kilometres away and visible through the heat haze as a pretty and tantalising blue line on the horizon.

The herd wasn't visible around any of the grassy areas, and even their hoof marks and droppings were quite old. On the western side of the last grassy patch, the stockman did find a lot of mixed tracks which, after a lot of churning up the ground, seemed to head off toward the sea. There was nothing for the cattle down by the creeks, apart from salt water, mangroves and the occasional crocodile calling them home.

It had been suggested by the Station Manager that maybe a large rogue male croc had moved into the area and might have been responsible for slowly eliminating the herd. But cattle aren't totally stupid, and if an apex predator had moved in, generally they'd stay well away or move out themselves. Still, the mess of hoof marks seemed to suggest that whatever had stirred the cattle, had done so with all of them, but he couldn't see any evidence of them down near the ocean, so didn't search further in that direction.

He spent more time examining the churned-up area, but ignored the human boot marks among the mass of cattle hoof prints.

Had he been just a little psychic, or at least a bit sensitive and not thinking about the new Jillaroo who had finally allowed him to share her bed and her body; he would have felt the gaze of three pair of distant eyes watching his every move. Tension increased between the watchers as the stockman examined the churned-up area, but they relaxed as he re-mounted his horse and moved away.

He had noted the boot marks, but decided against reporting that vital fact via the portable SatPhone he carried. Instead, he thought he'd tell the manager when he got back to the station in two days' time. As it happened, by the time he got back to the station, he was so keen to refresh his erotic memories of Leslie the Jillaroo, and her remarkably compliant body, that he delivered a perfunctory report to the Manager, by saying there was no sign of the small herd and promptly forgot about the boot prints in the scuffed up in the far south west corner.

They (the boot prints) popped into his mind again at a very inopportune time just as he was going through an encore performance with a very appreciative Leslie, but he managed to put those intrusive thoughts aside and rise manfully to the occasion. It wasn't until next morning he mentioned them to the Manager, but suggested that crabbers and barramundi fishermen had been duffing the odd one or two and the rest had bailed out. The Manager distractedly agreed with him, his mind pondering the problem of getting another pilot for the expensive and maintenance-intensive little Robinson R-22 helicopter that the owners had been bugging him to use more often.

NEXT DAY...SAME AREA

The new sun was just a dim promise when two fishermen in a 25ft half-cabin aluminium boat with a 200hp Yamaha outboard doing all the work, roared out of their overnight anchorage around the Mangrove Islands where they'd been successfully hunting mud-crabs. Two of the three freezers mounted in the cockpit were full of the succulent little darlings, properly cooked, cleaned and dismembered.

Still not satisfied with their haul, they were running hard up the coast, aiming for the mass of mostly nameless small creeks inshore from Cowle Island where reports said there were heaps of crabs and barramundi to be had.

The 25 nautical miles to Cowle Island only took about 45 minutes at 35 knots, a speed easily held at this early hour before the usual strong onshore southerly, whipped the shallow coastal waters into froth. But the fishermen planned to be well-ensconced up a small creek long before then, laying pots, retrieving them after just a few minutes then processing the delicious contents. They figured just one more good day would see the third freezer full and they could head back to Onslow to send their catch south to the lucrative markets in Perth. Just this three-day run alone would be worth several weeks' good wages for each of them.

Arriving just off the low-lying, mangrove-infested shore so beloved by mud-crabs directly in from Cowle Island, the driver slowed the boat right back to a slow idle. As the muted roar of the big V-6 Yamaha died away to a soft burble, the pleasant chuckle of water from the bow became noticeable. The two men scanned the shoreline; directions to the best spot were vague from here on, so they were using their years of accumulated knowledge and intuition to make the best choice.

A small inlet opened inshore of them, with a fork giving a choice of two shallow creeks to set their traps, so they headed slowly in, after shutting down and tilting the big motor to reduce drag. They lowered the small 20 horsepower back-up motor which was better for slow manoeuvring and probed as far up the right-hand arm as they could, before tossing over the first of a series of traps baited with smelly fish heads. Coming out of the right arm they moved up the left one, but were disappointed when the inlet shallowed very quickly. They laid a few traps anyway and as they moved back toward the mouth of the inlet, spotted a narrow, but much deeper little creek with a semi-concealed entrance on the north side that wound some distance into a little peninsula. Its banks were lined thickly with mangroves and even from the water; they could see holes in the steep banks that suggested the presence of mud crabs.

What they failed to see, being so focused on signs of crabs, were the heavily camouflaged sterns of several 25-foot RIBs just showing amongst the densely packed low mangroves a little further upstream. A closer inspection might have revealed, had such a thing been allowed, that several of the groups of mangroves were growing in floating boxes, cleverly connected and hinged so they could be easily and quickly drawn aside. When pulled aside, they gave access to a concrete loading ramp beside a short and solid wooden wharf painted green, grey and brown vertical stripes.

Such closer inspection might also have revealed that two of the boats were fully manned with heavily camouflaged and armed men whose undivided attention was on the hapless fishermen slowly entering their trap.

Finally, one of the fishermen, looking further ahead, saw something his brain had trouble identifying.

'Hey Jimmy,' he called to his partner, 'what's that in amongst the mangroves on the left?'

Jimmy looked ahead and toward the spot on the bank where his mate was pointing, but he too had difficulty trying to work out what he was seeing. 'I dunno mate. It looks like some funny mangrove branches, but mangroves don't normally have gun barrels, do they?'

'Oh, shit!' was the panicked reply. 'Let's get the hell out of here!'

Jimmy cranked the throttle open on the little 20 horse outboard, but on a 25-foot boat with the mass of a 200 horse outboard hung off the stern, it was sluggish in the extreme, although they did manage to spin around before the two camouflaged RIBs exploded out from concealment and were on them in seconds.

Jimmy didn't need telling to chop the throttle and sit quietly as the men in full camouflage dress and paint, holding loaded semi-automatic weapons on them, silently and efficiently took their boat in tow back to what was now a wide-open space with a concrete ramp.

At gunpoint, they were herded out of their boat and held while a black bag was pulled over each of their heads and their hands tied behind them. A sharp prod in the back was sufficient message to start stumbling in the indicated direction, even though the ground was very uneven. Finally, still in complete silence, they were halted, then pushed into what felt like a very small hut with rough wood walls and floor. The door was firmly bolted from the outside and they were left in darkness.

When they dared to speak, there was nothing they could do or discover about who their captors were or what their intentions were. Neither man was heard from again.

CHAPTER 8

As per my usual routine, I was awake just before sunrise and out of bed enjoying a hot mug of tea sitting right up in one bow on a small padded seat with my back against the pulpit railing, while my two ladies, Sandy who shares my bed, and our newest recruit Tracy, comfortably ensconced in the stern cabin, were still asleep.

Away from work and the associated rank disparity between Senior Constable and Inspector, both girls had immediately taken to each other in what promised to be a very harmonious relationship. Being of similar age helped the process and Tracy found Sandy to be a far more vocal source of information about our previous adventures than I had been. The telling of just some of those stories had kept both of them up until very late, aided by several of my traditional NQ teas, consisting of a mug of strong, dark tea heavily seasoned with Bundaberg rum liqueur.

By the way they parted last evening, I feared that it wouldn't be long before my dear, lovely Sandy would soon corrupt yet another female crewmember.

My reverie was disturbed by the buzz of an outboard, as Dave swept past heading for the stern. Wondering what was so important to get him up so early, since he's not noted as an early riser, I wandered aft to make him a tea.

'Gidday.' was the extent of his greeting until I had pressed the hot mug into his hand and he'd taken a sip.

'Great, thanks Harry, it's just what I needed, a straight mug of tea. Those bloody women and those blasted alcoholic teas of yours nearly did me in last night.'

I grinned at him, sitting shirtless with broad, muscled shoulders and not a gram of excess fat on his ridged belly. 'You poor old bastard, it must be hard getting to thirty years old. I don't know how you manage to keep going as well as you do.'

'Get fucked, Harry!' he grinned.

'Been there, done that and enjoyed it! Now...what's got you out of bed so early?'

He held up his mobile phone. 'I just got a text message from Corrine with another report. It's not very long, but she hopes to have more information later today.'

He passed the phone over and let me read it, which wasn't easy as she'd written it like a routine chatty note to Dave, with stuff like the food, staff and her palatial accommodation. She mentioned having a minor accident which hurt her arm when she slipped and was saved from falling by a very big and strong staff member who was escorting her to her quarters. When she commented that the slip was due to my usual clumsiness, I said to Dave, 'that's a warning. She's never been clumsy a single day in her life. Sounds like some goon tried to hassle her and damaged her arm.'

Dave face grew a very dark look, 'I didn't pick up on that. Do you think she's OK?'

'Yeah yeah, she'll be fine, dude. If she wanted to, she could've wiped the floor with this clown's face, so she's just into playing her part and holding back. Anyway, there's not much more of consequence, so we'll have to wait until she sends the next message.'

By then, Sandy and Tracy had joined us and as Dave was here and Sandy wasn't going to work, they set to making a very welcome hot breakfast.

EARTHCARE WELLNESS RETREAT... THURSDAY MORNING

At about the time the crew on the boat were sitting down to their breakfast, Corrine surfaced slowly from a deep sleep, having spent part of the night awake, but this morning, her arm was just stiff and a bit sore. The painful and movement-restricting damage of the night before seemed to have been repaired by the magic ointment, so with renewed appetite, she looked forward to her breakfast. It was delivered on time and proved to be just as perfectly prepared as her dinner was last night. After she'd eaten and cleaned herself up, a knock at the door announced the arrival of her escort to her first meditation session.

A young woman stood waiting patiently outside in the corridor, dressed in a tightly fitted and very revealing, one-piece jumpsuit in a pleasant blue-grey colour. It had an intriguing silver zip with a large and ornate silver ring dangling from the slider that ran from the scooping neckline to the well-defined division in her groin. '*They certainly don't believe in modesty pads,*' Corrine thought, '*but if you've got a body like she has, why not?*'

She seemed very comfortable wearing it and almost preened under Corrine's frank appraisal.

'Good morning, Miss Corrine, I'm Janine.'

'Hi. Nice jumpsuit you're wearing Janine,' Corrine commented, as the girl led her down the long corridor.

Janine smiled, 'Thank you. They're very comfortable and feel great.'

'Is it a uniform?' Corrine asked, 'I've not seen others wearing them.'

'Oh yes, it is a uniform, but they're only for those of us who perform escort duties around the Centre and serve in the guest wings.'

'It doesn't seem to allow you much choice in the way of underwear.' Corrine commented wryly.

The girl laughed. 'Underwear is optional, but Mr Terry really likes us to be without if we can. And I must confess that I prefer to go without. It makes me feel free and less constricted.'

She led the way, exchanging lightweight pleasantries on the long walk to the classroom block, where Corrine had to suffer through two back-to-back lectures with several other meditation hopefuls, although the slight residual ache in her arm kept her from nodding off too often.

Then it was time to visit Doctor Roger at the Medical Centre, and it was Janine who came back and led her the shorter distance to the Medical Centre, although there were still long corridors!

'What's with the long corridors?' Corrine finally asked. 'There must be better ways to design buildings.'

Janine giggled, 'True. But Mr Terry wanted it that way and his Head of Security, Mr Joshua, advises him on all that stuff. Still, it keeps us fit.'

She became solemn for a moment, 'Please, be careful if you meet Mr Joshua. None of the girls like him. He can be very cruel!'

Corrine filed that interesting little tit-bit away for future reference before asking, 'How many staff do what you do...that is, being an escort?'

Janine smiled again, 'Just six of us for now, but the meditation business must be good with more guests booking in every day, so there are another six girls in training.'

'Aren't there any men doing the escort job?'

'Oh no. Only girls, and we have to be very fit and conform to a set appearance, weight and height limits. We also have to train for two hours every day.'

She giggled again, 'If we don't measure up, literally, at our monthly medical, we get demoted and sent to the kitchens or to work as ground keepers, although Dr Roger is rather yummy, so none of us mind being examined by him!'

Corrine frowned, 'A medical every month seems a bit extreme. Why so often?'

Janine blushed slightly. 'We also get to look after Mr Terry and Miss Paula in their private quarters, so they want to make sure we're in the best possible shape, I guess. But still, the job does pay very well.'

It didn't take a Masters in Nuclear Physics to work out what 'looking after' Terry and Paula might entail, so Corrine refrained from comment, but filed that very interesting piece of info away with the rest.

Testing the water, she casually asked, 'Do you work with the volunteers as well as here in the Meditation Centre?'

Janine was quite happy to answer. 'Oh no. They have to look after themselves. They all take turns in doing what needs to be done, depending on their particular skills.'

She giggled again, something Corrine was suspecting might be a nervous response.

'If someone's only skill is being enthusiastic to help the 'Cause', they get trained in basic stuff like cooking and cleaning. The more skills someone has, the higher up the order they're placed.'

'Do you mean the volunteers are organised like a para-military group?'

Janine beamed, 'Yes, exactly. That's the term I was looking for. Just like the military. My dad was in the army, so I know what it's like. They're even assigned ranks the same as the army. I know they do lots and lots of training out in the bush and on the weapons range. We often hear guns firing!'

That news cheered Corrine up considerably, as it would seem she had an even better chance of being asked to join the radicalised volunteer group.

By then they'd arrived at the Medical Centre and Janine handed Corrine over to the receptionist. While she wasn't the same one as the previous night, she was equally pretty and bubbly.

'Hi Miss Corrine. I'm Abby. Please go straight in; Doctor's expecting you.'

Corrine smiled and went into the main examination room where Roger was waiting.

'Hi Corrine. I see that the arm is still giving you a bit of trouble.'

'Hi Roger. Actually, it's pretty good, considering. I'm sure it would have been a lot worse without your magic ointment.'

'Yes, it's good stuff. Now, if you would slip your shirt off please and sit on the examination table, I'll take a good look at it.'

She did so, showing that she usually chose not to wear a bra.

'Ahh, that's excellent. The bruising has started to fade already, even though it still seems tender. I'll apply another coating of ointment and a light bandage which will increase its effectiveness.'

Before he started, he looked out the part open door to see if Abby was at her desk, and reassured that she was, came back to Corrine. As he started to gently apply the pungent green goo, he spoke softly.

'I've heard this morning that based on your CV, Paula has you tagged as a potential recruit for EarthSquad. It has got them quite excited. I've also been told to give you a full medical workup as soon as your arm has settled down, so we'll do it tomorrow if you're happy?'

Corrine shrugged casually. 'Sure. No problem. But what happens then?'

'If you're willing to join their movement and I really have to advise extreme caution about doing so, they'll terminate your meditation booking and refund your money. You'll be transferred to the barracks area, but because you're being considered for immediate officer status based on your previous army training and experience, the change in comfort level won't be a lot different.'

She nodded, relishing again the buzz the ointment produced and particularly enjoying the tickle in her groin, especially with a handsome young doctor in close proximity. She noticed her bare nipples coming to attention, but didn't care he noticed as well.

Roger chuckled. 'That's one of the more pleasurable side effects of the ointment. It can get quite addictive.'

'By the way, I've taken the liberty of asking my partner Jill, who's also my Theatre Nurse, to drop in to meet you, particularly in regard to the enterprise discussion we had last night. She's generally in favour of a deal, but we'll need to meet your partner Dave and discuss it a lot more in detail at another place and time I'm afraid.'

As if scripted, there was a soft knock on the door and a blonde head poked around the edge, its owner sliding smoothly through the gap.

'Hi Dear, it's only me. Hi Corrine, I'm Jill.'

She showed no sign of surprise to see her partner chatting to a half-naked young woman, and quickly shook Corrine's hand, a broad smile on her pretty face.

She was short, but trim, curvy and moved with a feline grace that suggested she might be a gym-junkie. An air of vitality surrounded her as she moved to stand close to Roger.

'Roger told me about your offer of the use of your boat to visit this island in the Indonesian Archipelago. That would seem to solve one major problem with transportation, but how will your partner feel about making the trip?'

'Dave?' she asked. 'Oh he'll be fine. He's a bit of an adventure junkie too, so anything out of the ordinary will make him very happy.'

Jill smiled. 'That's good to hear. So how are you placed financially? I appreciate that since you've booked in for the meditation course, you must be fairly well off, but this trip will cost a lot, and Roger and I are still saving hard.'

Corrine shrugged. 'Funding won't be a problem. We're in very good shape.'

Jill's smile grew even bigger. 'Terrific! That's really good to hear. We're not asking you to fund the operation, since it was our idea to start with, so we want to pay our way, but since we don't know how long this gig will last, or when we can take this trip, it's good to know that money, or lack of it, won't hold us back.'

'Timing might be more important than having all your funding in place,' Corrine observed, noting that Jill was smiling slightly at her erect nipples. 'I appreciate you want to pay your way, but if you haven't got enough when we're ready to go, we shouldn't postpone the trip. We have plenty of money and you can pay us back out of profits if this stuff sells as well as I think it should. It's done wonders for my arm, not to mention the other effects I can feel!'

Jill giggled, 'I must admit Roger and I have played around with small amounts at times and it is very stimulating and great fun!'

'That's good to know. When we get some, I wouldn't mind giving it a try.'

Roger looked at Corrine, a speculative expression on his face.

'You know, getting back to the EarthCare business, when Paula gets around to inviting you to join their movement, you'll have to be a lot more enthusiastic than you have been here. I know the ointment affects you and I've told you we don't support these ratbags, so that's OK. In here you can relax. But with Paula and the others, you'll have to go back to being a rabid tree-hugger.'

Reality chewed through the euphoric ointment-induced haze, as Corrine realised that she could've blown her cover if she'd been with anyone other than Roger and Jill!

No wonder Harry had been so insistent about staying sober and sticking with her legend, which included the ways and means of lying with a straight face.

She nodded, 'Yeah, I guess you're right, but I've let down my guard with you guys because you definitely aren't with the program!'

Roger laughed, 'No problem, but you'll really have to be careful from here on in. There are very few others who will be around to help or protect you like we can.'

Corrine looked at them as carefully as her slight double vision allowed.

'Thanks for that guys, but where do you stand?'

Jill shrugged, 'When we were hired as a team to run the Medical Centre, it all seemed a dream come true—generally light work and hours that pays incredibly well. But lately what we've seen and heard suggests there's some very nasty business being planned, so we think we should cut and run before they decide to clean up loose ends like us who might have heard too much. We'd like to be able to walk out on our own terms, but we have some concerns about that. We might be simply taken out and I don't just mean out the front gate!'

'How can you be so sure that they'll resort to such violence?'

Jill gave a grim smile. 'That goon who messed up your arm was beaten senseless last night, and then strangled. Paula did it. It's one of her little fetishes.'

Corrine nodded, 'OK. That seems fairly good evidence. But how many more staff members don't like what's being planned? And while we're at it—just what is being planned?'

Jill looked at Roger who shrugged and said, 'Corrine seems to have guessed most of the story, and so she might as well hear the rest.'

Jill took a deep breath then moved a little so she could see that Abby was still at her desk, tapping away at the keyboard, before turning back to Corrine.

'We don't know about the volunteers, but there are perhaps six or eight staff who think like we do and could be relied on to help. As for what's being planned, they're going to seize the Barleyrock gas processing plant near Onslow in Western Australia and hold it to ransom.

The demand will be that the Federal Government withdraws all mineral exploration licences; permanently, and shuts down every gas and oil plant in Australia.

If those demands aren't met, they're prepared to blow up the Barleyrock plant as well as the gas field supplying it, 60 nautical miles to the north west of Onslow.'

Corrine's eyebrows had slowly climbed with this revelation, until she said, 'Bloody hell! That's insane! I mean, there's no way the Government will give in to those or any other demands! So then it becomes a game of chicken! Who'll blink first?'

Roger nodded grimly, 'You've got it! Terry might be charismatic, but it'd be a long stretch to say he's rational! And when it comes to stuff like that, Paula is even worse and she's pushing him. Anyway, there's more.'

Corrine groaned, 'Oh no. What is it?'

'Having locked their target in, they've already gone ahead and set up a base in the Pilbara region, just north of Onslow, but under the guise of a 'Marine Eco Study Centre' where their recruit volunteers are supposed to visit to study the delicate eco-systems that might be under threat from all the gas and oil operations in the area.'

Corrine thought a moment, 'Sounds like a good cover for an attack base.'

Roger gave a feral grin, 'Yep. You've got it in one. That's exactly what it is.'

'OK. So why not just send in the WA Police Tactical Response Group and clean them out?'

Jill took a deep breath and said, 'Because some time back, Earth-Care applied to the WA Government for a grant and permission to set up camp on a small spit of land along the useless coastal fringe, adjacent to Maude Station which is quite unusable for any other purpose, being virtually mangrove swamp. Therefore, with an election next year, the Government would lose a lot of face, along with the election, if word were to get out that they had spent public money to set up an eco-terrorism camp, right in the middle of Australia's largest gas and oil area.'

Corrine thought a moment more. 'That's certainly an 'Oh shit!' moment, but where is the rest of the money coming from to do this? I'm sure the WA Government didn't supply it all. And while we're on the subject, how come you guys are so well informed and seem to be sticking your necks out so far? I thought I was the only one who was a bit 'not quite what she seems'?'

Roger looked at Jill a moment and something passed between them.

'Let's just say for now that we're just concerned citizens who see and hear things they don't like and would like to be able to help stop it happening. By the same token, we don't know anything about you, either. As in...where you're coming from and what's your real reason for being here?'

Corrine had to think quickly and the euphoric, groin-tingling effect from the ointment was making that difficult. 'You've been honest with me and although I can't say too much, let's just say word has leaked to the extent that some highly-placed people are very interested in what EarthCare is really up to. I've been sent to find out what I can and get word back and from what you've told me, I really need to get this information out to them via my crew.'

Roger nodded, 'OK. Have you sent anything to Dave yet?'

'Sure have. But I tried to make it sound like just a light-hearted chat, in case they can monitor mobiles.'

Roger grimly nodded again. 'Yes, they can. The Head of Security, Joshua Koll is a very mean and dangerous bastard. I've had to treat a lot of injuries he's caused to staff, male and female although he prefers females! He's right up-to-date with electronic surveillance, so he's certainly tapped into your phone. Hopefully your messages were sufficiently innocuous that he doesn't suspect anything.'

Jill chipped in, 'I think if he did, he'd have let you know by now. You've been here 24 hours, so how many messages have you sent?'

'Just the one so far, to say I'd arrived here and I'd had a minor accident by slipping because I'm so clumsy. I tried to give a few more hints that things weren't right, but that was all.'

Roger laughed, 'Good one. But Jill's right. Joshua would've been on you straight away if he was suspicious, so things are OK for you for now.'

Jill looked at her watch, 'How's the time going for Corrine, Hon?'

Roger checked the clock on the wall, 'Oh shit! We're running way overtime. You should be at lunch then more meditation lectures this afternoon.'

'Can't you tell Paula that I need more treatment or something? I really need to find a way to pass this latest batch of information to Dave and my people safely. Can you help with that?'

Jill spoke up, 'I'll ask Abby to call Paula and say you decided to do Corrine's full medical today as she's much better and you're just doing the workup on her blood test. That should hold her for a while longer.'

Roger smiled, 'Great idea. I'll write up some plausible results while we think about safe communications.'

CHAPTER 9

The four of us sat around the cockpit table working on lists of stuff to do, so we'd be ready to move quickly if we got the appropriate word from Corrine and that really suited Jasper and Krazy who loved any extra attention they could bludge; from anyone. I'd called the FlexTank suppliers and they had all the tanks and fittings we wanted in stock in Brisbane and for guaranteed overtime, promised delivery for the next morning. They kindly offered to fit and test them all for us, something I was more than happy to let them do.

Routine maintenance items like extra oil for engines, fuel and oil filters and other spares in case of problems would need to be loaded, with all the heavy items going onto *Seeker*, since she was less affected by being overweight. Dave and I decided to get another two FlexTanks for new and used oil storage to save having to manhandle 60litre drums down below decks and I called immediately to add those to the order.

It was while we were talking about the flex tanks that Dave had a thought. 'Just to cover all possibilities, how about we get four, two-person inflatable kayaks in case we need to make a covert approach by water to a target? You never know...it might just happen.'

'Inflatable kayaks? I don't know about that. It doesn't seem like they'd be very stiff and probably a bitch to paddle.'

'Nah. One of the guys on a boat just down from *Seeker* has one and he reckons it's the duck's guts! It folds up into a backpack or small duffle which can be stowed anywhere. He's got a two-seater he and his lady have taken into all sorts of places. They use it a lot as a sea-kayak exploring rocky inlets they can't get their boat too close to. He says it's very stable, paddles easily and tracks well. He's even used it to do some surfing, but Helen doesn't like that, so he converts it to a single-seater in seconds and has some fun on smaller waves.'

'Well, if you think they'd be useful, sure. Let's get four. If they pack down as small as you say, there's plenty of space to stow them.'

So Dave ordered four Advanced Elements AF Convertible 2-Person Inflatable Kayaks and was assured that express delivery for an additional fee would have them at his door by tomorrow morning.

He'd just got off the phone when he had another thought. 'Portable comms!'

I looked at him.

'C'mon Harry. We need those little portable comms units with earplugs and mini-mikes. We can't do anything covert if we're running around with a bunch of hand-held UHF CB units squawking '10-4 good buddy, what's your 10-20' all the time!'

I nodded, the penny dropping. 'Yep, you're right. I'll just call the quartermaster.'

'*Hi Harry, what's going on?*'

'Just ordered the fuel tanks, but Dave pointed out that we don't have any covert portable comms. Can you lay your hands on eight sets of the earplug and mini-mike variety and get them to us by tomorrow morning?'

'*Good point mate. I'm sure we either have them or I'll get them sent down from Brisbane stores by patrol car immediately. Either way, leave it to me and I'll let you know when to expect them. Is that all for now?*'

'Yep, that'll be great thanks Greg. Cheers for now.'

In the absence of Amanda, our regular cook, Sandy and Tracy made a fair shot at checking the pantry and drawing up re-stocking lists, but they suggested that we hold off the shopping until the last minute when Amanda was on board and could check things properly.

Dave, who always did the catering and cooking on *Seeker*, chuckled at my concern, 'I've got my shopping list done. I'll make sure there's enough for all. We've got bigger freezers than yours Harry. But who's going to be my crew this time?'

I mentally kicked myself for overlooking such a simple but vital briefing item. I blamed the distraction of getting Tracy briefed and aboard. 'Sorry mate, I clean forgot to go over things with you in the rush. It's been a busy couple of days. Anyway, if we go, it'll be the same crew as at the end of the last job. You'll have Alf Story and Charlie Jakes with you again, but since you're missing Corrine, I thought Melissa would move over to *Seeker* until she returns. She and Charlie are still an item, so that should suit them fine.

That leaves me with Sandy, Amanda and Tracy, so the numbers are balanced and that will help with watch-keeping planning for all this non-stop cruising.'

'That's fine by me. You don't think Corrine can be extracted from the retreat before we go?'

'No, I don't; unless she blows her cover, in which case she's outta there immediately. She's keeping a low profile, so I think she'll want to stick with it and find out as much as she can. This means that if it's a go, we sail without her and she catches up when she can.'

He grinned, 'OK. I can live with that; but she'll be pissed to miss out on the trip around the top end.'

Just about then, Dave's mobile sounded a hunting-horn type call announcing an incoming message. He opened it, read a few moments then with a puzzled look, showed it to me. It read, 'Enable iMessage on an iPhone and advise number to this number via text, then standby for incoming encrypted voice message.'

I promptly passed it to Sandy, since she was our comms expert. She took one look, whipped her own iPhone out of her pocket, played with some buttons for a few moments and then grabbed Dave's phone, which was a Samsung something or other. She played with several more buttons, typed a string of some things, pressed a final button then handed it back to him.

'You can put it away now,' she advised, 'the message will come in on this one.'

Nothing happened for several minutes then Sandy's phone made a warbling tone. She pressed a couple of buttons again and Corrine's voice echoed from the tiny speaker.

'Hi Dave. I hope things are well with you and this is getting through. I also hope Harry and the others are with you, but if not, this message is saved to iCloud and can be retrieved but only on this phone since it's encrypted. I can't talk long even though this is being sent as a data burst and shouldn't be able to be intercepted.

I'm OK and have found some friends who are helping me keep a low profile, but I had to get this information to you urgently.'

There was a brief pause, before she resumed.

'Sorry about that. Another staff member we're not sure about came in, but she's out of hearing now. OK. EarthCare, aka EarthSquad, are eco-terrorists, and they've set up a base in the Pilbara, just up the coast from Onslow with, of all things, partial funding from the Western Australian Government who didn't know what was going on.

Their prime objective is to seize the Barleyrock LNG processing plant 14 kilometres west of Onslow and hold it to ransom. The demand will be for the Australian Government to shut down all oil and gas wells Australia-wide immediately and to cease all exploration immediately. If their demands are not met within 72 hours, they intend to blow the plant, any ships loading at the time and also the main production wells 225 kilometres north of Onslow. They are organised on para-military lines, are incredibly well-funded, and so far appear to be totally ruthless. The head guy, Terry Williams is a misguided wacko with delusions of grandeur and his sidekick, Paula Henderson is a vicious bitch who loves S&M and gets off on killing with her bare hands.

They also have a head of security, Joshua Koll, who's a sadistic arse-hole, but very skilled. He monitors normal mail and all phone calls, and that's why I'm resorting to this, but I can't do it too often, so keep the phone you've got charged and handy. If I get sprung, I'll just run, but at the moment I stand a good chance of being invited to join their happy band of terrorists, so naturally I'm planning to stay and see what else I can learn.

All I can say is that you need to head for the Pilbara ASAP. The base camp is right on the coast on the tip of a small peninsula, surrounded by mangroves and directly opposite a small island called Cowle Island. Co-ordinates are S21°15.047' E115° 47.726' and it's about 46 nautical miles up the coast from Onslow. I'll make contact again when it's safe to do so. Bye for now.'

There was a stunned silence at the final click as the message concluded. I looked around at the others.

'Well, I guess that answers the 'what are they up to?' question.'

I looked at my watch then at Sandy. 'Can you copy that onto a flash drive or something? I need to get a copy to Greg and Bob, and then we need to get Amanda, Melissa, Alf and Charlie aboard tonight.'

She nodded. 'I'll do that, email it to him and then call in the others. You call Bob and give them the good news.' She went to the Nav station where all the electronic stuff was kept and got busy.

Dave commented, 'We can't go until we get those bladder tanks fitted, so the girls can finalise the shopping lists tonight and do a shopping run first thing tomorrow. If we're lucky and there are no problems, we can be moving by midday.'

I nodded, my mind racing with planning, but Dave was right; there was nothing to do except wait until the tanks were fitted and tested, but for now we could get the rest of the crew aboard, briefed and settled. Leaving Sandy to do her tasks, I grabbed my phone and called Bob.

'Hi Harry. I presume you have news?'

'Gidday Bob, yes I have and it's not good. Corrine has made contact in a roundabout way, so Sandy's emailing you a copy of a lengthy voice message we received encrypted to dodge eavesdroppers.'

'That sounds like things aren't as peaceful as they should be at the peaceful Meditation Resort!'

Bob really shouldn't try to make jokes so I ignored this one. 'The essence of the report is that EarthCare is a bunch of over-funded eco-terrorists with high ideals. The military arm is called

EarthSquad and they've set up a base on the Pilbara coast, just north of Onslow with the approval of and some financial assistance from the WA Government. How that came about, we don't know, but it might be useful to find out. However, what the WA Government doesn't know about their new guests is that they intend to attack and seize the Barleyrock LNG processing plant at Onslow. They will then demand the Federal Government shut down all oil and gas wells and plants Australia-wide immediately and terminate all exploration licences. If those minor demands aren't met, they intend to blow the whole plant, any ships that happen to be loading at the time, and simultaneously attack and blow up all the main gas platforms feeding the plant.'

It must have been an afternoon for stunned silences, since here was another one, before Bob thought of something intelligent to say.

'Well fuck me! They don't mess around, do they? OK Harry, I guess you're going to activate your plan to get over there as quickly as possible?'

'Yeah, that's the go. Sandy's calling the rest of the crew to get aboard tonight, but we're still waiting for the long-range tanks to be delivered and fitted. The crew are supposed to come down from Brisbane sometime tomorrow morning.'

'Leave that to me. I've got the details on my desk now, so I'll call and have them on your doorstep at 06:00 tomorrow. Will that do?'

'That'd be great, Bob. We can get a good night's sleep, finish restocking food and other stuff while that's happening and be gone before midday.'

'Good work, Harry. I presume that Corrine is bailing out?'

'Ahh...no, she's not. She says there's an opportunity to get selected for officer status in their para-military organisation, so she's staying on for now. But in our absence, I'll ask you to be prepared to extract her quickly if things go pear-shaped. Apparently there are some very nasty people who've been attracted to this mob.

Oh, and we think it might be interesting to put a couple of your best financial investigators onto tracking the source of funding for EarthCare. There's way too much money for Terry Williams to have put up, and the Meditation Resort has only been in operation a few months.'

'*Copied all that, Harry. I'll keep an eye out for trouble from Corrine and with regard to the financial stuff; I have just the pair to do that. We contract the services of two ex-Tax Office investigators. They're like bulldogs when they get a sniff of dirty dealings and have proved very effective at tracing money trails.*'

'OK thanks Bob. I'll get going, and you have a listen to that voice message, but I don't need to remind you to keep it quiet. It needs to be booted up to the Commissioner immediately, so make your own copy.'

'*Got it, Harry. I see it's in my inbox now. Call me if I can help with anything, but keep me informed, please.*'

'Will do, Bob. Cheers.'

I hung up and Sandy reported she'd spoken to the four remaining crew and they were heading home immediately to pack. She'd also arranged for an unmarked police car to do a pickup run to each address and then deliver them to the Yacht Club.

With all that in place, there wasn't much else to do, so Sandy and Tracy poured beers and wines and we sat around waiting for the others to arrive. We were on our second round when there was a hail from the end of the Yacht Club Marina from a group of four young, lean and fit persons who managed to look exactly like what they were; a para-military group on a mission. I'd have to speak to them about that.

Dave did the taxi honours with his dinghy, leaving Melissa, Alf and Charlie to sort out cabins and stow their gear on *Seeker*, while he ran Amanda out to *Firebird*. He then went back to pickup his new crew and brought them over.

It was good to see Alf and Charlie again, since they'd often dropped in on Dave for a beer on a hot afternoon, but they'd only rarely visited my cat.

We held a briefing which brought everybody up-to-date and raised the crew's eyebrows somewhat. To Sandy's and my relief,

Amanda immediately took over the catering planning for *Firebird*, consulting with Dave about how much extra freezer space on *Seeker* she could plan on using.

I was interested to see how Tracy would fit in and noted that while she and Sandy got on extremely well, Amanda and Melissa were more reserved with her. Nothing that should be a problem, but it was a situation that needed watching.

I figured there would be plenty of time in the morning for the girls to do the shopping while the tank installation was going ahead, so told everyone to grab drinks and relax for the evening.

SOUTHPORT YACHT BASIN…FRIDAY

I was up early as usual and savouring my steaming mug of sweet tea on the bow seat, but was happy to be joined by Tracy as well as Jasper. Krazy was still curled up with Sandy, and Amanda was also asleep.

'Sleep alright?' I asked politely, offering her a sip of tea, but she shook her head.

'Yes, for a while,' she replied, 'being on a boat seems a great way to relax, but I guess that I'm a bit concerned how I'll be on this long trip. I'm not really used to small boats; my last sail was on a cruise ship!'

'Do you get motion sick?' was my next question.

She grinned, 'No, thank goodness! Nothing at all like that and I've been in enough situations where that affliction could have shown up and so far hasn't. I'm just concerned I won't be able to do my full share of work properly. You all seem to know what you're doing and while this is a beautiful boat, I don't know anything about sailing and it all looks very complicated.'

I figured this was more of her general insecurity coming out, and was about always needing to be in control of each situation, so I tried to be reassuring. 'I understand. But there's an easy way. Until you get used to shipboard routine, just start small and concentrate on the normal stuff you do know, like helping Amanda in the galley and doing general housekeeping. The boat and sail handling will come to you with exposure and experience and I can guarantee that by the time we get to Onslow, you'll be as expert as any of the others.'

'OK. That sounds like a good plan, but yesterday you and Dave were talking about watch keeping. How can I do that without experience?'

'No problem. For the first couple of days, I'll pair you with either myself or Sandy for each watch, which means that while we're all still fresh, we'll break the watches into 4-hour segments through the day and two 6-hours segments at night. That way, we can all get some decent sleep and you'll have somebody with you while you're learning.'

She still looked concerned, so I added, 'But don't be too concerned about the sailing or boat-handling part, since the systems are very automated and we don't stand at the wheel manually steering all day and night.'

That seemed to relieve her concerns and I'd just offered to get another tea each, when there was a shout from *Seeker's* berth on the outside arm of the Yacht Club marina. I looked over to see Dave standing in the cockpit waving, with several men armed with a variety of tools and equipment.

I waved back to show that I understood, told Tracy to hold the tea until I brought the tradies back with me, then jumped in the dinghy for the short trip to shore. The foreman introduced himself briefly as Reg and after indicating a pile of remarkably small boxes on a trolley, told me that he'd brought a variety of tanks with him so we could choose the best ones to fit the particular places on each boat.

'After a quick look at the big cruiser, I'd recommend two of the cylindrical 1250 litre ones strapped down in the side walkways on the boat's balance point. You can still walk on them—just a bit soft and squishy when some fuel is drained out. But one or even two of these other ones can go in the cockpit, and they're 1000 litre and don't take up much space as they're rectangular and taller than the cylindrical ones.

For your catamaran, as I understand it, you want just two tanks down as low as possible?'

I nodded, 'Yes, they have to be on the balance point as well because we're a sailing cat and trim is vital.'

He understood. 'So I should be able to put one cylindrical tank down on the cabin sole in each hull, centred on the balance point, but those ones only come as 430 litres each. The next size up is 800 litres and that might be a bit much. But the 430 litre jobbies are very compact at 1.5 x 0.6 metres when full, so they won't take up much room and can easily be walked on. To make up the lost capacity, I'd suggest fitting one more of those in your cockpit, and if it is as big as most other cats I've fitted out, you'll hardly notice it if we position it against the stern seat base. That'll give you 1290 litres and won't muck up your trim very much, especially if you draw fuel from the cockpit tank first.'

'Sounds reasonable,' I commented, 'but do you have all these tanks?'

He waved a hand airily at the loaded trolley on the jetty, 'Of course. I always bring several choices to a new installation because quite often the clients either give us the wrong dimensions or change their minds when they see how compact our tanks are and want bigger ones. So this way, if we're not sure what will fit where, we can mix and match.'

He undid one of the compact, colourful boxes on the trolley and pulled out a bright orange roll of stiff fabric which was much lighter than I expected. 'That's how the tanks will roll up when you don't need to use them. Just cap the inlet, outlet and vent and they'll stow almost anywhere. Then you can just leave the hard-plumbed valves and pumps in place for when you need to use the tanks again.'

'OK. Good plan. Both boats will have a lot more fuel than we need and that's good. I'll hang around here and take you out when you've done this one.'

'Nah. I've got orders from your boss to bring enough hands to fit out both boats at the same time, so the job's done as quickly as possible, and since he's paying the extra overtime, that's what we gotta do. I've got three more lads unloading more gear in the car park, so if you can run me out to your boat now with the bladders, pumps and fittings we've chosen, then come back and pick up two more lads to work with me, the rest of the crew will get stuck into this one. Let's get cracking, boys.'

I was almost cursing Bob's enthusiasm, but contained myself and went with the flow–in this case the mercurial Reg, who looked like he'd not stand for any argument. We loaded three rolled bladders, fittings and sundry boxes of stuff into my RIB and motored across the glassy-smooth water, just being softly kissed by the first of the sun's low, golden rays. I hoped Tracy had dug Sandy and Amanda out of bed–if not they were in for a rude awakening!

Which is what they did get! Tracy was still sitting up on a bow seat when we came puttering back and came aft to take the dinghy line.

'Gidday Missus,' was the nuggetty Reg's greeting, 'we've come to disturb your lovely morning for a while. Won't be long I hope, so long as everything behaves itself.'

'Hi,' Tracy stammered in reply, obviously having forgotten the work crews were starting so early, but recovered and helped move the pile of stuff we handed up to her to stow in the cockpit. However, in the rush, I clean forgot to warn Sandy and Amanda, so as I led Reg down below in the starboard hull to show him where the first of the two 430 litre bladders was to reside, we were greeted by a sleepy and very naked Sandy coming out of the bathroom.

'Hello Missus,' was the old fella's casual greeting, as he nevertheless cast an appreciative eye up and down her lush body, 'we've come to disturb your sleep-in I'm afraid, but we won't be too long.'

To her credit, Sandy did none of the usual naked female things, like shriek and try to cover herself, but simply wished him 'Good morning' in return, glared at me and brushed calmly past us to return to our cabin where she shut the door to get dressed.

'Sorry about that,' I apologised to the old fella, 'guess I forgot to let her know we were coming straight back.'

He chuckled. 'Don't apologise to me, boyo! That's the loveliest early morning sight I've seen in many a long year. But I do believe you might have to apologise to her unless you want to sleep alone tonight!'

I nodded ruefully then showed him where each bladder should be laid out on the cabin sole where it wouldn't affect the boat's trim. I also showed him the fuel filler lines that came down from the deck filling caps.

He nodded, 'No problem. They're easy to get at, so we'll splice a T-valve into those filler pipes each side, then you can pump from the bladders directly into each main tank. That way, your original fuel delivery system to the engines won't be disturbed and when you turn on a transfer pump, you'll just fill each main tank.

On the filling side, I always install filters and water traps in-line before the T-valve, to keep the supply clean. Just turn this valve to fill either main or bladder tank from the deck fill point. You won't be able to fill both tanks each side simultaneously, but it shouldn't be too much of a problem.'

'No. That'll be fine, but is the transfer pump manual or electric?'

'As the primary pump, I'll fit a high-flow electric pump to each side that's very reliable, but I'll leave you a high-rate manual one which can be fitted in parallel with the electric one to either side in seconds if necessary. It's very unlikely you'll need it, since the electric pumps have an excellent record, but at sea, it pays to be sure, to be sure.'

I wasn't sure if he was taking the piss with the Irish thing, but he seemed to know what he was doing, so after showing him where fuel and power lines ran, I left to pick up his two workers. Fortunately, Tracy had dug Amanda out of bed so she was at least up, dressed and brewing tea in the galley.

'I'm in the shit with Sandy for not getting her out of bed before I brought the foreman back, even though I didn't know they wanted to work on both boats at the same time, so could you tell her that I've just gone to get two more workers and some more gear, then I'll be back. I think she's holed up in the cabin with Jasper.'

Amanda laughed and pushed me out into the cockpit, 'Piss off, Harry. Go do what you have to do. She'll be fine and I'll have fresh tea ready when you get back.'

I gave her an appreciative grin and couldn't resist giving her firm bum an affectionate pat, much to Tracy's interest, then motored back to the jetty where two burly young guys and a small pile of gear stood waiting. There was much activity on *Seeker* with people laying out bladder tanks along the topside walkways and running cables to the switchboard, and pipes to T-fittings which mounted externally on the deck fillers. Dave wasn't in sight, although Melissa was sucking on a mug of coffee at the cockpit table, obviously staying out of the way of the action, so I just waved, then loaded up and motored back to *Firebird*.

Sandy was there to take the dinghy rope and gave me a quick kiss of forgiveness.

'You can be such a goose sometimes Harry,' she said with a grin, 'but I'm going to steal the dinghy so Amanda and I can go get the shopping. Does Dave need anything?'

'He said he's done it all,' I replied, 'but how about I run you ashore in case we need to get some more bits from the tradies truck?'

'How about you don't,' she countered, 'we've ordered everything on-line and it's being delivered to the beach at the end of the main street in about ten minutes. If the guys need anything, tell them to hold on until we're back. Should only be about 15 to 20 minutes.'

Her logic made sense, so I gave way gracefully and waved them away in a cloud of spray. Sandy loves opening up the outboard and I've often had to tell her to slow down around the other boats. For a Police Inspector, she could be a real tear-arse when she took those three pips off her shoulders!

Work on *Firebird* seemed to be going well and I knew when to stay out of the way and let the experts do their job, so I sat chatting with Tracy, trying to get to know the real person behind the mask of ambition to achieve perfection that seemed to drive her every step. It also seemed she either didn't know or had lost the knack of relaxing and doing simple, frivolous things that were pleasurable, like playing with a length of cord with a small, black kitten firmly attached by jaws and claws to the other end, while Jasper, as was usual when outsiders were aboard, stayed out of sight in my for'rard dressing room.

The pile of fittings and other equipment which had been scattered messily around the cockpit slowly diminished, although the stack of empty boxes grew proportionally, and as I couldn't hear too many curses directed at the installation, things must have been going well. Luckily, there was no need to fetch anything else and the girls were back in the promised twenty minutes, travelling considerably slower than the outward journey, since there was only a few centimetres of freeboard left, even on the RIB.

Amanda was pretty well boxed in by, well, boxes, and needed some removed before she could climb out.

Sandy stayed in to pass a seemingly endless stream of bags, boxes and mysterious parcels up to the chain we formed to get everything into the galley quick smart. Finally, she was able to get out and the three girls retired to the galley to unpack and carefully stow everything. The workmen weaved smoothly around them, avoiding the semi-controlled chaos in the galley as they came and went from hull to hull.

Finally, Reg the foreman came up, and after checking all connections on the cockpit mounted tank, attached a small compressed air bottle and very carefully inflated the bladder. He watched a pressure gauge like a hawk as the stiff fabric puffed up with a crinkling sound, stopping just as it assumed the correct shape and maximum dimensions. He noted the pressure reading, left it inflated, then went below to presumably repeat the process with the other two.

He then came up and plonked down in a chair, 'Now we wait to see if there are any leaks.'

Tracy offered tea or coffee and he accepted for the whole crew, telling her what each had. Tracy delivered the tea and coffee to the boys, since they stayed below watching the tanks and gauges, while the boss lounged in comfort in the cockpit. Two mugs of coffee later, he went around and checked all fittings himself and pronounced them air and fuel tight!

'As a final check please Skipper, we need to fill the tanks with diesel. Can this be done soon?'

'No problem,' was my happy reply. 'I need them filled anyway so we'll use the Mariners Cove refueller, I'll just call him.' I made the call to Ray and was graced with a grunt that I translated to mean we'd be very welcome to buy fuel off him at any time convenient to me. I knew Dave would get the Yacht Club's new mobile fuel tender to come visit him, so it was the work of minutes to fire up the engines, drop our mooring and motor the few hundred metres to Ray's re-fuelling jetty.

I had resigned myself to a very lengthy wait because Ray's bowser is so old and slow it'd be quicker to hand-pump the stuff, but I was very pleasantly surprised to see a pair of brand-new, bright-red bowsers sitting ready for action.

'Good morning Harry, I suppose you want your usual 25 litres in each tank?' was the sarcastic greeting after I'd shut down the engines and stepped down onto his floating pontoon. Ray loves to have a go at me about my strong preference for sailing almost everywhere instead of motoring, but my defence is always that when I'd spent so much money setting up my lovely big catamaran to be handled so easily under sail by one person, then why not accept the challenge to do so. It also improved my seamanship.

'Ha ha! Yep, yep, very funny Ray! You know, it's got me buggered why you persist in making a living serving over-priced, sub-standard fuel to unsuspecting boaties, when you could be on the stage telling dopey jokes to drunken yobbos.'

'Now listen here, you young whapper-snipper, I'll have you know my fuel is the finest and cheapest you'll get anywhere, that there then!'

Although I'd never admit it to him, his fuel is always clean and water-free, but it doesn't take much to get Ray wound up, and as much as we routinely pay each other out, I really like the old fart.

An annoying, gnawing sensation down in the region of my right ankle reminded me that there was one thing about Ray that I *didn't* like, and that was his ancient, dysfunctional, near-sighted, nearly-barkless and toothless Chihuahua; naturally called Fang. The useless bloody thing staggered about the jetty every day, farting an invisible cloud of Pal-flavoured noxious gas and wheezing canine defiance at everybody. The empty milk bottle cable-tied to it's collar was there so that when it fell in the water, which it did several times a day, Ray had time to fish it out with a pool-cleaning net mounted on a super-long alloy pole before it sank to the bottom.

Even with the new bowser running flat-out, it was still thirty minutes before all tanks were filled and *Firebird* sat a good 30mm lower in the water. Before we'd started fuelling, I sort of... well, kind of... forgot to tell Ray about the extra tanks, and I had great fun watching him trot up and down the inclined ramp that accessed the floating pontoon, getting more and more out of breath as he became more and more concerned about the quantity of fuel being pumped into my notoriously small main tanks! He was nearly pulling out what little of his hair remained, when the meter ticked past the 1000 litre mark, but refused to ask me what was going on, until I decided to put him out of his misery by announcing, 'Oh, by the way Ray. I've just had some long-range tanks fitted and we're checking for leaks.'

Ray stopped so abruptly in mid-stride that the half-blind Fang ran into his heels, frightened himself then tottered off the ramp into the water.

Ray cursed at both the dog and my laughter as he trotted up to the office to grab his Fang rescue net to retrieve the hapless little turd-burger.

While this bit of frivolity was happening, Reg and his boys were busy monitoring the fill and looking for leaks, or at least the boys were, since Reg had parked himself in the cockpit chatting up Sandy, no doubt still mentally reliving the pleasure of seeing her naked as he had earlier, and he was also much taken with Amanda and Tracy. Therefore, it was the boys who found and corrected several very minor weeps at joints until they pronounced the system totally dry, smell-free and secure. They showed me the correct way to fill the bladders and when to stop just as they were full enough, then how to transfer the bladder contents into the main tanks. It was a very simple and an almost fool-proof process, with a manual backup pump if the electrics failed. Nevertheless, I took notes and photos of valve positions so that any of the girls could do the job if I was asleep or busy.

Checking the contents of the bladders was as simple as walking on them to see how fat they were. The installation was very professional with all lines and hoses secured against chafing and even the smelly vents directed overboard via the holding tank breather.

When necessary, each bladder tank itself could be quickly emptied, disconnected from its various connections and rolled up to stow in a small locker.

After the workmen had packed up their gear, I looked across to the Yacht Club marina to see the fuel tender pulling away from *Seeker* who now also sat below her waterline marks, so I left the girls still stowing food and other supplies securely and with the tank crew safely aboard, headed across in the RIB to drop them off and then to see Dave.

His guys were just tidying up when we arrived, so they all stacked tools, leftover bits and empty boxes on the trolleys before wishing us a safe voyage. I'd mentioned in passing that we were heading for an extended trip through the Indonesian Archipelago and didn't want to trust local diesel.

'How did it go?' I asked Dave.

'Really good, mate. They did a top job and everything worked straight off and there were no leaks. Yours was good too?'

'Yeah. It is now. There were a couple of minor seeps at first, but they were quickly fixed and now everything is as tight as a fish's bum. They did a really neat job and I love the way we can disconnect tanks and stow them away, leaving the plumbing in place until we need them again.'

'It was a good idea to use those dudes,' he admitted. 'But Bob must have really lit a fire under them–like it's only just morning tea time and we're all done.'

'That's what I wanted to talk to you about. The girls are still stowing stuff away, but should be finished any minute.' I looked around at the scene of masterly inactivity that *Seeker's* crew were engaged in, sprawled back in the cockpit chairs sucking on tea and coffees and sweet bickies for morning tea.

'May I assume from this frantic activity that you're ready to go?'

'Smart arse! Yes Boss, we're all ready. Fuel, food and crew, but it's made the old girl a bit heavy, though a couple of days cruising will lighten that off.'

I looked at my watch, 'OK mate. How about we drop lines at 10:15 which will give me just enough time to secure the RIB.'

'Sounds good to me. Are we going out over the Southport bar, or up through Moreton Bay?'

'We need to make time, so straight out through the Seaway here and we'll stay a couple of miles offshore to keep in cell phone range as long as possible. This southerly will boost our speed, but I'll try to keep a minimum of 14 knots at all times if you can live with that snail's pace.'

He grinned, 'No problem. We'll hang in fairly close company and work things out as we go.'

I shook hands with Dave, sketched a wave to Melissa, Alf and Charlie and returned to *Firebird* to find the girls had finished their housekeeping. I started the engines, stowed the RIB for sea by hauling it up under the overhanging daybed, tightened the safety straps running under it, and got ready to back out of the fuelling berth. I'd squared accounts with Ray, including the massive one for the last fill, so he was happy enough to give us a wave as we dropped mooring lines and backed out.

Right on 10:15, we turned into the main channel and with *Seeker* in close company, headed north for the Seaway and the great cruise had officially commenced.

CHAPTER 11

After sending out the critical encoded message on Friday, Corrine had been waiting for Paula's goon squad to bash her door in and cart her off for interrogation, but nothing happened. She sat through more lectures on meditating, had a sumptuous evening meal and wandered off to bed feeling pleasantly tired. Nor was her sleep disturbed by any rude awakenings, so she was forced to conclude that the 'stealth' technology in her iPhone really was effective, and Paula and her security head, Joshua Koll, had no suspicions.

When she'd finished her breakfast in the dining room, Janine, the pretty guide in another skin-tight jumpsuit in a pale aqua colour this time but still without underwear, met her as she left to go back to her room.

'Good morning Miss Corrine. Miss Paula has asked if you would care to go to her office when you have cleaned up after breakfast? I'll come back to your room with you, wait until you're ready, then take you to her.'

Corrine's gut contracted as she imagined this could be a trap and maybe she should run now, but then she thought it through and realised that snatching her at night would have been much easier than doing it now. So she chatted aimlessly with the bright and breezy Janine as they made the trek to her room where she invited Janine inside while she tidied herself up a bit. A pee, a wash and a hair brushing did wonders toward making her feel better.

Minutes later, she was shown into Paula's spacious office and welcomed by the lady herself, who politely dismissed Janine, before seating Corrine on a comfortable armchair and taking a seat herself on the opposite sofa.

'Thanks for coming Corrine but I must ask, how your arm is feeling?'

'Much better thanks Paula. Dr Jacobs seems to have the magic touch, because I can hardly feel a thing now and have full use of it again, thank goodness and the doctor.' 'Excellent news, because I have a proposition for you.'

Corrine tensed, waiting for the much-anticipated pitch to be delivered. So she stitched an inquisitive look on her face as she asked, 'Oh? And what would that be, Paula?'

Paula crossed her long, shapely legs, an action that might have provided a momentary distraction to a man, but was lost on Corrine.

'You booked a fortnight of lectures and treatment through the Meditation Centre, and even though you've only been here two days, I'm told you are doing well. However, during the inter-active sessions, the staff reports you've said many things which condemns the lack of action taken by the present Government in the matter of pollution through the uncontrolled use of petroleum fuels. Not only that, but they are issuing new petroleum exploration licences every day! Is this a correct summary of the way you feel?'

With her best sincere look firmly in place, Corrine shrugged and replied, 'Sure. That about sums it up. It's one of the reasons I came here; I mean I was getting so frustrated and uptight, with all this waste and damage happening, while everybody just talks about doing something, but never does! So what's the big deal? Do I get kicked out for saying what is so obvious to anybody who cares to use their mind and wants to protect the Earth?'

Paula beamed. 'Oh no, dear girl, quite the contrary. We were very interested to hear your views! In fact, what would you think if I were to suggest that you could have a far more positive role in achieving what you've been worrying and complaining about?'

Corrine pretended to think a moment and then said, 'I'd say, bloody marvellous! But how's that going to happen?'

Paula ignored her question for a moment, asking instead, 'So you think being presented with a way to take positive action; to actually achieve what industry and the Government won't do would be a good thing?'

'Hell, yeah!' Corrine fired back without hesitation. 'All the Feds are interested in is making more money for their personal pockets! They'll never put the brakes on an industry which keeps pouring cash into their pockets, just because it's adding to the pollution levels every day!'

Paula nodded happily as if that sort of rhetoric was music to her ears.

'But,' Corrine continued, 'you still haven't told me how I can help make all this stuff stop happening!'

'Let me explain. We have another organisation here called Earth-Care, which, as the name suggests, is wholly dedicated to running projects aimed at reversing the destructive effects our greedy society has been having upon the Earth.'

Corrine jumped in, 'I've heard of it, but all these organisations seem the same; a set of lofty ideals, but as usual, no money translates to no action!'

Paula smiled indulgently. 'You're thinking and that's good. What if I said that these 'lofty ideals' are supported by several of this country's largest superannuation funds? Or that a small but vocal political party which has very substantial financial backing is also involved?'

Corrine relaxed and smiled, 'I won't ask for details, but I'd say it's about time some decent money got behind a well-organised eco group so something worthwhile can be achieved. Good work!'

Paula beamed as her star pupil ticked all the boxes. 'We have the backing and the credibility. All we need is a plan and the right people.'

'I could come up with a plan alright,' Corrine said, 'but it sounds like you already have one.'

An almost feral look slid over Paula's face. 'Oh yes. We certainly do, but let's talk about the right people first. For the action wing of EarthCare, we have created a para-military group called

EarthSquad with a military structure for its personnel. Since we already have a good cross-section of ex-military and ex-police who've joined, they fit right into that system but they are virtually all from other ranks. We're very short on officers at all levels and so far, only have one senior officer who can plan and direct operations in the broader picture.

We've examined your background very carefully and decided you would be very useful to us if you choose to join. We'd like to offer you the position of second in charge to our top officer, Colonel Antonio Bandolo. Antonio is ex-Spanish Army with wide experience both in peace and war, so we were lucky to gain his services. You'll be paid very well, and will have the rank of Major, as well as the comfort and privileges that go with being a senior officer.'

Corrine tried to hide her surprise at the offer, but nodded thoughtfully, 'That's a very generous offer Paula, but you do realise that I wasn't an officer in the SAS?'

'Yes, we noted that. But we were able to discover that you were offered promotion and entry to OCS many times and refused because you liked what you were doing; not because you weren't capable.'

The reach of their information gathering abilities surprised Corrine, but when she commented on it, Paula just smiled and airily said, 'We have friends in very high places.'

Corrine made an instant decision to stay on the inside, rather than run, based on the fact that as 2IC, she would be privy to everything going on and would be able to feed Intel to Harry much more easily.

'OK Paula, I'm in. It sounds like you have the backing and hopefully the resources to actually do something which will have a positive effect, particularly if we plan it properly. Which takes me back to what you said earlier about having a plan. Care to elaborate?'

Paula stood, clapped her hands in delight and pulled Corrine to her feet and hugged her fiercely. 'Welcome dear girl, or should I say Major! This is going to work out really well, I just know it!'

Yeah—but for whom? Corrine thought to herself. Better be our side if these turkeys have the backing they claim to have.

'Anyway,' Paula rattled on, 'I've asked Colonel Bandolo to come and meet you. I'll just see if he's arrived yet.' She used the intercom to check with her secretary.

'He's here,' she announced as the door opened and a tall, handsome man entered. He wore basic camouflage top and pants in a foreign pattern which Corrine thought might have been an obsolete Dutch design. The Colonel had curly black hair, flashing dark eyes, a moustache and beard that were maybe a clue to his deeper personality.

Nevertheless, on the surface, he was all very jovial and as a fairly typical Latin man in the presence of two very attractive females, very full of equal measures of testosterone and himself.

'Antonio, may I present Major Corrine Johns, your new 2IC and Executive Officer!'

With a beaming smile, showing his gleaming white teeth, he advanced to Corrine, snapped her a quick salute, to which she responded automatically, even though she wasn't used to another person saluting her. He then took her right hand and raised it to his lips in a very old-worldly gesture which Corrine found both amusing and touching.

He followed it up with a kiss to each cheek; the scent of his powerful aftershave almost making her sneeze, but at least his breath was sweet.

'Bienvenidos Major Corrine. I am most happy you have decided to join our little group. I agree with Mistress Paula we should use normal military ranks to avoid confusion and assist with discipline. Yes?'

Corrine shrugged, drew herself to attention, and threw him a salute. 'Si, my Colonel!'

He beamed and returned the salute, much to Paula's amusement. 'Very good Major, but also to avoid confusion, we will stay with the proper English, yes?'

'No problem, Colonel.' Corrine replied, not sure what to make of this character but prepared to play along to find out more.

'OK,' Paula said, 'let's have a break for tea or coffee, then we'll get down to details.'

Naturally it was Janine in her body-moulding jumpsuit that served them, the Colonel getting quite agitated by her proximity when she poured his coffee.

CHAPTER 12

After ten minutes of meaningless chitchat, Corrine was ready to run screaming from the building in frustration. Noticing this, Antonio suggested they resume the planning session.

'Good,' said Paula. 'Now you have accepted the position of 2IC in our small force, I'm prepared to tell you our planned target. Although having chosen it, we do not yet have a properly developed plan to achieve our objectives, so we need your experienced mind to help us refine that plan.'

Becoming slightly exasperated by Paula's waffle, but trying not to show it too much, Corrine replied, 'That's good, Paula. But you really need to tell me the plan before I can put my mind to work on it.'

Even Antonio nodded in approval, so Paula told Corrine of the plan to seize the Barleyrock LNG processing plant near Onslow and hold it to ransom. When she finished explaining that the Federal Government would be told they had to shut down all gas and oil production and stop all exploration, Corrine butted in.

'Before we get to the fine details, a couple of points jump out at me straight away that I'd like to have clarified. The first is, if the Feds stop all gas and oil production, industry would stop very quickly, like within days if not hours, because gas-fired plant and places like hospitals will be directly affected.'

Paula nodded. 'You're right. Natural-gas fired plant would stop almost immediately due to lack of storage reserves, apart from the main pipelines which will hold a small amount, and that's very unfortunate. Otherwise, our research indicates that stopping production will have a flow-on effect, where the energy supply rundown

107

will be a gradual process. There are more than enough stocks of oil to keep emergency diesel generators running for a considerable period provided it's not wasted on trivial stuff.

Our aim is to force the Federal Government into negotiations about limiting fossil fuel usage until renewables can come on line and effectively take over electricity production. We know it is happening already, but it's way too slow and we want that process sped up dramatically, although we do expect negotiations could take some time.'

That's an understatement! Corrine thought. Discussions would go on for years!

'OK,' Corrine said, 'that leads to the biggest problem of all.'

Paula raised her carefully trimmed; shaped and trained eyebrows in what Corrine took as an invitation to continue.

'I have had considerable experience in seizing assets like this and defending them against the original owners who generally want them back immediately. The one common factor is while a small assault and take-over force has the initial advantage of surprise, it cannot possibly expect to hold out against a determined and organised military response, especially if it's organised on a national scale, for any more than a few days. After that, whack! They're toast!'

Paula looked about ready to cry and Colonel Antonio was pouting as if his Mum had just tossed his favourite toy in the bin!

'Sorry to bring too much reality into the equation, but it is better we think of this shit now, than when people are dangling off a production platform with the Aussie Defence Force descending en masse!'

'But it has to work,' Paula tried to reason; 'we'd have the element of surprise!'

'Of course, we would, but that's not the point! Tell her Colonel, please.'

The Colonel nodded wearily, 'Our new and very talented Major is perfectly correct, Senorita Paula. The element of surprise would only get us in the 'front door' so to speak, but there's no way we could hold out for even a fraction of the length of time you're talking about for negotiations to take place.'

'So what can we do? I mean—our almost limitless funding has some very big strings attached, as you can imagine! We can't just say sorry, we can't hold the place hostage for more than a week. Terry and I will be in the hot seat!'

Corrine's eyes flashed dangerously, 'Your arses might be in the hot seat, but the troops trying to hold those three assets will definitely be wiped out after a couple of days!'

She opened her mouth to make an even more pointed remark, and then abruptly shut it and her expression went blank. Only the Colonel noticed, Paula having immersed herself in a bucket of self-pity, her dreams of the promised power and status in the new regime fluttering out the window on speedy wings.

Corrine let the silence draw on for a minute, then said, 'OK. If we're going to plan something which has a chance of achieving what you and your backers apparently want, you need to tell me everything you've already done toward setting up infrastructure to achieve these objectives, then we can discuss the only way to do it.'

Both Paula and Antonio looked relieved, and Paula seized on the chance to get her shapely little arse off the hot seat. 'So you're saying that there *is* a way to takeover these facilities and hold them?'

Corrine shook her head grimly. 'No, I'm not saying that. But if you want the truth up front, then here it is. We have to plan to infiltrate all three targets simultaneously and only hold them for a few days at most. You say negotiations will take some time? That can't and won't happen! There is no time! The Barleyrock facility should be seen to be the main target and should be held, so at least one of the offshore platforms must be considered to be disposable.'

Paula looked as if she was having trouble following the line of reasoning. 'What do you mean, 'disposable'?' We aren't supposed to even fire a shot, let alone blow something up.'

Corrine shook her head. 'Decide now, Paula! Either you want

this to happen or you will be making an empty gesture and Earth-Care will be yet another shot-duck on the world stage and you and Terry dismissed as useless wannabe's!'

She looked rather distressed with that frank statement, but finally asked, 'If I did say I really wanted to achieve the objectives I stated earlier, what would you recommend?'

Corrine relaxed a bit, careful not to let Paula or Antonio see anything in her face, 'Not much. Just as a demonstration of your power and resolve, the balls to actually blow one of the offshore production platforms as soon as it is seized. That's after you declare your demands, but you don't wait! Bang!

Then you need the resolve to be prepared to blow the second one if your demands aren't met within 48-hours. One minute over that time, bang, you blow the second one.

By then you really should have the Government's attention and it'll be a case of who blinks first in this game of bluff!'

'Then, if there's any more dancing around by the Government, you blow up the ship at the loading wharf. I believe there is one every two weeks and it takes two days to load. If I'm not mistaken, one docked there yesterday, so that also sets the timeframe for the launch of the operation. The Colonel and I will see how much training is required for the troops here and allow a week in the forward base to integrate the two groups. Then the troops head for the targets and things start happening.'

'That's my plan and it's the only one that will deliver what you and your backers want. But it's the old omelette analogy—you can't make one without breaking some eggs!'

Paula looked thoughtful. 'Let me talk to Terry and make a couple of phone calls while you and the Colonel work out other details. I'll be back within the hour, probably much less.'

Corrine nodded as Paula left and Antonio took over the briefing.

'We have established a base camp on the coast of the Pilbara region, 47 nautical miles north of Onslow in Western Australia and just 31 nautical miles southeast of Barrow Island, one of the largest oil and gas hubs in the region. The Barleyrock offshore gas platform is also 100 nautical miles to the NNW.'

'How did you manage to set up a base camp on the coast without being detected?'

'Apparently Mr Terry suggested making application to the Western Australian Government for a grant to set up an ecology monitoring camp close to the gas and oil fields, where our 'scientists' could keep a check on the effect the exploration and production might be having on sea and birdlife, and our 'Environmentalists' could visit to see the results for themselves. Amazingly, the WA Government not only gave permission to establish the camp, but it pays a hefty $250,000 per annum for a bunch of reports from our 'scientists' which say that the oil and gas production has little effect on the local marine flora and fauna and that fish life around the rigs has actually increased!'

One problem popped into Corinne's mind immediately. 'How do you stop the WA Government sending Inspectors or Environmental scientists to see what their money is being spent on?'

'So far it hasn't been much of a problem and the couple of enquiries we've received have been fobbed off by saying that before we can have visitors, we need more tents, swags and mosquito nets and to get the anti-crocodile electric fence modified to deliver lethal current and voltage since the present one only tickles them. That seems to deter even the most ardent Greenie.'

Corrine smiled and nodded appreciation, as Antonio resumed his brief. 'We've got boats, weapons and explosives and have built up good stocks of supplies. There are 25 men and women based there at the moment and they work hard to keep the place a secret. Despite what we've said to put off visitors, the accommodation is very comfortable with either solid tents or huts and everything is air-conditioned. Losing half the troops to sickness isn't acceptable.

Even though we've camouflaged the place heavily, there have been some un-avoidable casualties amongst local fishermen who got too close and saw stuff they shouldn't, so they've had to disappear and the crocodiles get blamed, even though there aren't very many around there.'

Corrine nodded, 'Sounds reasonable. That's how I'd do it too, but what about security in general?'

'Joshua Koll, our head of security, drew up the guidelines for that and they're followed very carefully. He doesn't travel, but sends his deputy, Drew Tallman every few months to check and he's good. But what we need to do, with your assistance, is to refine the broad, rough plan we initially came up with into a plan which could actually work.

As Paula said, there are no restrictions on spending to get what we think is needed, or to draw on any other resources necessary. We're backed to the hilt and beyond!'

Corrine had to draw this out, so thinking that a bit of ego-stroking might be in order, she raised her eyebrows and said, 'That sounds like a clever piece of marketing to attract so much backing!'

'Yes, it was a masterstroke on Paula's behalf, as it seems our manifesto fitted very neatly into the 'Grand Plan' of a small group of politicians who have been looking for a catalyst to kick-start their own plans for a major, long-lasting upset in the Australian Government. They are utterly determined to achieve their objectives and in that respect, we're small fish, but they have still opened the cash pipeline from one of the largest cash holdings in Australia; the Union Superannuation funds.'

'Brilliant! Thanks for the briefing. I'll get right onto it, but I suppose I'd better pack my gear first and move to the barracks with the troops.'

Antonio smiled. 'No need for that dear lady. As 2IC in the EarthCare Army, known as EarthSquad, you get to join me in the Executive wing where just the senior staff lives. Your gear has already been moved and I think you'll find that it is very comfortable.'

Before they finished the preliminary briefing, Antonio, who'd been very gentlemanly and hadn't displayed any of the macho bullshit she expected, suggested she should join him tomorrow for the regular morning inspection and parade so she could be introduced to the troops.

'How many are there?' she asked.

'There's forty-one here and twenty-five in Pilbara, making sixty-six in total. I haven't split them into sections or platoons yet, since the numbers are low, but I'm prepared to be guided by your experience.'

'Let's wait until I've seen how they interact first; but where did they get recruited from? As in, what are their backgrounds?'

He gave a shrug. 'Much of this work was done before I was recruited, so the records are either not available or have very little detail. By their accents, I'd say that there are a wide variety of nationalities. So far I can pick up Australian, American, South African, German and British, but there are others. You need to understand that we didn't have a lot of choice with these people initially, so there are a number of misfits who obviously weren't acceptable in more regular militaries. Most of them won't supply histories, although there are quite a few who have joined through our normal, local recruiting process, so we have details on them. One of the conditions of joining EarthCare is that we don't care where someone comes from, so long as they have the dedication and talents we can use. Therefore, we don't push them for personal details or even check if they are using their real identities.'

Corrine nodded, 'OK. I hope you realise I may have to cull some of the more useless or un-disciplined ones? Just a few bad ones can wreck the morale of the whole company. It does make it more difficult to have so few details, so I'll just have to weed out the bad and the useless when we start some training. Do we have any non-coms? Corporals or Sergeants to keep the troops in line?'

'Only two of each I could trust,' Antonio said sadly. 'So I have sent one Corporal and one Sergeant to the Pilbara camp and the other two are here.'

Corrine nodded. 'OK. I'll meet them in the morning. This raises another question. You mentioned boats at the base. What type? How many and what about personnel transfers and re-supply?'

He smiled, flashing those gleaming white teeth, 'More good questions! We have three 25-foot RIBs at the camp with 2 x 100 horsepower outboards on each. Additionally, we bought an old aluminium work barge at auction that's around 50-feet, has a small crane and that is our supply boat. We attached very big outboards to it, so if the seas aren't too rough, it's fast and being well-used, doesn't attract any attention.'

'OK. That's probably enough for my tired brain for the moment, thanks Colonel. I'll go over what files Paula has on the troops to get an idea of the material I have to work into shape.'

They were just about to leave when Paula swept back in, a grim smile on her face. 'Reluctantly, everybody who is backing this play or I should say project, has agreed and says to go with your plan, as radical as it is! They appreciate it really is the only way to force the Government's hand and get fast action, so one of two platforms going up in a fireball is a small price to pay.'

'OK. Thanks Paula. The Colonel and I will review the plan later today, but in the meantime, I'll go find my new quarters and go over the personnel files you mentioned.'

Paula nodded, 'I'll have Janine show you to your new rooms, and then she'll drop the files around straight after.'

Corrine nodded, 'Thanks Paula. Do I eat in the same dining room as I was?'

'No. The executive staff have our own dining room just around from the guest's dining area. Janine will show you where on the way back to your room.'

Corrine nodded and said to the Colonel, 'I'll see you at lunch Colonel, but we need to start refining the action plan this afternoon and I may have some questions about the troops after going over the files.'

He smiled genially, 'But of course my dear Major. There is a small conference room we can use beside the dining room, but I must mention before I forget, the parade tomorrow morning is at 08:00, with hand-to-hand combat and small arms training scheduled for 10:00.'

115

CHAPTER 13

Corrine's new quarters certainly were comfortable, although not as spacious as her Meditation Centre ones. Still, she'd never been one for huge living areas, which is why she loved living on the boat so much. During the previous afternoon, she and the Colonel had gone over the concept plan again, starting the long process of generating a step-by-step detailed plan to co-ordinate all elements of the actual assault.

Last night, she'd met the administration staff and others over dinner in the small dining room adjacent the customer dining area. She also made the very unfortunate acquaintance of Joshua Koll, head of security, a slim, slimy and thoroughly unpleasant man who had damp hands, a smarmy manner and couldn't drag his eyes above Corrine's crotch and breasts.

His deputy, Drew Tallman, was a very different type being a tall, good-looking man, well-built and very pleasant to chat to. Corrine had promptly made the decision to get to know the yummy Mr Tallman a lot better, since he would know the security set-up out west better than anybody.

Fortunately, Drew seemed to find Corrine just as desirable, so she spent considerable time after dinner with him, chatting about past experiences while knocking off a decent quantity of Terry's vintage Grandfather Port.

Drew also made it clear that he'd be very happy to share his bed with Corrine at any time, so she made another decision that if she had to 'take one for the Company' this would be a very pleasant way to get the intelligence they needed. Far better than getting into the clutches of Mr Koll's slimy paws!

Antonio had also made a play for her affections during their first planning session late Saturday afternoon in a briefing room in the Executive wing, but they both knew sharing beds didn't really work between officers trying to enforce discipline among subordinates. With that personal matter resolved, they'd made good progress on working out a functional attack plan for the LNG plant. Antonio had a mass of layout diagrams and photos of the plant, the loading jetties and the surrounding landscape.

Corrine had retired to bed very pleased with the progress so far, but not before she'd found out from Drew that while surveillance was continual on all meditation guests, including their cell-phone calls, text messages were much harder to intercept and he cursed the fact that iMessage, the default Apple Messaging application, was automatically encrypted and almost impossible to break!

She left him with the implied promise that it probably wouldn't be long before she'd share his bed and took the opportunity to compose an iMessage text to send to Harry, bringing him up to date on the latest happenings.

HARRY, *FIREBIRD*, AT SEA, MONDAY

For some reason, probably because we were between cell phone towers, we didn't receive Corrine's encrypted text until well after I'd wearily climbed out of bed at 07:00 the next morning to join Tracy and Sandy in the cockpit, since Amanda and I had taken the 18:00 to midnight watch. We'd been at sea for a day and a half and the crew were settling down nicely, although the two-person watch schedule was taking its toll. That was mainly because Tracy had needed close supervision, but she was a very fast learner and I thought just one more day of this schedule would see her standing day watch alone, although we always had two crewmembers on night watch for safety's sake.

So far, the southeast breeze had been fairly consistent, which gave the engines an easy time, and I found that I could maintain or exceed the required 14 knots by just using one at a time, which helped spread the wear and save fuel. We'd been travelling for just over 44 hours and had covered 616 nautical miles, which put us northeast of Bowen well past the Whitsundays, having given that whole area a wide berth.

As Corrine couldn't send encrypted iMessage texts to our sat phone, only standard unencrypted text ones, we had to stay reasonably close to shore to get good reception and that in turn meant we couldn't lay a straight course for long, because we had to dodge projecting bits of land. Still, the occasional sight of land made the scenery much more interesting than just water.

Sandy had just made tea and coffee for the three of us when the throwaway burner phone burped its message alert tone.

I read it first, shaking my head in wonder until Sandy kicked my shin.

'Stop being greedy and share, dearest.'

I took a moment, then said, 'The dear girl has not only found out full details on the objective, but she's got herself elected as 2IC in their para-army.'

Although Tracy hadn't met Corrine, she still appreciated the tremendous gain to our intelligence feed this would mean, so I read out the whole message to them.

Shrewdly, Tracy suggested. 'Based on what you've told me of Corrine's background, I guess if she's going to come up with some very tricky and effective ways to take down this LNG plant as well as take the off-shore platform, at least she'll be able to alert us in advance.'

'Good point,' Sandy acknowledged, 'and you're right. She certainly will be very innovative, but if she can let us know what she's planned, we should be OK.'

She looked at me, 'But what about this base camp? 20 or 30 well-armed and prepared troops are a bit much for us to take on. Have you thought of a plan to take these guys out yet?'

'No, I haven't,' I admitted, 'but if Mouse is planning most of the assault, then she should be able to feed us the best way to cripple them. She even might be able to build-in a few trapdoors for us to use to take bad guys out. We obviously can't make a head-on assault, and without Corrine on the ground, picking them off one by one will just alert them. I think we'll have to wait until we have Corrine's plan and also...maybe, until they have seized the plant.'

Sandy and Tracy nodded agreement, so we held off further discussion until Amanda woke up and we discussed things over breakfast. I also sent Corrine's text message over to Dave and chatted with him for a while about what we'd discussed. He was concerned Corrine was digging herself even deeper into the Earth-Care organisation, but admitted it probably was for the best, so we could know what was going on and have Corrine, who looked so sweet and innocent but was so incredibly deadly, available to subtly influence events.

While we waited for Amanda to rouse herself, Sandy started to prepare breakfast, knowing Amanda would chase her out of *her* galley ASAP. I sent Corrine's message to Greg and followed it with a phone call via the SatPhone.

'Good morning Harry, how's the grand voyage going?' was his cheery greeting.

'Hi Greg. Yeah, pretty good thanks mate. We're making good time and should be abeam Townsville by midday. We received an update from Corrine and I've sent you a copy of the text message. We've got full details of the LNG plant target and the dear girl has got herself elected as 2IC in their little para-military force, EarthSquad. So not only will we receive the very latest news, but also as one of the chief planners, she might be in a position to subtly sabotage the operation. At the very least, she can make life much easier and safer for us when we get there.'

'That's fantastic news. She's a wonder, that girl. I'll pass all this on to Bob and wait for the next instalment. Is there anything you guys need for now?'

'Nah. We're good for now, thanks mate. I'll be in touch. Cheers.'
'Yeah. Cheers Harry, take care.'

I stowed the SatPhone just in time for Tracy to present me with a beautiful, hot omelette and another mug of tea, contemplating our progress while I quietened my grumbling stomach. 'If we can keep going like we have been,' I announced to the crew, in between mouthfuls of succulent Spanish omelette, 'we should make Cape York by...'

Tracy grinned, 'Lazy bugger. I estimate we should make the rounding by mid-morning on Tuesday; perhaps about 09:00?'

I grinned at her, pleased with the way she was settling in with Sandy and Amanda, as well as how well she was adapting to her boating duties and interacting with the two pussies, which she adored. As well as being very decorative, particularly when she stripped down to bikini level, I was looking forward to the time when either Sandy or Amanda encouraged her to take that off as well. With all the rush of preparations and getting under way, there'd been no time for any of the usual fun games the ladies liked to play.

'So how do you ladies think we're going?' I asked.

'Great!' 'Love it!' 'Great to be back and sailing again!' the replies came, so no complaints from the crew.

'OK. We'll see how we feel when we get to Cape York, but we might plan to lay up for at least a day before we tackle the run across the top of the Gulf to Darwin.'

'Sounds good to me,' Sandy responded, while the others just nodded. 'Even though it hasn't been long, this the longest time I've been at sea. But I'm comfortable.'

We were certainly blessed in not having any seasickness problems; even Tracy, a total newcomer to boating, was comfortable. So the miles and the days ticked by filled with watch changes, sleeping and eating. Dave and *Seeker* held a steady station off to one stern quarter or the other just for variation, and I tried to keep our speed as steady as possible. We had one day where the wind picked up out of the southeast and blew around 30 knots for nearly 24 hours, which saved a lot of fuel and shaved a chunk of time off the estimated arrival at our first milestone, Cape York. However, in the aftermath of that blow, the winds were fickle and the engines got woken up again to maintain the 14-knot average I'd set as a target.

CORRINE...EARTHCARE HQ...MONDAY

She woke early, as was her habit, and spent a punishing hour performing an exercise routine which had been taught to her by a Norwegian Sergeant she'd met in the Middle East desert. A life of luxury aboard *Seeker* had corrupted her former strict habit of one hour of hard exercises to start each day, so she was determined to re-gain some of her former level of fitness, particularly if she was expected to be in overall charge of a bunch of hard-arsed mercenary soldiers.

She had a light breakfast and was ready to go by 07:45 when Colonel Antonio Bandolo came knocking on her door. She was dressed in a black SWAT-type jumpsuit and a black ball cap, chosen from a selection that had been left in her room the night before and which included several sets of BDUs in an obsolete Dutch woodland-pattern camouflage, camo T-shirts, two pair of the black jumpsuits, a German waterproof camo jacket and sundry socks, caps and scarfs. She was amused somebody, probably Jill Zellman, had got her sizes exactly right, but they'd stopped short of supplying bras and panties. It didn't matter since she'd brought a supply of her own, favouring sports crop-tops instead of a proper bra since she didn't really need that level of support.

She was also amused to find all the new clothing had her Major rank insignia of a single crown embroidered in muted black to the collar. The black jumpsuits had the crown in grey on the collar.

Antonio led the way outside where an electric golf cart with a canopy stood waiting. Antonio suggested that she drive and he would direct, so within five minutes they had left the resort buildings and facilities behind and after following a narrow gravel track through light scrub, came out into a large cleared area with several buildings scattered around. Corrine's practiced eye identified three barracks, each with an attached ablution block, a cookhouse and mess hall, plus several other buildings which were probably lecture rooms and offices.

A small parade ground lay immediately behind the buildings and it looked like some effort had been taken to de-militarise the appearance of the setup from the air. They drove between two buildings and stopped near two loose ranks of men and women in camo BDUs, drawn up on the edge of the parade ground with a sergeant standing in front of them. There looked to be only slightly more men than women, which Corrine found surprising, but several of the men were very big and strong. From past experience, she knew to expect at least one challenge to her authority from such a diverse group of misfits.

The sergeant saluted Colonel Bandolo as they walked up. 'Good morning Sir. Ready for inspection.'

Antonio returned his salute. 'Thank you Sergeant. This is Major Johns who has joined our ranks.'

The tall, burly sergeant looked at Corrine and snapped another salute to her, 'Welcome Major. I'm Sergeant Towson. I have been appraised by Miss Paula of your credentials and greatly look forward to working with you.'

Corrine smiled and returned his salute smartly, 'Thank you Sergeant. So do I.'

Antonio turned to face the double rank of troops who were still in a very 'stand-easy' position and made no attempt to smarten themselves up.

'Company, attention for the Colonel.' The Sergeant barked, but it made little difference and Antonio didn't really seem to mind. They were there and for him, that was the main thing.

'I'd like to introduce your new Company Commander, Major Johns. She brings a wealth of combat experience to our small force and will be directing training, so I'm sure we will all benefit from her knowledge and experience.'

'Bullshit!' The comment came from a huge man in the front row, muscles bulging everywhere. He stood about 6 ft 4 inches, which put him a good foot above Corrine and more than twice her weight.

'Trooper!' barked the Sergeant, and as Antonio went to speak, Corrine touched him lightly on the arm and murmured to the Sergeant, 'Is this one normally a problem Sergeant?'

Equally quietly he replied. 'Yes Ma'am, South African origin and a troublemaker. Vicious as well, so be careful about getting too close.'

She smiled sweetly, 'Thank you Sergeant. I suppose he'd be no real loss to the Company?

The Sergeant shrugged, not sure what she was getting at. 'No, I suppose not Ma'am, but he says he likes getting fed three times a day, having women to assault and a good chance of being able to kill someone. He's a real nutcase, but I don't think he's about to leave, no matter how nicely you ask him!'

She smiled again, but the Sergeant noted that this time there was nothing sweet about it and didn't make it to her eyes. 'Oh, I wasn't going to ask him to leave, Sergeant. I just wanted to know if he'd be missed.'

Still puzzled, Sergeant Towson replied, 'Well in that case Ma'am, the answer would have to be an unqualified, 'No'!'

Corrine stepped forward until she was very close in front of the huge man, and asked quietly, 'What part of the Colonel's introduction are you objecting to, Trooper?'

He lowered his head to gaze impassively down at her, 'Pretty much all of it, girlie!' he rumbled in his deep bass voice, 'but especially the bit where you're going to teach us stuff. You look like you're barely out of school, let alone in a position to know more than most of us here. We've been in wars and done the hard time!'

Corrine smiled up at him. 'So that'd mean you'd know all about un-armed combat, would you Trooper?'

He glared down at her, goaded by her patronising tone. 'Fuckin' sight more than you would, girlie! You're good for one thing only and that starts with you flat on your back!'

She looked thoughtfully up at him. 'And I suppose you'd be the best one to put me in that position would you Trooper?'

He looked around briefly at his mates, a brief smirk on his face, knowing he'd just faced down this smart-arse, chicky-babe Major in front of the whole squad. 'Well girlie, there are several guys here who could do the job but I'm closest, so I guess that makes me the best for now.'

Corrine nodded seriously and spoke even more softly, 'OK. That's good to know and we'll have a little talk to those gentlemen later, but for now, I'd like to remind you about a couple of things you might have forgotten about un-armed combat.'

His smirk returned in full strength, and he leaned forward a bit to get a little closer to her. 'And what might that be, girlie?'

'The first one is to never underestimate your opponent, and the second one is that being short isn't always a disadvantage.'

While his brain was still processing the meaning of her words, her hand flashed straight out and grabbed his very large nuts in a vice grip and squeezed much harder than such a small hand should have been able to. As a terrible agony seared through his lower body, effectively paralysing his limbs, his mouth opened to scream, but just a squeak came out as she increased the pressure, feeling the first signs of one or both testicles starting to rupture. Because only those close by the big man saw what was going on, there were some muttered comments from his mates behind and further away, that he should 'get on an' do the little bitch and let's all have some fun!'

Abruptly, Corrine let go of his irreparably damaged balls and flashed her hand up, fingers straight and bunched together, to stab him on his top lip, directly under his nose. As a source of intense pain, it was quite a showstopper in it's own right, but coupled with the agony from his crushed nuts, it was a fair bet that any thoughts about forcibly removing Corrine's pants were now long gone.

Still, he'd pissed her off sufficiently that she was determined to properly finish the job on the big goose, so she reached up with her left hand and firmly grasped the cloth of his jacket under his massive right bicep. Pivoting a smooth 180° to her left, she shoved her pert little backside against his thighs, braced her left leg back between his feet and heaved forward.

With seemingly little effort, the huge man slowly somersaulted over her right shoulder and crashed to the ground, flat on his back with a thump everyone felt. She straightened up and shook her jumpsuit straight, before casually stepping forward and planting the heel of her combat boot hard into his throat. The stunned troopers in the front rank heard a distinctive and sickening, crunching sound as his throat was crushed, his eyeballs distending as he frantically tried to draw air into his lungs through a throat that would never pass air again.

The front rank clearly heard her say, 'And that's for calling me 'girlie', arsehole!'

CHAPTER 14

Although all the troop broke ranks to stand in a loose semi-circle, well clear of the diminutive but lethal Major, there was total silence as the fallen giant's facial colour passed from mottled red to dusky blue, his heels briefly drummed against the hard-packed dirt, then he gave a final shudder and died – badly! Corrine gave the corpse one final, impassive glance and stepped back beside the Colonel who looked as though he was suddenly sharing intimate space with a hungry lioness, but didn't dare move in case she decided he was next on the menu. It was the Sergeant who displayed a commendable degree of equanimity and broke the stunned silence.

'This would appear to be a good time, Company, to fall out until the next assembly on the weapons range at 10:00. All may leave except for Troopers Botha, Nels, Venter, Smit and Chetty. You five come here.'

There was an almost frantic scramble by the others to leave the vicinity, although some furthest from the action couldn't resist a last horrified look at the corpse which seemed to have lost much of it's bulk and all it's former menace in death. There were also more than a few female troopers who gave their new Major some very appreciative looks.

With the five named troopers tripping over each other to form a line in front of the Sergeant, he turned to Corrine, saluted respectfully and said, 'Would you care to address these gentlemen, Major. They were Trooper Smith's closest companions and comprised his 'personal squad'.'

Corrine smiled at him and said, 'Thank you Sergeant, maybe just a few words for now.'

She stepped up to the middle of the row, looked them over, noting that while they weren't as big as Trooper Smith, they were still very big, tough men, and the thought occurred to her that it'd be a shame to waste their talent if she could control them for later use.

Without speaking, she moved along the short line, staring into the eyes of each until he dropped his gaze before moving to the next. When all five had dropped their eyes, she knew she had them, but knew it was best to reinforce the thought.

'It would seem, gentlemen, you have made a very poor choice of a companion to follow and try to emulate. Would any of you disagree with that statement?'

Silence greeted that question, so she spoke, 'Come on, gentlemen. Please speak up and correct me if I'm wrong. I dare say you six have had the run of the place since you were recruited, and I might even suggest you've terrorised most of the females here and forced your attentions on them whenever you wished. Any comments?'

Silence again greeted her question. 'Oh dear! It would seem, Sergeant Towson, that I might have to make another example of one of these gentlemen, since they won't even make a civil reply to my polite questions. Which one do you think would be the best choice to be the next example?'

While Sergeant Towson pretended to ponder the question with all due seriousness, there was an agitated stirring among them, until one mumbled something.

Corrine spoke up, 'I'm sorry, Trooper. Even though eliminating that last piece of shit has whetted my appetite for more, it must have impaired my hearing. I thought that I heard you say something, but perhaps I was wrong. Now where were we, Sergeant?'

'Ahh...Excuse me Ma'am,' came a voice from the end of the line, where a large man stood, head hung low.

Corrine walked to him and enquired, 'Yes Trooper; you wished to say something?'

He had enough guts to look her in the eyes. 'Yes Ma'am. I would like to say we agree wholeheartedly with your assessment of our poor choice of companion and we realise the error of our ways. We'd like to be given a chance to prove to you we can be soldiers worthy of your approval.'

Corrine pretended to ponder his statement for a few moments, before turning to Sergeant Towson to say. 'That's an improvement, Sergeant. What do you think?'

Sergeant Towson nodded, 'Yes, Ma'am. That's a definite improvement and I would suggest we place these five on probation for the duration. May I also suggest it be on a 'one strike and you're out' basis?'

Corrine beamed, 'Excellent suggestion, Sergeant. We think alike. I like that.'

She turned to the hapless five again and spoke sternly. 'Based on the Sergeant's recommendation, I'm inclined toward leniency at this point, *but*, as he has suggested, you are all on probation which means being under a suspended sentence. One misstep or strike against your record and you are out. You need to prove to me there will be no need for me to execute that sentence; pardon the pun! Ha, ha! Do we all understand?'

In best US Marine fashion, they belted out a ragged chorus of, 'Yes Ma'am—we understand!'

Corrine clapped her hands once. 'Excellent! Now you may stand down for breakfast, if your mates have saved you any, that is. I'll see you on the weapons range at 10:00. Sergeant!'

'Squad dismissed, but first fetch a stretcher from the first aid room and cart that pile of dog shit to the rubbish dump and cover it up. Report to the range at 10:00 as the Major has ordered.'

Corrine smiled slightly as one of the five double-timed away to fetch the stretcher, the other four standing in a tight group looking anywhere but at the corpse.

'I approve of your disposal instructions, Sergeant; most appropriate and should send even more of a message. You are proving to be most resourceful. Perhaps you would care to get the mess staff to send two breakfast orders to my office then join me there in a few moments. There are things we need to discuss.'

'Yes, Ma'am and thank you Ma'am. I'll arrange it immediately.' He saluted quickly then moved away to the mess hall where the non-coms had a separate small, partitioned off section.

Corrine turned to Colonel Bandolo who was re-assessing his new Major and wondering if he hadn't just let a lioness into the hen house. *Although*, he thought, and having a wry chuckle, *I don't have to worry about discipline any more. This Major doesn't just demote soldiers for discipline issues; she kills them—by hand!*

'Colonel? I think I'll be right now I have Sergeant Towson to show me where things are, if you could just point me toward the Admin block where I presume my office is located?'

'Ah yes! Certainly Major. And may I say that it was a most impressive display of your prowess and a remarkably effective method to eliminate discipline problems before they get started. We have obviously made the right choice, so I'll see you this evening for dinner at 19:00.'

'Yessir and thank you.'

'Oh, one last thing, Major.'

'Sir?'

'Perhaps try to leave *some* of the troops functional if you can. We need to reinforce our Pilbara base with as many as we can, as soon as you judge their training is complete. We'd like to be able to move people within 10 days.'

'That's a tight timeline but certainly Sir. I'll do just that.'

Over the working breakfast with Sergeant Towson, Corrine learned a lot more about the man himself and about the rest of the company, although size-wise, it was more an extended platoon. After having her initial impression of the man confirmed during the discussion, she said to him. 'We seem to be a bit light with NCOs, Sergeant. I believe there is one Sergeant over at the Pilbara base, but who do we have here?'

'There's just one Corporal, Ma'am, Corporal Julie Hegarty,

although she's had good training, having been in the British Army. She was given a discharge after a long period of sexual harassment. She did what she could to sort out the problem we had here, but hadn't made much headway.'

'So, is she suitable for promotion?'

'Oh, yes Ma'am. Very suitable!'

Corrine smiled, suspecting ulterior motives on the part of the handsome Sergeant, but not minding that at all.

'Very well Sergeant. I'd be obliged if you would ask her to report here immediately. And please return here yourself about fifteen minutes after the Corporal arrives.'

'Yes Ma'am!' He jumped to his feet, saluted and hurried out, as Corrine picked up the phone and pressed the button marked 'Colonel'.

'Yes, Major? No further problems I hope? Do we still have the same number of troops as when I left? Ha, ha.'

'Yes Colonel, very funny I'm sure. But I just called to inform you that I'm going to promote Corporal Julie Hegarty to Sergeant and promote Sergeant Towson to First Lieutenant. I'd like your approval for those promotions to be made effective immediately.'

'But of course, my dear Major. Excellent work and I'll see the records amended immediately. I'll have new uniforms with rank insignia issued and delivered to you instantly from the Quartermaster's store.'

Corrine blinked at the very positive response and decided that the good Colonel, despite his background, was not much of an action type and that her disciplinary action that morning had had a profound effect both up and down the rank hierarchy.

It was not more than five minutes later that a young man, dressed in civilian clothes, knocked at her door and entered, pulling a hand-cart with two small stacks of clothing. A small piece of sticky paper identified the person each stack was sized for.

'Good morning Major,' was his cheerful greeting. 'Two new sets of uniforms as requested. If you could have the persons concerned drop the old ones back to the store when convenient, that'd be much appreciated.'

Corrine stood and shook his hand warmly. 'That has got to be the fastest response from a Q Store ever! Congratulations!'

He smiled appreciatively, 'Thanks Major; we aim to please, but the truth is, we don't have a lot to do, so this was simple.'

Corrine nodded, 'Good work all the same. Thank you.'

Even though a civilian, he sketched a salute out of natural respect and left as quickly as he'd arrived.

Ten seconds later, another knock at her door preceded a tall, lean young woman with glossy auburn hair pulled loosely back into a ponytail and with the look of a swimmer, judging by the width of her shoulders and deep chest with small, neat breasts. She banged to attention, saluted and stated in a clear voice with a distinct English accent,

'Corporal Hegarty, reporting as ordered Ma'am!'

Corrine flapped a casual salute in return, but stood and held out her hand.

'Take a seat, Corporal. I'm pleased to meet you.'

Hegarty had a firm grasp, but sat tensely and was obviously unsure of the purpose of the summons to the presence of the new and very lethal Major. 'I'm very pleased to meet you too Major; I sincerely hope so anyway,' she added with a nervous laugh.

Corrine laughed in return to try to put her at ease. 'Please relax Corporal. I promise not to bite—or not you, anyway! I've noticed a generally relaxed discipline around here and I approve—to the extent that orders must still be obeyed.'

'Yes Ma'am, thank you,' she replied, relaxing fractionally in her chair.

'I won't keep you long, Corporal. I just want you to know I'm making some changes in the pecking order and you've been recommended as a steadying influence and a very capable soldier. Is that a fair estimation of your abilities?'

The Corporal looked Corrine straight in the eye without evasion. 'Yes Ma'am that would be a fair description. I haven't had much of a chance to demonstrate the skills my previous training taught me, but I haven't forgotten much.'

Corrine liked the way the Corporal, only slightly younger than herself, was prepared to acknowledge her attributes without false modesty. 'Good, I like that. So based on my assessment, you are now a Sergeant and will take over the duties formerly performed by Sergeant Towson.'

She pointed to a chair beside her desk. 'On that chair is a full set of all clothing, in your size, and has your new rank badge on it. Please return your old uniform items to the store when you change before we go to the weapons range. I want you out there as the Sergeant in charge.'

Julie Hegarty blinked a few times and then her face lit up in a beaming smile. 'Yes Ma'am and thank you! I'm not sure what I've done to deserve the honour, but I'll try my best to do the right thing by you.'

Corrine stood and held out her hand again, 'I can't ask for more than that. Congratulations Sergeant. Please take your new clothing and change as soon as you can. Should you find Sergeant Towson hovering about nearby, please send him in.'

Julie Hegarty stood, saluted and grabbed the armload of clothes and left, still in a daze. Sergeant Towson must have been really close since he popped his head around the doorframe moments later. 'Major?'

'Yeah yeah, come in and close the door. I suppose you ran into Sergeant Hegarty outside?'

'Ahh...yes Ma'am. She looked very pleased with herself.'

Corrine grinned, 'Well, you recommended her so you can take some of the blame if she bombs out, but I don't believe either of us think she'll do that.'

'No Ma'am, I'm sure she'll be everything you wanted.'

'Excellent! Because she's just picked up your old job and part of your new job is going to be to make sure that she does it. That pile of clothing is in your size and has all the new rank insignia fitted.

Congratulations, Lieutenant Towson!'

'Lieutenant! That's a big jump Major, but I'm up for it! What else am I to do apart from keeping a close eye on Sergeant Hegarty, that is?'

Corrine laughed, 'It doesn't have to be *that* close an eye, Lieutenant, except perhaps off duty. However, your main job, apart from keeping watch over everything, is to be my Executive Officer of this happy little band of misfits. I want you to make sure training goes well and the troops behave themselves and do what they're told. As I told Sergeant Hegarty, I'm not a strong believer in rigid discipline and drill bashing, particularly since we don't have the time and there are far more important things to do. People just need to know how to take orders without bitching, shoot straight and move quietly. Also, the demolition specialists need to show me they know what they're doing, but hopefully we can do that well away from the paying civilians.'

Her new XO looked down and shuffled his feet awkwardly, 'Ahh...I'm afraid we don't have any demolition specialists, Ma'am.'

'Oh, shit! Why not? Who the fucking hell is supposed to blow stuff up if we don't have specialists? We can't let just anybody play with the bang-bangs'

He shrugged, 'Good question but so far, it hasn't been an issue since we don't have any explosives either.'

'Fuckin' hell!' she muttered half to herself. 'What a shit-shower this is turning out to be. But just a moment, the Colonel told me there are explosives at the Pilbara base! Is that right?'

'Ahh...no Ma'am. We were supposed to get them, but whoever the supplier was, nothing turned up. I thought the Colonel knew, but obviously not.'

'Bloody hell! It almost makes me want to get rid of the whole bloody lot and start again! Oh, not you or Sergeant Hegarty, Lieutenant, you two seem just fine. I'm just a bit frustrated and blowing off steam. You'll get used to it.'

He grinned tentatively, 'Yes Ma'am, I'm sure I will.'

She grunted, 'Wait a moment while I just call the Colonel about getting some explosives. Shouldn't be difficult with the resources this mob seem to have.'

She dialled the number, 'Hello again Colonel.'

…'No. There's no trouble with the troops and the head count is the same as when you left.'

…'Well, I've just discovered we don't have any explosives on the base, there's none at the Pilbara base either and nobody is trained to use them properly, except for me.'

…'Yes, I know you thought that, but apparently the supplier didn't supply, so there aren't any. I understand, sir, but if we intend to blow up oil and gas rigs, we're going to need a shit-load of the stuff!'

…'Oh sorry, my bad! OK. To only look like we're going to blow up oil and gas rigs!'

…'Yes sir, I do appreciate that there's a difference. But does Miss Henderson understand that? She sounded pretty keen to see lots of big fireballs in the Indian Ocean sunset when we talked yesterday!'

…'Well of course destroying a rig would make a horrible mess! That's a given and is sort of the point of blowing it in the…'

…'Yes, of course it would harm the image of an earth-caring, ecologically-responsible Eco-terrorist organisation!'

…'Yes Sir. I do realise that, but with all due respect, sometimes bluffs get called. Then it's either piss or get off the pot.'

…'It's an Australian expression, sir. Translated it would mean that unless EarthCare wants to be laughed off the world stage, we need to be prepared to make some bangs to prove that we're serious.'

…'OK Sir. Got that. They're orders from the top. Little bangs only, no casualties and absolutely no gas or oil leaks. Sounds like fun. Are you sure Miss Paula is across this, because it wasn't on her agenda yesterday when I spelt out my plan.'

…'That sure, huh? OK, but maybe we should contract Howard & Sons to put on a show! It'd be cheaper!'

…'Sorry sir. I was being flippant. No disrespect intended. They are Australia's premier fireworks manufacturers.'

...'No sir. I wasn't being serious. It's an Australian tradition, something we resort to in times of adversity. A version of the British 'stiff upper lip'!'

...'No sir. My lip is fine. Nobody hit me. Ah...about the explosives? It's even more important, that if we're restricted to 'little bangs', we have some practice. Any dill can set off a big bang.'

...'I'd prefer Semtex, since that's what I'm most used to, but C4 will be fine. I'd prefer not to use any of the mining industry's water-gel explosive. They're harder to set off and in general, don't make such a big bang.'

...'Very well, thanks Colonel.'

...'Amount? Oh, well I was going to ask for about 300 kilos, but if it's to be 'little bangs' only, then probably 100 kilos should do for some practice and the real thing; if and when it's necessary. Bear in mind we actually might have to make a demonstration of our resolve and that would require a satisfyingly big bang! So, maybe 300 kgs would be necessary.'

...'Yes sir. I remember; no gas or oil leaks. But you can trust me to make a very good demonstration bang that will stay within Senior Management guidelines.'

...'Thank you Sir. I'll leave it with you and get on with seeing how well these people can shoot.'

...'No Sir, I promise I won't. I try to limit myself to one per day, unless I'm in combat.'

...'Yes Sir, that was a joke. See you at dinner.'

She looked at Lieutenant Towson who seemed to be recovering from a fit of the chuckles, 'OK. That's sorted. He seems to have a low opinion of my regard for human life for some reason. Anyway, let's go see what these rock apes can do with a gun or rifle. We do have some of those, I hope?'

Lieutenant Towson grinned, and dug a small electronic tablet from a pocket. After poking at it several times, he announced, 'Yes Ma'am. We've got a selection of rifles, sub-machine guns and handguns to choose from and plenty of ammunition for them. Most of it is either current or recently ex-Australian army stuff. As a general issue rifle, we have the latest F90 export version of the AusSteyr F88 in 5.56 NATO, a few SR98 sniper rifles, but I'm not sure how many are good enough to trust with one of those. There's also a thing called an AW50F that takes a .50 calibre round, but no one's been game to try that beast yet.'

Corrine's eyes lit up at mention of the AW50F. 'I know it very well. I used it in the Middle East.' That announcement raised Towson's eyebrows in silent surprise and he decided he needed to learn a lot more about the Major. Corrine noted that and hastily added, 'We'll have a show-me-yours-and-I'll-show-you-mine session soon, XO, but for now I can tell you I've spent too much time in the Middle East desert as a sniper, demolition expert and covert assassin.'

Towson's eyebrows went back up nearly to his hairline, but he gamely went on listing the equipment available. 'For handguns, we have the Glock 17 or the model 19 for those with smaller hands, and as a sub-machine gun, the H&K MP5 in a version called the SD6. There are three heavy machine guns, the Browning M2HB-QCB; that's a damn heavy thing. It seems to take the same .50 calibre BMP round that the AW50F takes and there are a lot of rounds for both.'

'Yeah, but it's very effective,' Corrine added, 'and also makes an excellent long-range sniper rifle.'

He smiled, 'I'll take your word for that, Major. It doesn't look like the sort of weapon I'd want to take on a 20-kilometre hike across the desert.'

'No. You don't want to do that unless you really need the fire-power, and then it's priceless. Anything else?'

He thought a moment, 'Oh, yes. There are two MK19 grenade launchers and 10 crates of the M430 rounds for it as well as 10 crates of the F1 hand grenade.'

Corrine looked pensive. 'That's quite a list of equipment and most of it is current Army issue. Someone has done some serious homework and dropped a lot of money in the right places to get most of those items.'

She looked directly at Towson. 'Do you ever speculate where all this money is coming from Lieutenant?'

He looked a bit evasive for a moment, as though he suspected Corrine was trying to trap him into some subversive statement, before guardedly replying, 'Yes, Ma'am. But in the privacy of my room and shared only with Sergeant Hegarty.'

She smiled at him, 'Don't look so concerned, Lieutenant, like you I'm only here for the duration, so I'd really like you to share your thoughts and concerns with me. Sergeant Hegarty can as well if she's of the same mind. I've not been brainwashed like some others I've seen around here and I need to get up to speed with regard to what's really been happening in the last few months.'

He relaxed a little. 'Yes Ma'am and thank you. I might just do that after I talk to Julie.'

'Good. Now let's finally get out to the range and see what these idiots can do.'

CHAPTER 15

I was happy with our non-stop progress, even though it was draining on everyone. Part of the problem was the constant battle to keep our speed as close to 14 knots as we could, and it meant sail trimming and engine throttle changes on an irregular basis. We ran on one engine nearly all the time, except for a few occasions when the wind was too light or dead calm, in which case two engines had to be run quite hard.

The other fatigue problem was caused by navigating inside the reef; a route I'd chosen to keep to calmer waters, but it meant a lot of course alterations to avoid lumps of the hard stuff. Lump dodging became worse the further north we went as the reef closed in on the coast north of Townsville, until off Cape Melville at midday, we were zigzagging constantly.

North of the hilly, but very pretty Stanley Island, where we were sorely tempted to stop to enjoy the beautiful white sand beaches and warm, clear water, the passages opened out considerably. By 17:00 that afternoon, we were abeam the remote settlement of Coen, inland from the coast with its population of 416 persons. To avoid an extensive series of coral cays which lay out like parallel ribs aligned north-east/south-west, I decided we'd stay to seaward of them. We'd lost cell phone coverage long ago even with the boosted antenna on *Firebird's* masthead, so it was worth staying wide of the coast to be able to steer a straighter course. The downside was that the ocean swells were more pronounced as the outer reef was, in some cases, just a few miles to the east of our course.

The general fatigue we all felt meant that although we were getting a reasonable amount of sleep, there seemed to be no time or inclination to kick back and relax. The booze locker had stayed shut by common consent, so we were looking forward to rounding the Cape next morning and having a day or two of rest at the creek estuary tucked in against Bay Point, just over one nautical mile west of Cape York.

On Tuesday morning, it was with an air of excitement and relief we rounded of the most northerly point of the Australian mainland, staying in very close to shore since we had deep water to within metres of the rocks. We were so close we were able to wave and call out to a few people who had made their way out onto the rocks so as to be able to say they were as far north on the mainland as was possible to get with dry feet!

Minutes later, we were heading south-west, crossing a shallow bay and staying well out from the beautiful glaring white, sandy beach because the water was still shallow two or three hundred metres out. Just inside the eastern side of the rocky finger known as Bay Point, we carefully felt our way in over a series of shallow sandbars, to a small sandy creek that afforded excellent protection from any weather.

Ever mindful of the exploding crocodile population, I dropped anchor just off a small sandy beach which had an expanse of shallow water to seaward, figuring if we were either wading or swimming in the shallows, we could easily see if a 'Saltie' was taking an unhealthy interest in some tasty two or four-legged snacks.

Seeker slid in beside us, dropped her own anchor then backed down until we were rafted up, making it easy to hop from one boat to the other. Even though *Seeker* now had the bigger, more open cockpit, *Firebird* was still the focal point of social activities and meals.

It was a real blessing to be able to turn off the engines and soak up the glorious peace and tranquillity of such a remote and beautiful place. Our arrival had set off a cacophony of birdcalls from the surrounding scrub, but after a few minutes they settled down and peace was restored. Several smaller birds we couldn't identify then visited us, but they seemed amazingly tame and just wanted to investigate these new visitors to their territory. Several pelicans gracefully dropped down from their endless food patrol to circle us, then landed close off our sterns, solemnly nodding their long, narrow beaks at us, hoping for a free feed.

Melissa was always a sucker for a pathetic look from a bird, so she dug out some frozen fish and while defrosting it in a bucket of seawater, had two of the birds swim up to the stern board and clumsily climb aboard, bobbing their heads and demanding to be hand fed.

Dave and I compared notes on fuel consumption and remaining stock and it turned out we were better off than we expected. We decided tomorrow sometime, we'd transfer the contents of one of Dave's extra bladder tanks to *Firebird*, which would then give me plenty to get to Darwin and avoid the need for a mid-ocean transfer.

It was Charlie who stirred me into action by saying; 'We'll give you a hand, Harry, if you'd rather get the job out of the way now. It shouldn't take long to do the transfer.'

I looked at Dave who shrugged and said, 'He's right. It'd be best to square everything away now; then we won't have to worry about it.'

I gave in to the logic of Charlie's idea, and helped along by Sandy giving me a pat on the bum as I dragged myself out of my comfortable chair, we set about laying out the portable pump and hose Reg had left for just such a purpose. Amanda roused herself to stir the galley into action to brew some tea and coffee and Sandy helped make piles of fresh, steaming pikelets with whipped cream and strawberry jam.

We made the various connections and I set the pump purring softly as it transferred fuel from Dave's cockpit bladder tank to the one in *Firebird's* cockpit, before we attacked the feast the girls laid out for morning tea; God bless 'em.

By the time the huge stack of pikelets had been reduced to crumbs and teas and coffees consumed, the fuel transfer was complete, so we uncoupled, disconnected and tidied things up. Then it was time to let the kitties have a romp ashore since they'd been remarkably patient in the preceding days. Since swimming ashore was ruled out as being way too dangerous, I launched the dinghy and ferried the pussies and Sandy ashore, still keeping a careful eye out for any beady little eyes that might be watching. Nobody else wanted to stir at that stage, so we were alone with the cats.

It wasn't much of a beach just where we were and the low tide had exposed isolated clumps of mangroves sitting in the warm, shallow water over a mostly sandy bottom. I'd told Jasper to be careful and not to go swimming because of crocodiles and once again he seemed to listen and comprehend, so he and the fast-growing Krazy kitten had a lovely time playing chase on the beach and in and out of some of the stunted mangrove trees and beach she-oaks growing in the sand.

We walked along to the main stretch of beach proper to get well away from the boats and the others for some privacy and a total change of scenery. With the low trees, it wasn't long before the boats were well out of sight. The first thing Sandy did was to take all her clothes off and roll them into one of the big beach towels she carried, so I did the same. Naturally enough, it wasn't long before the peace and privacy helped raise the mutual lust level to the point where we needed to look for a nice little shady spot to spread the towels out and indulge in our favourite pastime of releasing pent-up tension and lust, otherwise known as nookie. The cats respected our activity and kept away, but when we were still messing around about an hour later, they came closer and became just a little bit more vocal.

Sandy giggled when Jasper tickled her ear with his whiskers and suggested that as wonderful as it was, I might consider finishing things fairly soon before the crew sent out a search party. Always obedient in such matters, I did as requested to our mutual satisfaction and fifteen minutes later, we were strolling back to the dinghy, the cats galloping circles around us. Sandy had left her top off, which prompted Amanda to do the same shortly after we climbed back aboard when she went for'rard to lie on the trampoline netting.

That soon led to Melissa doing the same, although Tracy kept her shirt on for a bit longer, but finally took it off and joined the growing group on the trampolines.

For some strange reason I was overcome with tiredness, so despite the attractions of all the bare flesh on the foredeck, I went below and quickly fell asleep on the bed. I awoke an hour later to the sounds of laughing, happy people drifting down through the open hatch over the bed. Feeling considerably refreshed, I stood up on the bed with my head and shoulders out the hatch to find myself in the middle of a party.

The four girls were still topless and had been joined by Alf and Charlie, although Dave was apparently still sacked-out. The girls were sucking on Vodka Cruisers or wine, while the guys had a beer each and had joined the girls in taking their shirts off. Charlie had brought his guitar along and with his husky, soulful voice, was just finishing an Eric Bogle song that typically told a very poignant Australian story.

My appearance caused a round of cheers and a frosty bottle of beer was shoved into my hand. Although it was only mid-afternoon, R & R rules meant the bar was open on demand so I joined them by downing a large swig of the cold brew that seemed to claw quite delightfully at the back of my dry throat as it slid down.

'Bloody hell,' I complained in a mock-serious tone, 'how can a bloke get any sleep with you bunch of drunken, debauched jokers carrying on right over my head?'

That statement was greeted with a chorus of abusive comments thrown at me, along with a few pieces of ice from the esky. I stayed where I was and slowly sipped my beer, content to let the crew unwind in such a happy fashion as the afternoon slowly faded as the sun settled toward the west. Amanda and Melissa went aft, returning after a while with several plates of nibblies such as smoked oysters and sliced gherkins on small biscuits, several varieties of cheese in pieces, a bowl of green olives together with some plump, black Kalamatas and little rolls of succulent smoked salmon.

I'd finished my beer, didn't feel like another, so I found a Jackie's and cola pre-mix that I grabbed. It was refreshingly different after the beer and I had to remind myself to take it easy. Dave had joined the party by now and like me, he didn't feel like too much to drink, so he joined me in a Jackie's and cola as we wandered about the rafted-up hulls, making sure the anchor chains were laid out correctly. The light breeze was blowing from the east, so the two boats were lying back off the beach, but I'd put out the small stern anchor to make sure we both stayed there.

It was Dave who drew my attention to a fast boat heading our way, following the curve of the pristine white beach. It turned out to be a functional-looking 25-foot half-cabin alloy boat or 'tinnie' with four men aboard and pushed by a pair of 200 horsepower outboards. The boat was adorned with the obligatory array of rod-holders or 'rocket-launchers' attached to every conceivable vantage point, which made it one very serious fishing weapon.

The men were another story however, having obviously been hitting the booze pretty hard. I nodded to Dave as they recklessly roared into the creek mouth at full speed and broadsided to a stop just metres from our sterns. We left the others up for'rard while we tried to intercept them at the stern, although we could see their attention was already fixed on the four topless girls who weren't helping matters by waving happily and staying topless.

'Gidday gents,' one big man said, toasting us with a beer, 'nice pair of boats you've got here.'

We plastered silly grins on our faces, trying to look both dumb and pissed.

'Gidday fellas, how 'ya doing? That looks a fairly serious fishing rig,' I replied. 'Catching much?'

'Shit yeah!' another yobbo replied. 'It's the duck's nuts. We've caught so many we've run out of freezer space. If you're going to be here for a few days, maybe you could store some for us until we can run across to Thursday Island and buy some more eskies and ice. We'll give you a pile of fillets for your trouble.'

'That's very generous, fellas,' I said, 'but our freezers are pretty full up at the moment so we can't really help you out with storage, although we could use some fresh fillets for dinner if you do have some to spare. We've got a few mouths to feed.'

There were some fairly significant looks passed between the men, before the first one said, 'Yeah. No problem, but we haven't got any fresh ones aboard. How about we nip back to camp and get enough for all of us then we'll come back and have a good old cook-up and a few drinks together. It'd be nice to talk to some fresh faces for a change.'

I looked at Dave and shrugged, 'Yeah, well I guess that sounds OK. Why don't you go do that and I'll get the cooks organised.'

'That's the go, Skipper,' the Chief Yobbo said enthusiastically, 'and you can tell the little ladies that they don't need to change just because company is coming to dinner. We like your ladies as they are. In fact, if they wanted to lose the shorts as well, that'd be even better. Ha ha!'

That comment provoked a round of heavy laughs from his crew as they high-fived and backslapped each other.

'Well, I don't know if they'll want to do that. I mean, that's going a bit far, isn't it?'

Chief Yobbo looked like he thought they'd found Fool's Paradise. 'Nah! Don't you worry about that! We'll show you how it works, 'cause we've done this before and everybody will have a great time, especially the ladies with four new, healthy fellas for them to enjoy. We'll bring a stack of fresh fish fillets back if you really want to eat, or we can just get straight into the good stuff. We'll even bring an esky full of booze and there'll be something special to help the lovely ladies get right in the mood.'

I looked like I was considering his offer. 'Well, gee. I'm still not sure. We haven't done anything like this before and I'm not sure how keen the girls will be.'

I looked at Dave a moment, 'Do you reckon the girls would mind sharing for one night? It could be fun.'

Dave had caught the drift of what I was doing. 'Nah! I don't reckon they'll mind and like the man says, if there's a bit of good stuff to make them feel happy, they'll be right into it!'

I nodded agreement, all four hanging on every word, already getting excited with the thought that they were going to be handed four beautiful girls to do whatever they wanted with.

'OK. If you fellas go grab some fresh fillets, the booze and other stuff, we'll talk to the girls and get them sorted. We might just have a few cold beers waiting for you when you get back!'

'Good oh Skipper. You do that 'an we'll be right back. But make sure you tell the ladies that we guarantee they'll have a great time!'

'Oh I'll certainly tell them!' I waved acknowledgement as the outboards roared into life and with a burst of power and a twist of the wheel which nearly capsized the boat, the idiots blasted out over the shallows of the bar, leaving a rooster-tail of sandy wash behind them.

Dave looked at me as if he thought I was crazy. 'This is just a bit nuts mate! I went along with what you were saying because I guessed you're setting them up for one of your diabolical plans to take them down, but once those guys are aboard, there're going to be very hard to handle!'

I sat down on the cockpit surround and looked at him. 'Think it through mate. They'd already spotted the girls topless, most likely with binoculars. I thought I saw a flash or two earlier from way up the beach. Anyway, they approached us full of piss and attitude. Now we would have had a stand-up fight on the spot if we'd told them to just piss off, or they would have snuck back later tonight.

But this way, they come to us on our terms and our timing. As well as that, we're prepared. At the moment, they think we're just a bunch of dumb-arses who couldn't spot a gang-bang coming if it was being led by a marching band!'

Dave gave a wry chuckle, 'I seem to have heard this strategy before. OK, but what's our plan to handle these dick-wits. They'll be back with some fish, topped up with beer, drugs and pants full of raging hard-ons. Perhaps we should just shoot 'em?'

I gave him one of my manic grins, 'Nah, that'd be way too easy. I've got a much better idea. Did Corrine leave her special little medical kit?'

He looked puzzled for a moment. 'Yeah, she did. She didn't want to carry anything that might mess with her cover. Why, what's the plan?'

'Let's top four beers off with a pill and hit those idiots with one each as soon as they get aboard. We'll get the girls to play along by staying topless; maybe even get them to put bikini bottoms on. They'll be so busy looking at tits, pussy and bums they won't notice the pills. Although if I remember rightly, the pills were tasteless and they work in about five minutes.'

'Yeah, that's about right. They knocked those hairdresser girls for a loop. But then what? We'll have four drunk, unconscious yobbos on our hands.'

'Ah yes, but they're four unconscious yobbos who need to be taught a lesson.'

'Ah! So do I sense a diabolically cunning Harry payback plan being hatched?' Dave asked with a grin.

I shrugged, 'Maybe. But we need to talk to the girls first then get some stuff together. We don't have long, so you nip down and grab the medical kit and I'll talk to the others. As soon as we see them approaching, we can load up the beers.'

While Dave was fetching Corrine's special kit, I went for'rard and brought the others up to date and explained my evil plan. The girls were horrified at first that a potential gang-bang was headed back at them, but when I explained my plan to achieve diabolical revenge, they all loved it. The girls were happy to go and change into their smallest bikini pants, while Sandy, intent on playing her part to best effect, changed into a tiny, lacy pair of panties which hid bugger-all and looked stunningly erotic.

We lined up the beers and had four pills ready while Amanda and Dave ratted through both pantries and maintenance supplies for the other items I'd told them we'd need.

All the other stuff was assembled in the galley by the time Tracy called back from the foredeck where she was playing lookout with a pair of binoculars, to say that their boat had pulled out from the very far end of the beach and was heading our way.

147

CHAPTER 16

FIREBIRD, CAPE YORK, TUESDAY EVENING

Since they had total faith my plan would work, the girls were getting very excited about the upcoming encounter and needed to be reminded how they were to act and what to say. Then the fishing boat wheeled up to *Firebird's* stern and cut the motors. One glance showed that Dave's assessment was correct. The yobbos were even more pissed, but at least they had brought a bag full of beautiful thick fillets and passed them up as they all climbed out.

'Nice one guys,' I exclaimed, trying to slur my words slightly, but that bit of acting probably went unnoticed. 'What sort of fish are these?'

'Mostly Sweetlip, with some Barramundi as well.' They were all big fish.

'Fantastic!' I raved as I slurped on a beer. 'But here's the beers I promised you. I figured you'd like Great Northern or Fourex, there's two of each, so get into them; we've got plenty more.'

As arranged, Sandy brought the guys their beers and their little beady eyes nearly popped out of their heads when she walked up to them cradling the four cold bottles, the condensation running in a most suggestive manner down her bare belly and soaking into the waistband of her miniscule panties. It was quite funny to watch four sets of eyes track from her boobs to her crotch and back to her boobs, the cycle repeating over and over like they were watching a vertical tennis match.

They were so distracted by Sandy, they forgot to ask why the girls weren't naked and jumping in their laps.

Sandy very obviously enjoyed being so lusted after and nearly overplayed her part of distracting the four men, by putting on an impromptu show, doing a little dance around the table then propped up in front of them, carelessly lifting one foot up onto a chair as they downed their doctored beers without drawing breath. 'Nice of you boys to bring all that lovely fish back for us,' she said softly, 'and I believe that you've got some other nice surprises for us?'

'Oh yeah my lovely darlin',' the leader growled, his eyes still bouncing between her boobs and crotch. 'We've got some stuff that'll make things really buzz around here!'

She smiled sweetly and handed over four more beers that Amanda had popped a pill into as well. I shuddered to think what two of the powerful knockout tablets and all the alcohol they'd drunk was going to do to them when they woke up, but I figured if my plan worked, they'd have a lot more to worry about than feeling like they'd been run over by a herd of water buffalo. Sure enough, they'd barely had time to have the first swig of the fresh bottles, when first one, then two, three then the fourth yobbo slumped sideways onto the deck, beer bottles falling from unconscious hands to spew white, frothing beer over the white, fibreglass deck.

The crew gave a small cheer and stage one was complete. Amanda and Melissa were setting up the gun for stage two, so Dave and I hauled them back into their tinny and ripped the shorts off each, tossing them in a corner. They were already shirtless, with three of them having very hairy chests that fitted stage two very nicely. The girls giggled to see that only one of the yobbos could claim any sort of bedroom bragging rights, and that was only just! The girls rated the other three as being in the 'tiny' otherwise called the 'I think I can almost feel something, can you move it some more?' class.

Stage two of my evil plan called for several shots of liquid nails industrial adhesive to be pumped onto each man's pubic hair. Tracy was the only one keen enough to pull on a rubber glove and rub the sticky mess well into their hair and over their puny dicks. Thankfully, the smell of the adhesive overpowered the smell of four unwashed bodies.

The deviate girl lingered longer over the guy they'd awarded bragging rights to, but he still copped the same dose. For good measure, three had a large dollop rubbed into their chest hair and all four had a handful of the gooey mess spread between their bum cheeks, a less than pleasant task, but ultimately worth the horrible sights.

In case any of the girls were starting to feel we were going too far with the punishment, I reminded them that these fishermen had come to us with the declared intention of causing us trouble by feeding the girls date-rape drugs and lining them up for a gang-bang! At the very least we would have had a fight on our hands. I also pointed out that in this remote area, there was nobody to lend us a hand to deal with these would-be rapists.

Stage three was fairly easy and saw the girls using the cordless hair clipper to roughly shave the sides of each man's head leaving a wide Mohawk. We figured that they could either leave it and suffer the comments and questions from friends and family, or shave the rest off and start afresh.

We let the girls decorate them with spray cans of enamel paint, the kind that needs turps or petrol to dissolve and remove from skin. We thought the effect on sensitive skin would be interesting in the extreme! As a finishing touch, each limp form was carefully rolled slightly to one side and a squirt of Liquid Nails applied to the deck under each bum cheek, then they were eased back into position. I lashed each one upright against the cockpit side with some light cord I found.

For good measure, we solved their freezer-overcrowding problem by emptying one of all their choicest fillets, finding as a bonus a large bag of cleaned mud crab portions that would feed us for several meals.

The final task before we returned them to their camp was to interlace each man's fingers as tightly as possible, before squirting a good shot of thin Superglue over them, being careful not to touch them or even get too close. Their joined hands were allowed to rest on a bare thigh where excess glue made another firm bond.

We all admired the bizarre results of our handiwork, before I sent Dave to print off several copies of a note I wanted to leave with the boat when we parked it.

As soon as Dave was back, notes stuffed into envelopes, he launched *Firebird's* dinghy from between the hulls under the projecting shelf of the vast daybed, and I fired up the two huge outboards on the fishing boat for the short run up the beach. I was hoping their camp was deserted, with no other curious eyes watching as I wanted to be able to deny any involvement when these clowns were finally released.

With Dave ready, lines were dropped and I motored sedately out through the dimness of early evening, over the shallow creek mouth then accelerated for the run along the beachfront. I spotted the marks in the sand where they had pulled the boat up earlier, and although there were several tents and a few caravans back amongst the trees, the few people I spotted moving around paid no attention to the returning boat.

I ran the boat up on the beach and tilted the motors, before carefully taping the envelopes in several places where they wouldn't be missed by the first person to wonder why the boat was there with nobody in their camp. I knew camping people looked out for each other, but it was hard to imagine that anybody would have any affection for these clowns.

Dave was waiting, outboard idling quietly as I slipped over the side of the tinnie and into my own dinghy. He quietly reversed off and headed back to our creek and our crews.

Of course, the first thing they all wanted to know when we were back and had secured the dinghy up into the stowed position again was, 'what was in the notes Dave printed out?'

I was able to recite the text by heart. 'It said, *'These men planned to drug four ladies and subject them to multiple rapes. The drugs are in this boat and it is suggested they be turned over to the Thursday Island Police. They also intended harm to the other members of the crew who interfered with their foul plans. Liquid nails has been used for most gluing but their fingers have been joined with Superglue. The liquid nails can be softened by application of a vegetable oil—normal cooking oil will suffice, but it will be a very slow process. Soaking in acetone solvent can dissolve the Superglue, but this will also take time. The oil-based paints will need turps or petrol to clean off.*

Should the rescue process damage sensitive skin areas, we offer no apologies and urge you to remember these men attempted to imposed their evil intentions on a peaceful group of travellers and have paid the penalty! If the corrective measures are applied as suggested and patience exercised, the four men will not suffer any long-term effects, although a high degree of burning and itching of the more tender skin areas will be experienced for several weeks. Hopefully, this will serve as a reminder that sexually violent offences against women are not to be tolerated at any time!

Should they consider any level of retribution, we can only suggest they first consider our Biblical warning. 'The wrath of God will pale by comparison to what we are prepared to do should you cross our path again'.'

That statement was met with soft cheers and a hug from each girl.

'Thanks Harry,' Amanda said with suspiciously moist eyes, 'we really didn't know how serious those guys were.'

Alf and Charlie looked very ashamed to have missed the signs of what was going on and failing to back up Dave and me, but after I had a quiet word along the lines of, 'Never, ever let your guard down when you're on a job.' They took the message to heart and promised they wouldn't let me down again.

After all the excitement, I chased the girls into the galley to cook up some of the fresh fillets we'd scored, the rest saved for later meals. There was a large pack of frozen fillets, plus the beautiful crab pieces that Amanda found room for in the booze fridge, which was normally off-bounds for food, but in this case, I made an exception.

The rest of the evening passed peacefully, although Dave and I set the perimeter alarms and the electrical defences. I activated

Firebird's masthead-mounted infrared camera and set the motion detection alarm. With those warning devices activated, plus Jasper for close-in defence, we all slept soundly.

That is, everybody except Dave who was wakened by the perimeter motion detection alarm at 03:00. As he was hurriedly pulling on some pants, *Seeker* gave a lurch, so he grabbed one of his treasured Coonan .357 magnum pistols before hustling to the stern, where a strange scraping sound could be heard. Another sharp lurch made him stagger as he passed through the plush saloon, then out through the sliding doors to the wide cockpit.

At first, nothing seemed to be amiss as he quickly scanned around and all was quiet on *Firebird*. Then the scraping noise sounded again, accompanied by a soft, throaty grunt. Stepping quietly in an exaggerated crouch to the port access steps, he still couldn't see anything until he flicked the step LEDs on and got the shock of his life!

The front two thirds of a monstrous crocodile occupied the 6.5-metre-wide stern board which sat just above water level. The ugly beast had its massive head twisted sideways so that it rested up the access steps, the snout just a metre away from where Dave crouched, frozen in shock.

For some reason, the beast didn't get aggro and snap at Dave and the rotten thing actually seemed quite comfortable where it was, so he backed slowly away, before stepping over to the right-side railing where *Firebird* was tied up. In a hoarse whisper, he started calling out for Harry, which brought Jasper out but he stopped just short of the railing, knowing not to touch it while the lethal current was present.

'Jasper, get Harry please, Jasper,' he asked softly, feeling slightly foolish as he always did when talking to the big cat who had the most uncanny and surreal ability to understand humans better than they mostly understood themselves. Jasper blinked at him, then wheeled around and quickly padded back inside. Finally, Dave got a human response, except it came from Tracy who occupied the left stern cabin and slept with all portholes and hatches open for coolness. She appeared out of the large hatch over her bed, showing she didn't bother with pyjamas or nighties and Dave took a moment to admire her taut, sleek shape with all her nice bits on display.

'What's up, Dave,' she asked quietly, 'and why are you whispering? Is something wrong?'

The lack of clothing didn't seem to bother her as she lithely hauled herself up out of the hatch and stepped over to the railing.

'Please don't touch that thing!' Dave said, still whispering. 'The current's up at lethal level!'

'I remember,' Tracy said seriously, 'but what's the problem?'

'There's a monster bloody crocodile lying across my stern board, with its great fat head most of the way up the stern steps.'

Tracy became very excited; Dave could easily tell. 'No shit!' she exclaimed. 'Hang on and I'll turn the railing off, then I want to see it!'

'It's not a homeless puppy Tracy,' Dave told her sternly, 'it would have to be well over 20-something feet long and would easily weigh about one thousand kilograms! That's like one tonne! Anyway, turn the power off and come over. Harry should be on his way if Jasper understood me.'

She darted alluringly into the saloon and reappeared a few moments later, still naked and climbed over the railing, *Firebird's* UHD camcorder clutched in one hand.

'Bloody hell Tracy, you should have pants on when you do that. You look terrific, but fair suck of the sav! Remember I'm girl-less at the moment! '

She giggled at him, but sobered up fast as Dave took the lead, and I stepped quietly up behind them, taking a moment to admire Tracy's naked body.

'What've you got Dave?' I asked quietly.

'Big croc mate; bloody big! And it seems like it's settled in for the duration. Damn thing even looks comfortable! I've left the step's LEDs on, but it's lying on some of those. I didn't want to do anything else in case I spook it or stir it up. I'd rather not find out how a beast that big behaves when it's stirred up, thank you!'

I chuckled quietly as we stepped slowly closer around the inboard end of the huge daybed, Tracy tending to huddle back against me now the confrontation with the monster was at hand, although she had the camcorder up to one eye and in record mode. 'Where's its head?' I asked.

'It's lying up the stairway just ahead, with the snout almost at the top and the body draped right across the stern board. I haven't looked for the fucking tail yet!'

I motioned for them to hold position while I stepped back a few paces to the head of the other side stairway, confident that the creature couldn't see me from where its head was lying, and sure enough the whole stern board was covered in the massive spreading bulk of armoured hide, covered with lines of serrated fins and knobs. The huge back legs were trailing back parallel with its rear body and just reached the water, which left a fair chunk of the tail still in the water!

'How wide is your stern board Dave?' I asked softly.

'A bit over 6.5 metres full width,' he replied. 'Why?'

'Shit! In that case, I've got bad news. Given that the tail is about 45% the length of the rest of the body and head, this thing has to be well over 7 metres long! And in case your maths has become rusty, that's up around 25 fuckin' feet! We do *not* want to stir this thing up for *anything*! It could wreck both boats without even raising a sweat!'

'Terrific!' Dave muttered. 'So what do we do, Oh Great Crocodile Guru?'

I stepped back up beside them again, Tracy staying close. 'Fucked if I know, old mate! This is a bit outside my experience, but I just want to take a peek at the bitey end before we wake up the rest of the crew.'

With a now-trembling Tracy clinging to my arm with one hand and the camcorder in the other, I stepped slowly around the end of the daybed until the huge, ugly, misshapen head was visible; its massive jaws closed but with a picket fence-load of huge, polished white fangs poking up and down beyond the ragged edges of his jaw.

'Holy crap!' Tracy whispered. 'I can't believe the size of it! It's fuckin' gi-normous! Look at that bloody great head. It's got to be more than a metre long.'

I completely agreed with her sentiments and was about to slowly back off, when I saw a glint from one eye as it slowly opened, calmly appraising the puny creature standing just two metres away. Then it slowly opened it's massive jaws, causing Tracy to utter a whimpering sound as it displayed a very impressive full collection of teeth before just as slowly, closing it again and then closing its eye.

'I think it just yawned,' I said in wonder. 'You're right Dave. The bloody thing's got itself very comfortable and is going to sleep.'

I backed up slowly, taking a still-shaking Tracy with me, until the three of us had retreated to the safety railing closest to *Firebird*. Jasper joined us, looking inquisitively at me, so I bent down to speak to him. 'There's a very large, very dangerous crocodile wrapped around the stern of the boat. Its head is just the other side of the daybed. I don't want you or Krazy kitten to go anywhere near it.'

He cocked his head to the side, which usually indicates he's considering my words, something which still freaks me out a bit, and freaks visitors out a lot, and then he huffed loudly at me!

'Now come on Jasper. Don't do that! This is bigger than anything you've seen before and it's not a new playmate for you, so just leave it alone please. It could damage the boats if it gets annoyed!'

This was the most anybody had heard me talk to Jasper before and both Dave and Tracy were looking very strangely at me, but wisely stayed quiet as Jasper looked at the gun dangling from Dave's hand, then stood up, stepped past me and padded slowly around the daybed while Cameraperson Tracy and I trailed impotently in pursuit. 'Jasper! Leave it alone!' I demanded in a stern whisper, futilely it would seem since my lovely big cat just flicked the tip of his tail at me, and seemed hell-bent on being converted into a one-bite tasty snack.

He stopped a half-pace away from the tip of the huge snout then sat, staring thoughtfully at the croc. I saw its big eye open again and focus on Jasper, then the pair had a staring contest for a while before Jasper made a very strange mewling sound, reached out with one paw, rested it gently on the tip of its snout and then seemed to push its snout down to the top of the step. I was almost holding my breath when it opened its jaws a little, huffed a very fishy breath at Jasper who mewled softly again, then allowed its snout to be pushed down to the deck.

Jasper then lay down with both paws together and stretched well out in front, Sphinx-style, so they were just touching the tip of the croc's snout that stayed resting on the deck as it went back to sleep. Jasper kept his head erect and his ears were pricked alertly forwards as if he were scanning the dark waters of the creek behind his monstrous new friend.

'Jasper. Here boy,' I called softly, but my faithful, obedient cat just twitched the tip of his tail again and ignored all my pleas to come away.

We watched for a while, but nothing appeared to be happening, the croc seemed to sleep and Jasper stayed awake and alert, looking like he was keeping watch to make sure nothing bad happened to it while it slept.

Finally, I turned away and left him to it, seeing that Tracy had overcome some of her fear, and had stayed close enough to have recorded the entire surreal episode. She edged back a bit while I spoke to an anxious Dave but kept recording the view of the sleeping croc and Jasper sitting guard. 'What will be, will be! It's almost like they're mentally communing and Jasper's keeping watch over the croc while it is asleep. I can't explain it any other way.'

I told Dave about the surreal moment when Jasper reached out to gently touch the croc's snout and how the croc seemed to accept that all was well and it was safe.

'I got it all on video,' Tracy said proudly. 'The camcorder indicated there was enough light from the stern LEDs.'

'That's great, but it still doesn't answer the question of what we do about it?' Dave was still holding the Coonan .357, which maybe was why Jasper felt the need to defend the croc, which in fact, hadn't caused any damage apart from noticeably upsetting the trim of *Seeker*, jangling several sets of nerves and creating a lot of adrenalin.

'For safety, I think we should wake Alf, Charlie and Melissa and get them over to *Firebird*, or at least tell them to stay away from the stern. They can kip on the daybed or find a soft spot somewhere if they want to go back to sleep. It's just a precaution in case one of them decides to come topside for a leak or something.

I'm stuffed if I know what's going on between Jasper and the croc, but I have a feeling Jasper's got this under control and with a bit of luck, the croc will leave quietly when he's had a sleep. Let's leave Amanda and Sandy asleep for now. There's nothing they can do and Tracy's got the video, so someone might as well get some sleep. I'll park in a chair here and keep watch, if you guys want to go back to bed.'

'I'll stay up with you,' Tracy said, her trembles under control, 'but what about Jasper?'

'He'll be OK,' I said confidently. 'Somehow, and I'm buggered if I know how, he's managed to connect with that monster and they're sort of friends. I think he'd take a very dim view of things if we tried to shift either of them.'

Dave shrugged, 'Well, you know Jasper best. So we'll go with it for now. I'd better go rouse the sleeping beauties.'

'Can you bring them out through the forward saloon door, not these cockpit doors, please mate? And tell them not to go sticky-beaking too closely at our friend. I don't want to disturb anything.'

'Sure Harry, that's no problem and I agree. 'Let sleeping crocs lie', somebody wrote. Or some shit like that—or if they didn't, they should've!'

CHAPTER 17

As the first blush of daylight crept up the blue-black sky overhead and commenced the daily task of transforming the sharp, black silhouettes of trees and bushes around us into softer shapes, I yawned quietly and stretched. Tracy's head was on my shoulder as she snored softly in the recliner beside me, having quickly succumbed to the peace and serenity that had replaced the fright of the events of five or six hours earlier.

Dave had roused the rest of his crew and led them, still half asleep and grumbling, out through the forward saloon door and across to *Firebird*. I'd finally convinced Tracy to go and get some clothes on, stimulating as it was to see her naked. She'd returned in time to help me position two recliner chairs so we had a view of Jasper, still sitting guard over his monster friend who hadn't moved a muscle since Jasper had done the 'laying on of paws' trick!

It sounded like Charlie and Melissa had bunked down in Tracy's stern cabin, while Alf might have crawled in with Amanda in the forward cabin. Sandy slept on, utterly exhausted from events of the afternoon and still getting over the stress of the voyage so far. Despite my good intentions, I'd fallen asleep as well, but old habits brought me awake gently and without moving, to let me scan the surroundings. It was Jasper who wakened me, gently nuzzling my leg and when he saw I was awake, he gently took my hand in his jaws and tugged, wanting me to stand up.

Tracy woke up when I did and grabbed the camcorder again as I stiffly stood, letting Jasper pull me the two steps necessary to be within touching distance of the croc who still hadn't moved.

Jasper pushed and pulled at me until I got the idea he wanted me to sit down just in front of the croc's snout, a slightly intimidating position from my perspective, but as Jasper seemed to think I was safe, I had to trust both him and his newest bestie, the massive 24-odd foot male salt-water crocodile, fast asleep at my feet.

Jasper must have wanted to go to the toilet as I heard him peeing over the stern on *Firebird*, leaving me to commune with the big fella, but the only vibrations I got that morning were self-generated when I contemplated what it would feel like to have those metre-long jaws, just a few centimetres from my legs, snap closed around my flimsy body should he disapprove of finding a human standing watch instead of his new friend Jasper.

Naturally, before Jasper returned, my fears were realised when the croc opened one eye and gazed impassively at me. That was when I really felt vibrations, but I needn't have worried, since the big fella just grunted softly once and then closed his eye again. A movement off to my right turned out to be Tracy with the UHD video camera in hand again, recording the scene for later discussion. Finally Jasper returned, toilet complete and smelling of dry cat pellets. I brushed off a few remnants clinging his muzzle then with Tracy still videoing, he gently nudged me out of the way. I stiffly climbed to my feet and let him resume being a Sphinx look-alike, with his front paws pressing firmly against the croc's snout.

Without opening his eyes, the beast gave a soft rumble and stayed put.

Tracy stopped recording after a few more minutes when it was clear all was quiet again, and as she followed me back over to *Firebird*, she said, 'I saw it, but I don't believe it! Absolutely amazing! That creature knew Jasper asked you to take his place and approved of you. That's a totally wild animal, the apex predator, and he's behaving like a ... a....?'

'House cat?' I responded weakly, the adrenalin still pumping strongly from being in such close proximity to the monster croc and being part of something I classed as truly mystical. I made a mental note to call Greg and ask for the name of the best Estuarine

Crocodile expert and tell him about the event, complete with video proof! I belatedly remembered last night I'd set the masthead camera to motion-detect, Infra Red mode and it was still running. I shut it down and stowed the camera before checking the stored files that were very large.

From 21:00 when I'd activated it, up until 01:27, nothing stirred, not even the four fishermen still glued to their boat that was nearly 2 kilometres away, but showed up very clearly in high definition on the stabilised-zoom lens camera. Then the camera panned around, tilted down and there, in crystal-clear IR, was our croc carefully making his way up onto *Seeker's* stern board. It showed in fine detail how he wriggled around to get comfortable, before twisting his huge head to lie up the left steps. Soon after, Dave appeared gun in hand; peering around in the dark then there was flare of light as he flicked the stern lights on. It was almost comical to see his reaction to the massive croc's presence.

The recording also showed Tracy's nude appearance and all the subsequent action with Jasper. As the light level increased, the camera switched across to normal daylight, full-colour recording and caught all the action right up to our retirement from the stern of *Seeker*. I looked at Tracy who seemed to be having trouble sitting still.

'Being in action of any sort gets the adrenalin flowing and makes you jumpy afterwards. It's normal. You just need to go burn off some of that excess energy.'

She grinned back, 'It's that obvious, is it?'

I shrugged, 'Been there, done that way too often, so yeah, it's obvious that you're wired! If we were down south, I'd suggest a long swim, but under the circumstances, perhaps a long run will do the job. Even though there's no activity at the yobbo's camp, I wouldn't go more than halfway along the beach. Just to be sure.'

She nodded with a gleam in her eyes. 'That might be best, although if Sandy wasn't here I'd suggest something else, but I'll be a good girl and settle for the run.'

I chuckled, 'If Sandy wasn't here; I'd take you up on that offer.

Maybe when you both get to know each other better, she just might make it happen anyway, seeing as you two get on so well. She has an interesting viewpoint on things at times, does my lovely Sandy!'

Tracy raised one eyebrow, something I've never mastered. 'Interesting! So, I should keep those thoughts warm?'

I laughed, 'Oh, most definitely yes! I don't tell tales, but shall we say that there is some precedence.'

Tracy smiled contentedly. 'That'll hold me for now, but can you run me ashore in the dinghy. I've not had much chance to learn what goes where with that yet.'

'No problem, but I might row you over to keep it quiet for our sleeping guest.'

'Good idea, so I'm ready when you are.'

Ten minutes later, she was ashore and I was waking Sandy for some adrenalin-burning activity that left both of us pleasantly exhausted.

'That was a delicious way to be woken up, but what brought that surge of lust on? You've not been that vigorous since we left Southport, although I loved every minute of it!'

I smacked her bare bum. 'You'd better get dressed and we'll get the others up as well. We've got something to show you, but we all have to be very quiet for now.'

She looked suitably mystified, but we shared the bathroom and emerged more refreshed. 'Where's Jasper? He's normally on the bed with me if you're not in it.'

I smiled, leading the way up to the saloon, 'We have an uninvited guest, but at the moment he's behaving himself, Jasper has made friends with him and won't leave him alone. I need you to see him before he leaves.'

It turned out that Sandy was the only one who hadn't seen 'Saltie' as Tracy had dubbed the giant male, so after reminding her to be very quiet and not to make any fuss, I led her over to *Seeker*. 'What you are about to see will come as a shock and I think it's truly mystical, but judge for yourself.'

By now, with all my cautions, she was getting impatient with me, but I held her back as we eased across *Seeker's* wide cockpit.

'Is Jasper OK? I can see his tail.' she whispered.

'Jasper's fine, as you will see. He's just sitting close to his new friend and watching over him while he has a bit of a sleep.'

The next moment, all of Jasper came into her view, including what his front paws were propped up against.

'Oh, fuck! Look at that thing! It's enormous! Is it dead?'

'No no, it's just asleep. Jasper wove some of his magic over it last night when it came aboard, and apart from a couple of brief awakenings, he's been asleep since.'

'But how...'

I held a finger to her lips as the giant croc lazily opened one eye, looked at Sandy, who shuddered, looked at Jasper still sitting alertly, made another soft rumble, seemingly of contentment and went back to sleep. Sandy started to tremble like Tracy had, so I pulled her away. 'Come on. Let's go have a cuppa and I might toss a double shot in it for medicinal purposes.'

She let me drag her away, but kept looking over her shoulder as if the big male was going to chase us. While I made the tea with double shots of dark rum, I sat her down at the Nav station to look at the video. She reacted strongly when Jasper first padded up to the croc, but made even more fuss when she saw Jasper parking me in front of its snout so he could go to the toilet and have a bite of breakfast.

'Fuck it, Harry! You're an idiot! You could've been killed—eaten by that monstrous great thing! That's the most insane thing I've ever seen you do! I'm not ready to be alone yet...you...you arsehole!'

I looked suitably humble, 'I'm sorry to frighten you, my sweet, but at the time, it was quite logical, and very stimulating!' I added as a distraction that seemed to work since she got a silly grin on her face.

'Yeah, it did, didn't it? Just don't do that again! Oh...the flirting with the croc I mean, not the nookie. That was superb! But what do we do now? Do we just wait until he feels like lunch or something?'

I smiled pacifyingly, 'Basically, yes. We can't do anything that Jasper hasn't already done, so we just have to wait until he decides to go.'

The others slowly filtered out of their various beds, Alf and Amanda looking pleased with each other and Amanda with a healthy glow. We held a round table discussion after I'd retrieved a hot and sweaty Tracy from shore and came to the same conclusion that we just had to wait for 'Saltie' to decide to go. Fortunately, we weren't doing anything that day, so the lost time didn't matter.

Meanwhile, with Tracy in the shower, the girls organised a very welcome big breakfast and we'd just finished that, when Jasper appeared at my side, pawing at my leg, something he only does when he wants something important.

I glanced at Sandy, 'Quick. Grab the video camera on the Nav station and record this. Something is happening!'

Turning my attention back to Jasper who was still impatiently pawing at my leg, I said,

'What's up, boy?' Naturally he didn't reply apart from huffing at me, so when I stood up, he led me over to *Seeker's* cockpit, Sandy close on my heels and the others trailing behind. Making sure I was following, he padded up to the giant saltie who now had his head raised and eyes open. Stopping just in front of the slightly gaping jaws, he reached up and patted the croc several times on the tip of his snout, just like he had last night.

The croc made the same deep rumbling sound which seemed to come from his broad belly, currently out of sight down on the stern board, blinked at Jasper, and it seemed at me as well, before he gently eased his way backwards off the stern board and slipped into the sparkling water with hardly a splash, leaving only a few minor scratches and a lot of unforgettable memories, fortunately captured on video, or no one would believe our story.

CHAPTER 18

FIREBIRD, CAPE YORK, WEDNESDAY

The day drifted slowly after the croc had left, the tension slowly draining and leaving everyone feeling a bit flat. After we all went ashore, had a walk on the beach and a swim in the very clear shallow water off the beach, the general mood picked up a lot. Beers and wines with lunch lifted everyone further and set the tone for the afternoon as the usual party developed on *Firebird's* trampolines. I was pleased to see that Alf's early morning visit to Amanda's bed seemed to have paid off as they were cuddled up, leaning back against the bow railings, neither concealing their high degree of interest with each other. The only happening of any note was when a Queensland Police boat, in the form of a 6-metre RIB dropped in, carefully negotiating the shallow creek entrance and nosed quietly up to our sterns.

Dave and I left the others looking after the esky and met the officers at the stern. Dave took their bowline and offered tea or coffee, which was declined. The female sergeant and a male constable aboard didn't bother to introduce themselves.

'There's been a very strange incident concerning some fishermen who have a camp down at the other end of the beach,' the sergeant opened with, 'I don't suppose you saw four fishermen in a boat up around here yesterday?'

I looked at Dave who shook his head. 'Nope, I'm afraid not Sergeant, unless one of the others did. We pulled in here late morning and haven't moved since, although we'll be on our way west in the morning.'

'And your last port of call, Sir?' she asked.

'That'd be Southport,' I said helpfully. 'The crew were getting fatigued with the watch schedule, so we decided to take a break.'

'That's a long run Sir; you must have very large fuel tanks in the powerboat.'

Dave answered, 'We do Sergeant, but still needed to add some temporary bladder tanks. We plan to refuel in Darwin before swinging north.'

That comment raised eyebrows. 'A very long run indeed gentlemen; may I ask your destination?'

I shrugged, 'Sure. It's no secret. We want to spend time cruising and diving around the Indonesian Islands. It's something I've always wanted to do, so here we are. Have either of you been over there?'

They both shook their heads. 'No. Not had that opportunity, but it sounds an interesting place to poke around. Do either of you mind if we do a safety equipment check?'

I beamed at them. 'Of course not! Please come aboard and I'll dig out our registration papers and the safety equipment storage canister. There are two EPIRBs in the saloon and four PLBs in a rack beside the nav station.'

They made a cursory check of *Firebird's* safety equipment, had an even briefer wander around then checked *Seeker's* gear, naturally not finding anything that they shouldn't.

'So you're sure no one saw a 25-foot tinnie with four fishermen aboard come down this end of the beach at any time yesterday?'

'Dave and I didn't, but let me check with the others.' I swung up onto the side deck and called out to the pissy group on the foredeck. 'The Sergeant would like to know if anyone saw a tinny with four blokes in it anytime yesterday.'

Most looked blank, but Sandy, who had wandered partway aft and picked up on the drift of questioning, walked back towards the sergeant and me, not bothering to put her top back on, causing the constable to fall immediately in lust and to stare openly at her bare boobs. The sergeant curled her lip disdainfully and our reputation as a bunch of drunken fools with too much time and money on our hands was reinforced. 'Yeah, there was a boat that went past not long after we got here in the morning. I only noticed it because it stayed close into the beach then swung out past the headland here, but I didn't notice if it came back.'

'Was it a small dinghy you saw?' the sergeant asked casually.

'Nah! It would have been 20 or 25 feet long with a half-cabin. It had rods poking up all over the place. I hope there hasn't been an accident. Are they alright?'

The sergeant answered, 'Yes ma'am, we think they'll be OK. They just had a…bit of bad luck with their boat and had a bit of an equipment malfunction, you might say. If everybody had the sort of safety gear you fellas have, they'd be a lot safer. We're the bunnies who have to go help these idiots when they get into trouble.'

After we made the suitably sympathetic noises and exchanged pleasantries for a few moments more they left, heading back to the east along the beach.

'That seemed to go well,' Dave commented as we made our way back up for'rard. 'Do you think they suspected us?'

'Shit yeah!' I grinned, as I thanked Sandy with a rub on her lovely bum. 'How many other groups of fairly tough-looking individuals are here at the moment? It could only have been us or maybe a group of campers down the other end of this beach. Still, they haven't got much to go on and I'm sure those yobbos won't be making any complaints.'

'Fair enough. It'll be good if that's the end of it.'

'Here, here, brother,' I said, handing him a cold beer. 'Let's enjoy tonight and get going first thing in the morning. For what looked to be a quiet little anchorage, it's been rather eventful.'

That comment sparked off another round of discussion about the surreal experience with the giant croc and Jasper, our mysterious enigmatic cat. He'd taken to his hidey-hole up in my forward cabin dressing room when the Police Officers came aboard, although little Krazy stayed on deck all the time, having great fun being played with by everybody. She had come aft, peering down on the officers from the safety of the cockpit roof. Jasper joined us when I whistled down the forward hatch and accepted the admiration, the scratching from all and sundry, and of course, any food scraps handed out as being his due.

CAPE YORK TO DARWIN – THURSDAY

We were on our way before the sun lifted its orange glare above the horizon, 14 knots as the target speed and quickly fell into the passage-making routine again, although perhaps not as rested as we'd hoped. Still, the crew were much more familiar with watch-keeping and it was a lot more relaxing. By choice, the bar stayed closed. I knew Alf would have liked to have transferred to *Firebird* to be with Amanda now they'd hooked up, but it would have meant transferring Tracy over to *Seeker*, a move I didn't want to make as she'd just started to learn the complexity of *Firebird*, plus I wanted her close for more personal reasons.

We took the main channel away from our exciting little creek, tracking west then southwest through beautifully clear water which was various shades of green through to blue in the deeper patches. A typical south-easterly breeze sprang up and helped with our speed as we tracked past the rugged and scrub-covered Entrance Island, then past Muralug or Prince of Wales Island, the largest island in the Torres Strait group, where just 20 or so original Indigenous owners, the Kauraeg People, still live.

Once clear of the south-western corner of Muralug, we turned west into clear, open water and headed for Darwin. With some 740 nautical miles to cover, we expected to be there around midday on Saturday.

The next planned landfall was to be Cape Wessel at the tip of a long, skinny finger of islands that stretched up from the bulk of mainland Arnhem Land, pointing at the former territory of Irian Jaya, now West Papua, to the northeast. I was tempted to drop in at Cape Wessel since the beaches are reported to be absolutely beautiful, as was the fishing and diving, but decided it might have to wait for another, more leisurely time.

FRIDAY

After an uneventful night, and promptly at 06:30 the next morning as predicted by the know-it-all Chart plotter, the low-lying mass of Cape Wessel appeared out of the slight sea mist, confirming our position. As we had progressed further west into the Arafura Sea, the winds had backed around the compass until we had a general west to northwest airflow, unfortunately making the use of both engines a full-time necessity so we could maintain our 14-knot average speed.

That landfall meant we were still on target to arrive in Darwin harbour around midday the next day.

SATURDAY

The navigation plan worked out well. In the wee small hours we gave Cape Don a healthy clearance while entering Van Diemen's Gulf. From there we had a straight run past the Tiwi Islands, home to the Indigenous Tiwi people, numbering some 2,500 and renowned for their art, music and sporting prowess on the footie field. The Darwin Harbour small boat advisories insist all refuelling and mooring requirements must be pre-booked. Once within range, I was on the phone making arrangements firstly for fuel, then booking a mooring each for two days at the Stokes Hill Wharf. It was hoped Darwin would prove to be less exciting than Cape York so everyone could actually get some decent rest. When the Stokes Hill lady asked for the draft of each boat, she was very surprised when I replied, 'Oh, about 0.6 metres for the cat and 1.3 for the powerboat.'

Both the refueller and the Stokes Hill people were happy to accommodate us and when we found the refuelling jetty, a crew was there to take our lines.

'Gidday Skipper,' a cheerful young fella called out. 'D'ya know how much both boats need?'

'Gidday mate. Yeah, I'll take about 1500 litres and my mate there with the Italian jobbie will need about 9500 litres.'

'Holy crap! Where'd you come from?'

'Gold Coast,' I replied.

'Shit! That's a friggin' long run. OK for you with sails, but the fast jobbie must have bloody big tanks.'

'We fitted some bladder tanks before we left,' I informed him, then trying to sow a few seeds of misdirection. 'We want to spend some time poking around the Indonesian islands and didn't want to have to trust their fuel quality or availability.'

He nodded wisely, 'Bloody good idea Skipper. I've heard some bad stories about boaties getting stuck with watered and dirty fuel up there. Made a real mess of one bloke's engine, I heard. Best if you only buy from one of the big centres where there's lots of turnover but make sure you both filter it well.'

'Yeah, that's what we thought.'

He got the pumps started and handed a nozzle to me to control the delivery, so I made sure there were plenty of rags around the filler neck and turned the job of watching the nozzle, which had the fill lever clipped down, over to Tracy who wanted to help with something. I went below and made sure that the transfer taps were set for filling the main tanks first, then re-joined Tracy listening to the tanks fill, an activity which is similar to watching the grass grow, but far messier if you don't pay attention.

Firebird was low on fuel because the last day and a half of motoring in light headwinds had eaten most of the fuel we had aboard, although Dave had enough spare fuel on *Seeker* which would have kept us going for at least another day.

My Platinum Visa card copped a hammering when all tanks were finally full and we thanked the staff for their help then headed for our moorings at Stokes Hill Wharf. Once again the staff were very helpful, especially when we said a swing mooring each was actually desirable and we didn't need to tie up alongside the public wharf itself. That was something I always tried to avoid since a boat at a public wharf is somehow considered fair game by most visitors and tourists who seem to wander past at all hours of the day and night.

Therefore, as far as I was concerned and liking my privacy, a swing mooring is infinitely preferable to a public wharf at any time!

The ladies in particular, loved the next two days where they could dress up a bit, go shopping and not do any cooking, since we ate out each night at the Wharf's excellent restaurant and bar. That was the place where we guys spent quite a lot of time while waiting for the girls to return from shopping. After the first foray, I had to remind them space was limited aboard, but that thought fell on deaf ears as they bought up choice selections of the beautifully patterned and coloured, multi-national fashions that were very good value.

I took the opportunity to try to make contact with Corrine, using a method we'd devised before we'd left. Therefore, I fired-up the throw-away mobile and texted the letters 'DW' I hoped she'd recognise as meaning that we were back in cell phone coverage at Darwin, but it was more than two hours later when an encrypted text pinged for my attention.

'Good progress guys. I'm still OK and training the troops hard. Some are good, others hopeless. I've been told we are to deploy to the Pilbara camp in ten days from now, which would be about Tuesday week, and those who aren't considered useful will be dumped. From what I've seen of how these guys operate, that means Paula, who loves that sort of thing, will probably play with them, then terminate the rejects permanently.

I've had to waste one guy who challenged my authority, so they all know what to expect.

My position seems secure with EarthSquad and I'll be going to the Pilbara Camp. A Boeing 737 has been chartered to carry the troops and a large quantity of supplies to Onslow, where EarthSquad boats will ferry everything up to the camp. There's a lot of stuff to transport and they don't seem to have many boats, but I guess I'll find out what they plan. Even though they somehow got funding for the place from the WA State Government, they can't afford for outsiders to see the camp 'cause they'd realise it's an armed camp, not an environmental monitoring camp for tree-huggers. They're rather serious about that since several fishermen who blundered onto the camp have already been fed to a local big croc.

I'll not be able to reach you until I get to Onslow or the camp where they don't have this totally creepy Security head, Joshua Koll who insists on being called Mr Joshua. I'll call on the SatPhone since you're bound to be away from a cell tower. Try to stay close if you can, please guys. There are some seriously dangerous people mixed up in this.'

CHAPTER 19

FIREBIRD, TUESDAY, DARWIN TO ONSLOW

All good things had to come to an end, so with reluctance and just after first light, two weary crews motored quietly out between the breakwater arms of the marina and set course down harbour. Once around the tip of the Cox Peninsula, we stayed offshore and laid a steadily changing course that headed more and more southwest as we headed across the Joseph Bonaparte Gulf to Cape Londonderry. This was the top end of the fabulous Kimberly region, a boating area that many described as the Whitsundays of the West with a fraction of the overcrowding and overdevelopment.

WEDNESDAY

01:00 on Wednesday morning saw us skirting Cape Londonderry in the darkness with just the occasional distant loom of vehicle headlights to visually mark where land was. It was just after breakfast when Sandy and I were off watch, that she said, 'You know I was on watch with Tracy last night.'

'Yes, and I'm on with her tonight. Did you want to change or something?' It wasn't usual for Sandy to fluff around a topic; she's normally very direct.

'Oh no nothing like that, in fact, quite the opposite! We spent a lot of our time talking, as you do on night watch when things are quiet, and I came to understand the real person behind her facade of super efficiency a lot better than I did. It seems a lot of it goes back to her childhood, growing up with four older brothers who were very competitive in everything they did. I won't bore you with details, but I've come to realise I really like her a lot and we seemed to strike such a responsive chord with each other, it's almost like we're twin sisters. Super scary!'

She giggled, 'But I did learn she's got the hots for you…big time!'

I sat up and concentrated. 'No way!' I looked pointedly at her chest. 'I mean, you can't be twins, her boobs are a lot smaller than yours!'

I ducked away from a finger stab to the ribs. 'But seriously, that's the first I've heard of it. I mean, she's very sexy and pretty, but…'

She giggled again, 'Lots of things get talked about in the 'lonely' night watch hours, my lovely man. Being at sea on a boat seems to bring people out of their shell for some reason. Anyway, just remember I'm not the jealous type.'

'Yeah, I remember and understand.'

She smiled enigmatically, 'You're a male so you probably don't, but let's just say that I think she's pretty and sexy as well.'

'Ah…Do I detect a desire to set up another fun thing like we had with Janice?'

That earned me an enigmatic smile that the Sphinx would have been proud of, a passionate kiss and she was off to bed, leaving me to mull over what she'd said and might really have meant.

As the coming of daylight had placed us abeam Admiralty Gulf and among the first islands of the Bonaparte Archipelago lying off the coast of the Kimberly region, I was happy to weave our course between the profusion of beautiful islands which lay offshore of a contrastingly bleak and inhospitable coast. I went to bed in the afternoon to get some sleep in readiness for my night watch, but was up and showered by 18:30 when we left the close confines of the island chain and headed seaward again for the night run south, staying clear of the rest of the islands.

THURSDAY – VERY EARLY

During Wednesday night and the wee dark hours of Thursday

morning, we passed the fascinating and beautiful islands of the Buccaneer Archipelago unseen and un-encountered in the darkness. Dawn on Thursday lit up an empty ocean, with the historic old pearling town of Broome some 50 nautical miles off to the ENE of our position as we made a straight course across Roebuck Bay with the intent to close the coast at the next town of Port Hedland, but we stayed further out to sea to straighten the course as much as possible. Port Hedland was passed at the watch change at 21:00 that evening.

Despite the long trip and lots of engine running, the catamaran was in good condition and the list of problems was quite short with nothing serious, since I'd been doing maintenance items during the day as they occurred. When we had enough wind to maintain speed, I'd done an oil and filter change on one engine at a time so they were in good shape too.

Our fuel was lasting well. The winds over this side of the Continent were generally easterly, but since they weren't very strong, one engine was kept running all the time, and we were swapping the task between both engines at each watch change.

With the crew now more experienced in watch keeping and boat handling, we just had one person officially on watch throughout the day since there were usually one or two others up and about doing various things if assistance was needed. Because of that, I'd extended the night watches out to nine hours, from 21:00 to 06:00, which gave the two off-watch crew a good night's sleep. Tracy and I relieved Amanda at 21:00 and she headed for a shower and bed as Tracy made us a mug of tea each and we sat and sipped quietly as *Firebird* purred along. With the radar target alarm set and two chart plotters driving the autopilot, there wasn't much to actually do on these extended offshore runs, apart from monitoring their state of health. It was open water ahead.

We were on our second cuppa and I just finished one of my usual rounds of inspection of the deck, when Tracy hesitantly said, 'I talked to Sandy last night and she's really cool. I hardly knew her before, but as you said, she surprised me with her very open attitude. She wants us to get to know each other a lot better, but I got a bit confused when she said she's not a jealous type.'

I chuckled. 'From what she said, I gathered she added that bit because you gave her the idea you wanted to go to bed with me.'

'Oh, shit! Did she tell you that? I know I sort of hinted at it to you back at Cape York, but Sandy seemed so understanding, I just told her what I was thinking and feeling. Now I feel like a right goose!'

I chuckled and patted her hand, 'You shouldn't feel that way. Saying what you really feel is called being honest with yourself as well as with others close to you, and that's a very good thing.'

'Yes, but...'

'No buts about it! Sandy appreciated your honesty and she was honest with you in return. She really isn't jealous of me being with other ladies she approves of and now it seems she's put you in that category.'

She thought about that for a few moments. 'So if we actually did go to bed together, you're saying that she wouldn't come at me with a sharp knife?'

I laughed quietly. 'No! Of course not and as she's already suggested, she's far more likely to drag you to our bed anyway for a bit of fooling around, provided you want to of course.'

Tracy thought a bit more. 'That's an interesting thought and I confess I've only ever kissed another girl once before when I was a bit pissed and certainly haven't done anything else or gone to bed with a girl. I don't know how I'd handle it. What if I don't like it and don't want to do anything?'

I smiled gently, 'You just say 'that's enough' or 'stop' and you don't have to do it. It's as simple as that. I don't tell tales out of school, but this has happened before and the lady liked it very much! I can say for sure Sandy would not have invited you to try if she thought you would be turned off by it. She's very, very gentle and doesn't have any deviant habits.'

'Oh!' was the reply as Tracy thought further.

'Anyway, all I can suggest is you try it once and see. I'm sure Sandy would go very slowly with you and make it really good fun.'

'Could I do that? If I did try, would you be there as well? The first time I mean?'

I shrugged, slightly uncomfortable with giving such advice to another female and probably sounding like Sandy's pimp, but she did ask! 'It's totally up to you. I can be or not; whatever you prefer.'

She grinned and started to look excited at the idea. 'If you are there, do you and I get to...sort of, fool around as well, or is it to be just with Sandy?'

I chuckled, 'Once again, it's what you want to do. When you're there, the only rule is that everyone is to have fun, no hurting any-one else and with no regrets afterwards. But if you do want me there, we'll have to wait until we're anchored or tied up somewhere. We can't leave Amanda on her own on watch, that wouldn't be fair.'

'No, you're right. But I think I'd like you there now we've talked about it. That would be good. Although I suppose if I really wanted to, I could be with Sandy while we're still at sea if it's just the two of us?'

'Sure, that's no problem. You work that out with Sandy.'

'Hmmm. I'll have to think it all through. But the way you've described it, it seems like fun.'

'It is and I think you'll love it, but do consider. We won't mind if you decide not to, but then you'll never know, will you,' I added with a cheeky grin which drew a laugh from her at last and a light slap across the arm.

'When do we get to port?' she asked, smiling cheekily.

I consulted the Chart Plotter, which informed me that if the present average speed of 14 knots were maintained, we'd be in Onslow harbour on Friday afternoon.

THURSDAY

'So, this is now Thursday morning, just. Which gives me time to have a think, if that's all right?'

I touched her hand again. 'Of course it is. It's whatever you want to do. No pressure from either of us.'

She seemed happy with that and was then quite keen to cuddle up and be held for a while and I must admit that her lean, well-muscled body did feel very pleasant parked against my side. I didn't try to fool around, letting her get her thoughts in order, so we just chatted about lots of different things and exchanged some personal information which seemed to relax her further so the rest of the watch proceeded smoothly to the extent that I didn't wake Sandy until 06:00 with a steaming mug of tea.

'Shit, Harry. Look at the time! Why didn't you wake me?'

'It was all going quietly so Tracy and I just kept chatting and you were still asleep and I was still awake, so I let you sleep in.'

She yawned, stretched and the sheet falling away from her naked body turned the movement into a very provocative action. So much so that after the quite stimulating discussion I'd been having with Tracy, my thoughts were on one thing only. Sandy saw the look in my eye and the bulge in my shorts. 'If Amanda's not up yet, do you think Tracy would mind being on her own for a few minutes more?' She inquired innocently.

My answer was to drop my shorts and crawl up the bed, straight into Sandy and her welcoming embrace. Under the circumstances, we couldn't take our usual leisurely time about our pleasures, but the end result was still very satisfying. While Sandy cleaned up and dressed, I brought her up to speed on the discussion I'd had with Tracy.

'Oh, good man!' she said warmly. 'I was hoping you'd manage to do that. So, do you think she wants to give it a go?'

'Yes, I really do. In her usual way, she's probably over-thinking the whole scenario but you might be able to straighten those thoughts out. I'll stay down here and have a snooze to give you two a chance to talk.'

She smiled happily and patted me on a sensitive portion of my anatomy, 'Lovely man. This could be really good fun! I'll see you at breakfast.'

While the Chart plotter talked electronic stuff to the Autopilot to get us to Onslow without hitting any hard stuff, I called Dave and chatted about our planned arrival in Onslow the next afternoon and the story we would be telling anybody who asked. I had briefed my crew with the same cover story; we were wealthy layabouts with more money than sense, looking for good fishing and diving up and down the Western Australian coast as part of a meandering, no fixed schedule circumnavigation of the continent.

I also asked Dave to think about whether we should base out of Onslow, further north at Dampier or further southwest at Exmouth. It appeared that mooring space at Onslow was very limited and free anchoring seemed to be not permissible.

There was also the 5-metre tide range to make life difficult for an anchored boat.

He called back at midday with some thoughts that he and his crew had put together.

'Basically, we thought since Onslow is probably the place EarthSquad people would fly in and out, and given the limited berths available, it might be best to base somewhere else. This leg will take a little over half the time of the first very long leg, we've only just used the bladder tanks, therefore, the main tanks are still full, and I imagine you would be in a similar condition. We could get some more fresh food, but it will only be three and a half days since we re-stocked in Darwin, so we've got enough to feed everybody very well for another month.'

'Yeah, copy that Dave. You are right about the fuel though, I'm still drawing on bladder tanks and with just the mains full, *Firebird* feels much lighter and responsive so I'd like to keep her like that as long as possible. I might even roll the bladders up when I empty them. It'll make it easier to get around down below at least. Then depending on where we lay up, we shouldn't be far from a fuel outlet. So you're suggesting we give Onslow a miss for now and look for somewhere else to lay up?'

'That's the idea. We thought if we were holed up at an uninhabited island, we wouldn't have a problem with security, except for fishing and charter boats and to them we're just another couple of cruising yachts.'

'OK. Works for me, but where do we hole up? We don't want to be too close to EarthSquad base in case they get suspicious.'

'Way ahead of you there, sport. The crew have been checking places since this morning and they have what looks like the perfect spot. It's a weird-shaped island called Hermite Island in the Montebello Group. You know, where the Poms let off a few atom bombs last century. Anyway, we don't have to go to Ground Zero on Trimouille Island since Hermite Island looks like it's got very good weather shelter from any direction and a lot of lovely beaches with good fishing and diving. The bonus is that it's only 50 nautical miles across to EarthSquad. If we track directly to Hermite from our checkpoint abeam Karratha, we should be dropping the anchors in a nice, calm anchorage before 10:00 or thereabouts on Friday!'

I chuckled at his enthusiasm. 'You make it sound so good, so let's lock it in. I'll go check the charts and consult the internet, but it sounds an excellent choice. Well done to the crew!'

'Thanks mate. They worked all morning researching this and I'm sure it'll be just what we want.'

We exchanged some housekeeping information before hanging up and I could go and boot up the Mac mini. When I had an image of the Montebellos on the big screen, I called my crew in since all were awake at this hour, and showed them our new base. I chuckled to myself, and I could see Sandy grin slightly when Tracy casually asked, 'So we're not going into Onslow at all now?'

'Nope, at least not for now. We have plenty of fuel, we haven't been hitting the booze and there should be plenty of food, so we're going to track direct from Karratha to Hermite Island in the Montebello Group. That places us just 50 miles from the EarthSquad base and out among the islands, security will be easy as there'll only be charter boats or the occasional cruiser like us.'

The others saw the sense of that and Amanda added, 'We're

pretty good for supplies. I built up the stocks of bread-making doings and there's plenty of long-life milk.'

Tracy displayed her new talent for being a smart-arse, 'Staying there will be neat. I've always wanted to glow in the dark!'

That raised a few chuckles, so I said, 'The shortcut will put us in an isolated anchorage a day early at about 10:00 on Friday, instead of getting into Onslow just on dusk and having to wait until morning to refuel. There's also a low tide range, no crocodiles and great fishing!'

'What's the go from there then?' Amanda wanted to know.

'There's not a lot we can do until we hear how Corrine's getting on and what she recommends we do, so I guess we just kick back, relax and play at being degenerate yachties!'

That did raise a laugh, as we continued on a course straight for a point close to Legendre Island which was the outer-most of a cluster of islands off Karratha and riding easily over a long swell of perhaps a couple of metres in height. Unfortunately, we were also heading almost straight into a light southwest breeze with meant that the sails were furled and both engines were running at 75% power.

With nothing but the endless rolling sea to look at, the crew relaxed as the day progressed, Sandy trying her hand at trolling by running a lure on a heavy line out well astern to see what might be interested. I snapped a safety line on the reel so if some deluded fish did decide to commit suicide; we wouldn't lose the lot overboard. Nothing happened for an hour or two and she had almost forgotten about the line, when the ratchet on the reel clattered into life and line spun out astern at a ridiculous rate.

She grabbed the rod and looked pleadingly at me. 'What do I do now?'

I pushed her down into a chair, turned the rod so her hands were ready to grasp the winder and when she was a bit more composed, tightened the drag slowly. By the way her arm muscles tightened up and the rod tip bent, I could see there was something substantial on the other end.

'Ah...shit Harry!' she panted. 'This bloody thing's going to pull my arms out! Can you give me a hand?'

By way of answer, I took the rod and sat myself in a chair, feeling the fish on the other end, still running; it was slowing although still pulling like a truck.

'Get yourself comfortable, spread your legs and put a quad-folded towel between your thighs and tucked up into your crotch, pull the butt of the rod in as hard as you can then take the load of the fish with your arms. I don't have a harness, but the way this thing's pulling, I don't want you to get pulled overboard!'

She did as I asked, so I stood with some difficulty and poked the end of the rod into one of my very favourite places. 'What are you grinning at you degenerate arsehole?' she giggled. 'And don't you dare start making depraved suggestions!'

'Sorry dear! Yes dear, no dear', I replied, bracing the rod while she got a good grip. 'Now I want you to lower the tip and then lift it sharply to hopefully set the hook. If you get it right, the fish may go a bit berko for a minute or two, so just be ready.'

She did as I asked then cursed as the fish did go a bit nutso, but she gamely hung on and after some 30-minutes of give and take, finally got it turned around and heading for home. It made a few more bids for freedom, but Sandy was reeling in a decent amount of line by now and getting very excited to see what it was.

'I think my fucking arms are going to drop off!' she grunted for the fourth time. 'Doesn't this thing know when to give up?'

I looked at where the line was entering the water. 'It looks like you've got it pretty close, so not much more now. Hang in there.'

'You'd better have a boathook or gaff or whatever it is ready; there's a lot of weight out there.'

Suddenly, there was a violent swirl of water ten metres astern and a grey fin broke the surface. 'Oh bugger,' I said, 'it's a shark and a decent size one too! It gave you a good fight but I was hoping for a dolphin fish or a big barramundi.'

The shark looked to be a good two to three metres long and

although not fighting as much as it had, it clearly wasn't happy.

'You're not going to try to take the hook out, are you?' Sandy asked, getting awkwardly to her feet.

'Yeah, we'll try. I don't like leaving hooks in fish even though it'll rot out fairly quickly. If we can sling a rope around it just behind the head, we can pull it up against the stern and I might be able to release the hook.'

'Please be very careful. I don't like the look of that thing and I don't think Jasper can do anything to help you this time.'

I laughed, 'Yeah, you're right. He couldn't help with this, even though he's lying on the cockpit roof above you watching every little thing going on.'

Sandy snatched a quick look up and laughed. 'I should have known he'd not miss out on the action. Is that Krazy sitting on his shoulders?'

'Yep! They're both staying well out of the way. Anyway, back to your fish, we'll just have to use the old brute force method to hold him steady, so you keep as much tension on the line as you can.'

So with Amanda helping, Sandy dragged the shark right up to the stern, where Tracy and I jiggled a rope around its tapered head then I had them haul as hard as they could until it was jammed against the stern platform. The shark didn't like being trapped like that and thrashed around for a while before suddenly quietening down.

Carefully, I eased closer to where the hook was caught in the flesh at the very corner of its jaw. It'd already started to tear loose, so it didn't take much to cut it with a small pair of bolt-cutters, not risking my hand or arm to try to clean out the last tiny piece. I stepped back and called for the girls to let just one end of the rope go.

It took about two seconds for the shark to realise that nothing was holding him as we motored away from him at a steady 14 knots then he rolled over and with a great flick of his tail, disappeared back into the depths. Sandy gave a shaky laugh as she sank back in her chair, loose fishing line and heavy trace wire laying in coils at her feet, 'Bloody hell that was an ordeal! I thought we had fresh fish for a week. But shark is edible, isn't it?'

'Yes, it is, and rather good too with no bones, but at that size, they cause way too much fuss to try to bring aboard and kill it, so it's much safer to let them go.'

She grinned tiredly. 'Amen to that! I might go have a wash and clean up.'

We motored past Port Hedland at 21:00 that evening, but were too far out to sea to see anything. Finally we were blessed with an easterly breeze that was just strong enough to not only allow both engines to be switched off, but to maintain our average speed. The silence was almost deafening after the last twelve hours of constant engine running and when they cooled down, I checked them carefully. Everything was in order and once again I mentally thanked the installers for taking the time to set all the systems up properly to start with.

The extended run had drained the two bladder tanks laid out on the cabin sole and most of the one in the cockpit, so I disconnected the two hull tanks and rolled them up. They compressed down to a surprisingly small package and with bungs fitted to prevent any dribbles of fuel, were easily stowed in a cockpit locker. We all appreciated being able to walk normally down in the hulls without having to stumble over the tanks.

Friday proceeded without any further incidents, with Sandy leaving the fishing gear stowed until we were anchored and she could almost choose what she wanted to catch. Sail adjusting gave those on deck something to do, even when the strong breeze backed more to the south east, the big Code Zero screecher still set well and helped keep our speed up to around the mid-teens.

FRIDAY

Around 04:00 Friday morning, our course skirted the west point of the long, skinny Legendre Island, the double flash of its warning light visible as a faint pulse on the horizon long before we passed within half a mile of the Cape. The light itself is just a stubby fingertip of white fibreglass sitting like an afterthought in the low, tangled scrub, 170 metres or so back from the low cliffs. Originally built in 1927, the light was replaced in 1963 then again in 1989; except a cyclone struck the island the day after it was replaced and destroyed it. It was rebuilt yet again and the builders must have done a much better job, since it's still there.

Once past Legendre Island, the Autopilot bent our course slightly to the right to head directly for the Montebello Group and our chosen laying up place. Dawn was just breaking when the phone rang with Dave on the other end.

'Hi Dave, how's it going?'

'Yeah, pretty good, Harry. I've been considering our arrival time, which at the moment is still around 10:00 and after looking at the chart and the satellite map, and it would seem trying to find our way to the best anchorages inside all the arms of that weird-shaped island might be a bit un-necessary.

An easier alternative would be to maybe track straight in, to one of two lovely-looking beaches on Renewal Island. Our track would just clear two small islands close to Renewal, but it's a straight run with nothing else in the way.'

'Yeah, good thought, mate. I hadn't looked that far yet – I'm glad someone's on the ball. I'm just looking at the chart now and it's a good plan. We would still have shelter from the breeze but we can move deeper inside the island if we want to. Let's do it!'

'Good-oh. Now that's sorted, lead on dude!'

So I did and as the night was pushed westward by the spreading glow from the sun's imminent arrival on the eastern horizon, we approached the Montebellos. The very oddly shaped islands were part of a long finger of shallow water reaching from close to the Pilbara coast some 87 kilometres north into the Indian Ocean. The largest island by far was Barrow Island, a large oil and gas hub and processing plant, with a scattering of small, picturesque and rocky islets running up the shallows to the Montebello group.

Most of those small islets had beautiful white sandy beaches with brilliant fishing in the vicinity, but it was the Montebello islands that caught and fired the imagination. That such beautiful islands should have been subjected to the insane devastation of three aboveground atomic bomb tests was an obscenity. It seemed anomalous that 66 years later, the islands showed almost no sign that the outrage ever happened. That is, if one were to exclude the remnants of the British occupation that had been left scattered around where they fell.

If one were to look in the right place, there was even a deep hole, some 500 metres across, still showing in the seabed where the first bomb was exploded in1953.

Our first landfall was the very appropriately named Renewal Island, where two pretty little bays, quaintly named Whiskey Bay and Stout Bay provided a safe refuge for two boatloads of weary travellers. Although both were open to the north, around to the southeast the shallow water and surrounding islands tended to stop or deflect any swells pushing through in all but very heavy weather. With the south-westerly breeze still blowing, we were in sheltered water tucked in close on the north side of a small projecting headland.

By 10:00 the anchors of both boats had rattled down and briefly disturbed the peace, setting thousands of birds squawking. It took just a few minutes more to make sure they were set securely and the necessary fenders put in place so we could raft up as usual, before the engines were shut down and the bird population slowly quietened to their usual dull roar that sounded like surf on the shore.

Sandy and I had shared this watch, but the unfamiliar rattle of anchor chain, plus the deafening silence of the engines being switched off wakened Amanda and Tracy who wandered blearily out to see where we were. Once I was happy with our position, Sandy and I headed for bed, leaving the girls to work out what they wanted to do, although as I drifted off into an exhausted sleep, I heard the sound of silence as they returned to bed.

It was after midday before we were all up, with the breeze whistling happily through the rigging and the smell of bacon cooking dragging me out of bed. Sandy was already up, along with Amanda, Alf and Tracy; all looking excited to be in this lovely, isolated spot. Amanda's 'new' boyfriend, Alf had transferred across when we rafted up last night. Sandy gave me a good morning kiss and said, 'Jasper wanted a run ashore, but when I told him I'd take him soon, he was too impatient to wait. He just jumped into the water, paddled around to the stern platform so Krazy could climb onto his head, then swam ashore.'

I looked over to the glaringly white beach to see my strange, beautiful cat and his tiny, inseparable companion playing chasing games in the dry, soft sand. 'That's a new twist, although I guess he took what you said to mean that it's OK to go.'

'Really? A big stretch even for Jasper, isn't it?'

'Nope. That session with his mate, the big croc, must have stirred his mystical senses up more than usual. Did he have a feed before they went?'

'No,' Sandy replied with a giggle, 'he was too keen to get off the boat to wait for that.'

I nodded, 'In that case, they'll be back as soon as he smells cooking and sees movement.'

Sure enough, it wasn't long before he did just that – encouraging Krazy to perch high on the back of his long neck, then stepping smoothly into the water, trying to keep her as dry as possible as he paddled steadily back out to *Firebird*. At the stern boarding platform, he let Krazy step off before he climbed out using the piece of boat carpet I always hang over the stern when we're at anchor and Jasper wants to swim.

I made sure I was there to greet both wet, sandy pussies with the freshwater shower, although Krazy didn't like it at all, voicing her displeasure very loudly. In contrast, Jasper loved being washed off. Sandy did the honours with a towel before either of them had a chance to rub or shake water over any human in range, after which Krazy retired in disgust.

We ate what amounted to a light brunch, after which Dave and I spent some time checking each boat over for wear and tear that could be repaired on the spot, but didn't find much. The crews decided that we all needed to go ashore and have a run after our long stretch at sea, so we launched both dinghies and ferried everyone ashore, Jasper included. Krazy was quite happy staying behind as she was in her favourite position, curled up on one of my very old soft flannelette shirts on the inner corner of the chart table where she could keep an eye on everything when she wasn't asleep.

I kept forgetting that apart from Dave, Sandy and me, the other crewmembers had done Special Emergency Response Team training and desperately needed to regain an acceptable level of fitness. Therefore the super-fit ones headed off along the 200 metre-long beach at a very fast pace, intending to do multiple fast laps. Their initial plan to run all over the small island was quickly abandoned when they discovered that the predominant plant was Spinifex, a charming cluster of needle-sharp spines sprouting out from a central core. Each spine needle was tipped with a point of brittle silica that broke off easily in anything that touched it.

Human legs ended up covered with a rash of little sores which had to fester before the silica points were expelled—not a pretty sight!

The athletic types sprinted on ahead of the senior staff, doing two laps to our one, but we did start to feel better. Running in the soft sand was very hard on the calf muscles, so we tried to stay on the thin strip of harder wet sand. Jasper bounded along effortlessly beside us, mouth open in his big pussy grin, his four broad feet barely sinking into the sand at all and delighted to have so much company on a decent romp.

An hour of sprints and steady trotting was enough for the most diehard fitness fanatic. Alf and Charlie, competitive to the end, pulled up to stand hands on knees as they tried to suck air into their starved lungs. Amanda, Melissa and Tracy staggered up next, the three promptly sitting down on the sand, with their heads on knees, chests heaving. We seniors drifted up more gracefully, having backed off the pace much earlier, but still breathing hard and sweating profusely from what was exactly the workout we all needed.

Alf seemed to recover first and picked Amanda up from her sitting position and walked into the water, releasing her when it was waist deep. Charlie grabbed Melissa and dragged her in, while the rest of us followed what seemed to be a bloody good move.

Being crystal-clear and slightly cool, the water was instantly refreshing and it wasn't long before the first clothes started being pulled off. Within minutes everyone was naked, splashing each other in chest-deep water, just relaxing and blowing off steam. Sandy stayed close to Tracy and she was staying close to me, so I copped a lot of splashing from the pair and was ducked several times. It was extremely stimulating to feel slippery, naked female bodies sliding against mine and, surprisingly, I quickly developed a very full erection which made the girls giggle and try for even more body contact as we wrestled in the shallows.

Jasper quickly joined in the fun, his agile furry body snaking between pairs of legs, his muscular tail acting as both rudder and propulsion.

All the guys sported erections to one degree or another and I could see the ladies quietly checking out each one.

After another round of wrestling involving a lot of full-body contact, Tracy made a quiet comment to Sandy who giggled and replied, 'Oh, he can do better than that! He just needs a bit more stimulation.'

Both giggled at my obvious discomfort, normal for me when confronted by naked females in this sort of situation, but at the same time, I was thoroughly enjoying myself. When the fooling around started slowing down; everybody decided to swim out to the boats so Dave and I got the dinghies and swam them back the short distance. We tossed all the clothing in a heap to be rinsed and sorted. While we were doing that, the others were queuing for a turn at the closest freshwater shower which happened to be on the stern of *Firebird*, while Charlie and Melissa had *Seeker's* all to themselves and seemed to be making the most of it. From what we could see, there wasn't a lot of rinsing off happening, unless Charlie was just being very diligent at getting every trace of salt water out of every crease, crevice, nook and cranny on Melissa's body that he could reach.

A cheerful chorus of 'Get a room you two!' drove them inside to their cabin, both blushing at getting so carried away in front of the rest of the crew. The crews normally followed the common boating convention that accepted running around naked and doing a bit of fooling around in the open was fine, but getting more seriously intimate was usually conducted at least semi-privately.

Nevertheless, after playtime in the water and the rinsing off process on *Firebird*, everybody was obviously feeling very horny and minimal time was spent under the wash-off shower. Dry towels grabbed off a stack were shared before couples dispersed to their cabins. Tracy and Sandy had apparently worked out an arrangement, for as soon as I'd washed off, they both hustled me off to our cabin for the much-discussed and long-awaited encounter.

Despite the prior stimulation and faced with the reality of being in private with all three of us naked, Tracy became a bit shy and hesitant, so to get out of the way I climbed up on the bed and sat cross-legged against the side wall. I let Sandy do the talking to help Tracy sort her thoughts out and she said much the same things she and I had said previously.

Finally, Tracy grinned contritely as she climbed up on the bed, 'I'm just being stupid by messing around, aren't I? I really have been looking forward to this, but just this minute, I got a little nervous.'

As Sandy joined her, I stayed where I was with Tracy stretched out just beyond my feet. Sandy lay beside her and murmured soft words of encouragement as she very gently stroked her back and smooth flanks. I had a very good view of her shapely bum, but that was about all and resigned myself to the fact that a nice view was about all I was going to get that day.

And that was mainly how things played out, as Tracy seemed to greatly appreciate the little things that Sandy did and encouraged her to reciprocate. So after a while, I decided to stretch out as far over as I could and get some sleep.

It's said that all good things come to those who wait and in my case a warm, firm female form snuggling up, woke me from a light sleep. A quick exploratory feel suggested it wasn't my delightful Sandy's lush roundness that had parked against me, but a leaner, more muscled bum that pressed against my crotch causing a very predictable response. As that response quickly firmed up, there was a slight re-arrangement of legs and position before I was able to savour the exquisite feel of Tracy.

It was just as well that I'd had a sleep, as our first time was very successful and led, after the obligatory short break, to a second and then after a longer break to a third encounter that left both of us sweaty and exhausted, much to Sandy's amusement. I had my suspicions that she'd been having a little play with Tracy at various times, but that was all to the good.

A short rest, then Sandy chased us down aft to the shower, making a threesome in the cubicle that was just big enough to allow a reasonable amount of movement. There must be something about naked, wet female bodies in close contact with a weak-willed male that produces such a strong aphrodisiac effect, but whatever it was, I managed to perform yet again, leading Sandy to exclaim in mock disgust, 'Now you're really making a pig of yourself, Harry! Let the poor girl have a few moments to herself!'

I hadn't noticed Tracy complaining about the additional attention I had paid to her delightful internals, but was glad Sandy waited for the proper time to say that, because we all cracked up.

Dried, dressed and presentable, we joined Alf and Amanda then met up with the others over on *Seeker*; already getting stuck into strawberry daiquiris which Dave had made in a six-litre bucket. Everyone was tired, but very upbeat and relaxed from the day's very therapeutic activities. Interestingly, Tracy, Amanda and Melissa all chose to remain topless with Tracy looking still very excited.

'What's the plan for tomorrow boss?' Alf asked, with Amanda snuggled up beside him.

I slurped, as one is supposed to, on my daiquiri before answering.

'First up, I'd like *Dragonfly* launched for an over-flight of the EarthSquad camp. Staying well above visual and audio detection range, but try to make a few passes both directly overhead and a couple of oblique ones. Hi-Res colour daylight and Infra Red as well please. I'd like to look as closely into the camp as possible.'

Sandy nodded, 'No problem. We could make a run this afternoon if you like. There's still plenty of light and maybe the low sun angle will show up some features a more overhead sun might lose, even using IR.'

I thought a moment, looked at the sun and as usual, she was right. 'OK. Let's do it, but I'd like another run in the morning, fairly early, then late morning, early afternoon, etc.'

Sandy nodded. 'That'll build up a good set of camp movements at different times. There are supposed to be about 25 personnel in camp, if I remember Corrine's last message.'

'Yeah, that's about right, but she's supposed to bring another 20 or so, so we need to have regular runs. Have you got plenty of fuel?'

Amanda fielded that question. 'Sure have. We can use the outboard fuel if necessary, but we've enough for now. I presume we'll be refuelling the boats at sometime, so we'll top up then, but there's some 40 to 50 hours of flight time with just the fuel we brought, without touching the outboard stock.'

'Great! But stay on top of maintenance, because we need it to be our eyes. I've been thinking about moving us closer to the coast which would reduce the flight time.'

'Where are you thinking about?' Dave asked.

'We've a couple of choices. If we want to stay as remote as

possible, right here is as good as anywhere, although if the winds change to the south, east or north, we'll have to move. So the first option is to move south toward Barrow Island to a quaintly named place called Ah Chong Island, that's just 4nm away, but it has a number of good, sandy anchorages that cater for what looks like most wind directions. Although close to where we are now, we should be safe there unless a bunch of other boaties decides that it's a nice spot as well.

The next choice would be a lot closer to the coast and that is Bridled Island just north of the big Lowendal Island that has oil storage facilities, although Bridled Island is deserted and has a lot of islets scattered around close by, that would be handy if we need an alternative. I don't want us trying to fly the UAV with other boaties watching so we may have to stuff around finding a deserted anchorage.

Another choice a lot closer at just 12 nautical miles off Earth-Squad base, is North Sandy Island, a very small, shrub-covered bit of sand offering very little swell protection from any direction.'

Dave was scanning a chart he'd grabbed off the nav station. 'Found all your choices Sport, although I'm in favour of staying a bit further out, so Ah Chong or Bridled Islands look good with Bridled Island being my pick. They both have multiple anchorages and other little islands close by if things get too crowded in one particular anchorage.'

'Good call, Dave. Bridled Island is probably my best pick; it's 6nm closer to the base at 39nm away and there's a neat little bay with a westerly aspect on the northern tip of Lowendal Island if wind or swell change too much.'

Dave smiled at my sales pitch. 'OK, you've sold me. Bridled it is. We can head there in the morning.'

While we were discussing the merits or otherwise of the various islands, Sandy and Amanda had set up *Dragonfly* and were nearly ready to launch off *Seeker's* broad and open foredeck. Amanda crossed back to *Firebird* to ask, 'Is there anything else we need to program into *Dragonfly* before we launch?'

I thought a moment, 'What height have you set?'

'Two thousand feet,' she replied, 'guaranteed soundless and invisible. There are no reflective items on it apart from the camera lenses and they're recessed or shielded, but to be sure, we've set up north to south passes tracking from overhead and working to the west for the oblique ones. That way there definitely can't be any sun flashes!'

'OK sounds good. Launch please.'

CHAPTER 21

As the compact Ground Control Station was set up in the saloon, Amanda returned to Sandy on *Seeker*. I followed, fascinated as always by the operation of this highly automated and very capable surveillance Unmanned Aerial Vehicle. By the time I stepped over the railings between the two rafted-up boats, Sandy had pressed the 'Start' button on the GCS and the twin cylinder engine in the hybrid UAV cranked over then fired immediately, emitting a soft purr as it warmed up.

It was an odd-looking device as it sat in the slightly recessed and carpeted launch pad created by eliminating the huge sun-lounge area originally on *Seeker's* wide foredeck. It looked roughly like a patriarchal cross with two sets of equal-length wings placed one behind the other. The nose section was relatively short, while the body behind the rear wing was longer. A change had been made to the forward body from the last time I'd seen it, where the whole nose section was now a broad, flattened shape like a cobra's head with the mantle spread.

'What's with the new nose section?' I asked Amanda as she monitored the engine temperature on the GCS, the idling engine almost inaudible now I was inside the saloon.

'Ian did that so the two cameras could be placed side-by-side, as well as creating more space for payload, in this case, a much better satellite communications setup with more bandwidth. Another benefit was that the shape of the nose flare also increased lift in forward flight by 15%, which in turn reduces the load on the engine and motors. He found there was a gain of a nearly 35 minutes endurance with a full tank of fuel, so if we regard that as a safety reserve, there's a full 8 hours useable endurance.'

I shook my head in wonder at the innovative features that had gone into creating this cutting edge technology aircraft produced by the 72-year-old inventor and designer who was an old age pensioner. Somehow, I had trouble imagining this clever old fart guiding his wheelie-walker – if he had one – into the local RSL for a bingo session with the blue-rinse set. Someday, I'd love to meet him!

As Sandy activated the pre-set flight plan by pressing a button on the GCS, and under command of the Autopilot, the UAV throttled-up then lifted smoothly on the thrust of it's four electric motors until clear of the foredeck. The autopilot, which was no bigger than a matchbox, looked after everything to do with the aircraft; flying it and navigating. As required in the programmed flight plan, it tilted the four power nacelles slightly forward, causing the aircraft to accelerate toward the coast in a slow climb to a cruise altitude of 2000 feet. The muted roar of the engine at full power cut back more and more as the wings and body shape took over the lifting duties from the propellers and that prompted the autopilot to continue to tilt the nacelles forward until they were horizontal with the props providing forward thrust only, with no further need for them to provide lift. It was literally only seconds before the pale blue mottled undersides blended totally into the sky and *Dragonfly* disappeared from sight and hearing.

'Are there any other changes to *Dragonfly* Ian has made apart from the nose?' I asked Amanda as a sharp, vibration-free picture popped up on the second display screen set into the lid of the GCS.

'Yes. He's added a mini wireless modem with a signal booster to the GCS so the video signal in 1920 x 1080 full HD can be sent to another Smart TV or display up to 80 metres away, or it can be uplinked to a satellite for distribution via a dedicated encoded website as required. If you were to turn on that big-screen Smart TV on *Firebird*, the upscaler feature should boost the resolution even more. Naturally, everything is being recorded both on-board and here in the GCS onto a 2TB solid state drive that will hold all the video data from 200 8-hour duration flights.

Anyway, let's go look at EarthSquad's happy snaps on the big screen.'

Sandy unclipped the Controller laptop from the GCS and led the way over to *Firebird* where I turned the TV on and she set the laptop up on the dining table. It displayed all the operating parameters and navigational details of *Dragonfly*, and let her change the flight plan in mid-flight if required. After some searching, we found the GCS WiFi signal and a breath-taking picture filled the big screen as the ocean rolled past at 60 knots. I was briefly concerned that the flight path was too close to Lowendal Island, a big oil and gas hub, but it seemed with most re-supply done by boat, there was very little helicopter activity and at 1.5nm off to the east, *Dragonfly* would be invisible to even the keenest eye.

With nearly 50 nautical miles to fly, *Dragonfly* would take about 50 minutes to reach the EarthSquad base camp, so there was no necessity to hang around looking at the empty ocean sliding by. I was concerned we'd launched too late, but Sandy was confident we'd still get some good Intel from the flight. Due to the distance, we couldn't receive full HD video and had to wait until *Dragonfly* returned and she could download the on-board recorder. And so it proved as the smart little UAV tracked between Passage and South Passage Islands, then over tiny Cowle Island that laid just 1.5nm offshore from the desolate, red peninsula where EarthSquad had set up camp.

The only relief from the endless, red earth was a narrow triangle of green, nearly 500 metres wide at the top end and nearly one kilometre long. The other end of the green patch blended into the mangroves lining a small tidal creek that nearly cut the peninsula off from the endless expanse of iron oxide rock and soil that makes up the Pilbara. This particular peninsula sported another nine creeks snaking partway across the rocky red soil, suggesting that when it did rain, it must fairly bucket down! Each small creek was lined with mangroves and *Dragonfly's* probing cameras revealed all the clever design that had gone into the base.

Substantial looking tents made up a lot of the base construction, but there were quite a number of small pre-fab and transportable units spread across the green area. The whole site had been covered in mottled green and red shade sails that a paranoid would call camouflage netting or simply decorative shade protection if one wanted to appear more innocent.

There was no road access and not even any tracks in the vicinity, although a rugged four-wheel drive vehicle could get through to the highway, which was some 35 kilometres away in a straight line. Therefore everything had to come in by boat. The cameras showed a timber wharf jutting out into the creek on the southern side of the camp; the IR camera providing the detail since the wharf and surroundings were covered in shade sails.

'Someone's dropped a huge amount of money to set this base up in such a remote area,' I commented to Sandy as we counted four large RIBs with two huge outboards on the stern of each, parked in the creek just upstream of the wharf. 'They must own or charter a much larger boat to ferry the biggest items up here and even just the fuel and food for the twenty or so persons means a regular delivery service.'

The IR camera had already spotted the camp generator, with several large aboveground fuel tanks beside it, located as far from the main body of the camp as possible. It was impossible to confirm the number of people in camp, although I did notice that tied up further up the main creek from the two big RIBs, was a decent size half-cabin tinnie that looked like a fisherman's boat.

Sandy had programmed six north to south passes, each pass displaced 500 metres further west from the last one, but after watching the tracks on the navigational display of the GCS, I suggested that she cut it back to just four, then bring Dragonfly home. Re-planning took just moments before the UAV completed the last run and smoothly peeled off and headed southwest for *Seeker's* position.

With *Dragonfly* safely recovered, fuel drained and batteries charged in readiness for the morning flight, I took the flash drive which held a copy of the flight record and gave it to Dave to plug into *Seeker's* computer so we could all watch in the larger saloon on the big Italian speed cruiser.

I asked Tracy to take notes of what each person said or noticed to help build a picture of what we were facing. Once the long list was condensed, we realised we were facing a formidable organisation with what appeared to be unlimited funding. And there were another twenty or thirty troops on the way from the HQ near Beaudesert in SE Queensland!

Most of the personnel we sighted were under the age of forty and were a fairly even mix of male and female, but only about ten were dressed in camo clothing and were armed with H&K MP5 sub-machine guns. It seemed the only permanent guard post was near the wharf where the RIBs were tied up on the upstream side.

'If there's a guard post near the wharf, there must be roving patrols around the perimeter,' Alf suggested, 'therefore a frontal assault at the wharf would be suicidal and penetration of the perimeter very difficult. With those guards armed like that, it'd just be a shoot-out and the fuss would stir the whole camp.'

'True,' I commented, 'but despite the possibility of roving patrols, maybe a quiet night landing away from the wharf would be more successful if we used those inflatable kayaks you talked me into getting, Dave. Perhaps we should dig a couple out and have a practice setting up and using them.'

'Sounds good boss, we can do that in the morning after we shift camp to Bridled Island.

SATURDAY

Everyone felt good to be doing something pro-active again, so after a comfortable and uneventful night, when even Tracy took a rest from exploring her new and awakened sexuality by staying in her own bed, we woke refreshed and ready for action. The first step was to move anchorage before the wind shifted, although since we arrived it had blown hard from the southwest in the mornings and quietened down toward evening. Still, given it was very exposed to open ocean, neither Dave nor I wanted to be caught on this particular lee shore if the wind shifted.

'Please Harry; tell me again why we're leaving this beautiful little cove to go just ten miles away?' Tracy asked as I fired up the engines to let them warm.

'OK. Short version is we need to anchor in a location which gives as much shelter as possible from the wind and the waves it generates. We can withstand being exposed to wind speeds over 80 knots, but strong winds make big waves which are uncomfortable or even dangerous.'

She nodded understanding.

'That's why we find somewhere downwind of a piece of land with good holding for the anchor. Hence the move of ten nautical miles to Bridled Island since it offers a choice of several lovely sandy coves offering shelter from any wind direction.'

She smiled and gave me a quick kiss. 'Thanks for explaining. I didn't realise even the choice of where to anchor involved so many considerations. It's so different to a road trip where you just pick a motel with a vacancy and stop for the night without having to think about stuff like weather or holding ground.'

I smiled back. 'That's the attraction of boating for those of us who love the life, despite it being very uncomfortable at times. Unfortunately, life ashore for many has become way too easy with too many modern inconveniences. The various Governments try to protect people from their own stupidity, but that process just dulls the senses and an insidious type of boredom sets in. In the so-called civilised countries, very few people have to fight to stay alive as so many in Africa have to, and I believe that's why so many turn to drugs and excessive drinking in an effort to escape from their dull, cosseted, comfortable reality! It's a pity more don't realise a challenging existence is available and doesn't have to be expensive.'

I waved around at *Firebird*, 'I freely admit to appreciating my luxuries like automated systems and plenty of water and power, so I'm almost totally independent. But even with all this, I'm always thinking and planning ahead or the ocean and the weather will swat me down like an annoying insect!

So that attraction becomes addictive; the endless challenge and the opportunity to experience the raw beauty of nature first-hand, instead of having it pre-digested via some TV station's carefully made-up weather person who wouldn't know a Force 9 gale at sea from a blow-job in the dressing room!'

I stopped to draw breath and grinned sheepishly at Tracy, who'd been joined by Amanda and Alf listening intently, which encouraged one final rant. 'Sorry to rave on. It's a bit of a sore point with me when I hear about all the problems young people have and the huge amounts of money spent by parents and Governments who give them things like more computers and skate parks to try to spark their interest. Most of them would turn out to be really good, well-balanced adults if they were sent as crew on a sailing ship like the superb *Leeuwin II* sail training ship or even the *Young Endeavour, Enterprize* or *Lady Nelson*.

If the Federal Government were to fund a program to both support the existing programs and built more tall ships like the *Leeuwin II*, rather than replicas, all the money being wasted on crap they don't need, could actually start producing a new generation of self-reliant, self-respecting young adults who have some decent core values!'

To my surprise, they all nodded seriously. 'Well said, Harry,' Alf spoke for them. 'I certainly hadn't thought of those aspects of this lifestyle, but from the small exposure I've had so far, I can appreciate that while this life isn't for everybody, a training scheme like you talked about would be fantastic for kids. As coppers, we get to see the bad side of misspent, over-indulged youth, way too often and despair of ever finding a way out of the downward spiral for them.'

I nodded, 'Good points Alf, and I keep forgetting that you guys see more of this problem first hand than I ever will!'

I turned to the control panel to get on with raising the anchor and getting underway as Dave already had *Seeker* un-rafted and was idling slowly seaward to clear the little headland, before making the turn south toward Bridled Island.

Sandy had stayed on *Seeker* for the run south and with Melissa's help, was preparing *Dragonfly* for the next overfly of the EarthSquad camp. As we motored towards Bridled Island at an economical 10 knots, a brisk south-westerly breeze of 20 knots with higher gusts came in over our right bows. I thought the turbulence might make launching *Dragonfly* difficult, but was delighted once again with the behaviour of the UAV as it lifted smoothly, the autopilot making the instant corrections necessary to keep it steady in the disturbed airflow across *Seeker's* deck.

Once again, it accelerated slowly, then as the wings and nose shape took over lifting duties, the power nacelles inclined further toward the horizontal and the grey, low-visibility UAV lived up to the designation and disappeared.

Our ten-mile run took us close to several islands that were part of the Montebello Archipelago, then over the shallow bank the islands were anchored to. We passed a pair of tiny islets which were nothing more than small piles of sand and rock, then had to dodge around a few more close to Bridled Island. Sandy was the only one who had tried to look at the live video return, but at that distance and relatively low altitude, there were only low-resolution, intermittent frames of vision available, so she joined Dave and the others in looking out for unexpected hard bits in the poorly mapped shallow water approaching Bridled Island. Dire warnings were in the Sailing Directions for the area, so even with the Forward Looking Sonar running and the high-resolution digital radar in short range mode; human eyes were necessary to supplement the electronics.

I'd opted to head for the main, northern-most bay which was conveniently inside a hook of land promising to provide very good shelter from most winds and waves. The run took an hour, and *Dragonfly* had completed its surveillance runs over the camp and was heading back to its relocated home before we had even dropped anchor.

By the time we had anchored securely and rafted-up, Sandy had triggered the homing beacon on *Seeker's* foredeck and shortly after, *Dragonfly* smoothly touched down.

<h1 style="text-align:center">CHAPTER 22</h1>

With *Dragonfly* safely recovered, Sandy downloaded the data from the on-board recorder and we sat down to watch the HD video. There wasn't much to see that was different, although in the brief time taken by each pass, it appeared there were one or two of the camo-clad para-military types strolling around the camp perimeter at irregular intervals and even from 2000 feet, appeared to have a serious lack of enthusiasm for the job.

After seeing nothing more of particular interest, I thought a few moments, which encouraged Sandy to make some rude comments about gears grinding slowly, but I managed to ignore her comments and presented my plan. 'Don't bother with any more over-flights today, but please make sure *Dragonfly* is ready for a run tonight at about 22:00. If you were to set it to make the tracking runs a bit higher to be absolutely sure they don't hear the UAV, will that still give us good resolution on the IR camera?'

Sandy replied positively, 'Definitely! At 3000 feet the IR video will still be super-sharp and can be blown up to least plus 6 before there's any risk of pixilation. And even if there isn't a sound in the camp from humans or the wind, it won't be heard; there's a generator that probably runs 24/7 so I can guarantee they won't hear *Dragonfly* at all.'

'Great! I really want to see if those couple of perimeter guards are still on patrol at night, how keen they are on the job and if any of them are using night-vision goggles. I also need to know if they have any sort of radar installation, although I didn't spot anything on the daylight videos. Therefore, I'll need you to program it to fly orbits one kilometre wide, centred on the middle of the camp so we get continuous IR video for at least 30 minutes to establish a movement pattern.'

She nodded, game face back on. 'No problems doing that at night with no reflections to worry about, but you're planning something and I don't think I'm going to like it!'

I laughed at her perception and nodded. 'You're right as usual. I want to grab one of those guards for questioning.'

There was a chorus of objections from Sandy, Alf and Dave, so I held up a hand to quell the babble. 'I know the idea sounds dumb, but we need the Intel. At the moment, we know bugger all and that means we can't plan on how to pull the pin on these turkeys. We don't know when Corrine is coming over with her extra troops or what their timetable is. Just remember, they're very well equipped and most likely have a lot more in the way of weapons we haven't seen yet.

They certainly won't try to take over a plant the size of the Onslow one, or the two production platforms with just pistols and a few MP5s.'

Dave was the first to fire another round of objections. 'Assuming we manage to grab a guard without raising the immediate alarm, there'll be a big fuss when he's discovered missing. Then there's the problem of getting him to talk and what to do with him afterwards.'

There was more babble as the others tried to add their two cents worth, so I held up a hand again. 'Stop please; let me answer Dave's questions which might just answer your own.'

They quietened down and I explained my nutty plan, which raised a lot more questions, but they became more constructive as they saw that the plan could work. It took a while before the details were worked out, but by then we all felt there was a good chance we could gain some good Intel and the bad guys should remain ignorant of the fact that an attack on them had started.

It was nearly lunchtime when I called a halt to the discussion. 'Let's wait until we see the results of this evening's flight before we discuss this any more. The afternoon is free to relax and enjoy this rather delightful little bay.'

So that's what we did, starting with lunch, then we all ferried ashore to get off the boats and explore, including both cats; Krazy now big enough to romp around on her own, although she rarely strayed far from 'big brother' Jasper. We found the land was a mix of sand and sharp limestone fragments with a thin scrub covering, although the beaches were nice enough with patches of mangrove trees thriving in the sand and in the water. The bay had a clean, sandy floor offering excellent holding for our dependable Aussie-made anchors, and the extensive seagrass beds further out, suggested there should be a few dugong around.

Both Tracy and Sandy were keen to have another romp after we were back on board so we retreated to our cabin for a couple of hours of light-hearted and very enjoyable fun. The evening cocktail hour was a bit subdued with the impending night run by *Dragonfly* but since nobody was actually controlling it, so long as the flight plan was correct, it wouldn't matter if the person pushing the start button was totally bombed out. Nevertheless, it was a point of protocol that at least the operator was sober, but the rest of the crew wanted to be involved as well.

Sandy pushed the start button and it fired up and departed as usual, the autopilot not caring about the time of day or the weather conditions. As we were closer to the coast, it was only a 40-minute run to the EarthSquad camp and at the higher altitude, it allowed real-time full HD video.

Sandy fired up the IR camera as the UAV closed in on the coast, and although the infra red picture coming back was grey-scale only, it was in full HD and showed amazing detail, even at 3000 feet. We watched as *Dragonfly* swung smoothly into the pre-set one-kilometre wide orbit around the camp which showed up as though it was daylight! If anything, the detail was sharper than it was in colour.

Not many personnel were moving about at 22:45 and of those, most were in camo gear rather than civilian dress. There appeared to be several females in camo outfits and while the civilians were unarmed, all troops were armed with the standard MP5's. We spotted a heat flare coming from a hut on the far northeast corner of the camp area that was well separated from the other buildings and had to be a generator that was kept running all night. There certainly weren't any neighbours to complain about the noise!

Finally, we saw what I was hoping for, which was a couple of figures in camos strolling along a narrow path circling the camp's outer perimeter. During the time we watched, they kept a degree of separation, but didn't get fussed if they met up and patrolled together for a while. Occasionally, one would stop to pee on a bush, but in the 45 minutes we watched, they took no other breaks. We also noted that they didn't stray off the path to the outside at any time, especially on the northeast side furthest from the boat wharf and close to the next little waterway, Peter Creek. The normal activity around the main wharf had ceased and no one seemed to be stationed there at night.

Finally, *Dragonfly* rolled out of the constant turn and headed seaward, so Sandy turned the camera off and we were left with just the telemetry tracking trace heading back toward us, looking like a fat yellow worm crawling across the map overlay.

'Thoughts, anyone?' I asked, kicking off the analysis session while the images were still fresh in everyone's mind and we waited for *Dragonfly's* return.

Charlie broke the silence as everyone digested the images. 'Looks to me like most of the camp go to bed early and the guards aren't very vigilant. There's no permanent guard at the wharf and the generator runs all night. Based on that, it shouldn't be hard to pick off a guard and cart him away, but I don't know how you can hide the fact from the rest of the camp. I mean, we all saw the way those two clowns bumped into each other every so often, so when one goes missing, they'll have to suspect foul play.'

I grinned at him, 'Good assessment! So let me tell you the rest of my cunning plan.'

Sandy groaned theatrically, 'Shit Harry. The last time you came up with a cunning plan, we had to wipe out forty bikies! Is this going to be a repeat performance?'

I laughed at her black humour, 'Not quite that many, well not just yet. In fact, with a bit of luck, none for the moment. But I am planning some serious mayhem. I can't see any other way to stop these idiots without some very damaging publicity. We'd have at the very least, the Western Australian Government pissed off at us, if not the Feds and our respective bosses as well! Anyway, here's what I was thinking.'

That part of the plan at least got grudging approval from the crew, so we packed it in at that and went to bed.

SUNDAY

Over breakfast, Alf asked, 'Any change to the plan you hatched last night, Boss?'

'Yeah, just one thing. I think we'll wait 24 hours to make this raid in case we hear from Corrine with fresh information. I couldn't think of anything better, so we'll go with it for now, unless anybody comes up with a better idea!'

He smiled, 'Good idea. Another time-out day in this beaut place will be more than welcome.'

'OK. Done. Rest day today and raid night on Monday.'

So we had another quiet day, relaxing as best we could. Dave, Alf, Charlie and I went over and gently scrubbed the waterlines of both boats with pot scrubber pads. Jasper and the girls ended up joining us after making up a bucket of Pina Coladas, though Alf, Charlie and I restricted ourselves to two each. There wasn't too much messing around, although the temptation to get naked in the soft, warm water was irresistible.

We took the opportunity to dig out the two inflatable kayaks stored in *Seeker's* bow cabin, blew them up as per the instructions, and with a series of painting drop sheets draped over *Seeker's* fore-deck, we gave the white and orange hulls a quick coat of matt black from a few spray cans that promised 'quick dry enamel'.

While the paint dried, we returned to the water with the naked ladies and the remains of the Pina Colada. After lunch, the paint on the kayaks was also quite hard and it was time to make sure the boats were as stiff and seaworthy as the makers claimed. To my relief, they proved to be very easy to paddle, were plenty stiff and stable enough to get in and out of easily, so we pulled them up onto *Seeker's* foredeck again and strapped them down in readiness for tomorrow night's adventure.

The usual sun downer party was a bit more subdued with every-one still tired as well as thinking about the raid.

MONDAY

It was another quiet day, although there was no word from Corrine, so I declared the raid was on for that night.

The plan was for Dave, Alf, Charlie, Sandy, Melissa, Jasper and me to head for the coast in *Seeker*, departing Bridled Island around 22:00, travelling at 45 knots. Dave said it would be easy travelling in the calmer conditions at night. He'd maintain speed until about 4nm off the coast, making the approach to keep Little Cowle Island between the camp and *Seeker*. At that point, we'd slow down, shut down the diesels that even at idle made a deep bass grumbling, and fire up the gas turbine which only made a soft, high-pitched whistling at idle, which would be more than sufficient thrust to carry us closer inshore.

Moonrise was at 01:30, so we had to be well clear of the place by then. Though the sky was clear, it was still very dark and Dave reckoned he could safely take *Seeker* just past Cowle Island before the risk of being heard became too great. That wasn't a big paddle in the sleek kayaks so it seemed a good plan.

I had Sandy ready to launch *Dragonfly* as soon as we slowed at the 4nm point, to provide safety surveillance for us via the mini comms units that Alf, Charlie and I would be wearing. Alf and Charlie would be in one kayak and Jasper and me in the other.

'I swear that cat looks like he knows we're going into action and he's looking forward to it,' Sandy observed.

I chuckled, the usual pre-operation nerves kicking in, 'I'm sure he does. Maybe it's the seal suits and face-black that gives the game away.'

At the last minute, when Greg had the mini comms units delivered by a very curious Senior Constable from the Brisbane Highway Patrol, he'd included ten sets of the latest body-suits worn by the Special Emergency Response Team when they were going on marine operations. They were almost one size fits all, although happily some were larger than others, which still made for some hilarious try-on sessions. The suits were virtually the same as those worn by the Australian swimming team, but with a very thin layer of woven Kevlar® cloth covering all vital parts of the anatomy. Melissa found the smallest and the suit fitted her delightfully snugly. Sandy was the biggest lady in the crew and once pulled into place, looked absolutely stunning and raised instant erections on every male. For we males, the suits were almost embarrassing, and Tracy didn't help by commenting, 'Oh look. I can almost see what you had for breakfast, Harry! Is that your packed lunch?'

On the two girls, they literally were like a second skin, but once they were on and warmed up to body temperature, they were still snug, but comfortable. There was probably no real need for the girls to have them on, but they wanted to be ready in case they had to become more directly involved in the action.

The ride was very comfortable as Dave had suggested; the superb shape of the AB100 hull almost ignoring the residual wind waves and the larger southerly swell, allowing 45 knots to be easily maintained. At the six-kilometre mark, Dave pressed a couple of buttons on the instrument panel and a soft but growing whine sounded beneath our feet. As the pitch of the whine climbed, Dave cut the throttles to the diesels; let them idle for a minute to cool the turbochargers and then cut them completely.

Since all three engines drove water jet units, there was no drag from propellers associated with shutting down an engine or two, so the big hull just slowed down, dropping off the plane as the turbine ramped up to idle; the twin oval exhausts exiting either side of the cockpit, but angled outboard to avoid frying any overly-curious passengers, while emitting a soft, high pitched whine that really couldn't be heard more than a coupe of hundred metres away.

At that point, I had Sandy and Melissa fire up *Dragonfly* and launch it into the same one-kilometre wide orbit of the previous night. Her instructions were to keep us informed of any unusual movements or signs of alarm in the camp while the operation was in progress.

The big sleek boat with its dark blue hull whined softly past Cowle Island at a sedate 12 knots, until the GPS readout showed we were 1.5 kilometres off the peninsula where the camp was located, at which point Dave put the drive into neutral, leaving the turbine running to avoid the change in sound level that might alert a conscientious sentry. I was relying on the latest update from Sandy and *Dragonfly* to decide whether to land at the wharf or on the other side of the peninsula, but landing there would involve a slog through mud and mangroves; better avoided if possible. A quick check of the IR video feed showed the wharf wasn't under dedicated guard and the same procedure of two guards plodding the perimeter track was maintained.

'OK,' I briefed my black-clad crew, including the furry one as well, 'we'll go in via the wharf, park the kayaks under it and wait for the first sentry to walk past. It makes no difference which one we grab. Either one will have enough information to be useful so first one to arrive is it. I'll be point with Jasper, Charlie and Alf are on the ground as backup. If there's a problem and fuss is made, we grab who we can and bugger off fast, but if we have to do that, try to slip a knife into all the other RIB hulls before we leave, but absolutely only if we get sprung. Otherwise, we want to leave no trace of our visit to arouse suspicions. Is that very clear?'

They both nodded seriously, 'Yes boss. Got that. Covert unless sprung, no problem'

In short order we donned headsets, launched the kayaks and stroked smoothly and quietly away from *Seeker* toward the faint loom of blackness that was the land. Jasper sat quietly in the front seat, looking around with fascination and delight like a dog with its head out a car window. I felt obliged to run the plan for the rest of the operation past him, mostly for my own benefit in case I'd forgotten something important, but he turned his head and started at me intently until I'd finished. He gave a 'Huff' that was his usual sign that he had heard and understood the briefing.

It still freaked me out to be conversing with a cat, albeit a very mystical one and having him prove time and again that he understood what I'd said.

Under whispered directions from Sandy who was watching us on the IR video, we angled toward the creek on the south side of the peninsula where the wharf and main access to the EarthSquad camp was sited. I paused my paddling to key my radio, 'Any activity at the wharf?'

'Negative, but a sentry is about 250 metres away, heading in that direction. At this stage, you'll be well ahead of him if you keep paddling.'

'Smart arse,' I said softly, 'but a very nice one!' then clicked off and picked up the pace, heading straight for the wharf, now visible not far in from the mouth of the creek. With two paddling, Alf and Charlie were right on my tail as I glided soundlessly in under the grey, sun-bleached wood making up the sturdy wharf. As the tide was in, there wasn't much room and I had to lean back to clear the main crossbeams, stowing my paddle as Alf and Charlie slid in beside me.

'Do we want to grab this one?' Alf asked murmuring, as that sound carries far less than whispering where the higher pitched sibilants could be heard further away on a quiet night.

'Hang on. Let me check in with our eyes.' I triggered my radio and queried Sandy as to the position of the both sentries and was told that the closest one was still a hundred metres or so away, but still coming slowly toward the wharf. The other sentry was almost diametrically opposite our position and wouldn't be a factor if we were careful. Sandy added a final bit of information that the first sentry seemed to be a bit smaller than the other one.

'Let's grab this one,' I said. 'Sandy says he's a bit smaller than his mate, so that'll help. If we can knock him out cleanly, then provide the diversion, we can get gone.'

Following the plan, we pulled both kayaks up on the sandy shore on the far side of the first of the big RIBs, where they were out of sight. Alf climbed out of the front seat of his kayak leaving Charlie in the stern seat, a child's clicker toy in one hand, his paddle ready in the other. Alf, Jasper and I got into position below the shore bank, tucked in the blackness at the end of the wharf on the sentry approach side and waited. With the tide in, the water level was nearly up to the underside of the planking. I told Jasper again he was to help subdue the sentry, but not to make any noise. To Alf's amusement, I was loudly 'Huffed' at for my trouble.

The sentry's approach was nearly soundless, with just an occasional crunch of a pebble to track his progress, but the generator was running, providing a soft background rumble that should've masked any small incidental sounds we might make. I also double-checked the pair of elastic bands around my left forearm where one of Corrine's hypodermic syringes with a good dose of the knockout juice was loaded and ready for discharge.

I just had to be careful who got stuck.

Finally, and much closer than we'd expected, a dim figure in dark camo gear materialised out of the gloom, and conveniently turned onto the wharf, walking slowly to the end, which was less than ten paces away. In seconds, Alf, Jasper and I had darted up from under the structure and were stepping soundlessly in our padded slippers up behind the unsuspecting sentry

His MP5 was slackly slung from his left shoulder instead of across his chest where it would be ready for immediate action, but that just confirmed to me that these troops were not very well trained and certainly not expecting to be raided.

It was almost ludicrously easy to step up behind the sentry, make a quarter turn to the left to shove my right hip hard into his backside and throw a choke hold around his neck with my right arm. Bending him back over my hip all but eliminated the chance that he might kick back at my sensitive parts, as well as pulling him off balance. I was able to grab the MP5 with my left hand before it clattered to the decking and passed it behind me to Alf.

The sentry let out a stifled squeak of fright and immediately clawed with both hands at my arm that was stopping the supply of both breath and blood.

'Jasper,' I called softly and a black shadow leapt up against the sentry's chest and gripped one wrist in his bone-crushing jaws, hauled it down and held it immobile. Twenty seconds later, the sentry went slack in my arms, but I held on for another ten second count just to be sure and a sharp hand stab to a kidney produced no response, so it was safe to assume that temporary unconsciousness had set in.

Gratefully, I released the chokehold and lowered the limp form to the planking, pulled the syringe from its restraints and injected the contents into the sentry's neck. Within thirty seconds, the pulse rate had slowed, but was strong and steady. It was only as I was checking pockets for other weapons or papers, that I felt the pleasantly familiar rounded bits of anatomy and realised that our captive was female.

'Ahh, fuck it!' I cursed softly, 'we've grabbed a female sentry.'

'Does it really matter?' Alf murmured, 'Male or female, they should still know the same stuff and she'll be lighter to carry.'

'True. But who's going to do the female scream? The male yell was going to be easy, but I'm not good on falsetto!'

'I'll do it' Alf volunteered, 'I've always been able to hit a high note when singing.'

'Good oh, you've got the job. But wait 'till I tell you and remember that a crocodile's just grabbed you off the edge of the wharf and dragged you in. You just have to scream for a second or two then stop abruptly. Is that alright?'

His black shadow nodded, 'No problem boss. I'll be a good little terrified girl.'

I smacked him lightly on the upper arm, 'Smart arse! Anyway, let's push on with the rest of the plan, then get the flock outta here!'

Improvising to set the scene, I undid the girl's combat boots, removed them and took her camo pants off as well, leaving the three items of clothing on the edge of the wharf. Alf passed the MP5 down to Charlie who'd brought both kayaks back from hiding to the edge of the wharf where we could slide the girl into the front seat. It was difficult to tell what she looked like in the blackness of pre-moonrise, but that would have to wait. I asked Jasper to climb in and sit on her lap, although I was sure she wouldn't be waking up any time soon.

I stepped in the back seat, Alf stepped in the front seat of his and we pushed off. As we drifted out, I made a loud disturbance with my paddle and splashed several loads of water over the end of the wharf and her boots and pants. As I did that, Alf gave out a surprisingly realistic female scream that cut off with chilling finality.

As the echoes of that desperate-sounding scream were still fading away over the camp, we dug our paddles in and stroked hard for the creek mouth and the open sea. Behind us, nothing happened for a good minute before a couple of lights flickered on and there was a faint shout from the far side of the camp.

By the time several bobbing torches could be seen converging on the wharf, we were heading straight out to sea, stroking as hard as we could. Charlie had thoughtfully tied a cord to the front of my kayak while he waited for us and they increased our speed by partly towed me along, although I kept paddling.

Behind us, our wake disappeared within metres, and although I listened carefully for the dreaded sound of 250 horse-power Suzuki outboards being fired up, the gods looked favourably upon us that night as the camp staff came to the most obvious conclusion that their sentry had taken her pants off to pee or poop off the wharf and a croc had grabbed her.

Human nature being what it is, there seemed to be a distinct lack of interest in mounting a search in the utter blackness which was the croc's undisputed territory. Though fading in the distance, some hurried glances over my shoulder showed the torches winking out one by one as their holders returned to either bed or to the mess hall for a tea or coffee and a tension relieving talk.

Suddenly, Sandy's crystal-clear, dulcet tones spoke to my ear, 'Well done guys. That's a clean getaway, but Harry, did you really have to take that girl's pants off? I mean, it's just so you!'

'Just setting the scene, dear lady, just setting the scene. And it does seem to have worked; can you confirm?'

'I'm delighted to confirm the camp is settling down nicely, with most returning to their beds, although several persons are in the mess tent having hot drinks. There doesn't appear to be any attempt to launch one of the RIBs to check around, so I think your misdirection has worked. Well done again!'

'Thanks Sandy. Where are you?'

'Approaching, but keep paddling for now, the greater the distance from the camp for the pick-up is better.'

'Amen to that, sister,' panted Alf, 'but if Harry were to actually paddle a bit and take some of the load, it'd really help!'

'Cheeky bugger! I **am** paddling!'

'Ah yes. But you actually have to use that fibreglass pole with the blade at each end!'

Ten minutes later *Seeker's* dark blue hull, looking huge from our low position, loomed out of the darkness and slid to a smooth halt beside us. The single water jet driven by the quietly whistling turbine, sat frothing under the stern board while the drive was in neutral, but that was the loudest noise.

Dave reached down and carefully lifted our unconscious, half-naked captive out of her seat, Jasper having vacated her lap as soon as the stern board was in reach, and couldn't resist having a friendly shot at me by saying, 'Gee Harry. It didn't take long for you to get her pants off!'

Alf passed up the acquired MP5 and I told Dave, 'Actually, she offered to take her pants off if I gave her gun back, but I'm such a devious bastard, I took both. When we see Corrine, you can tell her that this MP5-SD6 is mine – all mine!'

He laughed as we hauled the kayaks up on deck and lashed them down against the railings up for'rard for the run back to Bridled Island. With them both secured, Dave headed for Bridled Island, staying at low speed until we were at least ten kilometres offshore and with Cowle Island between *Seeker* and the camp. During that time, Sandy had kept *Dragonfly* over the camp to observe any change to activity, but reported no change, except that a replacement sentry was detailed to patrolling and both sentries stayed away from the wharf. The lights in the mess tent were finally turned off as the last person went to bed.

'Do you want me to keep *Dragonfly* watching the camp?' She asked.

I thought about whether it would gain much, but if they were suspicious, the RIBs would have been sent out long ago. 'Nah I think that'll do. Bring it home and put it to bed, please. I'll go see how our captive is doing.'

'OK. Landing in a couple of minutes.'

CHAPTER 24

Right on time, the UAV appeared; tracking in on the little homing beacon placed in the middle of the landing pad and making its usual gentle touchdown. While Sandy put it to bed and downloaded the recorded video, I went forward along the deck to a large hatch set in the left side of what had been the big sunlounge. The stairs led down to a pair of small, two-berth cabins for the crew, in case the owner needed the ego-massaging luxury of a paid crew. The triangular-shaped cabins had a small ensuite between them and two spacious and comfortable bunks each, although as soon as Dave and Mouse had taken over the boat, they had used the space for storage of odd items. On the old boat, the AB68, the crew cabin had been used as a temporary lock-up once on the Victorian operation and it was easy to have one of these meet that requirement again. The addition of a very substantial sliding bolt fitted to the outside of one of the cabin doors made the subtle conversion from cabin to cell.

Alf was sitting on a stool dragged in from the galley, leaning comfortably back against the centre bulkhead reading a book and chewing on a sandwich, as he kept watch on what was now revealed as an attractive girl laid out on the lower bunk. Incongruously, she was still wearing the camo-pattern T-shirt, brief panties and wool socks. She was snoring softly, and looking as though she wasn't going to wake anytime soon.

She appeared to be in her early twenties and in good shape and condition.

'All good, Harry, but how long is that shot supposed to last?' he asked. 'It's been about an hour so far and she hasn't even twitched.'

I felt her pulse in her neck, finding it strong and regular. 'The last time Corrine used it, she said using that dose with the average male would knock them out for at least an hour, unless the antidote was given, in which case the recovery would be almost immediate, so logically, it will knock a smaller female out for longer. I don't see any need to rush this one into waking up, so we might just let her sleep it off, but if she still isn't stirring after another hour, we might have to give her a shot of the antidote.

What we must do is plan the scene for when she does wake up, so we can make the most of the opportunity to start playing with her head. In the Middle East, we found that was the best starting point with prisoners when we wanted Intel. From what I've seen of this particular cocktail, she'll be disoriented for a while.'

'So, this cocktail isn't the one which induces a degree of amnesia?'

'Nah! That's yet another one Corrine's got tucked away in that amazing little medicine kit of hers. She's got it in the form of either a pill that dissolves very quickly and tastelessly in drinks, or as an injectable liquid. There's an antidote or wake-up potion in the form of a pill or a liquid as well. She's expanded the kit since I came across her and Dave in the Gippsland Lakes, two operations back.'

'Oh, that's all very confusing and I'm glad I don't have to sort out one from the other, but presumably you've got it all under control.'

I grinned, 'I'm as confused as you are, but hopefully I've got it right. We don't want her waking up with amnesia yet. Yell if she stirs.'

I left him on watch, and headed for Dave in the wheelhouse, via the galley with some ideas bubbling up in my brain.

As we passed the 10nm mark from the coast, Dave started both diesels and let them warm up before shutting down the turbine. The small swell was out of the southwest and for comfort, Dave kept the speed to around 40 knots, which was still very quick in the open ocean, but the superb design of the AB100 allowed it to stride effortlessly over the one metre swell. Dave kept his eyes on the digital radar and the overlay of its display on the chart plotter that was a marvellously convenient aid to navigation, but occasionally wasn't totally accurate. Therefore, because the radar overlay was totally accurate, it kept the plotter honest.

As we loped along with an easy motion across the smaller swells, the twin 2600 horse-power diesels dialled back to a muted thunder, I asked Dave, 'I don't suppose you've got one of those voice synthe-sizers aboard, have you? You know, like the Darth Vader kits that used to be all the go with kids years ago?'

He nodded enthusiastically, 'Yeah, as a matter of fact we have. Funny you should ask. Angie and Zoe gave us one just before we left Melbourne to move to the Gold Coast before the bikie opera-tion. They came down with Janice, Hilary and Debbie to visit a few times and we all went for a run down to Phillip Island. We were a bit intrigued since they said it was a memento of that paedophile operation where they first met you. Are you thinking about playing some mind games with our new captive?'

'Yeah,' I grinned at him, 'and I figured the more tricks we throw at her, the more disoriented and off-balance she'll be. I've always found that to be very effective in extracting information.'

Sandy was sitting on the dual helm seat beside him, and said, 'If I remember rightly, those things are very effective, depending on the quality in the first place. You'll need to have a speaker in the cabin though, if you're going to keep her there.'

Dave chuckled, 'I remember Zoe telling us that it wasn't just a cheap toy, but was quite expensive, so it should do the job all right. And there's already a speaker in there, hooked up to the intercom. You just have to select the crew quarter's button on the sub-panel over there on the lower right of the main panel. There's a switch to select for either ship-wide broadcast or just for the crew quarters. The crew selection gives two-way comms and there's a separate mike in each cabin so the crew only have to speak normally to be heard clearly back here.

That mike on the front of the bulkhead just below the panel with the long curly cord is the one to use.'

'That's great, Dave. Can you lay your hands on the unit easily?'

'No worries. If you'll just take over here for a few moments, I'll go dig it out.'

I assumed command, carefully checking radar and the chart plotter. The new digital, pulse-compression radar gave a very sharp, clear and accurate depiction of objects down to 50 mm in diameter at the close range of 6 metres, right out to 48 nautical miles or 89 kilometres. Therefore, it was nearly always overlaid on the chart plotter; both to pick up temporary obstructions like other boats, ships and shipping containers, and to verify or refute what the chart plotter reckoned should be safe water.

Dave was back in five minutes, a colourful square box in his hands. 'Here it is and it's still got batteries fitted.' The plastic box had a few buttons on the front, a small mike on a short lead and a small built-in speaker with a volume knob. When turned on, it proved to have a Darth Vader-style voice selected, and provided one spoke fairly slowly, the altered voice coming from the speaker was very different to my own, but quite understandable. The volume knob made it more than loud enough.

'Perfect,' I said into the little mike, 'may the Force be with you!' The resultant output voice was only a little bit like Vader, but more than spooky enough for my purposes and gave the crew a good laugh. To test the intercom, I selected 'Crew Cabin' and pressed the call button. 'Alf, this is Harry. Do you hear me all right? Just talk normally, there's a microphone in the speaker.'

'I hear you loud and clear Harry,' the reply came, 'how about me?'

'Loud and clear also. I've just thought of something so I'll be back up there in a minute.'

'OK.'

To a set of questioning looks from the others, I went back for'rard through the galley and to the cell.

'That's a bloody good intercom unit,' Alf commented, 'you were crystal clear; there was just a slight click when you pressed the button to speak and I could hear the engines softly in the background.'

'Excellent. But what I'd thought of was that Missy here may just piss or crap herself when she wakes, so I think we'll strip her, which I wanted to do anyway as part of the interrogation process, then put her on the floor in the ensuite. That way if she does mess herself, it won't foul the cabin and she can clean herself easily. If we leave the door open and the intercom on, we can hear when or if she stirs.'

Alf nodded acceptance, 'Suits me fine. I'd rather be aft chatting with the others than playing nursemaid, so let's do it.'

It only took a few minutes to awkwardly strip her clothes off, check the cabin for anything she could use to escape, tie her wrists in front of her with several large cable ties I'd brought with me, and lay her on the floor of the ensuite with the door open. Dave had thoughtfully secured a large sliding pad bolt to the outside of the ensuite as well as the cabin door.

With her clothes in hand, we left the cabin and checked that the ensuite door was secured as well. Back in the saloon, only Sandy showed any sympathy for the girl's plight and my treatment of her. I cranked the volume up on the intercom, but heard nothing.

'We heard you very clearly when you were discussing what to do,' offered Sandy, 'so it's working well as a baby sitter.'

Even though we had to slow for the last approach to our anchorage at Bridled Island through the scattered islands large and small, we had dropped the anchor and rafted up to *Firebird* at 01:00, less than an hour after leaving the camp. Amanda, Tracy and Krazy were overjoyed to see us and the little puss in particular gave us an enthusiastic welcome, Krazy going over Jasper with a fine toothcomb! Sandy had kept them updated via SatPhone, so they knew our mission had been successful. I managed to dissuade them from going forward to have a look at the captive, promising they could see all they wanted of her in the morning.

'But right about now, I'm going to have to wake her up. She's been sleeping a bit too long by my rough reckoning.'

Sandy was against the idea and was supported by Amanda who claimed some prior experience with these drugs, something that hadn't been revealed before. After further questioning of both Alf and me about the girl's appearance and condition, both ladies were strongly in favour of letting the girl sleep.

'If she's snoring softly, it means that she's in a deep natural sleep and it'd be better if she was allowed to sleep off the effects of the drug.'

'But I want her to be woozy and disoriented,' I protested, 'not wide awake, refreshed and ready for action!'

Sandy smiled and shook her head, 'When she wakes up, she won't be any of those things, especially if you're going to mess with her mind.'

Finally, I bowed to their opinion and let her sleep on, with the proviso that I would sleep on the lounge in *Seeker's* saloon where I would be able to hear any sounds coming from the crew cabin via the intercom. Tracy sealed the deal by volunteering to stay up to take the first half of the watch while I actually got some sleep on the very comfortable white leather lounge and for once, didn't offer to keep me company on it.

The rest of the raiding crew were all stuffed and gladly went to bed. They were asleep in minutes, leaving Tracy sitting in the Captain's chair reading a book with just a dim light on in *Seeker's* saloon and the intercom speaker by her right elbow turned down a bit.

Happy with that arrangement, I relaxed and slept deeply.

CHAPTER 25

It had been a rather busy three weeks since Corrine had been delivered to the reception of the EarthCare Meditation and Healing Resort and being recruited into the EarthSquad para-military as a paid Major and 2IC under a Spanish Colonel who was an administrative type. Despite Paula's enthusiastic review of his background at her induction, he was neither well trained nor suited for action. Corrine wondered time and again why he'd been hired, but acknowledged that he was an excellent administrator with an uncanny ability to procure or organise everything and anything at very short notice.

The brief demonstration of her hand-to-hand combat abilities, plus allowing stories of her Afghanistan wet-work jobs in particular to leak to the troops, had at least ensured there were no more challenges to her authority.

She was also delighted with the competence shown by her new Executive Officer, Lieutenant Howson and his girlfriend, Sergeant Hegarty, the only Lieutenant and Sergeant in the HQ squad, although apparently there was a Sergeant and a Corporal at Pilbara.

Another plus was the escalation of the relationship with the deputy head of Security, the handsome and manly Drew Tallman who congratulated himself for finally talking Corrine into joining him in his bed! He would have been only slightly less happy if he'd known that the delightful sex they both enjoyed, was a calculated plan by Corrine to get an inside look at the security plans for the EarthSquad operation.

Her other motivation, apart from the personal satisfaction gained, was to keep away from the thoroughly unpleasant Head of

Security, Mr Joshua Koll, who apparently was an extreme deviate and renowned for damaging female staff.

Unfortunately, that was one of very few things to delight Corrine over the next week as assessments of firearm skills, hand-to-hand combat and bushcraft skills showed an almost woeful lack of overall expertise, with only a few bright sparks amongst the herd. A surprising inclusion on that very short list of noteworthy troopers was Trooper Chetty, one of the late and very un-lamented Trooper Smith's former acquaintances, who showed above average firearm skills, had good hand-to-hand abilities and was surprisingly agile for such a big man.

He was, in fact, the same Trooper who'd spoken up for the other four when hauled out in front of Corrine after the brutal demise of Trooper Smith, and following discussions with her XO and Sergeant Hegarty, Corrine sent for him.

The big man knocked and then eased his head and broad shoulders through the doorway as she called, 'Enter.'

He came to a rough form of attention and not knowing the reason for the unusual summons, said warily in his gravelly voice, 'You wished to see me, Ma'am?'

Corrine closed the folder she was studying and took her time looking at his impressively large frame. He was quite a handsome man, she thought as a by-the-way, but still very dangerous despite his good behaviour over the last week since seeing his role model taken down and killed in front of him.

She remained seated and indicated the chair on his side of the plain steel desk, 'Please be seated Trooper Chetty.'

He inclined his head and sat carefully, 'Thank you, Ma'am.'

'I've been observing your behaviour and performances over the past week Trooper.'

'Yes Ma'am. I trust it has been satisfactory. I've been trying hard to do the right thing.'

'Yes, from what I have seen, your behaviour has been fine, I'm glad to say. Do you have any problems with the other troopers you'd like to mention to me?'

'No Ma'am. I've been getting along just fine with everybody.'

'Good. So, tell me, have you noticed a difference in general behaviour and attitude amongst the others since the demise of your associate, Trooper Smith?'

'Yes Ma'am, I have noticed a big difference. They all seem a lot more relaxed and happier.'

'Good! Would you say therefore, they are working more as a team and much less as a bunch of individuals; always on the defensive and watching their backs?'

He looked a bit shame-faced and nodded soberly, 'Yes Ma'am. I know what you're saying and once again I apologise for the damage my associates and I have caused. We allowed Smithy to influence our behaviour way too much, although I have to say, if I may, that he was a very forceful individual!'

'I can certainly appreciate that, although I didn't call you here to get another apology. As far as I'm concerned, all that is over and done with, although I'm pleased to hear you say that and glad you realise the problem. I'm far more interested in your honest assessment of the performances of the other troopers on the range and in hand-to-hand combat.'

He looked a bit puzzled, but thought a moment before speaking. 'Most are below what I'd consider even adequate with weapons, although there are several who are very good. The .50 calibre weapons scare the hell out of most of them. Their hand-to-hand combat skills are very sub-par, as is the ability to move quietly in the bush.'

Corrine nodded, 'I concur, so it's just as well we don't have to attack a target in the bush, but they do have to be able to shoot and maybe fight up close and personal.

Has the Colonel explained the plan to everybody?'

'No ma'am, we've heard some rumours, but they are very vague. I don't think anybody in the squad really knows what the target is.'

Corrine smiled, 'That's probably for the best right now since it is becoming obvious we're going to have to lose some more of the squad before we deploy.'

Chetty looked interested at that piece of information, but knew when not to ask for more.

'I'm asking your opinion of the performance of the others, Mr Chetty, because you have shown you are very competent in most areas and that pleases me considerably. For that reason and because you seem to be trying hard to fit in with the others, I'm promoting you to Corporal, answering to and working with Sergeant Hegarty. Will you have any problem working with her? Please be honest.'

For the first time, the big man gave a smile of pure delight, before responding with. 'That's a very big pat on the back coming from you, Major. Thank you! And no problem, I will be pleased to work with the Sergeant. I never hassled her before and I respect how she stood up for herself and some of the other women who weren't so... strong-willed.'

Corrine stood and shook his huge paw, 'In that case congratulations Corporal Chetty, because you've earned it, but you still need to show me you can do the job. We have to straighten these people out as quickly as possible. It's taken a week to assess them and we might only have another two weeks to improve firearm and close combat skills before we deploy. Can you work with that?'

Corporal Chetty nodded, 'Yes Major. It's a stupidly tight time-frame, no disrespect intended, because I'm sure it's not your call. If we had the time, we could bring most of them up to a reasonable standard, but two weeks is only just enough time for the Sergeant and me to concentrate on the ones showing the most promise.'

'Good. Can you and the Sergeant make up a list of all the troopers and rate them as 'Keep' or 'Drop'? Be ruthless, but bear in mind there will be some who might improve enough in the next two weeks to be rated 'Keep'.'

'Yes, Major, we can do that and we should be able to let you have it tomorrow morning.'

'Excellent Corporal. If you would care to stop by Q Store, they'll have a new uniform with your rank insignia on it. Please exchange clothes immediately, since your duties commence as of now. After changing uniform, please report to Sergeant Hegarty for further instructions. Make me happy, Corporal!'

He jumped to his feet with a renewed energy and enthusiasm, 'I look forward to doing just that Major, and may I say that you're the first person who's ever given me any encouragement to better myself. Thank you.'

He actually fired off a sort-of salute, which at least showed his good intentions, and left.

Following a few choice words from Corrine, the new Corporal and Sergeant Hegarty actually did get on remarkably well. It proved to be a masterstroke of promotion as Chetty's size and changed personality quickly brought the entire Company into line without resorting to extreme measures, so the four training leaders could get on with the job without undue distractions.

However, as predicted, when Corrine went over the performance lists handed in by her new Corporal and Sergeant, she found that ten or twelve troopers were listed as 'more dangerous to our own troops than anybody else' with weapons. Likewise, they weren't much better in field craft and in hand-to hand combat, so Corrine made the decision to get rid of them.

Her decision was the 'why', but the Colonel had to make the 'how' resolution, since any rejects posed a strong security risk, and for that discussion she thought she'd better jump in the golf cart assigned to her mini-HQ and visit the Colonel in his palatial office in the main EarthCare admin block.

He stood and made a courtly half-bow, waving her to the comfortable leather chair on the other side of his polished wooden desk. 'Please be seated Major. How may I be of assistance on this fine day?'

'We have a problem with some of our troops, sir. Twelve of them have been consistently underperforming and for most of those, their lack of weapons skills has caused them be assessed by my NCOs as being more dangerous to our own people than to anybody else. They can't be used on any proposed operation, unless it is in a purely administrative role, and even then, some are just plain incompetent. Fortunately, they all seem to realise it without having to be told.'

The Colonel looked unhappy, 'Twelve out of 41 leaves just 29 to send to the west to boost the 25 already there. Is there nothing that can be done?'

Corrine gave a mirthless laugh. 'Sure, after maybe another year of intensive training they might be useful, but here and now? No way! We'll have to make the most of the ones we do have. But that's only half the problem.'

The Colonel gave a very expressive eyebrow lift, inviting her to continue, so she lobbed the hot potato right into his lap.

'What do we do with the twelve rejects? Do we send them home where they will talk about this training camp and what's been going on; including the rather strict discipline I've had to impose at times? I can certainly eliminate them permanently, but that could raise some questions elsewhere. What do you think?'

The Colonel gave a delicate shudder at her blunt and terminal suggestion. 'Have any been told of their objective?' he asked.

'No sir, and to the best of my knowledge, only the Lieutenant and the Sergeant are aware of the full target plan, while the others haven't even trained on particular aspects of the operation, like boarding a platform from a boat. So that makes them less of a security risk.'

'Do you have any suggestions, Major?'

'Only two. Either eliminate all twelve or absorb them into administrative or housekeeping functions here or at the Pilbara camp.'

The Colonel gave another little shudder at Corrine's repeated elimination suggestion, but seized on the second like a drowning person would grab a hold of an empty coffee tin floating past. 'Yes, yes! That is much more acceptable. I can have them transferred to the Admin section and assess them for a different set of skills. We can use some here and maybe send some to the Pilbara base. They have asked for more support staff.'

She smiled at his obvious relief, 'OK. I'll have the rejects pack up immediately and transfer to the other barracks with the EarthCare people and then come up here for interviews.'

He frowned. 'That might be a bit rushed. I'm not sure we're quite ready for them yet Major.'

Corrine's expression hardened. 'With respect, Colonel, you'll have to make it happen because I need to get them out from underfoot immediately. They're a pain in the arse and dangerous, and their continuing presence is undermining the little bit of morale that's built up, so the sooner the better. If you're not ready for them, I'll at least have to get them into some new accommodation with the other EarthCare lot so they're out of sight. I've only got four days left to try to make this mob capable of pointing a weapon in the right direction, and frankly, it's not enough time, but Paula says we have to head west by next Wednesday.'

He held his hands up to stop her tirade, 'Very well, Major. It shall be as you say. Do what you think is best and I'll take it from there.'

'Thank you Sir, I'll get on it immediately.'

The remaining four days were frantic with some last-minute training, and then the task of making sure all those deemed suitable to go, had their full kit of clothing and weapons. The Colonel had come up with around 150 kilos of C-4 explosive and despite his warnings that no targets were to actually be blown up, Corrine trained up six other troopers which included Lieutenant Towson, Sergeant Hegarty and the continually surprising Corporal Chetty, to handle and effectively use the innocent-looking stuff. They could only afford the time for three sessions out on the southern boundary of the EarthCare property, but nevertheless had a wonderful time blowing up trees and the resulting stumps.

It was in her own bed the previous night that she realised she'd taught her demolition squad quite enough to actually take out the targets, and had to remind herself that her job was to sabotage the whole operation, not make it work! However, to assist with that objective, she had held back two of the more incompetent, but likeable misfits to Lieutenant Towson's complete mystification.

After dealing with a seemingly endless stream of dramas and hassles generated by the transportation of 35 EarthSquad personnel, their personal kit, weapons, ammunition, explosives and other supplies to the Pilbara, Corrine was becoming increasingly frustrated. There had been no confirmation regarding exactly when the move was to happen, or how weapons, ammunition and explosives were going to get past Airport Security!

Finally, after snapping at her NCOs once too often, she jumped in her golf cart and once again, roared up the hill to the main Admin block and barged into the Colonel's office.

He took one look at the expression on her face before pasting a welcoming smile on his face and coming around the desk to close the door, ushered her into a comfortable armchair away from the desk.

'My dear Major. You look…how you say…frazzled! How may I assist you?'

'Colonel you could start by telling me about the transport details to move our troops and their gear to the Pilbara. I'm trying to organise everybody to move out tomorrow but I haven't got a clue regarding the finer details! So, with respect sir, please start talking!'

He looked puzzled for a moment, 'But I sent a detailed list to you in a sealed envelope by messenger at 09:00 this morning. Didn't you receive it?'

Corrine glared at him, 'Obviously not, sir or I wouldn't be here asking you. No message, no knowledge, total fucking confusion!'

The Colonel allowed his smooth, unlined forehead to wrinkle slightly in consternation, 'Oh dear! I gave the memo to Janine, that delightful young lady who's been helping me with some administration work. She was to deliver it to you personally at 09:00.'

Corrine guessed that as pleasant as she was, the only administration work Janine could help him with involved pulling down the silver tag on the full-length zipper closing her skin-tight body suit!

She shook her head. 'Nope! No Janine, no message!'

She gave a dry chuckle, 'Mind you, if she came down to the bar-racks area wearing just that jumpsuit, she may never be seen again! Or at least not in the same condition she was!'

He allowed another slight frown to crease his face. 'Hmmm. I see your point. But not receiving my message is most unfortunate. Let me print you a copy first then we'll discuss the transport arrange-ments. I'll sort out the problem with Miss Janine later, if as you say, she is still around the Admin area!'

Corrine smiled slightly, hearing in her mind Janine's silver zipper sliding down to Ground Zero as the Colonel investigated why his message had gone missing. She noted the comfortable couch on the other side of the coffee table from her armchair and her deviate mind guessed that it was the principal investigation site.

Once the Colonel got his mind focussed on the transport prob-lem and away from Janine's silver zipper, he quickly and efficiently briefed Corrine.

'So, to summarise,' she said when he'd finished, 'all personnel fly out tomorrow on a chartered Virgin Airlines Fokker 100 Regional Jet from Eagle Farm Airport, departing at 06:00, with a refuelling stop at Alice Springs then terminating at Onslow.

With time on the ground refuelling, the total time will be just over 5 hours. Is that right?'

The Colonel nodded, '5.1 hours in fact. The Fokker is really too big for the group we have, but that allows the crew to load more fuel, and there's still plenty of space for our gear. The cost isn't a consideration.'

Corrine nodded. 'That's fine Colonel, but how are we going to take weapons, ammunition and explosives through the airport secu-rity and onto an aircraft?'

He smiled gently. 'We have an arrangement with airport Secu-rity where the four aircraft-compatible containers which hold all our special equipment will be pre-sealed and not subject to further inspection. All personnel will, of course, pass through the security checkpoints the same as usual, so warn everybody they must not carry any contraband into the cabin.

I need you to make sure everything which shouldn't be looked at by Security, is in those containers. They should have been delivered to your compound by now, ready for you to have them loaded.'

'OK, Colonel, that sounds all right, so what are the arrangements at Onslow?'

He nodded. 'Ah yes, a good question. I've decided it will be better for your supplies to be sent on ahead to the camp on the transport barge, if you will get the troops to help load them soon after you arrive. As you will all be staying in town for the night, I've booked one of the local motels, the Sun Motel and they assure me there will be plenty of room for the whole party. Just one word of caution, when in public, please make sure that the personnel don't look too military. I have noticed you have allowed them to grow their hair and largely dispense with saluting and standing for an Officer, so that will help the image.'

'Yessir. I did it deliberately for just that reason. There hasn't been time to process them through basic training as would be the case in the regular military as you so well know.'

He nodded sagely, dropping back into a moment of reminiscence, 'Ah yes. How well I do remember…'

Corrine jumped to her feet to shut down yet more wasted time as the Colonel relived the glory days when he stole weapons from his own armoury and sold them to the Separatist Rebels in the north of his beloved Spain, although love of country didn't stop him from keeping all the proceeds of the weapons sales for himself.

Waving her copy of the movement orders, Corrine snapped off a salute. 'Thank you Colonel. I must return to my work immediately now you've clarified what's happening. There is still much to do and so little time to do it.'

The Colonel jumped to his feet, managing to look slightly disappointed that he couldn't regale the pretty Major with more stories of his administrative prowess. 'Of course, my dear Major, but I am further remiss in not telling you that you will have three additional passengers on the journey, since Miss Paula, Mr Terry and Mr Drew are all planning on being on hand to decide when the time is right to commence the action.

As much as I would love to be joining you, alas, it is my job to stay behind to organise supplies and anything else you might need.'

Corrine frowned briefly at that news, although she should have expected Paula and Terry would want to be present for the kick-start of their warped dreams. Having Drew along just meant he'd want more sex, but at least she could stay well informed about the security aspects of the operation and should be able to twist plans to suit her own ends.

'No problem sir. There will be plenty of room now we have the bigger and faster aircraft.'

He beamed at her agreement, 'Yes indeed Major. Why have all this money lying around and not spend it? What is your expression, 'hold onto the expense'?'

'Ah…I think that should be 'hang the expense' sir, but close enough. Oh, just one final request. Do we have any SatPhones for communications away from the mobile network?'

'Ah yes, we do and I'd forgotten to give these three to you and your senior staff. There are three others already at the camp.' With that, he went and dug around behind his desk a moment, before producing three plain white cardboard boxes. 'Here they are. Brand-new, but already on contract and linked to the service provider. I am told they will need charging, but are otherwise ready to go.'

With the boxes under her arm, she escaped his office, carefully avoiding his customary pat on the bum that usually lingered a bit too long for comfort.

Back in her office, she called for Lieutenant Howson, Sergeant Hegarty and Corporal Chetty and briefed them on the instructions she'd received, then started firing off orders to cover the rest of the preparations. She also handed the Lieutenant and Sergeant a SatPhone each and as soon as they'd left, put her own on charge.

That evening, under the pretext of checking on some troopers who'd suffered minor injuries during training, she visited the Medical Centre and was able to have a lengthy chat with Roger and Jill.

237

CHAPTER 26

SEEKER, TUESDAY AM, BRIDLED IS

I was pulled unceremoniously out of the depths of an exhausted sleep by a crocodile that had my left arm locked in its massive jaws and was dragging me to the water's edge. Determined to face the reality of my impending demise, I forced my eyes open to find the lovely Tracy, a worried frown on her face, hissing at me as she shook me by the left arm.

'Stop fucking around Harry and wake up! We've got action up front.'

I did a quick stocktake of limbs, digits and sundry appendages and found all present and correct. Gee, dreams can be vivid! I'd not had one like that for years, so maybe I was stressing a bit too much about this job.

'OK, OK! You have my full attention. I'm awake. What's going on?'

She finally stopped pulling on my arm, which was a relief and let me swing my legs off the lounge. I'd been covered with a light cotton blanket as the winter nights at this latitude did become cool in the early hours and woke with the usual male erection caused by a full bladder.

The sight of it was enough to make Tracy giggle as I growled, 'Let me up. I need to pee!'

After negotiating the stern steps and reaching the safety of *Seeker*'s wide stern board, I did so with a feeling a great relief. Finally drip-free, I made my way back to the saloon where I retrieved my pants and slightly restored my dignity, although occasionally, Tracy still broke into a fit of giggles.

'Right! Now, what's going on?'

Putting on a partly serious face, she reported, 'Stirring in the crew cabin finally. It started about fifteen minutes ago with a few groans, then silence for a while, then more grunts and groans. While you were peeing and losing that rather nice pump handle thing, I heard her say 'What the fuck...' in a slurred voice. She's been quiet since then.'

I used the sink in the corner of the cockpit to quickly wash my face, chasing the last cobwebs of sleep away until I felt more on the ball.

'OK. Let's see how responsive she is,' I said, heading for the helm position where Tracy's e-reader still sat propped up against the throttles. It was then I noticed the faint glow in the sky and looked for the clock on the vast spread of the instrument panel where gauges, dials, switches, buttons and screens capable of reporting on every function and condition possible, whether it was needed or not, were laid out with Italian style in a gleaming swath of money. When I finally found the clock amongst all that glitter, despite having four hands and five minor dials, it at least indicated the time! That is once you'd sorted which was local time. There was the choice of London, New York, Venice and a place called Sorrento which I was fairly sure was the boat's original Italian home port and not the somewhat pretentious suburb on the Gold Coast or the one on the Victorian coast!

'It's after six! You were supposed to wake me hours ago!'

She shrugged, 'Nothing was happening and you needed to sleep, and sleep is what you got! So stop complaining and do your Darth Vader bit. I want to see what her reaction is.'

I tried to put on my 'Pissed-off Commander' face, but she giggled again so that failed miserably. I turned on the voice-changer box and found someone had cunningly taped the crew cabin mike to the back speaker of the voice-changer so I didn't have to hold it separately as I did before.

Nodding appreciation, I stood as far from the box as the mike cord allowed, turned my back for good measure, pressed the button and said slowly, clearly and loudly, 'Wake up! Wake up!'

I hate to think what it must have sounded like in the crew cabin, but the effect the deep, gravelly voice had on Tracy, was to send her into fits of hastily stifled giggles as I sternly shooed her out into the cockpit. There was a muffled shriek from the crew cabin speaker, before a tremulous voice asked, *'Who's that?'*

'Never mind who I am,' I replied, forcing myself to keep speaking slowly and distinctly, 'I need to know who you are.'

'I... I'm Brianna Welsh,' she replied, her voice a little stronger. 'Where am I and where are my clothes?'

'You're secure; on a boat; and nobody is coming to get you because all your friends and workmates think you're dead! For now, that's all you need to know. However, there won't be any clothes or food unless you answer all my questions truthfully and follow the rules.'

'What rules?'

Shit! Good question. I hadn't thought up any rules!

'Listen very carefully. I will say this only once! You will answer all my questions truthfully and without hesitation. You will not try to escape, but if you do manage to, we will not make any attempt to rescue you from the sharks and crocodiles that haunt these waters. A failed escape attempt will result in a water-only ration for three days. Any attempt to damage your cabin will result in you being fully restrained, gagged and locked in the toilet for three days.

Water will be made available for a five-minute period, three times per day at 06:00, 12:00 and 18:00, so you had better learn how to save water, not waste it. If you attempt to clog your toilet, we will not fix it until we have disposed of you. Therefore, you will live the remainder of your very short life literally in your own shit! Do you understand these rules?'

'Yes, I understand,' came a very subdued voice, 'but does that mean you're going to kill me anyway?'

'Not necessarily. But we are quite happy to do so if you cause the boat or us too much grief. Understand that very clearly. If you co-operate, you will be looked after and probably released when your misguided associates are eliminated, so you can consider yourself very lucky.'

'*You said earlier my friends and workmates think I'm dead. Why would they think that?*'

'Because we staged a fake crocodile attack when we took you. You may be disappointed to learn they didn't even try to look for you after they thought you'd been taken by a croc. So you're all alone now, dead and disposed of.'

'*Oh. I see.*' *she replied in a very despondent tone and it sounded like she was crying softly.*

'Now. Are you prepared to co-operate and answer questions about EarthSquad?'

'*Yeah sure, why not. Just don't put me over the side. I can't swim very well and I'm terrified of sharks.*'

'OK. Let's start at the beginning. How did you come to be here in the Pilbara with this para-military group called EarthSquad?'

Bit by bit, the story came out how she was recruited as an idealistic, young greenie who attended the Meditation Centre to commune with nature, then discovered she liked shooting at things which might be considered harmful to the earth. From there came a series of intensive 'motivation' lectures and suddenly she was on a chartered airliner headed for a remote camp on the Western Australian coast where she was issued a uniform and a semi-automatic carbine and told she was a soldier, 'defending the earth against those who would rape and pillage Her Bounty until the air and sea was poisoned and the Noble Earth died'.

Much of this sounded like pure propaganda designed to brainwash young impressionable minds and make them malleable to take in the sort of insidious crap any radical militant group seems to spout at will. It also sounded like the sort of bull-shit a marketing expert like the much-exalted Paula would come up with.

With any luck, maybe this girl could be still turned aside from venturing any further down that very dangerous path.

And maybe, she could even be turned to work on the side of the good guys.

All this information came slowly, as she needed to be constantly prompted with questions, and several times needed to have a drink and to pee. Our crews slowly woke up and drifted over to *Seeker*, attracted by the Darth Vader voice and soon lovely smells were drifting up from the galley, so I told the girl we were taking a break and might give her some breakfast, since she'd behaved herself.

'We need to feed her so she doesn't get sick' Sandy stated, 'so far, she's co-operated, so we have to do our part.'

'OK,' I agreed, 'work out what she can eat with her fingers, without knife, fork or spoon and not on a ceramic plate either, just in case. I'm not prepared to trust her yet.'

'How about a bacon, egg and cheese sandwich?' Amanda suggested sticking her head up the stairs from the galley. 'Dave's got some on now. We could serve it on a paper plate, so that'd be safe enough. Better give her a plastic or paper cup for water.'

'Excellent idea! In fact I wouldn't mind a couple myself. I'm starving!'

She grinned, 'Coming right up.'

'And how do we get the food to her?' Sandy asked. 'I presume we shouldn't show our faces or let her know how many we are?'

'Exactly right. Come here and try saying something into the mike. The output should be very similar in tone, although your phrasing will be different.'

She did and since her voice was deeper than most females because of her larger frame, it didn't sound a lot different to me. 'OK. That's good. As long as we're keeping her under wraps, only you or I talk via the box. As far as food goes, we'll keep it simple, but still three meals a day. Fruit juice for drinks at mealtime in case we need to give her a sleepy pill, and I've already told her the water will be turned on only three times a day. We'll make those times 07:00, 12:00 and 18:00 and that can do for her meals. I'll tell her those times as well as how we'll deliver the food. Do we have a spare bucket?'

Dave had heard the request and dug in a galley locker and came up with a medium size mop bucket that was nearly square, with a strong wire handle.'

'Perfect! I'll tie a line on this and it can be pushed in the door. How about I tell her the lights will be left off all the time except for meals, then when food is due, she has to go into the ensuite and close the door? Whoever delivers the food can take one of those very bright LED torches and shine in the cabin. If we tape over the portholes on the outside, the cabin will be very dark, so a bright light shone in there will blind her enough that she won't be able to rush the food deliverer. How does that sound?'

'Too bloody complicated, mate,' Dave said, having turned the bacon and egg sandwiches over to Amanda to finish off. 'Blacking out the cabin is good value, but forget the torch and the ensuite. Just tie a cord to the door latch to stop it being pulled wide open, push the bucket in and stay out of sight behind the door until she gets the food out, then pull it back out. She may try to either see who you are or to bust out, but I'm sure you'll have some very diabolical punishment waiting for her if she does.'

I laughed, 'OK. Good point, and I do have something lined up for her attempt to escape. I just don't want any of us getting hurt when she does. Maybe just Sandy and I will do the food runs as well.'

Sandy nodded, 'That'll work. It'll be best if she thinks there are only two of us on one boat.'

There were some protests, but finally they all saw the wisdom of keeping Miss Welsh as isolated as possible in case she did make an escape. So Dave tied a line to the mop bucket, we put a plastic bottle of fruit juice and two sandwiches heavily wrapped in paper towels to keep them warm, into the bucket before I grabbed the mike again and turned it on.

'Your breakfast is about to be delivered. There will be a penalty for any minor disobedience and attempted escape will result in terminal punishment.'

'*OK. I'll behave! I've already said I would and I've told you every-thing you asked!*'

'That is why you are getting breakfast. You have to earn your keep.'

'*Ah... crap, the same old bullshit all over again! So when you run out of questions, I have to turn it on for all the boys, is that the deal? Well, no way, jerk-off! Cause I'm sick of that gang-bang scene and having to lie down on demand for every dick wit who wants to get his rocks off! No more! You might as well toss me overboard right now and you can shove your food fair up your bum while you're at it! The condemned prisoner isn't hungry any longer!*'

I looked at Sandy and Dave and shrugged. 'As you wish. No breakfast it is. You may wish to talk later.'

I cut the mike, but kept the intercom on 'receive' so we could listen only.

'Well! That's interesting. She's been through the wringer by the sound of that. But let's eat while these bacon and egg sangers are hot. They smell fantastic!'

'But what about Brianna?' Sandy asked, a worried look on her face. 'We can't leave her without breakfast.'

'Sure we can,' I mumbled around a succulent mouthful, while wiping at an errant dribble of egg yolk that tried to make an escape down my chin. 'You heard her instructions, but I must say this tastes far better going in this end than her suggestion.'

That crass statement earned me a full 1500W Inspector Thomson glare that was probably going to see me sleeping on the daybed for a night or two.

'C'mon Sandy, when she calms down around about lunchtime with a grumbling tummy, I'll have another chat, because I want to find out what she's been told about why they're in an armed camp in the middle of a stretch of dry, red nothingness.'

My attempt at reconciliation sort of worked as I was favoured with a wintery smile.

TUESDAY, BRIDLED ISLAND, LOWENDAL ARCHIPELAGO

For safety's sake, we started a watch routine where one person stayed in the wheelhouse of *Seeker* to listen to the intercom feedback from the crew cabin for an hour at a time. It was mostly a boring detail, but there were several requests to talk to 'Mr Vader', or to scream abuse, or beg for food. She must have forgotten about the water being turned off and not saved any, since there were a number of requests for drink. But we chose to ignore her until lunchtime and apart from the watch person, we all went swimming, staying either under *Firebird*'s raised bridge deck in the cool shade or swam ashore and ran on the beach and looked for mud crab holes in amongst the mangroves.

The head of the bay where we'd anchored had quite extensive clumps of mangroves, so Dave and I fetched a couple of buckets and two fish gaffs and went probing crab holes. We were quite successful and managed to find ten of them, but four were females so we did the right thing and let them scuttle indignantly back into their holes.

While we all loved the taste of mud crab, catching the feisty big buggers was a different matter seeing that they can move very quickly and tend to object very strongly to being poked with a curved metal hook then dragged out of their half-submerged holes. They can also jump out of plastic buckets quite easily, slashing at everything within reach. Their claws are incredibly powerful and once clamped onto whatever they fancy, they won't let go, even if the claw is torn off.

We were no experts, so were very careful handling the muddy beasts.

Both cats joined in the water games to everyone's delight, with little Krazy braving the water briefly on her own a few times, but after a few minutes solo, would paddle back to her usual perch clinging to Jasper's thick neck with her head well above wave splash. Amanda had the last 'intercom watch' before lunch and had made platters of toasted sandwiches with little rolls of wafer-thin smoked salmon wrapped around smoked oysters decorating the edges of the platters. As per my instructions, she had put the two B & E sandwiches and bottle of fruit juice from breakfast in the bucket again, grinning at me as she handed it over.

'You can be a stubborn old sod sometimes can't you!'

I accessed the crew quarters via the galley and answered as I passed through, 'Yep, but I'm buggered if anyone is going to waste good food just because she's chucking a hissy fit. If she's as hungry as she says, she'll eat it!'

Sandy got on the intercom again and did the Mr Vader persona, 'Food and drink are coming. Get ready to unload the bucket. It'll only stay there for a few seconds. There will be severe consequences if you try to fuck around or get out. What's it to be? Food or starve?'

'I'll eat,' came the sullen despondent voice. 'I'm fuckin' starving and very thirsty. There's no water in the bathroom and the toilet stinks because it won't flush!'

'I told you the water would be off except for three times a day at meal time. You were supposed to save some to drink through the day, so you'd better sharpen up your memory! OK. The door is being unlocked and the bucket is coming in. Unload it quickly or it goes.'

'I'm getting it. Don't take it away yet. OK, I've got it now thanks, I think.'

I pulled the bucket clear of the door and bolted it closed again, before heading back to the saloon where Sandy handed me the mike.

'OK. You behaved, so there might be an evening meal if this continues. I'll give you a few minutes to eat then I have some more questions.'

'Terrific!' came a mumbled reply. 'I can hardly wait.'

'You'd better lose the attitude, because you *really* do not want to piss me off any more than I am! I'm so completely over all you smart-arse, greenie tree-huggers who think you're justified in bringing the country to its collective knees, just so that you can pretend you're doing the planet a favour!

When you stop pissing in each other's pockets and telling yourselves what a fantastic job you're doing, just consider the tens of thousands of people whose lives will be placed at risk when the oil, and particularly the gas supply is turned off! I'm talking about hospitals, nursing homes and every person who is sick at home and depending upon a steady supply of gas or electricity for medical appliances, heating and cooking throughout the winter!

And don't give me the bullshit argument that 'Saving the Earth' needs strong and violent action! Violent action has never solved any major problem, ever! So instead of feeling smug and self-righteous, try reading some history and see how well these half-baked, radical action plans have worked in the past! We should save ourselves a lot of trouble and just get rid of you. I've always wanted to catch a Great White shark and I'm told there are a lot of them in this area. They like live, moving bait best of all, especially if it's bleeding a bit. We'd just have to make a few nicks here and there; you'd hardly feel them. Anyway, eat up for now, while I think about what to do with you.'

When I finally wound down and put the mike down, there was a stunned silence in the crew cabin as well as around me in the saloon. Sandy came back from stowing the food bucket and put her arms around me giving me a little hug. 'Are you OK? That was very cruel, what you said. She'll be terrified.'

'Yeah, well I'm not sorry about that. I'm all right though. I'm just letting these idiots get to me and I shouldn't. I must be tired. We all know we're polluting the world by every means at our disposal, but these clowns don't realise that they're not really helping by trying to stage this radical action-plan crap. Change on the scale they're demanding is impossible within the timeframe they want. The problem is the built-in inertia of mankind's resistance to change. It makes the necessary changes to our way of life a long, slow process. It is actually happening, but apparently not fast enough to suit these fucking idiots! Corrine and I have each personally paid a steep price when we fought against similar idiots on the other side of the world, who also wanted to impose their narrow-minded ideals on everybody else, and the reality is that these greenies are no different to any other religious fanatic, now or in the past!

And as the complete opposite to true beliefs which are what each person privately believes, religions are just a set of beliefs and rules someone else has thought up and can be about origin of the species or saving the whales or exterminating ethnic minorities! The only real difference with the radical minority is that they have the necessary mix of arrogance and stupidity to feel compelled to try to force the rest of humanity to believe the same thing!'

Sandy looked thoughtful, 'So you're saying radical greenies or tree-huggers who drive spikes into tree trunks, or chain themselves to bulldozers are no different to radical fundamentalist religious wackos?'

I grinned, 'Well put. That pretty much sums it up. You always did have a way with words my sweet! So, if I sound less than concerned about the welfare of any of these misguided fools, that's why!'

She patted my arm. 'Sure Harry. But even a radical bitch needs feeding.'

'Ah yes. But first she has to 'sing a bit more for her supper' as the saying goes.'

So I wandered back to the Darth-box and climbed back into my new persona, imagining the weird, distorted voice booming and rattling around the small cabin.

'Before you were fed, you were saying you were sent to that camp and given a carbine and a uniform. Did they tell you why or what was the purpose of it all?'

'Not at first. But after a few weeks of bullshit, they said we were

all going to strike a blow for the earth by attacking some facility to do with oil or gas or something. They made it sound very exciting and for a while all us new recruits were quite keen to be getting ready to do something meaningful and effective, but then nothing happened; except all us new female recruits were told we had to service all the more experienced men or we'd be kicked out of EarthSquad and EarthCare and dumped in Onslow! And that's not the sort of place a young girl wants to be dumped! Oh, they made lots of promises about promotions and better duties, but in the end, we were just hookers at their beck and call, day or night!'

Sandy poked a face as I asked, 'Did they mention what the actual target was going to be, apart from something to do with oil or gas?'

'*Nope. We were just that we'd be heroes to the environmental movement all around the world. It made us feel special.*'

'How special do you feel right now after I've told you that all your so-called friends think you're dead and didn't bother looking for you, not even your body?'

There was the sound of a sob or two, before a soft little girl voice said, '*Pretty shitty right now. I guess I didn't make any friends in that place after all.*'

'No, it doesn't sound much like it!' I replied. 'Just out of interest, if you had the chance, would you go back there?'

'*Fuck no!*' was the emphatic answer. '*I was looking for a way out before you guys rocked up, although I'm not sure this is much of an improvement, but at least I'm not spending half my time on my back with my legs in the air! Or not so far, anyway!*'

'You don't trust anyone, do you?'

'*Why should I? Every time I do, I get screwed. Literally! As far as I'm concerned, you guys just haven't got around to it yet, but you will.*'

I gave a dry Darth Vader chuckle that raised Sandy's hackles, let alone hers. 'I hate to disillusion you, young lady, but you really aren't good enough to appeal to me, so you're safe from that. But the shark-fishing thing does interest me, so let's keep that one in mind.'

As a conversation ending, it was remarkably effective, so I killed the mike and we listened to her soft keening distress for a while, but she didn't utter anything of interest after that.

Nothing much of note happened the rest of Tuesday and the day drifted quietly and peacefully away as we swam and played with the pussies. We ate, got thoroughly pissed drinking lovely cocktails in the cockpit with the sun setting in a blaze of orange light over the low sandy, scrub covering Bridled Island and followed that with a feed of fresh-cooked mud crab. The lovely tucker was well worth the effort of catching, handling, killing and cooking the feisty creatures.

Needless to say, our captive in the forward holding cell didn't get mud crab sandwiches! Cheese and tomato were good enough for now, although she was remarkably quiet and made no complaints when her sandwiches and fruit juice were served in the bucket.

Dave had a thought to put a video camera on a broom handle and hold it through the open door when the food was delivered so we could check on her general appearance and health, but she seemed to be holding up all right. Sandy thought to toss a hair brush into the bucket and I mentioned she should ask if there was anything she urgently needed, apart from getting out of there.

CHAPTER 28

After a quiet night, with no alarms or excitement, we were startled to have breakfast interrupted by the trilling warble of the SatPhone. I was left to grab it and was delighted to hear Corrine's voice. 'Harry's Café de Wheels. How many pies do you need?

Big fella, it's so good to hear your voice, you wouldn't believe it! But for now, don't ask questions; just listen because this has to be a very quick call. There're people everywhere, including Terry, Paula and Drew, the Deputy Security head. They've chartered a Fokker 100 twinjet airliner and we're at Alice Springs Airport, re-fuelling, and expect to be landing at Onslow in about 3 hours from now. I'm too tired to work out the time difference, but you can do that.

We're bringing in 35 troops, including myself, two NCOs, a lieutenant plus the other three I've just mentioned. We'll be staying overnight in a motel in Onslow, so I'll try to get clear and call you again tonight. We expect to move up to the camp tomorrow morning on the high-speed barge they've got. Our gear goes up this afternoon. You'll get a full update on what's going on tonight. Love to all and gotta go. Bye!'

The SatPhone shut down and I was left digesting all she'd said before relaying it to the others.

'I'm sorry you couldn't speak to her, Dave, but she was in a real hurry with people all around, it was lucky we got this heads up.'

He nodded, 'Yeah. I understand. We'll catch up when we can.'

Sandy impatiently asked what they were all thinking, 'What the hell did she say, Harry? Stop fucking around!'

I gave a sheepish grin, 'Oh, yeah. Sorry. She's on the way here now with another 34 troops, including Terry, Paula and some dude named Drew who's the Deputy Head of Security.'

'Well it's great Corrine is heading this way, but we could have done without the extra 34 troops to boost the numbers in the camp. How many were there to start with?'

'Twenty-five until we nicked one,' I replied, 'so 24 plus 34 adds up to 58 that we have to look out for. Not good numbers, my dear lady.'

Sandy poked a face, 'Harry, they're fucking terrible numbers! These are para-military dudes armed with serious weapons! They'll be a lot tougher to take down than the last lot of bikies! Please tell me you've got a plan to deal with this mob!'

I was just about to say no, when my rampant imagination kicked several germs of ideas into life and they all started running around in my head at the same time. Fortunately, Sandy recognised the effect of thought overload and let me cogitate in peace.

Finally, I focussed on the present and replied to her earlier question, 'As a matter of fact, I think I have, but I need to make a couple of phone calls before I can spell it all out for you. Just talk amongst yourselves for a few minutes or so.'

That raised a few eyebrows, but they were getting used to my weird ways, so a bit of offhanded behaviour wasn't a problem. I left *Seeker* and went to *Firebird's* nav station, fired up the SatPhone and called Bob Casey, the Southport Superintendent responsible for our movements.

'Good Morning, Harry. I hope all is well with you?'

'Morning Bob. Yes, all good thank you, but I have a big favour to ask.'

'Go ahead.'

'At that first briefing you gave us in Southport, you said this operation could have the complete co-operation and support of the Australian Military. Is that offer still on the table?'

'Ah...yes, I do believe the offer would still be open since the operation is still running.'

'Excellent! You'll have to run it up the pecking order, but here's what I need.' I quickly outlined what I deemed necessary and after a bout of teeth-sucking which sounded like he was in agony, he reluctantly agreed to process my request.

'*They won't like it Harry, it's a very big step for them to be asked to operate like this.*'

'Yes, I realise that Bob, but surely being a full Commander counts for plenty? And they did say we'd have full resources at our disposal, and maybe just remind them the operation is about to kick off; big time!'

'*Yes Harry, I take your point and I will talk to the right people. Immediately! This should be loads of fun at this hour.*'

It's unlike Bob to make a joke about anything, so maybe I had lit a fire under his bum after all.

'Thanks Bob. You'll call as soon as you have the details?'

'*Yes Harry. Trust me, immediately I know more, then so will you! Please be careful and plan well.*'

As the phone terminated itself, I sat back to mentally review what I'd put in place but to me, it all seemed to fit together, even though it would count as one of my more bizarre plans.

And so I was told in no uncertain terms when I went over the broad details with the crew back in *Seeker's* cockpit.

'Geeze, Harry. You've come up with some pearlers before, but this really raises the bar!' Dave commented with a cheeky grin. 'I love it!'

As always, Dave supported my usually radical ideas without much in the way of reservation. This was in contrast with Sandy who nearly always was a counterpoint to my more outlandish plans.

I grinned at him, 'Thanks mate. But we have to start setting things up, soon as, in case Mouse comes up with an early kick-off date. Hopefully we'll find out tonight.'

Sandy looked a bit concerned. 'It could be very soon though. I mean if the extra troops are almost here, they must be planning to make the attacks within days. From what we know about the camp, it'll be bursting at the seams with the extra people in it!'

'Yep, it certainly will be, and that's a fair assessment of their intentions, which is why I want to set up our assistance package right now.'

Finally, everyone agreed that I wasn't quite the whacko I'd sounded like when I first laid out my ideas.

I spent an uneasy time waiting for the next phone call and wasn't disappointed when the SatPhone sounded off again and an officious female voice announced, *'This is an incoming call for Commander Stevens from Fleet Command Australia. Is this Commander Stevens?'*

I raised my eyebrows at her tone and speech manner, tempted to bung on a smart-arse act, but figured that maybe I was really going to speak to the top man, 'actual', so I restrained myself to a polite, 'This is Commander Stevens.'

'Connecting you with Fleet Command Australia now Commander, please go ahead.'

There was a series of clicks and hums, then a gravelly voice that generated visions of a grizzled old seadog spoke in my ear, *'Com-mander Stevens, I presume?'*

'Yessir, this is he. Thank you for your time.'

'No problem. I enjoy some fantasy early in the morning. It sets the mood for the rest of the day. Now Commander, and might I presume that your rank is not a Royal Australian Navy one?'

'That's correct, sir. I'm with the Australian Commonwealth Police on temporary duty heading a Queensland Police covert marine task force, although I am a former SAS Major.'

'Hmm. Yes, I gathered something like that. You appear to have some very high-powered associates pushing your cause Commander, but I'd better hear directly from you just exactly what's going on and what it is you want from the RAN.'

'Yes sir. This is the situation at the moment.'

I quickly outlined the situation in the form of a concise briefing, sticking with the known facts and leaving aside all speculation.

'So that's the situation to date sir, although we expect to receive an update this evening with regard to the timing for the attacks.'

'OK. That's the first part and it's raises enough questions, but how sure are you of this Intel you're getting?'

'One hundred percent reliable sir. For your ears only, we've infiltrated one of our own operatives into the EarthSquad force and they have assigned her the rank of Major with the position of 2IC. She will be the ranking officer in the Pilbara operation; although the civilian principals are coming along to see all the fun, so they can over-ride her, but they have no knowledge of military tactics and to date have relied on her very heavily.

Because of that, we know we're getting good Intel and we have the opportunity to mess around with their plans to a fair extent.'

'You said 'she'. You must have a lot of faith in this person.'

'Yes sir, I do. She was part of my squad in Afghanistan. We were both injured together in a dust-up with the Taliban.'

There was a moment's silence where I thought I heard him bellow at an aide, and then he was back.

'Christ, I hate incompetence! I'm surrounded by people who are supposed to brief me on everything, but half of them couldn't find their arses with both hands in broad daylight!

*My apologies, Major. So you're **that** Harry Stevens. It's a very great pleasure to speak with you and I have to say it changes the dynamics for me knowing you're running the show out there. So let's cut the bullshit and you tell me exactly what you want.'*

'Yes sir and thank you. Basically, I need the loan of one of your patrol boats for a few days and a skipper who will do as I ask without needing to get clearance every five minutes from your office. I'd prefer not to try to go into the fine details at this time since I haven't worked everything out just yet, but I'd like to be able to talk to the Skipper directly or even face-to-face to issue instructions. There are too many loose tongues and listening ears out there for my comfort and our safety.'

I heard him draw a deep breath.

'That's asking a great deal Major, even for you. To expect me to turn over a patrol boat and crew without knowing what you intend doing with it, although I do realise the magnitude of the threat you're facing. I might have to consider this a bit more carefully.'

'I understand, sir, but let me say we cannot afford any delay with the deployment of this asset. Consider this instead. Will you release it to my control if I undertake to brief the Skipper directly; and provided he accepts the risk and is agreeable to being under my direction, I will allow him to communicate the plan directly to you alone via a secure link?'

There was a longer pause while the SatPhone made soft little whistles and crackles in the background, then, '*Very well, Major. On those terms I will contact the nearest boat to your position and have my staff advise you of the Captain's contact details. Are you able to use the RAN's frequencies?*'

'Yes Sir. I have a full suite of frequencies and encryption devices.'

'*OK. That sounds interesting. I'd like to talk to you further when this is all over, but in the meantime you can expect a call from my XO shortly and I'm holding you to the briefing of the Skipper. I can assure you, the shit will fly thick and fast if you fuck-up one of my boats!*'

I swallowed, the threat of retribution by a Rear Admiral being something even the two letters 'VC' after my name couldn't protect me from.

'Fully understood sir and thank you.'

The connection cut immediately as I let out a big breath before heading out to tell the crew that we might just have our very own patrol boat to play with. Sort of!

CHAPTER 29

It was late afternoon following a slow lunch which was eaten with some the crew sitting on the stern-board of *Seeker* and the rest of us floating in the water beside it. It was an even slower afternoon spent splashing around the back of the two boats and playing with the kitties who relished the extra attention. The one bit of excitement was when a small yacht puttered into the bay where we occupied the north eastern-most corner, took one look before turning around and heading further south down the eastern face of Bridled Island then anchored. Being nearly a kilometre away, they hardly intruded on our solitude.

As the day wore on, the whole crew was getting edgy, knowing the clock was definitely ticking, with Corrine and her troops now on the ground at Onslow, and their gear on the way up to the camp.

Despite the other yacht further down the island, we decided to send *Dragonfly* out to have a look and being a bright afternoon with clear skies, I suggested to Sandy and Amanda that they set 3000 feet as the cruise altitude. The extra height certainly avoided attention, while the sharp high definition video showed a camp humming with activity as all hands pitched in to unload the 50-foot work barge tied up at the wharf.

There was a steady stream of movement to and from the wharf as they worked to stow all the extra equipment and supplies in their proper places. We noticed a lot of extra tents were being erected to house the new troops due to arrive the next morning. I also checked that the four camouflaged RIBs were present beside the stubby wharf, as well as the half cabin fishing boat tucked under the mangrove branches further up the little creek.

With the un-detected UAV safely homeward bound, the Sat-Phone sounded off again and I was again tempted to be a smartarse when answering it, but as there is no indication of caller ID on these things, I behaved myself. Well, everyone behaves differently under stress and this was one of my quirks.

'Hello.'

'Is that Commander Stevens?'

'It is. Who are you?'

'My name is Lieutenant Commander Zellman. I'm the XO for Fleet Command Australia and he has given me an odd set of instructions which I hope mean something to you. I'm to tell you that Lieutenant Commander Henderson of the HMAS Broome *may be reached on this SatPhone number—064 8816 978 59567. I am further instructed to tell you that HMAS Broome is currently at Broome on a good-will visit to her naming port, but is scheduled to depart on Friday to return to regular patrol duties. There is one final part of the message. Lieutenant Commander Henderson has been instructed to comply with any reasonable request from you with regard to establishing a face-to-face meeting in a timely manner.*

I do hope that all this means something to you Commander, although I asked Fleet Command to repeat most of the message.'

'Thank you, Lieutenant-Commander for passing the message and please extend my thanks to the Rear Admiral for his faith. Tell him I'll not let him down.'

'Now I understand even less, Commander but I will do as you say. Good evening, Sir.'

As the SatPhone went through its disconnection cycle, I looked over the message I'd scrawled on some scrap paper and thought 'no time like the present!' Someone should be awake—it's a boat after all.

Turning the phone on again, I dialled the number for *HMAS Broome* and was rewarded with a warbling ring tone, followed by a crisp female voice.

'HMAS Broome. How may I help you?'

'This is Commander Stevens for Lieutenant-Commander Henderson, please.'

'*Yes, sir, patching you through.*'

There was a brief period of relative quiet, then over a noisy background a male voice said, '*Hello?*'

Gritting my teeth to hold back a rude remark, I asked again, 'Lieutenant-Commander Henderson please.'

'*Oh, yeah sure. Hang on, here he is.*'

The background noise immediately faded and a crisp voice said, '*This is Lieutenant-Commander Henderson. Who's calling please?*'

'This is Commander Stevens. I believe you had a conversation with Fleet Command Australia a little earlier?'

'*Ahh, yes Sir, I most certainly do recall that conversation. I received some very strange instructions from the Rear Admiral, some of which I'm not very happy about.*'

I bristled slightly at his tone. 'I trust one of the instructions you **are** happy about is the one which says you should try very hard to achieve a face-to-face meeting with me ASAP and then report the outcome to the Rear Admiral.'

He backed off the attitude a bit, apparently recognising I wasn't going to meekly go away. '*Yessir. That one seemed entirely logical and I'll be happy to do what it takes to link up with you. We wind-up our Naming Port courtesy visit on Friday and are scheduled to return to regular patrol duties. Perhaps arrangements can be made after that, to meet somewhere on our patrol route, although I have to warn you that we might be heading straight out to the Christmas Island area. I reckon it might make it a bit difficult to have this meeting, but we'll see what my orders are.*'

By now, frustration with this complacent, condescending idiot was making me angry and Sandy who'd followed me over the *Firebird* to sit with me recognised the signs and shook her head in warning. 'Tell me Lieutenant-Commander; are there any other patrol boats in the area?'

'*Yessir, there is another boat, the Glenelg. I know her Skipper,*'

Lieutenant-Commander Davy and she was due to sail from our Darwin base a couple of days after us. Her patrol route should have her in this area about now, since she was heading down as far as Exmouth before swinging north to Ashmore Reef. May I ask why you needed that information?'

Under Sandy's calming hand, I took several deep breaths and prepared to shut this patronising prick down.

'Yes Lieutenant-Commander, you may well ask why I need the services of another Captain. Regrettably, I find you would be totally unsuitable for the vital mission I have been tasked with, and shall be informing the Rear Admiral when I call him in a few minutes to request the services of *HMAS Glenelg*. I hope you enjoy the remainder of your time in port and have a safe and uneventful patrol.'

There was an excited rush of words from the speaker as the errant Commander tried to stop me hanging up.

'Ahh…Can you wait a moment please Sir, before you take action like that? If I've given the wrong impression, I apologise most sincerely. I didn't realise there was an important mission which had to be carried out, and I'd like the chance to be able to assist you in everyway possible. Can we start this all over again?'

With a twisted grin at Sandy I replied, 'Disappointingly Lieutenant-Commander, you have already shown you have an inflexible attitude towards change and I stand by my assessment that your attitude and patronising manner renders you totally unsuitable to be involved in the mission for which I required the personal intervention of Fleet Command Australia. Please excuse me now, as I have to call the Rear Admiral and start the selection process all over again. Goodbye.'

Sandy clapped as I hung up. 'Well said! What a prick he was, being so smug and patronising. I hope the Rear Admiral gets stuck into him.'

I grinned, 'Yeah, he will. I reckon it'll take about 10 minutes after my next call before he develops a new body orifice! There's no way that total arsehole would fit into what we need done. Anyway, I'd better start the process over again, but at least I should be able to go direct to the Admiral. Let's see.'

18:00 LOCAL, *FIREBIRD*, BRIDLED ISLAND

'*Commander Stevens…unless you're suddenly in command of one of my boats, I'd hoped not to hear from you tonight. What's the problem now?*'

'Sorry to trouble you again sir, but I have to report that Lieutenant-Commander Henderson would be totally unsuitable to carry out the mission as I require. He also displayed an unfortunate attitude problem which would have ruled him out anyway. He did volunteer the name of Lieutenant Commander Davy who should be in this area in *HMAS Glenelg*. May I request his contact details, please?'

The Admiral was silent for a moment. '*I've checked up on you since we last spoke, Commander Stevens and I'm prepared to trust your judgement, although Mitch Henderson is a very experienced Skipper.*'

'He may well be sir, but he's temperamentally unsuited to the job I need done, so in that respect he's utterly useless. With respect, Sir.'

The Admiral chuckled. '*I was told you don't pull too many punches Commander, and I appreciate that. I also gather time is running out, so I've got Glenelg's number here. Based on your feelings about Mitch Henderson, I think Paul Davy might be just the man you're looking for. Let's hope so anyway, because I'm running out of boats for you to chat to.*'

The number he carefully read out was just a few digits off the one I had for the *HMAS Broome*, so after thanking him again, I hung up, then waited the requested 10-minutes while he spoke to his man, Paul Davy.

When I called the *Glenelg*, once again a female sailor answered crisply, '*HMAS Glenelg, how may I help you?*'

'Lieutenant Commander Davy, please. This is Commander Stevens.'

'*Yessir, one moment please…*'

'*Commander Stevens, this is Paul Davy. I've just spoken with*

Admiral Stallman and he says you might have some work for us. How may I be of assistance?'

'Good to talk to you Commander and yes, I do have a bit of a job for you, but whether you want it or not will only be decided after we meet up. What's your location, please?'

'The plot shows that we are 96 nautical miles northeast of Port Hedland and we're tracking 245° at 15 knots.'

'Standby one, Commander.'

'Glenelg standing by.'

I quickly consulted the chart and plotted his position, looking ahead for a suitable rendezvous point, discovering that North Turtle Island would be ideal, particularly at night, unless there were other boats already there. But if we thought it was a problem, we could always check it by sending *Dragonfly* out to have a look.

I called Dave over, 'What's the best speed *Seeker* could make in this breeze and sea condition?'

He looked at the readouts on *Firebird's* nav station panel which showed a steady southerly at 10 to 12 knots. 'There'll still be some swell out there, but running with it we should be able to hold 55 to 60 knots without shaking our teeth out. Where do you want to go?'

I laid a finger on the chart, 'Right about there. It's called North Turtle Island and I'd like to get there ASAP.'

Dave looked and measured. 'Allowing for the time to get clear of the shoals around here, the run should take about 3 hours.'

'OK. It's just on 18:45 now, so we could be there at 21:45. Go get *Seeker* fired up while I organise the Navy to be there as well.'

Dave left at a run, or as much as you can on any boat smaller than a cruise ship, while I picked up the SatPhone handset.

'Glenelg this is *Firebird,* still with us?

'Still here Firebird. *Go ahead."*

'Commander, we're going to have a private meeting in three hours time. If you look at your plot, you'll see an island up ahead called North Turtle Island. It is 29 miles bearing 026° from Port Hedland. It doesn't have much in the way of an anchorage, but we both should be able to drop a pick in the lee on the northern side. Because it's such a lousy anchorage, there shouldn't be any other boats overnighting there.

'Can you organise yourselves to be there in three hours?'

A genuine laugh came from the handset, *'I think the Navy can manage that, Commander. We'll see you then. Glenelg clear.'*

I hung up and made a quick check of who wanted to go and who was staying. It ended up that Sandy, Amanda, Jasper and Krazy kitten stayed to look after *Firebird* while the rest of us scrambled over to *Seeker* where Dave had the diesels rumbling, the anchor raised and just a single bow line attaching it to *Firebird* which was quickly dropped off. With the radar operating in close-range mode and both the depth and scanning sonars painting a three-dimensional picture of the sea floor below and out in front for 600 metres, we moved out of the anchorage as Dave checked actual radar bearings with the chart plotter to keep it honest, which wasn't always the case.

Once clear of the confines of the bay and sure of our position, he warned everyone to sit or hang on and smoothly opened the throttles to 75% power.

The grumbling of the twin MTU 2600-horsepower V-16 diesels was replaced by a rising roar, then a glorious bellow that shouted defiance across the quiet, evening ocean as twin white rooster-tails of water-jet thrust rose higher than the cabin top behind us.

Within moments the digital water speed indicator showed nearly 50 knots as we shot out between the islands of the Lowendal Archipelago before turning slightly left to a course of 077° for the 193 nautical mile run to North Turtle Island.

Seeker sat stable and almost level as we thundered across the small sea swell, the hull hardly moving; such was the brilliance of the Italian design, so after a few minutes to make sure all was well, Dave reached over to a sub-panel on the right of the main panel, turned a key and pressed a green button with no discernible effect. Thirty seconds later after checking several gauges, Dave slowly advanced a small lever poking up like a finger from the sub-panel and finally a rising whistle was heard above the bellowing thunder of the diesels, although it sounded almost effeminate by comparison to the macho bass thunder of the diesels.

The effect it had on the boat was anything but effeminate however, as the stern sucked a bit lower in the water and quickly grew a third white rooster-tail that rose above the other one's either side of it. The other effect on the boat was to cause the water speed indicator to steadily rise past 60 knots until it hovered around 70 knots or 130 km/h as a significant portion of the 5500-horsepower available from the gas-turbine was unleashed.

A gale of wind exceeding that of a Category 3 cyclone was swirling around the cockpit, threatening to drag any unsuspecting soul or unsecured gear out of the boat. With a struggle, I slid the two heavy glass doors at the rear of the saloon closed and the relief from the scream of the turbine and howling of the diesels was an incredibly stark contrast. Dave turned around with a manic grin on his face.

'This is the fastest I've ever gone in open water and she's riding flat and smooth. I might try to go a bit faster since she's riding so well. Corrine's going to go ape-shit when she finds out we're doing this!'

He moved the little lever a bit more and the scream obligingly escalated, pushing the speed needle towards 80 knots! At this speed the howl of the engines was nearly drowned out by the scream of the wind past the wheelhouse, as it probed with hard, scrabbling little fingers of racing air at every tiny crack, each one producing its own scream of energy.

'How long can we keep this up for?' I spoke loudly into Dave's ear after thirty minutes at that speed, a silly grin still plastered onto his face as he jammed himself into the dual helm seat and held the tiny wheel very carefully.

'As long as we like if nothing gets in front of us,' he yelled back. 'We have to make a slight jig around Legendre Island off Karratha, but we can go as close as we want there, so it's almost a straight shot for North Turtle Island. The diesels are at 75% power and the turbine is still only 70% usable power so there's no strain there.'

I looked at the speed indicator again. 'Maybe we should back off just a little bit, say to 70 knots. That's still pretty awesome!'

Dave nodded, 'Yeah. You're right. This is a bit crazy, but shit! It's brilliant fun! Corrine is going to love it! I reckon we could top 90 knots in flat conditions and that's not too shabby for a 100-footer that weighs about 90 tonne!'

He pulled the turbine throttle back a trifle and let the boat slow to 70 knots which dropped the noise level a lot and it made the boat feel a lot less nervous, even though we were still rushing toward our rendezvous at a crazy speed for open water.

With the chart plotter and the radar in agreement, we roared past Port Hedland way off our starboard side with just the faintest loom of its lights showing above the horizon. Little Turtle Islet was just a blip on radar off to starboard while North Turtle was right on the bow. I reminded Dave that I'd asked Commander Davy to anchor on the north east side of the oddly-formed island with the dry land portion completely surrounded by a very shallow, circular reef.

CHAPTER 30

SEEKER, WEDNESDAY NIGHT, BRIDLED ISLAND TO NORTH TURTLE ISLAND

Dave pulled the turbine throttle back before we reached the island, letting the engine cool down for a couple of minutes before shutting it down. The speed quickly dropped back to sane levels again, although the speed readout still showed around 40 knots, which seemed like idling compared to the pace we'd been maintaining earlier.

Finally, two hours and fifty minutes after leaving Bridled Island, we swung around the west side of the flat piece of reef and dry land and Dave throttled the diesels back to idle, letting them cool. We'd already spotted the lights of a long, low boat riding at anchor, surprisingly close in to the reef edge and commented that the thing was lit up like a cruise ship with spot lights and flood lights everywhere.

When I'd spoken to Commander Davy earlier, we'd agreed on a short-range UHF radio frequency to use, which was well away from the usual marine band, so with the radio already fired up, I found the right mike and made the call.

'*Glenelg, Glenelg*, this is *Seeker, Seeker*, how copy?'

'*Seeker, Seeker, this is* Glenelg *actual. Go ahead.*'

'I propose to anchor 50 metres off your starboard quarter. Then it's my place or yours.'

A chuckle preceded the reply. '*How about your place. Our radar indicated some serious, if not impossible speeds on approach, so I'm curious to see what that thing is and also, we might have more privacy. This bridge crew are a very nosy bunch.*'

There were some background noises which could have been well-blown raspberries and general protests indicating a relaxed

"

but competent crew.

'Roger that. Come on over when you're ready.'

'*Will do; Glenelg clear.*'

By the time we'd anchored, secured the engines and brewed up some decent coffee, Dave mentioned we'd forgotten all about Brianna Welsh, our captive in the bow cabin.

'Oh, fuck! I didn't give her a thought!'

'Not your fault,' he replied, 'I'm the Skipper and should have included her on my checklist!'

'Is she still alive?'

'Oh, yeah!' he poked a face. 'I reckon there must be a few dents in the door by now.'

I had a few moments where I felt really bad about forgetting her, but then reality kicked in and I thought of the havoc these idiots had planned. That quickly helped me rationalise that it was the rush to get to a meeting with what we hoped would be a main defensive element against them, which had made me forget all about her.

Anyway, as I went to meet and greet our visitor at the blunt end, Dave, Alf and Melissa went forward through the galley to the bow cabin with a powerful torch, a pillowcase to use as a blindfold and gaffer tape for a gag and handcuffs if necessary. As a last resort, they had Corrine's little knockout kit.

'Do whatever you have to,' I said emphatically, 'but keep her absolutely quiet for at least a couple of hours or until the patrol boat skipper leaves. We don't want to have to explain keeping a prisoner, in case they feel obligated to take some sort of action. Knocking her out might be best, because we'll probably stay the night here after all this. Another high-speed run locked in the cabin would probably kill the silly bitch.'

So while Dave and Alf did what they could to quieten Brianna, I stood on *Seeker's* broad stern board watching one of *Glenelg's* 24-foot RHIB attack craft, motor the 50 metres over to us. I was pleased to see the Skipper had elected to dress down for the occasion and was wearing his workday SW12 Disruptive Pattern Navy Uniform.

He was tall and slim, with an open, smiling face and a shock of bright red hair that was a lot longer than his superiors would probably like. His boat crew nosed the mean-looking RHIB, complete with a mounted .50 calibre machine gun, up against the stern, letting him step easily and lightly onto *Seeker's* stern board where I was waiting to greet him. The RHIB crew backed off and hovered around until he waved them back to the patrol boat.

He grinned at my sea-going uniform of ragged shorts and an old red T-shirt faded to a dusky pink and soft as silk from hundreds of washings.

'Commander Stevens, I presume?'

I grinned back, taking an instant liking to his easy manner and ready smile, 'At your service, Commander. Welcome aboard.'

From there on, it was Harry and Paul as I led him up to the cockpit and introduced him to Tracy and Charlie. All was quiet up front, so Dave, Alf and Melissa must have been doing a good job.

I offered him tea or coffee and when Tracy served that, she and Charlie went down below to the galley lounge area to give us some privacy. I suggested a tour of the boat, but he declined, saying, 'I want to look over the boat later, particularly the engine room, but for now I just need to hear what's happening down here which requires the services of a patrol boat and what part I get to play. The Rear Admiral wants to be called directly as soon as I have heard the proposition and made a decision.'

'Good oh. That was the deal I made,' I said, 'so here's the deal for you, but when considering the proposition, you must bear in mind there is a strong political element in all of this. The Western Australian Government is shaping up for major embarrassment by allowing a bunch of eco-terrorists to set up camp right in the middle of the biggest collection of oil and gas fields in Australia and virtually paying them to do so.'

He nodded understanding before I stepped him through the whole situation, as we knew it, right up to Corrine's morning phone call and the UAV over flight of the camp that afternoon. I also mentioned we were expecting another call from her at anytime soon. I was about to explain his part in the operation, when the SatPhone rang.

'Speak of the devil,' I said lightly to Paul, digging it out of my carry bag. Taking a chance, I hit the right buttons and said, 'Hi Mouse. How's it going?'

'*Smart arse! Hi Harry, I'm going well, but I still have to keep this short. The deputy security dude, Drew Tallman has taken a personal interest in me and stays fairly close. The Sit-Rep is our gear and supplies have been taken to the camp and we're due out on the work barge at 08:00 tomorrow.*

I discussed the kick-off with Paula and Terry on the way over and they want to go ASAP, like in the next day or two. However, I've convinced them of the impossibility of that date because I need some time to integrate both sets of troops, select the three separate assault squads and then do some training with them. This is where I need to hear what you've got planned to counter all this and when you want me to set the kick-off day for.'

'Copy that. Stand-by a moment please Mouse.'

I looked over at Paul. 'You're going to hear some of the finer details of the operation that I haven't even told my crew yet, so if you decide not to join in the operation, I'd appreciate your silence. The Admiral doesn't need to know either, so your message to him would be that you deem the risk to your boat and crew to be unjustified and I'll try to think of another way to get help to deal with these people.'

Paul smiled gently, 'Why don't you just get on with the briefing and let me work out what I'm going to do. This all sounds way too fascinating and your young lady is waiting.'

I gave him a hard look which reminded him that patrol boat skippers might be king of the heap on their own bridge, but there were bigger and nastier dogs around and I was one of the biggest and nastiest in this area.

'Sorry Mouse. I have a gentleman with me who may or may not

be willing to assist us, although I've had to promise a 2-star Admiral I'd let him make the decision alone once he heard the facts. But there's one important question you can answer first. Have the EarthSquad troops been told of their targets yet?'

'*Yes, they've been told. Paula briefed them on the flight over. Why is that important?*'

'I'll explain in a moment, but I need to know how they reacted when they learned of the targets and the overall objectives?'

'*Most went off their tits with excitement. Bloody near foaming at the mouth, the fuck-wits. Or to put it in a way that my dear Sainted Mother would respect, the news was very well received and nearly all were very enthusiastic and couldn't wait to start shooting and blowing things up!*'

'Hang on. You said, 'nearly all'. Does this mean that some are against the plan?'

'*There are two who I'm certain won't go along with the plan and strangely enough, they are my XO, Lieutenant Towson and his girlfriend Sergeant Hegarty. I'm pretty sure they can be easily turned away from the Dark Side, but I'd like to pull them out with me regardless. It's quite possible there will be another, a Corporal who came over with us.*'

'Great! That's the info I wanted. Anyway, the plan depends on this gentleman here to look after the off-shore platforms, while we attend to the processing plant defence.'

'*How the fuck are you going to organise that? You do realise we'll be fielding 59 heavily armed troops to take and hold three targets? I haven't worked out the split of numbers yet, but that'll happen in the next couple of days once I see what the other 25 are like.*'

'Don't worry about that too much, its big Navy muscle I'm trying to get. But tell me the calibre of the ones you got with you?'

'*Generally very ordinary, although there are a few outstanding ones. Most are just mercenaries who've been kicked out for incompetence, brutality or both. I deliberately kept a few hopeless ones, but they won't really affect the outcome with the numbers they've got. I'm really afraid we're outnumbered on this one Harry, so you'd better dig deep into that big bag of dirty tricks or we're going down!*'

'Working on it, my dear Mouse, as we speak; but the plan is really very simple. Because we have to keep this whole mess low profile, we take all the attack boats out well before they get within range of civilisation, let alone near the targets. I just need some time to co-ordinate the timing and weapon systems. Look, this is Wednesday night and you won't be in camp until tomorrow. Then you reckon you'll need at least two or three days to integrate the two sets of troops, so what's the latest you can postpone the raids?'

Her reply was swift and confident, 'I'd need a month of Sunday's to get this bunch of fuckwits ready for a piss-up, let alone do some actual fuckin' fighting, but I'm going to tell Paula that we move out on the evening of next Monday, which is five days away. Will that suit you and your plans?'

I glanced at Paul who had his whole attention riveted to the phone. 'Yeah, that should be plenty but regardless, I'll make it suit, thanks Mouse. But don't you forget to plan your escape. Let us know where you're going to be on Monday so we can have an extraction ready. There'll be no good guys going down with this shit-wreck!'

'Understand and concur most heartily, Harry.'

'Very good. I won't be able to contact you, so please call when you can to let us know the latest schedule, plan of attack and division of numbers.'

'Will do, but it will probably be a text message for safety. See ya, Big Dog!'

I shut the phone down and laid it on the cockpit table, where Paul eyed it carefully.

'Not only should a civilian not be able to get that series of Sat-Phone, but that particular model is several ahead of what the Navy has. I don't suppose you're going to tell me exactly who you are?'

I grinned disarmingly, 'Personally it might be best to leave it a bit murky for now, although the name is my own. What I can tell you is that this boat, and my own back at our lay-up site and the eight crew, comprises the Special Marine Strike Force; an official covert unit of the Queensland Police Service.'

Paul looked really puzzled. 'Hang on. Police. Two boats and eight crew? Is that it? What about the lovely Tracy and Charlie who I just met? Where do they fit in?'

'They're part of the eight crew. Five of them are Police Officers and have trained to the equivalent of the SAS. I know since I used to be part of that organisation.'

He looked thoughtful again. 'I've heard of a Harry Stevens, ex SAS, but he dropped off the grid a few years back. Probably just what a careful ex Major and VC winner would do if he were to join the spooks and head up covert special units staffed liberally with lovely young females as cover. It's an honour to meet you, Major.'

I waved the compliments away as un-necessary, but he carried on. 'OK. Your inside girl is high-ranking, so that's a great advantage, but as she says, they have fifty-nine warm bodies to your eight. I'm not much of a gambler, but those are terrible odds. What can we do to balance things up?'

I eyed him off, checking for genuine enthusiasm. 'Are you offering to help without knowing what it is I want you to do?'

'Almost, but not quite. So, if you do want help then stop fucking around and tell me!'

CHAPTER 31

I'd been trying to decide how much to tell him, but there really wasn't anyway to hold information back, so I told him the full plan as I saw it.

'OK. As I have said, there'll be two separate attacks on the offshore production platforms. From what our UAV has shown of the camp, they have four 25 foot RIBs and a 50 foot work barge capable of quite high speed in low seas. We spotted what looked like a 25 foot half-cabin fishing boat with a very large outboard on the stern tucked back up the main access creek, but I can't see that taking part in any of the attacks.

I expect one RIB will be sent to each platform, while the work barge and the other two RIBs will be sent to hit the on-shore gas plant and the loading facility. There's no ship docked there at the moment, but that could change by kick-off time next Monday night.'

'OK. And my role is?'

'Your role is to take out the two RIBs attacking the offshore platforms, long before they get within range. It won't be good enough to arrest them when they board, because they can't be held incommunicado for too long, because word will leak out to the press and its game over. Both the State and Federal Governments will be tipped out and the Australian political scene will be in chaos for years with the Labour Party running the country uncontrolled and on yet another of their spending orgies, buying votes.'

Paul nodded, 'I can appreciate how that could happen, but if we stop them reaching the platform, what do we do with them after that. I do have a refugee holding compartment, but then what? Who do I turn them over to if nothing is supposed to leak out about the raid in the first place? There'd be too many loose tongues to expect total silence.'

I waited a moment to see if he'd make the connection, but he didn't. 'The short answer Paul, is that you can't turn them over to anybody without risking a media blowout. There can be no survivors.'

He looked stricken. 'Bloody hell Harry, that's not what we're here for.'

I shook my head, 'Sorry, I hate to disagree with you Paul, but from where I sit, that's *exactly* what you're here for. To defend Australia from those who would do the country harm, whether internally or externally. And these people positively do intend to cause harm to Australia!

I should add that all of them are mercenaries, in it just for the money, despite the lofty ideals spouted by their so-called 'spiritual leader', Terry bloody Williams. And on top of that, 95% of them are foreigners.

Now you heard Corrine say there are two or perhaps three, who are worth saving, but the rest have to be toast. This is why I had to keep the Admiral out of the loop since he needs to be able to deny any knowledge of this mess. You and I, however, are paid to be at the coalface and get to do the fun, dirty work!'

He still looked unhappy. 'Is this the sort of shit you had to put up with in Afghanistan? I mean, so far in my career my orders have been fairly benign, even with the odd intercepted boatload of refugees. I've never been expected to deliberately wipe out people.'

'It will probably make it easier, Paul, when these people start shooting back at you and your crew with deadly intent. They will not be messing around and you will have to tell your crew that. With respect, may I guess you haven't faced live, hostile fire before?'

He shook his head, 'Nah! Refugees might be potentially danger-ous, but they don't shoot at RAN patrol boats. They tend to save that violence bullshit for when the pollies have given them a house and a pension for life. And Indonesian trepang fishermen don't shoot back either.'

The last was said with a slight chuckle, so I dared to entertain a hope that he might be willing to embrace my plan.

'Well. I did it for a living for too bloody long and I can assure you that the experience wears very thin, very quickly! So that's the guts of it, Paul. We'll be able to put our UAV overhead to feed you live video as to their movements, then you need to use all the resources available on your boat to intercept, and take out the entire raiding party. All you have to do is tell your crew they are weapons-free from the get-go to return hostile fire with everything they have. And don't forget to make the point that these clowns won't give up and will need to be ruthlessly put down. No prisoners!'

He still looked unhappy at the prospect, so I went on.

'You'll have to come up with the Captain's pre-action motivational speech and you may have to say a few words afterwards to calm the odd ruffled conscience, but really, you just expect your crew to do their duty. If you'd like me to talk to your XO, I'll be happy to'.

He looked up with more resolve in his expression, 'No problem, Harry. I'm on-board with it, although I'd like my XO in on all future briefings, if that's OK. Now you've explained the situation fully, I can see 'the what **and** the why', so I'll tell the Admiral it's a go. I might as well do that now from here.'

He pulled what looked like the junior twin of my SatPhone from one of his voluminous pockets and fired it up. The number must have been programmed as a speed dial because he was connected within a minute.

'Good evening, Sir.'

'...Yes Sir, and I'm still with Commander Stevens as we speak.'

'...No Sir. No problems and I wish to advise that I'm happy with the mission information Commander Stevens has given me, and am willing to accept his directives and take on this task.'

'...Yes sir, I understand and accept it without reservations.'

'...Unfortunately, not at this time sir, since there are several security considerations that mean it would be best if I did not communicate that knowledge right now, but I believe I will be able to before long.'

'...Thank you sir, I was hoping you would and I do appreciate it. I'll put Commander Stevens on. One moment.'

'Good evening Admiral, this is Commander Stevens.'

'Your powers of persuasion are impressive, Commander. Lieutenant Commander Davy is not noted for taking undue risks. I thought you would fail to convince him, but you must have made a convincing case.'

'Thank you, sir, although I prefer to suggest the case sold itself. Saves me from making up embellishments.'

*'Very well Commander. You seem to have achieved the impossible by gaining control of one of my boats and left me hanging by 'the whatever's', still not knowing what's going on, but if you bend my boat or **any** of my people, I'll be a **very** unhappy 2-star. Copy?'*

'Yes sir, copy and sorry about the security clampdown. However, if plans work out well, I'll personally brief you fully about the operation. Will that be acceptable?'

'Obviously, that will have to do Commander, since I've just had my boss remind me I have to go along with whatever you ask. I'm not used to that level of power resting with a Commander, so you'd better live up to your reputation or else get yourself promoted up to my level.'

A solid click and various noises indicated that he'd hung up, so I handed the thing back to Paul who disconnected his phone before letting out a big breath. 'It's not every day that a humble Lieutenant-Commander gets to tell an Admiral to back off and keep his trap shut. And as for you? Bloody hell, big balls, Harry! How the hell did you get the Admiral of the Fleet, telling a 2-star Admiral he has to do what you say? Unbelievable! I feel that I should be saluting you all the time.'

I grinned, 'Give it a rest, Paul. You're being a goose.'

He grinned back and saluted, 'Yessir!'

I laughed, 'Welcome to my world. I get to tell Admirals and

Generals what to do all the time. It can get quite addictive as well as being good fun!'

We enjoyed a good laugh together at the Admiral's expense, before he sobered up and said, 'OK Harry. As I seem to have placed my boat under your indirect control, what's the plan for my movements?'

I stood, grinning with relief and shook his hand. 'Welcome aboard. You've just taken a huge load off my shoulders, especially as I don't have a Plan B at this stage!'

'Now as far as the operation goes, the objectives for your targets are 63 miles bearing 343° from where I'm based at the moment, and that location is 39 miles bearing 340° of their camp. That means the track from the camp to the target platforms runs right past our laying-up location.

At this stage, I'd like you to come south to our anchorage, so we can plan our movements face-to-face, and you'll be in a good ambush position. We can also supply you with live info from our UAV, which should help. Corrine will give us the heads-up when the launch is scheduled, but before then, you'll pre-position on the track just out from where we are, then deploy your two RHIBs to head back east to intercept them. If the RHIBs happen to miss one or both, you'll still have a shot with the main boat.

We can cover you with our UAV to make sure there are no problems and that should give you a good advantage.'

Paul asked. 'So how far is it from Bridled Island to the camp?'

'Just 38 nautical miles,' I replied, 'although for our work, we have to travel 64 miles to Onslow if, unfortunately, we have to go all the way.'

He nodded. 'Thirty-eight miles seems reasonable, but you're right that we'd need to be lying in wait ahead of them to be sure of stopping them. The main boat couldn't catch those RIBs if they get in front of us, although my RHIBs can and the .50 calibre is very effective against soft targets.

That sounds good for the preliminary, and I want to go over it in more detail with you and my XO in the next day or two. But tell me about this UAV you keep mentioning. We've got a couple of drones, but they're only good for about 20 minutes flight time at best and aren't very fast so they can't go far. The way you're talking, this thing can cover some territory?'

I chuckled at his scepticism. 'You can have a look at it anytime you want; it's on-board although it might be better to see it in daylight. But to give you a better idea of what it can do, here's a sample mission. It can fly out 150 kilometres, loiter over a target at max endurance low speed for 5 hours, then return home with stabilised 1080 HD colour and IR video recorded on-board, while a stream of 1080 HD still-snapshots have been sent back via the satellite linkup. It has up to 8 hours endurance, which is naturally speed dependant, vertical take-off and landing, full autonomous flight including auto land and take-off and return-to-home. There's an 80-knot top speed with extended hover capability, Electro/Optical and Infrared stabilised cameras, up to 75 kilometre full HD data-link range or Sat-link for hi-res snapshots, or 500GB on-board video or data storage. There's more, but I'll get Amanda, our expert, to go over it with you and your XO when we get back to Bridled Island.'

Paul looked suitably impressed. 'That sounds incredible. I'm on a Committee that assesses UAV and drone developments for the Navy and we've never heard of anything like that. What you've just described is the UAV at the top of our wish list, but the experts tell us we won't see it for several years! Yet, you say that you've got this capability now?'

I grinned at his disbelief and slight outrage that a civilian group should have better technology than the Military. '*Dragonfly* is down below right now and does all that and probably more stuff that I've forgotten, but we'll show you tomorrow. Don't worry, it's real and we've got it!'

He didn't want to let go of the UAV and asked, 'But where did it come from? I mean, like who made it? The Chinese? I know they're doing some good things with UAVs.'

I laughed, 'I'll get Amanda to fill you in on the fine details, but it's a great story.'

It was designed and built here in Australia by a retired helicopter pilot and life-long aero-modeller who lives in country New South Wales. He proposed the concept to several organisations, but they told him he was dreaming. One company rejected his ideas outright because he didn't have an Aeronautical Engineering degree and consequently couldn't possibly know what he was talking about.

So apparently, being a stubborn old bastard, he told them all to get stuffed and went ahead and built the prototype himself. Amanda used to work with him at some stage and kept in touch after he retired, so he loaned her the prototype to do his beta field-testing. We used it on a job earlier this year and it worked perfectly. This one we have now is the MKII version, with more range and is a bit faster, with some more space for payload items and a better layout for the cameras. There are several other improvements, but Amanda can tell you about those.'

Paul was shaking his head in wonder. 'How come we've never heard of this UAV?'

'This is the only one he's released. He's really only just refined the design and being a bit anal about it, he didn't want to start producing it until everything worked properly. I believe Amanda spoke with him recently and he said that he's finally hooked up with a small company to go into limited production, maybe 6 or 8 per year.'

'If it can do only half of what you claim, it's a giant leap ahead of anything the Military has in service right now or even planned. The trouble is, we've never heard of this fellow or his UAV.'

'Well, I think you'd would want to find out all about him after you see *Dragonfly* in action tomorrow.'

I checked the time and was surprised to see that it was 01:15, which explained why my crew had disappeared. 'As this is now Thursday, let's get some sleep and head down the coast for Bridled Island in the morning. There'll be all the time you want to play UAVs, but your crew might appreciate some leisure time there, although there's no pub or any social life. The fishing is terrific and the mud crabs superb, so that might help a bit. You've got 21 crew in total, I believe?'

Paul nodded, 'Yep, 21 including myself. And you're right; they would appreciate a few lay days. We've been moving non-stop for ten days now on 24-hour watches, so a rest on a deserted island without a pub will be very good. So how far from here to Bridled Island?'

'Just on 193 miles and it's almost a straight shot with a slight kink to the west to clear Legendre Island off Karratha, so is that going to take you around 10 hours at cruise speed?'

'I know Legendre Island and 10 hours for us is about right. You look like you'd be quicker. What does this thing cruise at?'

I grinned, 'We made the run up in 2 hours 50 minutes!'

Paul's jaw dropped comically as he quickly did some basic sums in his head, 'Bullshit! There's no way this thing can be that fast!'

I had a sudden thought and grinned at him. 'If you trust your XO to run your boat, why not do part of the trip with us. Let your XO take *Glenelg* out and head off on course, while you stay here with us for a few hours. Then we'll do a speed run and drop you off when we catch her up.'

He looked intrigued by the suggestion. 'Barbara can do anything I can. In fact, she's more than ready for promotion into her own command, but the modern Navy has too many Officers and too few boats to put them in. So I might just take you up on it, although I'd like them to get away by 05:00.'

'No problem. Come over when you're ready, we'll have breakfast and then talk further.'

He whistled up his taxi with a tiny hand-held UHF radio and was promptly whisked back to his orderly, rule-bound domain. I was very surprised he'd accepted my offer. Since becoming ex-military, I'd noticed that many current military types tend to be uncomfortable if they have to interact with civilians for too long, although Paul was pretty laid back for a Navy Skipper.

Due to the temporary change in crew, Alf and Charlie shared one twin cabin, leaving Tracy and Melissa the other twin and I grabbed the very comfortable guest queen cabin.

281

THURSDAY MORNING, NORTH TURTLE ISLAND, BRIDLED ISLAND

It was promptly at 05:00 that I woke to the slow, deep thrum of large diesels right alongside my ear, or so it seemed. I threw the covers off, pulled my old, battered shorts on and headed topside at a rush. Towering over *Seeker* in the pre-dawn gloom was the massive grey shape of the patrol boat with several curious sailors of both sexes peering down at *Seeker's* low, sleek hull. At 186 feet in length as opposed to *Seeker's* 100 feet, we looked a lot shorter and much lower than big, grey brother. The aft deck of *Glenelg*, as the only deck close to our deck height, was held a careful half metre off our side and perfectly in line with the cockpit.

As I reached the cockpit, Paul Davy was just casually stepping over the rail and as soon as he was safely aboard, the Patrol boat eased carefully away. It was a very impressive display of boat handling and I guess his XO was taking the opportunity to show off a bit.

I invited him down to the galley where I put the kettle on, discovering that contrary to Navy practice, Paul was a tea person, so while it brewed, I put on some bread for toast. The smell of fresh toast is rather compelling and it brought Tracy and Melissa out of their cabin, delightfully draped in sleeping T-shirts and very little else; much to Paul's and my pleasure.

While I had been talking with Paul last night, Dave, Alf and Melissa had had a long talk with Brianna and extracted a promise that she would behave if we let her out. Based on that long chat, they'd made the call that she could safely appear in the morning since Dave, Alf and Melissa hadn't met Paul yet. Bree was only too happy to gain freedom and join our crew, although she would have to continue using the bow cabin she was already in since there were no other beds.

Still, with the door unlocked and wearing clothes donated by the other girls, she cleaned up very well and it meant she could travel in a lot more comfort than the trip up allowed.

After I'd introduced Paul to Melissa, who'd been up for'rard last night, they both demanded coffee and more toast so I set to, letting them chat up Paul. The noise woke Alf and Charlie, so they joined the breakfast party, with Charlie meeting Paul. Dave then wandered out, scratching himself.

'Good to see you doing something useful for once Harry,' was his greeting as he introduced himself to Paul before pinching Melissa's toast.

There were way too many bodies for the little breakfast nook which was designed more for just the four paid crew, so we moved up to the saloon.

'I'll go get Bree out of bed,' Melissa said before she sat down, 'if we're up, she might as well be too.'

Paul looked around, 'There's another one? I thought I'd met everybody in the crew.'

'Ah...yes. But strictly speaking, Bree is a very late addition and not crew. She was with the EarthSquad gang and decided to swap sides. She gave us a lot of very useful Intel, but at this stage, I'd class her as a non-combatant.' That he understood, but still approved of her presence.

I could see Paul was amused by the casual nature of the crew, but hopefully I'd told him enough about everyone's credentials for him to have confidence that they knew what they were doing. In turn, I was also amused to see that Paul was the first to prop his feet up on a long alloy case parked underneath the dining table.

When there was a break in the various conversations, I said to Dave, 'In case you missed the discussion, Paul is along to experience a speed run when we leave and catch up with his boat further down the track; so to speak. He was a tad disbelieving when I said that we took just under three hours to get up here, and that was after we had slowed down.'

Dave flashed a cheeky grin. 'In that case, we'll have to take the combined power beyond the 70% mark, 'cause that's effectively all we've been using.'

Paul took the bait as intended, 'OK. How about you show me your engine room?'

He and Dave didn't wait to see if Bree was going to present at early breakfast, and headed aft to the engine room.

Shortly after, Melissa led Bree up to the saloon and I realised she hadn't seen anything of the boat apart from the forward crew cabin. She shyly said hello to everyone and was pleased when I parked a mug of steaming coffee and a plate of toast in front of her.

Just to remind her about the agreement we'd reached the night before, I said, 'Our Navy visitor is on a tour of inspection, so once again I ask that you watch what you say. Anything about the camp and EarthSquad is fine, but nothing about being locked up.'

She nodded seriously, 'I understand, Harry and I won't let you down. I appreciate now what you've done for me and I'll help all I can.'

I formally shook hands with her to seal that deal. There was no opportunity to discuss things further as Paul and Dave returned, deep in discussion about relative power to weight ratios. When he had met Bree and taken his seat again, I said, 'If you don't want to wait until you meet Amanda, you can ask Melissa just about anything about the UAV since she's one of the operators. And that box you've got your feet on holds *Dragonfly*!'

At that point, I went to wash and clean up, leaving him and Melissa in animated conversation. Thinking about our little ego-tripping demonstration, I thought that if we up-anchored at 08:00, the *Glenelg* would be about 57 miles away at that moment and if we could hold 75 knots, we'd catch her in about 53 minutes.

I passed those thoughts on to Dave when I stumbled out of the guest bathroom. 'I presume our guest is impressed with your power arrangements?'

'Hell yeah,' Dave grinned, 'he set to working out the relative power to weight ratios and came up with the fact that *Glenelg* weighs 8.3 times that of *Seeker*, yet has only 24% more power. He's very smart, but also a funny guy. I like him.'

Dave was ready with all three engines on-line at 08:00, the big turbine whistling softly like an overgrown teakettle. We burbled around the outside reef in the broad light of day with all engines idling, before he smoothly and steadily opened up the diesels until they howled.

'Seventy-five percent again,' he yelled as the speed indicator rose to 50 knots, which was highly impressive when you weren't used to it, as Paul clearly wasn't!

The seas had subsided a bit more overnight, so Dave got his usual manic grin on his face as he smoothly slid the little chromed lever of the turbine throttle forward. There was the usual steady push of almost unlimited power as the torque gauge ticked off the numbers until it was on 65%, the same as yesterday.

With the smaller swell and almost no breeze, the boat sat even better, hardly moving around as the speed indicator slid up to 75 knots -- Paul watching in disbelief.

After stabilising at 75 knots for a few minutes, Dave yelled, 'Let's try another 10% power.' I nodded and moved the throttle for him since he was reluctant to let go of the small wheel to make the adjustment.

Of course, what he didn't say was that power delivery with a turbine isn't linear; it's exponential with most of the power being generated toward the top end of the throttle travel. In this case we were still well short of full power, but that extra 10% made a huge difference, pushing the noise level up along with the speed reading, which steadied on 85 knots.

Paul was beside himself with excitement and I admit to feeling pretty revved up myself. Once again, the screaming of the airflow past the cabin and windows almost drowned out the thunder of the diesels and the howl of the turbine doing it easy at 75% power and

I was glad Dave didn't try to push the power up further, because this was an insane speed on the open ocean.

In any event, we were skipping from small crest to small crest so quickly it was almost like a low frequency vibration, but the boat didn't feel distressed in any way.

It didn't seem that long but at the 45 minute mark, the radar showed a bright blip which resolved visually into a grey smudge on the horizon, then the menacing grey form of *Glenelg* surging along at 19 knots, a huge mass of white water piled up at her stern.

Dave smoothly throttled back as we came up on her and Paul's XO did the same until both boats were steady at 10 knots.

With his own bit of show-off seamanship, Dave angled in toward *Glenelg's* stern quarter as Paul and I made our way up to the bow.

I shook his hand, 'Hope you enjoyed that as much as I did,' I commented. 'You know where we'll be and there's good water even for you in that little hook of the bay. See you about 15:00 or so this arvo.'

'Thanks Harry. That's been a whole new experience. Wow! See you soon.'

With that, he stepped over the rail onto his own deck as Dave smoothly brought the bow to within centimetres of the grey warship, before easing away. The many sailors clustered around to welcome their Skipper back waved cheerfully as Dave started to throttle up and I hurriedly made my way aft before I got blown off the exposed foredeck.

As it was, I'd barely made the safety of the cockpit before I felt the diesels stabilise at 75% and was nearly deafened by the howl of the turbine throttling up as Dave put on a show for the Navy. Within 30-seconds, the grey warship was out of sight astern. After the initial burst of high speed, Dave, with no further need to be a show-off, pulled the speed back down to 65 knots with the diesels at 50% and the turbine at 60% power.

At those power settings, we travelled more comfortably and were sliding in beside *Firebird* at 11:15 to a very big welcome from the kitties and also from Sandy and Amanda, who were both quite surprised to see Bree wandering around.

'Been having fun I see,' Sandy said dryly, eyeing off the salt crystals that had dried into a thick white rime over most forward-facing parts of the upper-works and windows.

'Great fun,' I agreed, 'we'd better use some fresh water and get rid of that. There won't be rain to do the job anytime soon.'

'And the trip was successful, I presume?'

'Oh, apart from forgetting Bree was locked in the crew cabin for the speed run north, it was very successful!'

Sandy fairly erupted, 'You did what? Forgot about her! How the fuck could you do that? Oh, the poor girl. Was she hurt?'

'Settle petal! She's fine as you can see for yourself and glad to be joining the crew. She accepted it was a genuine mistake and not torture, although she confessed to having some dark thoughts at the time. We let her out last night and Tracy and Melissa have donated some clothes. She's fine!'

Sandy grumped a bit more before settling down so I could finish the briefing.

'In around four hour's time, expect a Navy Patrol boat to park beside us with a bunch of randy sailors aboard. The Skipper is with us 100%, so that's the good side. They'll take care of the two RIBs which will be heading past here for the offshore platforms, but are going to hang with us until kick-off time. Corrine has told us that Monday night is fireworks night, but we'll be having a few briefings and planning sessions before then.'

I scored a smack on the arm for being a dickhead and a belated kiss for being a clever little vegemite. I hugged her and patted her shapely bum in return before attending to Jasper and Krazy who wanted attention from everyone, so after bringing the others up to date on the discussions with Paul, I warned Amanda to get *Dragonfly* ready for an inspection by Paul and his XO, as well as to make a camp surveillance flight. Then we tiredly settled down to rest.

It was closer to 15:30 that afternoon when the now-familiar

long, grey shape slid quietly into the bay, turning to stay close in to the north-eastern shoreline where the water was much deeper, before nosing into the southerly breeze to drop anchor. It was a very neat and economical manoeuvre that brought the warship to rest, anchor set, just 50 metres away from where *Seeker & Firebird* were rafted up together.

The high-band VHF radio that was set to the pre-agreed contact frequency squawked some unintelligible message so I grabbed it and requested a repeat.

'*Firebird* this is Glenelg *actual*. Care for a couple of visitors?'

'Come on over. We'll put the kettle on.'

'*Roger that. There in five*. Glenelg *clear*.'

There was the usual trampoline party already happening up for'rard with Alf, Charlie, Tracy, Amanda and Melissa introducing the new crewmember, Bree to the pleasures of sprawling around on *Firebird's* trampoline netting while sucking up the odd Pina Colada or three. I was interested to see that Bree seemed to be fitting in very well with the others and they in turn accepted her. The girls had all stripped down to bikinis and the guys were in shorts only and the little party had attracted the notice of several sailors of both sexes on *Glenelg*. The fact that Bree looked very neat and trim in her donated bikini attracted my attention as well and I had the fleeting thought that it must have been Tracy who donated the bikini since the top fitted Bree's smaller breasts quite neatly.

Dave joined Sandy and me in the cockpit to greet Paul and meet Barbara, who were both on their way over in a 25-foot RHIB attack boat. Barbara turned out to be a tall, attractive brunette with long-ish hair, and a slim build. She carried a competent air and appeared to be treated very much an equal by Paul. It hadn't taken them long to get into casual mode as both had ditched their uniforms and were in normal civvies gear—shorts, loose shirts and joggers. The boat crew who dropped them off were also in casuals and were preparing to ferry a load of off-duty crew ashore to have a run and feel dry land under their feet again.

'Welcome Commander,' I said. 'I'm glad to see it didn't take long to go casual for the off-duty watch.'

She gave a husky chuckle, 'Barbara, please. No, it doesn't take long when we have a few days off in a beautiful place. We insist that both watches get plenty of opportunity to relax which is good for morale. Are there any nasties in the bay that might affect swimming or other water sports?'

'Nah. Not that we've seen. Certainly no sharks or crocodiles during the day at least. The fishing is excellent and there are mud crabs in the mangroves, but tell the crew to be careful of their claws. Anyway, come for'rard and meet the crew then we can come back here and go over plans.'

'Great, but first I'll just pass that to the duty Lieutenant.' She pulled a small hand-held UHF radio from her shorts pocket and relayed the info to be passed to the shore parties. I noticed there were two uniformed sailors on deck armed with rifles just in case a bitey or two decided to swing into the little bay to see what all the activity was about.

We went for'rard and I introduced the two officers to the tramp party, then we retired to the cockpit to talk business. Paul had obviously told Barbara the whole plan, but she had some excellent questions of her own which helped us refine things further. Interestingly, she apparently had no qualms about wiping out the attack force and accepted it was the price the bad guys would have to pay for electing to be on the wrong side. She seemed to have my attitude to business.

With their role and action plan as sorted as it could be at this stage, both Barbara and Paul were interested to look at *Dragonfly* so I asked Amanda and Melissa to dig it out and prep it for a recon over the camp to see what changes had happened since yesterday now Corrine and her additional troops had arrived. While they did that, we moved over to *Seeker's* saloon for more privacy, because the trampoline party was getting noisier with some of *Glenelg's* senior off-watch personnel being invited over for drinks and a chat.

It wasn't long before the RHIB shuttle boat dropped 5 or 6 crew off at *Firebird's* stern and they joined the rowdies for'rard.

Paul and Barbara were fascinated by the arrangement of the UAV and the simple solutions that had been applied to so many complex problems. Amanda explained the changes made to create the MKII version, the most obvious of which was the flared cobra head nose which allowed the two camera systems to be mounted side-by-side, as well as providing significant additional lift, reduced power needed, and increased endurance and range.

They were even more impressed by the quick setup of the UAV and the Ground Control Station. With fuelling complete, Amanda placed the homing beacon on the padded mat we used as a take-off and landing pad on *Seeker's* foredeck. Leaving *Dragonfly* switched on, she retired to the GCS in *Seeker's* cockpit, performed a quick pre-start check and pressed the start button. The Navy was surprised and delighted when the engine burst into immediate life, quickly settling down to a steady and quiet idle.

With cylinder head temps in the green, Amanda hit the 'Flight Plan Execute' button and our visitors were entranced to see the four engine nacelles swivel fully upright so that the props were horizontal, then they all spun up together. A moment later, the engine revs increased and the engine note deepened as the ungainly-looking craft lifted smoothly off the deck, hovered for a moment, then transitioned sideways to clear the deck before accelerating forward at ever increasing speed as the wings carried more and more of the weight, allowing the nacelles to rotate forward so the props could provide forward thrust. As it climbed steadily away to the east, the mottled, matt grey and blue colouring meant that it was lost to sight within seconds and the sound faded a few moments later.

The Navy was quiet until Amanda called for them to view the display on the GCS.

'Here we have the Electro Optical or daylight colour camera view in real time, overlaid on a map of the region which we can zoom in or out as required. These ribbons on either side show the aircraft data like height, speed, heading, fuel state and other information as well as a continuous GPS position in Lat/Long. Any parameter that gets out of spec range is flagged as a flashing red icon.

Flight planned track shows as a yellow line and the small red arrowhead is the actual position of the UAV.

We can't fly the aircraft directly with a joystick or anything like that, but by clicking and dragging the heading bug on the display, we can make turns or by moving the altitude bug we make height changes. Of course, we can completely change the flight track or the entire flight plan en-route and send it somewhere else and bad weather doesn't seem to fuss it too much. A mission can also be aborted immediately by pressing that red button in which case it will execute a return-to-home manoeuvre, including auto-land at the take-off point. Data download, either direct in visual range or off the satellite, can be broadcast on a LAN via a modem built into the GCS. It's good out to about 80 metres, but if we fire up an amplified booster, we can push the signal out to 200 metres or more in the right conditions. For instance, while our boats are close like this, I can give you the password to tap into the data feed and watch it on *Glenelg*.'

Paul and Barbara seemed speechless, although Barbara finally asked, 'Do you have any control over the cameras from here?'

'Oh sure,' Amanda replied brightly, immensely proud of *Dragonfly*, 'we can zoom like this, or pan and tilt like this.'

In response to her tiny joystick commands, the crystal-clear picture of water whizzing past under the UAV suddenly rushed up at the screen, then spun dizzyingly side to side when the camera twisted and turned in its stabilised gimbals.

'Wow!' was the response from Barbara.

'Or,' Amanda added, 'we can add Auto Track by selecting this switch, which brings up a set of cross-hairs which are placed over the target using this trackball, then when I press this button, the cameras are slaved to the cross-hairs, regardless of what manoeuvres the UAV makes.'

'Yes, we're used to that feature and it's a great thing, but as a package with everything *Dragonfly* can do, especially being VTOL, this thing would be worth millions to the Military,' Paul said. 'As I said earlier, at all the conferences and committee meetings I've been to, it's what everyone has been screaming out for. Has your designer friend set a selling price on them yet?'

Amanda shrugged, 'The last I heard, he was going to ask $350,000 for one complete system.'

Paul shook his head, 'No way! That's way too cheap! They'll be regarded as junk and the specs considered faked at that price, but if he charges $1.5M apiece, he'll sell all he can make. I'd love to be his agent.'

That statement made Amanda think carefully for a few moments and file some thoughts away for later, before she went back to extolling the many other innovative features of the UAV. She pulled the camera zoom back to wide-angle, which let the occasional island pop into view, since it was clear their visitors weren't going to miss a moment of the flight.

Barbara had another question. 'This designer friend of yours must be an electronics expert as well as an aeronautical genius? There are some very complex programs running that thing.'

'No, he's not. As you say, the various electronics packages are very sophisticated, so he teamed up with a young guy who's a self-taught electronics expert and a genius in that field. Ian told him what he wanted the various modules to do and then Robby just had to design and build all the modules to those requirements. They worked closely together to get it all working and I believe they've taken out patents on some of the circuit designs, although if the Chinese get hold of them, they'll be duplicated within days.'

Barbara nodded, 'I have a Masters in Electrical Engineering and I'm not sure I'd know where to start designing and writing code for the processors in that thing. Those two guys make a formidable combination to have done all this without having degrees in Electrical and Aeronautical Engineering.'

Amanda wholeheartedly agreed with that. 'They're both very unassuming guys, and I don't think they realise how much knowledge they've absorbed over the years in full-scale and model aviation. I guess that's why they didn't bother with University degrees! They already know all the stuff they need.'

The flash of another small island flicking past the camera lens warned that the target was close and with the UAV maintaining 3000 feet altitude to be certain it remained undetected, the stubby peninsula came into view. Amanda zoomed in on the camp, the auto focus and auto exposure functions keeping the picture sharp and clear. While the scene was new to Paul and Barbara, for the rest of us who had seen the images yesterday, the difference in activity was remarkable. It was as though a small boy had viciously stirred an ant's nest, with people moving quickly from place to place, seemingly without a pattern. New tents were still being erected and it looked like the mess tent had already grown an extension.

'Look at this Harry,' Amanda said, zooming in more, 'there are a lot more weapons on display than yesterday, and see this bare ground just inland of the green bit? That looks like a couple of squads practicing something. And there's the supply barge they use, still tied up at the wharf.'

She also pointed out to Paul and Barbara the four RIBs pulled up on the shore near the wharf, along with a 25-foot half-cabin fishing boat with a large outboard hung on its stern. Paul looked and said, 'The RIBs look to be about the same size as ours, but without the .50 cal machine gun. They've got big outboards instead of the diesel water jets ours have, so they'll need extra fuel tanks to have the range to get there and back. Except they won't be coming back, but they don't know that!'

We watched the video feed until *Dragonfly* had completed its four programmed passes and turned for home. It was a 40-minute flight time until the approach and landing, so Barbara looked at me again, 'You have the exact co-ordinates of the offshore platforms I presume?'

'Yep. Even though we weren't going to let the raiders anywhere near the platforms, I asked for them anyway. You guys should have them as well.'

'Yeah we do, but could you dig out yours, with a ruler, pencil and a chart, please?'

It took a few minutes to find the scrap of paper with the co-ordinates on it, and then I took everything, along with a local area chart and spread it on the cockpit table. Barbara checked the co-ordinates and made a small mark on the map before drawing a line from there to the location of the EarthCare camp. As I'd advised Paul up at North Turtle Island, the line passed just east of Lowendal Island, then just one nautical mile north east of our present location and then passed through the Montebello Islands.

'This seems like a good position for an ambush and should make your job a lot easier.'

Paul smiled, 'Yeah, I reckon it will, especially if your inside girl can get them to track just to the east of the Montebello's. But we don't want to start a bunfight within sight or sound of Lowendal Island with that oil facility and its personnel, so I reckon on Monday we'll deploy further north to this Ah Chong Island. It's only 6 miles or so away and won't take long to get there.'

He traced his finger over the chart and indicated a bay on the north east side of the intriguingly-named island.

'If we were here, just inside the little hooked headland with the engines running and the RHIBs deployed about half-way back toward this place, they'd be in an ideal position to intercept the bad guys. Especially if you can put *Dragonfly* over-head tracking the attack force and letting us know their exact position. Our radar isn't too good at picking up very small targets like RIBs unless they are much closer than these will be, so we can't use that for early warning.'

I nodded. 'Yep. We can do that and relay the relative positions of everybody. We don't have the remote-access website download facility set up yet, but we'll make this work.'

'If the RHIBs have any problems and one gets away, it'll probably head west to get in amongst these islands near Ah Chong and we'll be ready and waiting with *Glenelg*. Our 25mm cannon has a range of 3 kilometres to 6 kilometres, so we should be effective backup to our RHIBs and their .50 calibre machine guns.'

Sandy was taking some notes as I replied, 'that sounds like a good plan. I'll ask Corrine to get across that on our next phone call.'

Just then, there was a round of cheering and clapping from the foredeck party, so I stood up to see one of *Glenelg's* RHIBs whizz past our bows towing, of all things, a female sailor on a single water ski! They came around again and circled both boats, before heading back to drop her off close to shore where another hopeful water-sport enthusiast was waiting.

I grinned at our two visitors, 'That's an interesting use for Navy equipment.'

Paul laughed, 'Oddly enough, that activity is officially sanctioned as being good for morale. You'll also see they're setting up for a beach party on-shore tonight with a bonfire and a BBQ. We'll leave a skeleton crew on watch and rotate them, so all the crew get to have some fun. Your crew are welcome to join in and have a feed. There'll be beer and wine, but no spirits ashore.'

Sandy and I nodded, 'Thanks. We might just do that. Our extended foredeck party is already corrupting your guys and girls by getting them pissed, so I'll make sure they don't take any cock-tails with them.'

'Oh, don't worry about that. The little bit they might share won't make too much difference.'

I laughed, 'OK. I'll let it go then.'

It wasn't long after that when a mottled grey dual-winged shape suddenly appeared overhead as *Dragonfly* returned, lining up for approach to *Seeker's* foredeck. Watched avidly by Paul and Barbara, it came to the hover, slid smoothly sideways to the landing pad and lowered itself gently to the soft matting where the engine throttled back, entering the idle cool-down phase. One minute later, it shut down and waited for its human attendants, Amanda and Melissa to take over.

Amanda popped a hatch and slid a flash-drive into a port which triggered a download of the video data, and handed it over to me on completion.

'You're welcome to go over the video if it would help,' I offered it Paul and Barbara.

Paul took the drive, 'Thanks Harry. We probably have seen enough, but we wouldn't mind showing a few other of our crew in case there's something that would be useful.'

They spent some time talking with Amanda and Melissa and examining *Dragonfly* very closely, finally finishing up quite blown away by the unconventional but clever design that worked so well.

'We probably won't get our hands on one of these anytime soon, but at least we can benefit from it on this operation,' Paul commented.

I turned the chart around. 'I expect both attacks will be planned by Corrine to occur at the same time for maximum surprise, so when she phones through the time, we can launch *Dragonfly* and have it shadow the two RIBs heading your way.'

Paul was pleased, but voiced a concern. 'It'll make it almost too easy if our RHIBs can make a stealthy approach in the dark guided by the UAV. But won't you need it over at the main plant for your mission?'

I smiled, 'That's the other part of the plan that needs careful co-ordination since there will only be *Seeker* to do the intercept of three boats, although I'm going to have Corrine and her crew occupy the lead RIB with maybe a dim light on the stern. So that cuts it down to two targets for us to take out. Because of the different distances involved, the offshore group will be launching well before the Onslow plant group, so your targets will get here first. That way, we can give you coverage by *Dragonfly* before pulling it over to cover us. Provided you guys don't fuck around too much!' I finished off with a grin.

Paul and Barbara quickly looked at each other and then at the chart, Barbara's fingers quickly measuring.

'There's bugger-all difference in distance, Harry, between the distance to Onslow and to the intercept point between here and Ah Chong Island. That plan won't work!'

I grinned, 'Not if the bad guys thought they were only going as far as the intercept point, it wouldn't work. No sirree! No way!'

The penny dropped. 'Ah, shit! I should have seen that. They're planning on going 103 miles as opposed to 47 miles, so they'll allow for just over twice as long to cover the distance and will therefore be well ahead of the Onslow group.'

'That's what I'm counting on so you guys have the UAV first, then when you've cleaned your targets up, we'll scoot it across to our area. If you get a bit delayed, we can just move the intercept point forward a bit closer to Onslow, but we don't have a lot of wiggle room to do that, so shoot straight! Fortunately, our radar is the new digital pulse type that resolves down to two centimetres, so we should be able to pick up the attack RIBs and the work barge and shadow them from seaward until the UAV is overhead.'

Paul looked a bit worried, 'That's still very tight timing. What if we move our intercept point a little closer to the coast? That way we hit them earlier and can release the UAV earlier.'

We spent the rest of the afternoon having fun kicking plans around and trading off distances and proximity to civilisation, before I deemed that the sun was most definitely over the yard-arm and we could break out the rum. It turned out both Paul and Barbara like rum drinks so I made a batch of Pina Coladas. The foredeck party had graduated to Margaritas, becoming even more raucous in the process. At least everyone still had most of their clothes on!

We'd just started on our second round when I raised the subject of weapons.

Paul cocked an eye at me, his nose buried in his glass of lovely cocktail and dryly replied, 'I think we're pretty well off for weapons, thanks Harry. But good of you to consider the point.'

I smiled a little grimly, 'Well, we're not! Not long-range stuff anyway. We've got a useful arsenal of close-in toys, but nothing that would take these guys out at a safe distance. You get to play with our UAV, how about the loan of something heavier than an H&K MP5?'

Barbara went serious fast, but alcohol had brought out the smart-arse in Paul. 'You want the loan of one of our guns? Fuckin' hell, Harry. What'd you think this is, Toys 'r Us®?'

I started to wind up until Sandy nudged me and I realised that he was yanking my chain.

'Yeah, well, you know how it is. We've got this big, bad-arse, fast boat and I thought a pair of .50 cal machine guns would mount really well either side of the main cabin.'

'Oh! You did, did you?' he replied, a glint in his eye.

I held my glass up to him in salute, 'Yep, that's what I was thinking.'

He shook his head, 'Nope. No can do. We've only got two and they go on the RHIBs, but I do see your problem.'

He turned to Barbara, who was trying not to laugh, 'Could you call for Weps to join our conference immediately, please Barb?'

'Sure Paul,' she replied easily, a little grin hovering around her lips as she made the call to the Duty watch on *Glenelg*.

'*Roger that, XO. She's actually mobile at the moment so we can drop her off in two minutes.*'

'That's good service,' I commented, topping everyone's drink up from the bucket of brew.

'The Navy always comes through,' Paul threw in, 'regardless of the circumstances.'

It was less than two minutes when the RHIB attack boat doing water-ski duties swung past the stern of *Firebird* and the skier at the end of the rope let go, sinking neatly into the water just a metre from the stern boarding platform. I didn't immediately make the connection until a tall blonde female in a rather small bikini trotted up the steps and called, 'Permission to come aboard, Sir.'

Sandy elbowed me in the ribs again, 'That's you, dopey. As Captain, you're supposed to make a response and invite the young lady aboard, so get off your arse!'

Belatedly, I scrambled to my feet and said, more or less formally, 'Permission granted, Lieutenant. Welcome aboard. Care for a drink?'

She grinned and padded wetly over to our group, who were sprawled in approved relaxed fashion, drinks in hand, as she accepted the tall, frosted glass of Pina Colada. 'Thank you, sir and a good afternoon to you, Commanders.'

Paul waved his glass vaguely in my direction, 'He's one as well, Lieutenant, so you're surrounded by them at the moment. But please be seated, as we have something to discuss with you.'

At close range, she was very easy on the eye and Sandy had that patient, indulgent look on her face as I surreptitiously eyed her off with the wet bikini showing very interesting bits of her anatomy, further boosting her appeal, at least in my eyes.

'This is Commander Harry Stevens and Inspector Sandy Thomson, Lieutenant. Clare Stahall guys, our highly talented Weapons Officer.'

Hands were duly shaken, before Paul resumed giving Clare a quick briefing.

'Before I outline why we're here water-skiing and sucking up alcoholic beverages, I must say that no less a person than the Admiral of the Fleet has seen fit to allow Commander Stevens here to have control over *Glenelg*, all our movements and arrangements for the next week, an action which I believe, to the best of my knowledge, is unprecedented in Australian naval history.'

Lieutenant Clare's eyes widened in surprise as she looked more carefully at Sandy and me, taking in the tattered shorts and faded T-shirt. In turn, I took in the very pleasant, but incongruous sight of the Weapons Officer of an active RAN warship dressed in a small, wet bikini.

'That's a rather extreme step for the Admiral to take Sir,' she replied, 'and as Weapons Officer I'm obliged to ask if you have verified Commander Stevens' authenticity and the origin of the orders? No offence intended, Sirs,' she hastily added, glancing at Sandy and me.

Paul inclined his head, 'Well said, Lieutenant, but both the XO and myself can guarantee the orders from both Admirals are genuine, as are Commander Stevens credentials. It may help your concerns to know he is fully entitled to, but rarely does, display the letters VC after his name.'

Clare's eye really did open wide as she stammered, 'Yes Sir. In that case, my apologies Sir. It'll be a pleasure to work with you.'

I spoke up, 'I'm sure it will be, Lieutenant. You are doing your job as it is supposed to be done, so there's nothing to apologise for.'

She bobbed her head, 'Thank you sir. Now, Skipper, you were saying?'

CHAPTER 34

Paul delivered a concise briefing of the situation and it was clear that both he and Barbara held the Lieutenant in very high regard. With the basic situation outlined, Paul got to the heart of the matter and why they called for their Weapons Officer.

'We have the classic division of forces here Lieutenant, although it would appear Harry has given us the easy task since we have to take out the two RIBs, only being equipped with a patrol boat armed with a Bushmaster cannon and two attack RHIBs armed with .50 cal machine guns. He, on the other hand, has awarded himself the task of taking out one RIB and a fast work barge with nothing more than a few shotguns, handguns and a couple of 9mm sub-machine guns. Based on that information, what do you recommend we do to correct the imbalance of the situation?'

Unfazed by the company and her lack of clothing, Clare took a good pull at her drink as she carefully considered his words.

'Given the directive issued by the Admiral of the Fleet, the obvious step would be to improve Commander Stevens' weapons load out to the stage where he is no longer at a disadvantage. Since we only have two .50 cal machine guns and will need those, might I suggest that we allocate the two Mark 47 Strikers we carry to *Seeker?* I can have our fitters knock up some brackets to support the mounts and we'll just need to have a look where it will be best to position the launchers.'

Paul beamed at her. 'Well done Lieutenant. Excellent suggestion and I'm sure you can choose a crew for each weapon.'

'No problem sir. The guys and girls will be falling over each other to get in on this gig!'

'That's good, but keep in mind when you choose, they will be firing at night with both their boat and the targets moving.'

'Won't be a problem, sir. I'll pick the best.'

'Excellent Lieutenant. You've been most helpful as usual, so you're free to resume your leisure time, or you can stay if you wish.'

'I'd prefer to stay sir, if that's OK with Commander Stevens. I'd like to hear more of this operation. It makes a change from chasing trepang fishermen.'

I grabbed the bucket of cocktail juice. 'You're very welcome to stay Clare, but only if you let me top you up with this very pleasant brew. But would someone please explain what the hell is this Mark 47 that's going to be secured to *Seeker*?'

Clare laughed as she held her glass out. 'Easy to explain, Commander. The Mark 47 is a 40mm automatic grenade launcher, that's virtually a close-range cannon. It has an integrated fire control system with laser range-finding and can fire a wide selection of 40mm grenades out as far as 2 kilometres, including a smart grenade that can be set to airburst over the heads of the target. And it can fire continuously at a rate of at least 60 rounds per minute. But because of the heavy recoil, it jumps around a lot unless it's well secured to something solid, rather than just sitting on the ground on a tripod.

We've not had ours very long and haven't had a chance to play with them yet so this will be an excellent opportunity to learn what they can do.'

Paul looked at me, 'There you go Harry. Will that restore the balance?'

I laughed, 'Absolutely Paul and thanks for the explanation Clare. It sounds like a real beast, but if your fitters can make up a pair of secure mounts, we'll be happy to use them. I hope there are waterproof covers for them as well, since things can get very wet on the exposed foredeck, if that's where they go.'

Clare answered, 'That's no problem, ah…Harry. We have covers, although I might have a look around the rest of the boat to see if there is a better place for them.'

'No problem, I'll call Dave down from the party to help you. It's his boat anyway.'

I went forward and waved for Dave to come aft, but had a quiet word in his ear first. 'The young lady in the bikini is Clare and she's their Weapons Officer. Paul is going to loan us a pair of 40mm grenade launchers for the Monday night fireworks show and Clare is looking for the best places to mount them. You'd best go with her to see if there's a better place other than the bow for them since I suggested that things would get a bit wet and bouncy up there. Apparently they aren't heavy but they do buck around a lot when fired so they need to be held down well and there has to be room beside it for the box of grenades that feed the thing.'

'No problem, Boss. I'll look after her.'

I grinned at him, 'Maybe not that well. Corrine's only a few days away.'

He grinned back, 'I'll be good…maybe.'

'I hear that you are very good, my friend, but will you behave? That's the real question!'

He laughed, collected Clare and went exploring *Seeker's* upperworks looking for mounting points.

By mutual consent, we stopped making plans and just chatted, comparing past experiences and consuming more than we should of the brew in the bucket. At some point, the trampoline party came aft and dragged us ashore to the bonfire BBQ where we mingled with a very happy crew and were served some really good tucker. The cooks had been busy since they'd arrived, since there was plenty of fresh fish and even a few succulent mud crabs.

In deference to the booze limitations, we switched to beer or wine of which there was plenty. There was even live entertainment with several guitars, a violin, a clarinet and a trumpet, which was an odd mix, but they managed to blend fairly well and kept punching out tunes that most seemed to enjoy singing along with. I was surprised to see the number of girls in the crew! They were a very happy bunch and even when a bit pissy, they treated Paul and the other officers with the relaxed respect that's the mark of a good Captain. As Tracy was the only unattached female in our crew, she had more than her fair share of attention and every time I saw her, she seemed to be more dishevelled than before although she was always smiling.

The Petty Officers kept things under control and the party wrapped up at a reasonable hour, although the huge BBQ was left set up on the beach for the traditional after-party breakfast.

Somehow, we ended up with Lieutenant Clare sleeping on the stern daybed, or at least that's where she was when I blearily wandered out just after dawn to have my traditional pee off the starboard boarding platform.

I'd just finished when there was a plaintive whisper from the daybed, 'Can you do one for me, please? I don't think I can make it.'

My laugh wasn't cruel, it was what she said that just sounded funny, but then I realised that she was serious about needing help.

'If you're really desperate, I can help you down here,' I offered and she groaned.

'Bugger modesty, I have to pee and I'm not sure I can walk. Help! Please?'

So I carefully eased her off the daybed, mindful that I could cop a stream of vomit any moment, but she didn't need to bring anything up just then, so we tottered slowly down the steps until I was able to sit her down on the broad bottom step, her legs dangling in the water.

'Pants on or off?' I asked, holding onto one arm lest she slip off.

'Off!' was the croaking reply, so I awkwardly leant her back, still keeping hold of one arm and she was able to help tug her bikini pants down. Getting them down her legs and untangled from her ankles was not exactly elegant and I was glad for her sake that the morning was still too early for any of *Glenelg's* crew to be up and about.

I tried not to look too much. Really! I did try, but semi-naked ladies deserve to be looked at!

Finally, I was able to retrieve the pants and holding her arm, got her seated normally whereupon she spread 'em and gave a huge sigh of relief. Any thoughts about girls having thimble bladders were well and truly dispelled by Clare as she peed for what seemed a couple of minutes.

'Oh bugger, Harry. I'm sorry,' she mumbled, 'I peed all over your lovely boat and I'm sitting in it as well!'

I laughed. 'Well, you haven't hurt the boat and it'll just wash off you, it's only pee. I have a shower here to rinse you down when you've finished, so no one will ever know.'

'You're a good man.'

'Yeah, I can be on the very odd occasion,' I replied, moving to help her up, but she suddenly said, 'Uh oh. I think I'm going to upchuck.' I leant her forward, holding firmly onto her arm and the other shoulder as Clare disposed of all the rubbish in her stomach. She stayed like that for a while before croaking, 'Done now. Thank you. So sorry Harry!'

I sat her up again, but kept her where she was in case of more, but she must have done a good job first time around and after a few minutes, said she was feeling better. I made her hold onto the rail on the outside of the stern while I opened the locker under the second step and pulled out the shower head and some soap. Setting the temperature to warm, I washed all residue off the step and sprayed Clare from the waist down.

'OK. Spread 'em,' I instructed quietly which she did without comment, keeping her eyes closed as I sprayed.

'That feels nice,' she murmured as the warm water cascaded down over her from the waist down, so I kept it going a bit longer before helping her to stand. She was very wobbly and when I said that I had some soap so she could wash off properly, she pleaded, 'My head's spinning and I can't let go or I'll fall over. You do it. Please?'

I had to ask her to spread again and as gently as possible, washed her. I behaved myself and confined my movements to only what was required for actually washing, glad in my own way that nobody was around to see what was going on. I did admit to myself that I found the task quite pleasant and consigned all thoughts about the softness of fine blonde hair to the far corners of my sex-addled mind. Once dried and dressed, she wanted to lay down on the day-bed again and promptly went to sleep, so I took my stimulated self below to wake Sandy who took a while to get wound up, but when she did, it was a memorable half-hour or so.

After the second round and as we lay in recovery mode, she giggled and asked, 'What on earth got into you?'

I leered at her, sprawled naked across me, 'I think that you'll find it was the other way around young lady. That's the way it normally works!'

That earned me a couple of sharp pokes in sensitive areas, so when we finally moseyed aft to the bathroom, I looked up to see Clare sitting at the dining table, her head resting on the table. I ventured up two steps and asked softly, 'Are you alright?'

She opened her eyes and giggled to see me naked and still show-ing signs of recent activity. 'I'm OK, thanks Harry. It got a bit hot out there.'

'I'll just have a shower then I'll get you something for your stomach.'

She looked me over carefully then gave a wan smile, 'That'd be good. I don't think I'm in much shape for any of the other just now, as nice as it looks.'

That was my cue to be embarrassed, so I retreated as gracefully as I could and told Sandy of the events of the morning. She was still having fits of the giggles when we made it up to the saloon and I presented Clare with a fizzy glass of Eno's. Ten minutes later she was looking a lot better until she looked at the clock and nearly had a relapse.

'Holy crap! It's quarter to eight and I'm the Officer of the Fore-noon Watch. Can I borrow a something to put on over this bikini please Sandy? And can you run me back, please Harry?'

We both laughed, but I quickly went topside to check the RIB was ready, while Sandy grabbed a pair of shorts and a top that Clare hurriedly pulled on as she scrambled into the RIB and we roared over to the *Glenelg* where the cooks were just pushing off to go and start the beachside breakfast.

The seaman manning the companionway access saluted and said, 'Welcome back, Lieutenant,' as I spun the RIB about and headed back to *Firebird* to pick up Sandy who first yelled out for any more starters for breakfast. There was zero response, except from my beautiful big cat, Jasper, who'd been keeping a low profile while strangers were aboard.

'He was cooped up all yesterday,' Sandy commented, 'and has only just had his morning pee after Clare left. He needs a good run on the beach.'

I looked at Jasper, nuzzling my leg and making noises like a 3-cylinder diesel engine, looked over at the shore, and then at Sandy.

'I was just thinking that with everything that's about to go down with these people, showing Jasper to them will be the least of our problems. Let's take him ashore now and he can play with the sailors and bludge some food off the cooks.'

She was pleased with the decision and Jasper as usual, seemed to understand what I said because we were treated to one of his rare 'Merowls' of approval. So with Krazy still asleep on someone's bunk, it was just the three of us who made the very short trip to shore. There were several cooks and mess attendants firing up the BBQ and lighting the heated Bain Maries before filling them with hot dishes of hash browns, grilled tomatoes and trays of poached or scrambled eggs that they'd prepared aboard.

The first boatload of sailors was on its way in as we pulled our small RIB up on the beach, Jasper leading the way with a loud 'Merowl' of delight at the sight of strangers to play with and food to bludge.

To the uninitiated, the first sight of Jasper is somewhat intimidating, as being all black, he looks like a 2/3 scale black panther. The first cook to spot him nearly dropped a tray of bacon in shock, but quickly recovered as I led Jasper over to them, holding his collar.

'Good Morning Commander, and Ma'am,' the head cook said politely, obviously briefed by Paul or Barbara. 'That's an interesting cat you have there, sir. I've not seen an animal like that before.'

I addressed them all, 'Good morning gentlemen and thanks for feeding us so well last night. This is Jasper, my cat and while he is a bit bigger than most, he's very obedient to me. I've told him that everyone here is a friend, so he'll behave himself. He loves company and will try to bludge food from you. He needs to have a run around, so if you could, please spread the word he won't bite anybody, provided they don't bite him first!'

That drew a laugh, so I had another whisper in his ear about the rules of behaviour and was promptly 'Huffed' at in return which was his way of saying that I should stop talking and let him go smooch up to the cooks who might hand over some food.

So with a laugh, I let him loose and true to form, he went straight to the head cook who was a bit wary at first, but then was won over by Jasper's extraordinary people skills and soon all the cooks and mess attendants were making a fuss of him. They in turn told the new arrivals about him and before long, Jasper was romping with the sailors who threw things for him to chase and chased him in turn. A football being thrown around was the perfect thing for Jasper to jump for and I heard the cry of 'Mark!' several times.

The smell of fresh-cooked bacon and sausages seemed to draw the rest of the off-watch crew ashore, including Skipper Paul and XO Barbara who grinned when we all complained of sore heads this morning.

'Those cocktails were lovely,' Barb commented, 'but I don't know what you put in them. It might be a day or two before I try them again!'

I was about to reply when Sandy poked me in the ribs and said, 'Jasper.'

I looked around to see what trouble he was in, and then understood what she meant.

Looking back at Paul and Barbara, 'I have another crew member for you to meet.'

'Huh? Another one? I thought that Brianna was the last one.'

I smiled and shook my head, 'Not quite. This one usually hides away when strangers are around. Not everyone appreciates his talents.'

Paul looked around, 'I see the boys and girls are playing with a big black dog up the beach. It must have come from someone else's boat. Where's your crewie?'

'That's him, I'm afraid. I'll call him over.' I whistled loudly and Jasper immediately broke off the chasing game he was playing with three sailors and came bounding joyfully over the sand to us.

It was comical to watch Paul and Barb's reactions as he got closer and it became very obvious that this was no dog!

'Holy crap!' was Paul's reaction when Jasper sat in front of us, a big grin on his face, not even breathing hard from all the running around he'd been doing. 'That's no dog! That's a cat, but what sort of animal grows that big except for a jungle cat.'

Sandy grinned as I explained, 'He mostly is a jungle cat, but he was supposed to be a Chausie cat cross-bred 50:50 with a jungle cat. But the Korean cook who gave him to me said that he had been bred specially and was more like 75:25% jungle cat to Chausie. For your ears only, he's been proven in combat and has recorded several kills protecting Sandy, me, the boat and others who we had designated as friends to be protected.'

Paul involuntarily moved a half-pace back on hearing that, but Barbara was made of sterner stuff and dropped to her knees in the soft sand to look more closely at him.'

'Jasper,' I said, 'this is Barbara and Paul. They are our friends and are to be looked after.'

My big cat with the very mystical habits lowered his head and took a small step forward, then lifted his right front leg with the huge paw and lethal, but sheathed claws attached and held it out to Barbara.

With a grin of delight, she grasped his paw and gently shook it. 'What a great trick you've taught him, Harry. I've never seen any cat trained to do that. Very cool!'

I smiled gently. 'I'm afraid I didn't teach him anything Barb. He just does it with people he likes.'

She looked a little bemused. 'That's bizarre! And you say he's killed people defending you and the boat?'

'Oh yes. If he decides he doesn't like somebody, then its game over and lights out. He doesn't mess around!'

'But we saw him playing with some of the crew and he seemed to be enjoying that immensely. They certainly were!'

'I had a word in his ear when we brought him ashore and told him that everyone was a friend and he could enjoy playing with them. So, he was!'

'But he doesn't really understand what you say to him, does he?'

'We've asked ourselves that many times and the answer keeps coming out that yes, he does understand. Try this. Jasper. Do what Barbara tells you to do please.'

He looked at me, looked at Barb and then huffed.

'What was that?' she asked. 'He blew out his breath at you. Is he angry about what you said?'

I laughed, 'No. That's his way of saying that he understood perfectly and that I should stop doubting his ability. Go ahead and ask him to do something I couldn't have trained him to do.'

She thought a moment, then addressed him directly, 'Jasper. I left a red towel in the Navy inflatable boat. Could you fetch it for me please?'

Jasper cocked his head and gave her a look, then looked at me, huffed again and trotted off to where the RHIB pulled up on the beach, a sailor sitting on the bow. Ignoring the man's alarmed protests, Jasper jumped aboard, dug around for a minute with only his long thick tail visible above the sides, then reappeared with a neatly folded red towel in his jaws. He trotted the 20-metres back to us over the sand and sat in front of Barbara. She gently took it from him and thanked him.

He turned and came to sit between Sandy and me, looking at Barbara and Paul.

Barb looked thunderstruck. 'That was totally surreal, as well as being utterly impossible! I didn't say anything before, but Paul can verify the red towel was with two others in my beach bag which was closed with a rope threaded through eyelets and tied with a reef knot. I could see the boat watch didn't do anything to help, so Jasper has found the bag, undone the knot and picked out the red towel from the other two, one of which was for Paul. And he's brought it back, still folded.'

Jasper tried to look suitably modest, but failed, so I scratched his head and said, 'OK Mr Super-Pussy-Cat, that's enough showing off for one day. Why don't you go back playing with the nice boys and girls and try not to kill or maim anybody – please!'

He gave me a look; huffed in disgust and bounded away to resume play with the two girls and one guy who were tossing a frisbee and cheered when the big black cat re-joined them.

Barb stared after him, still in awe of his intelligence and antics. 'I need to have a long talk with you and Jasper, if you don't mind Harry. I'm doing my Masters thesis on human animal interaction with regard to military applications and need to find out more.'

'No problem, Barb, but good luck finding out more, because I don't know. But maybe we'll both learn something.'

CHAPTER 35

We left the Navy to do their own thing after breakfast with the catering crew cleaning up, although I noticed that the huge BBQ was left set up on the beach for possibly a lunch and evening meal again as well. The sailors were obviously rotating in watches and in the early afternoon, Clare had the duty-taxi RHIB drop her off for a chat.

'Actually, as well as returning Sandy's clothes, I wanted to apologise for my behaviour last night and this morning. I shouldn't have drunk so much and I still don't know how I ended up sleeping on your daybed!'

Sandy grinned, so I replied, 'There's no need to apologise. I think we all had a bit too much to drink last night, but it was fun! As for ending up on the daybed, I think you must have swum out, or one of the taxi-boat crews would have mentioned dropping you off.'

She looked a bit stricken, 'Oh fuck! That's worse than I thought. Anyway, I just wanted to thank you for looking after me and not telling anybody else on *Glenelg*. That little episode would have been hard to live down.'

Sandy added with a grin on her face, 'Harry never has problem with helping semi-naked females, but I have to say it really worked for me this morning as well, so if you want to repeat the performance, go right ahead!'

Clare shuddered at the thought, but then caught on to what Sandy was saying.

'Oh? Oh! I see! So when I saw you walking past as I was curled up in the saloon, I thought Harry looked rather, well...'

'Yes, well, he is and he does look like that a lot,' Sandy laughed.

'Almost any pretty face will do it, in fact, so it's just as well we understand and still love the old bugger!'

Clare joined in the general laugh although she directed some curious looks at me. She seemed to fit in with us really well so we invited her to stay for afternoon tea and drinks later.

'I'd love to,' she said, 'especially as I'm better dressed than yesterday, although I definitely won't be overdoing it again. I'm buggered if I know how I got through my Watch, but I almost forgot to tell you and Dave that I've got our fitters lined up to come over and look at where we can mount the hold-down brackets for the MK47 grenade launchers. Would now be OK for them to come over?'

I shrugged, 'I guess so. Hey, Dave,' I yelled and his tousled head popped up from where he was dozing in a chair in the next cockpit.

'Afternoon Harry, hi Clare. There I was having a lovely dream and had just about got to a really good bit when…wham. You called! How can I help you and your lovely ladies?'

'Clare wants to get the fitters over to look at where they can attach brackets to hold your new weapons. But we can tell them not to worry if you want to get back to your lust-filled dreams!'

'Piss off, Harry. I'm not passing the chance to get some new toys for anything. Clare, you can call them over any time that suits them.'

'Actually, they're probably ready now. Can I use your radio please Harry?'

'Yeah, of course. The UHF is already set to your frequency. It's on the Nav station panel.'

She went inside and made the call, reporting back that the Duty Taxi would drop them off in five minutes. Dave dragged himself out of his chair and Clare went to join him wearing her metaphorical hat of Weapons Officer. I left Sandy, too comfortable in her chair to move, and just out of interest tagged along.

The two fitters who were dropped off with a pile of gear were in camo uniform and were soon inspecting *Seeker's* upper works, tapping, poking, measuring and prodding to find a secure and effective place for the launchers.

'I reckon the forward section of the sundeck would be perfect, Ma'am.' the senior Fitter said to Clare. 'These handrails are strong enough, although the gunners will have to kneel to shoot, but that shouldn't be a problem.'

He looked at Dave, 'Will that be OK, Sir?'

Dave shrugged, 'No problem for me, Chief, go for it.'

So they did, using adjustable clamps on the handrails and adapting the MK47 mounts to bolt securely to them. Since they had all necessary gear with them, the job didn't take long and without being told what they were for, they could have been mounts for big spotlights.

'When can we go play bang-bangs?' Dave asked Clare. 'I presume the crews will need some practice?'

Clare nodded, 'Yes, they will. Not only is this a very different platform, but also we haven't had much to do with the MK47 at all since it's only just replaced the old MK19 launcher which was inferior in just about every way. This one shoots further, faster and a lot more accurately, especially if the mounting is held down tightly like this. It's probably a bit late now, so we might bring the launchers over in the morning to set them up which won't take long, then we should go find a quiet spot without spectators and blow up some sand.'

Dave beamed and rubbed his hands together. 'Outstanding! I can't wait. Finally *Seeker* gets to be properly armed, even if it is just with grenade launchers.'

Clare grinned at his enthusiasm, 'Don't underestimate the 40 mm grenade. It has a hell of a punch and when you can toss one per second from each launcher at something more than two kilometres away, it has a devastating effect.'

He nodded, 'Good point and I'm very glad we'll have them if the bad guys are going to be shooting back at us.'

'Harry was saying you've already had that experience.'

'Yes, but only to a small degree compared to what he's had. And we had the element of surprise at the time which always helps.'

At that point, we declared work over for the day and invited the two fitters to have a beer with us. They looked at Clare, who said 'go ahead, it's after 16:00 so you're off duty now.'

They looked at each other, before the senior one said, 'We'd love to have a beer with you Commander, thank you.'

'Harry please! Excellent, walk this way. No, not that way, this way! Sorry, old joke.'

The fitters only stayed for two beers, appearing slightly uncomfortable drinking with what they regarded as senior officers, but they were nice guys and we said we'd catch up ashore for the evening BBQ.

It was a much quieter evening, although Clare chose to hang out with us before heading back to her boat before midnight. I introduced her to the pleasure of NQ Tea with the triple-shot of rum liqueur and we sent her off on the Duty-Taxi with only slightly wobbly legs.

SATURDAY... BRIDLED ISLAND

We didn't bother getting up for the beach breakfast again, settling for tea & coffee and loads of toast on board, but several sailors passed by asking if Jasper could come ashore to play and run with them, so after a quick word to him about behaving, he happily hopped into the RHIB taxi and went to play with the boys and girls. We watched him romping with several groups who were all competing to attract his attention, but the frisbee crew always won.

It was a bit strange to see him playing so happily with a large group of strangers and I made a mental note to include that in the discussions about Jasper that Barbara had arranged for after lunch.

Of course, the big event of the morning was the fitting of the two MK47 grenade launchers and the scheduled testing by their crews.

Promptly at 08:30 the two fitters from yesterday, together with four competent-looking young sailors, two men and two women, in addition to Clare as Weapons Officer, were ferried over to *Seeker* along with three small crates, one of them very heavy.

'The MK47 itself is only 18 kilos,' Clare explained, 'much lighter than the MK19 which was over 35 kilos. The heavy crate has boxes of rounds for today's practice, but we'll supply more for Monday night.'

The crates were hoisted up to *Seeker's* sundeck and the various parts of the launchers were taken out and assembled by the crews, although the fitters grabbed the tripods and started clamping them firmly into the brackets that had been installed yesterday. There seemed to be a lot of parts to each launcher, but the crews knew what they were doing and made short work of the assembly. By the time the tripods were fixed in place, the launchers were ready to be lifted into place where they clicked into place as though, strangely, they were meant to go there.

A box of linked rounds sat neatly beside each launcher and they were spaced far enough apart that there was plenty of room for the gunner and loader on each.

'OK, Dave,' said Clare, 'we're ready when you are. I'd like to find a small islet not too far away, but without anybody there, if you can.'

'OK. We might head north toward the Montebello's. There are some small islets on the way. It's only two or three miles so we'll hardly get the engines warm.'

He started the big diesels, letting them rumble quietly as they warmed up while we sorted out who was going and it turned out that everyone wanted to see the effect of the MK47s so while the temp gauges slowly climbed, we got the tribe loaded and settled.

We rumbled out past *Glenelg* and after turning the corner of the bay, Dave pointed the bow slightly west of north and slowly wound the diesels up until we were doing around 40 knots, which was fun for the crew who weren't used to anything over 25 knots. He had us running up past a string of islets that stretched half way to Ah

Chong Island. The one we were hoping to shoot up was at the end of another shorter string which angled more to the northwest. It was clearly visible since it was only a couple of miles away and at 40 knots, it took all of three minutes.

Throttling back to a more comfortable 15 knots, we circled the little islet which was just 200 metres long by 100 metres wide, with a tiny appendage hanging off its north-western tip. The water surrounding the little island was very shallow and there appeared to be a small beach where the baby islet was attached. The main thing was, there were no boats at the island or in the vicinity so we were free to make some noise.

Clare took over directing Dave to nose in toward the shore near the narrow neck of exposed limestone where there was a low cliff. At about 100-metres range she called for the two gunners to load weapons, waited for their return call of 'loaded' then directed them to fire alternate short bursts at the low, vertical part of the cliff.

There was a loud banging sound from the boxy weapons and a series of explosions against the cliff brought down a small cascade of pulverised rock, and sent a large cloud of dust climbing skyward. The downside was a cascade of hot cartridge cases and belt links over the sundeck floor, but that was a minor problem.

'Cease fire and clear' Clare ordered and waited for the response before asking Dave to turn and head back out away from the shore. When the Chart plotter showed we were just over one kilometre away, she had him turn and hold position again. She issued the fire order again and the loud banging and the shower of spent cases and links littered the floor, yet again the small cliff was chewed up by a series of small explosions, the dust cloud rising to join the first that was slowly dissipating.

'Cease fire. Good shooting people!' Clare ordered. 'Dave, would you take us further out to two kilometres offshore please?'

'No problem,' he replied, eyes alive with the excitement of both shooting and blowing things up. While he did that, the fire teams checked their remaining loads and decided they had enough for a few short bursts at the more extreme range. I heard them being coached by Petty Officer Jane Glen regarding what they needed to do to make proper use of the range finder and firing solution processor to be able to lay their first rounds on target.

'Two kilometres Clare,' Dave said quietly.

'Fire teams load. Same target. Fire when ready.'

I noted this time that although the banging recoil was obviously quite strong, the grab rails weren't flexing and the boat didn't vibrate so the fitters had done an exceptional job.

There was a cheer from the fire teams as all their first rounds impacted the target area again. This time, they ran out of rounds before Clare could call a cease-fire.

'Excellent job girls and boys! Right on the money, although that's from a stationary platform at a stationary target. Let's see how you go with the boat moving.'

'Dave, can you swing further away, then track in at the target at a shallow angle so the range is closing and there's some relative lateral motion? Set your speed at 25 knots please.'

'Will do.'

While we swung away and accelerated, the fire teams lifted up fresh ammo boxes and reloaded their obviously very deadly little weapons. Once back inside the two-kilometre range and closing the target on an oblique angle at modest speed, Clare gave the open fire order.

This time the first few rounds exploded wide of the target, but the savvy gunners were using short bursts and correcting visually for the shortening range and sideways movement, so that the next short bursts were right on target.

'Cease fire. Well-done teams. Standby for re-engagement.'

'OK Dave, can you do a 360° turn and up the speed to say 45 knots? Still angling in toward the target. We can't turn side on to the target since the launchers won't slew too far but the higher speed might make them work a bit harder.'

'Coming up.' *Seeker* leant over and the stern sank a bit more as he advanced the throttles and cranked on a turn, coming out of it doing rather more than the requested speed, but it was still good training since on Monday night, the bad boys wouldn't be just sitting there watching incoming rounds without firing back.

This time the first rounds were much closer to the target and the second burst was right on. Clare let them get a few more bursts in before calling for a cease fire.

She called up to the fire teams, 'That was really good work, but what angle of slew can you get on those mounts?'

Petty Officer Jane replied, 'For safety, ma'am, the left unit can only do 0° right and 45° relative left, while the right unit is vice versa.'

'Understood. Make that set procedure for this installation please.'

'Yes Ma'am. Will do.'

Clare asked Dave for one more run in, starting from nearly two kilometres out, but to zigzag in at speed and on legs that were at 45° to the target. This time only one gun was firing at a time so it was easy to see if they were accurate and they were, scoring hits from the first rounds. Inevitably, it became a competition between the two teams and by the time Clare called for a cease-fire and clear the weapons, they were pretty even.

Behind them, we had worked out a process that collected the cases and links into a large rubbish bin.

'Thanks Dave, take us home please.'

'Yes Ma'am on our way,' he said with a grin, shoving the throttles well open for a bit of fun on the way. At 65 knots, it only took a few minutes to enter the narrow passage just off our sheltered bay, where he swung in at speed in a showy gesture, before slowing abruptly and idling up to drop anchor beside *Firebird* again.

CHAPTER 36

After the fitters had checked the mounts and pronounced them unaffected by the firing trials and the crews had serviced their weapons, secured the covers over them and cleared all the debris away, Dave pulled me aside.

'I'm going to have to refuel before Monday night. All this running around has run the tanks a bit too low for comfort, so I'd be happier filling up sooner rather than later.'

I thought a moment, 'OK. That sounds good. I wanted to see Onslow so I'll come and Barb wanted to talk about Jasper, so we could take them both and I could chat on the way. Sandy might want to come as well, but I hear Alf was saying they were going to have another tramp party on *Firebird*.'

'Well, it's still only 10:30 so if we go shortly, we can be back in time to have a relax.'

I called Barb on the Inter-ship UHF and she happily accepted the offer, although she suggested that the fitters come back and un-clip the MK47s from their mounts and stow them below out of sight. It was a two-minute job Dave and I could have done easily and we told the men we'd re-mount them on our return.

Sandy was keen to come along, and because it was Clare who dragged Jasper away from playing on the beach with the *Glenelg* crew, she came as well. At 10:45, we dropped lines to *Firebird* and hauled the anchor, idling quietly out of the bay before Dave opened the throttles again. He held the speed to 55 knots as I placed a SatPhone call to the refueller at Onslow, to make sure he would be in attendance. He sounded most obliging and was happy to look after us in about 70 minute's time.

I refrained from saying where we actually were at the time to avoid stirring up unnecessary discussion about our speed, although we were going to stand out since there wouldn't have been many boats like *Seeker* running down the remote west coast.

On the way down, Sandy and Clare had a chuckle as Barbara grabbed the chance of a captive audience to explore Jasper's mystical doings with me. The best example I could tell her about which had been seen by several others, was his encounter up on the Cape with the giant crocodile. That story fascinated her like nothing else and she wouldn't let up on it, by trying to analyse the encounter and his behaviour every which way. She was even more excited and captivated when I told her we had video back on *Firebird*, both from the Handy-Cam and the masthead camera, of the entire encounter with the croc.

To most of her questions I couldn't offer an explanation for his behaviour.

'I must say Barb, that in the two years I've had him, I've almost taken for granted his ability to apparently read my mind and to understand what I say in plain English. I know that's a terrible thing to say, but we've lived together in the same relatively small space and no matter how clever or mystical he is, after a while these 'miracles' seem almost commonplace.'

We paused the discussion when Dave called out that Onslow was close and I needed to get Jasper under cover.

It was right on 70 minutes from the phone call that we entered the narrow entrance to Beadon Creek, with a man-made finger breakwater on the right and a dredge working to realign the shifting sandbar on the left. It was an uninspiring landscape with flat expanses of red sand replacing flat expanses of red rock as the dominant background. According to directions, we had to pass the extensive oil and gas rig service wharf to get to the refuelling wharf.

I'd briefed the three ladies that it would be best if they played the part of the attractive but dumb companions of two wealthy playboys on a cruise around Australia just for the fun. Clare and Sandy got into the spirit of that theme and took their shirts off, but kept their bikini tops on. Barb just didn't manage to get into the 'dumb blonde' companion image, but still looked very attractive anyway. As the fuel flowed into *Seeker's* tanks, I casually mentioned that as we were on an anti-clockwise circumnavigation, we were heading south from Onslow. I mentioned having the long-range tanks fitted to explain why the fuel meter happily ticked on past the 6000 litre figure without any sign of the tanks being full but the refueller dude couldn't have cared less, and apart from perving on the girls, seemed more interested in getting rid of us as soon as possible so he could join his mates in the pub for the afternoon.

We were nearly an hour re-fuelling so Sandy and Clare took a break from looking decorative and made sandwiches for lunch. There wasn't much point in going ashore since the town centre was a fair walk away and there wasn't anything we needed immediately. Amanda had already bludged a fresh supply of bread-making ingredients off the *Glenelg's* head cook so we relaxed in the cockpit, acting the part of bored, rich layabouts until the re-fueller called out that everything was full and who was going to pay the bill?

Dave grinned as he dug out his Visa Black card with the 'no spending limit' and followed the dude back to the office. Shortly after, with the paperwork complete, he re-appeared and five-minutes later, we pulled our lines aboard and headed back out from the wind-swept red desert coast. To reinforce our story, I asked Dave to swing around the point and head south, staying in close so we could take a look at the facility that we were preparing to defend. It certainly was a massive, sprawling complex with a long jetty poking out into the ocean where a tanker was tied up, presumably in the process of taking on another load of gas for South East Asia.

'Another good reason to keep the whacko's away from this place!' I commented to the others as we stood in the saloon watching the targets drift past. Once well past the plant, Dave swung out to sea in a big arc until we were heading northeast for the east side of Barrow Island. He kept the speed down on the return run and Barb sat down again with Jasper and me to probe at his mystic nature. I noticed Sandy and Clare spent the time out in the cockpit sitting close and chatting cosily and was glad since Clare seemed like a really nice girl, but there was an aura of loneliness about her.

I'd already noted that she didn't mix with her own peers very well, so it was good she and Sandy were getting along so well.

The diversion and slower speed meant it was getting on for 15:00 when we rumbled into the little bay to a scene of activity with the Navy RHIBs shuttling crew to and fro as well as towing water-skiers around the area. Another bonfire had been set up on the beach in readiness for the Saturday night BBQ and beach party as Sunday was the last free day as designated by Paul. Monday was designated as pre-action day where everything was checked and double-checked, so the crews were really making the most of their bonus free time.

After running off a copy of both videos of the 'Croc Encounter', Sandy ran Barb back to *Glenelg* then continued on to shore where she and Clare let Jasper have another play while they went for a run together up the beach.

I helped Dave re-mount the MK47 grenade launchers and secure their covers, a quick and simple job and then relaxed in *Firebird's* cockpit. The trampoline party that was underway when we left for Onslow had moved on-shore, joined by several off-watch Navy guys and girls who were hell-bent on getting a head start on the evening's party, so we had some peace.

'The timing is going to be fairly tight to get *Dragonfly* back to cover our assault,' Dave commented.

'Yeah. I was telling Paul and Barb that your radar should allow us to pick up the EarthSquad RIBs and the work barge, but that's only going to work at short range, given your Radome isn't mounted very high.'

'That's why we're going to need *Dragonfly* overhead as soon as the Navy has done its bit. I reckon it's at least 50 miles from where the Navy will be to where we should be hoping to intercept our group. That's at least 40 minutes flight time at full bore for it to get to us.'

I fetched the chart from the Nav station. 'Part of the problem is that we don't know if they'll be tracking close inshore, or will swing out to stay clear of this maze of little islands.'

'Why don't we get Corrine to just tell them. She's the boss. That'll make it easier to position ourselves on their track and even better if she tells them to stay close inshore where the channel is narrow.' He traced his finger down the chart, 'Look here. If she makes them track just inside Weld Island and Mangrove Island, then to the outside of Direction Island, we can ambush them when they get to Mangrove Island.'

I considered the position and distance to Onslow. 'I don't know, Dave. Even though it gives us extra time to get *Dragonfly* on station over us, I don't like hitting them so close to Onslow. How about we lie in wait at Weld Island and if it looks good, we hit them? If it doesn't work, we can sprint on ahead to Mangrove Island at best speed. How would that be?'

He took his time working out distances, before speaking. 'Yeah, that's not a bad compromise. If the situation looks good even without the UAV, if we have a good radar plot, we ambush them from Weld Island. It's far enough from the camp that no sounds or lights should be seen. Okay, you've sold me.'

I smiled, 'Good. We'll lock that down for now, but we'll still be trying to get the UAV overhead ASAP.'

'Shit, yeah!' was the stern reply.

I felt happier now we had a workable plan for both parts of the operation and had even allowed for contingencies, so by mutual agreement, we declared the bar open. By the time Sandy and Clare came back with Jasper, Dave and I were getting a bit shit-faced and the girls were not amused we'd started without them, so they tried to catch up which was a very bad mistake since by the time we were due to go ashore to eat at the Navy BBQ, they were having giggling fits for no apparent reason and had trouble standing.

'What do we do with them?' Dave asked. 'I wouldn't like to leave them on their own.'

'I'd chuck them overboard if we weren't so close to the beach, but how about we hose 'em down on the stern steps.'

'You are a brave man Harry Stevens! I get the feeling that this will one of your less popular decisions.' Dave laughed.

'Nah! They'll forgive us!' So with difficulty we wrestled the very wobbly pair down to the lower starboard stern step, dug the shower out of its locker and turned the cold on. As a quick sobering method, it was very effective, although some of the threats that were directed at us were truly vile and totally unthinkable!

'OK. Enough you rotten bugger!' was the instruction from Sandy, so I complied, noting that Dave had fled some time before, leaving me to cop the abuse. I couldn't help laughing at the two very bedraggled females who were still wobbly, but could at least talk.

'Come on Clare. Get out of those wet things and we'll get dry,' was Sandy's suggestion as they climbed very unsteadily back up to the cockpit. It was lucky the cockpit was mostly facing away from the beach as she unbuttoned her shirt with considerable difficulty. She managed to remove her shorts more easily and bra and panties followed. Clare had no concerns about doing the same and moments later; both ladies were delightfully naked and looking for towels.

'See?' mumbled Sandy, pointing at the front of my shorts. 'I told you it didn't take much to make him big. Hang on, that should be very big! How could I have forgotten?'

Clare peered at me intently for what seemed a long time, so I did the same, happy to check her out again, but she made no comments, which was probably just as well.

Once dry, they padded down below to the bow dressing room, still very unsteady on their feet so they bounced off a few bulkheads on the way, each time breaking out in fits of giggles. I followed to make sure they were OK.

Sandy dug out shorts and a top for Clare, but they both needed help to get them on. Neither bothered with bra or panties and their wet hair was just pulled back into a limp ponytail before they pronounced that they were ready to join the party.

Dave appeared to help with getting them into the RIB and that was more fun as Clare tripped on the side of the RIB getting out and did a face-plant into the sand. We got her up and de-sanded and steered her toward the BBQ, which was putting out some beautiful smells. I made up a couple of plates of lovely grub and sat them down on the nearest lump of driftwood.

'Get that into you, ladies, and you'll feel much better.'

'That's very fucking doubtful,' growled Sandy, picking at her lovely steak. 'Why the hell did you let us drink so much, you bloody big goose?'

Wisely, I kept my mouth shut, which 'shows to go' that sometimes I can learn from past mistakes. The night followed the format of the first one where there was live music and a type of dancing in the loose sand that was cause for a lot of laughs. Some of the Navy crew had beautiful voices and even Skipper Paul was game to try a song.

It was a happy night with no aggro, although the Petty Officers were there to keep things sane and started wrapping it all up before midnight. Dave got tangled up with a bunch of Navy dudes so at about 23:00 I went looking for Sandy and Clare. I'd caught glimpses of them throughout the evening, still together, but hadn't seen them for a while.

Finally, I checked with the RHIB taxi driver.

'Oh! Yes Sir. I dropped Inspector Thomson and Lieutenant Stahall off on *Firebird* about an hour ago.'

'Thanks, Leading Seaman.'

'You're welcome sir and if I might add, I'm looking forward to being in your crew on Monday night. I'm Terry Boone, one of the grenade launcher gunners.'

'I'm sorry I didn't recognise you Terry. There was a lot to take in then and I've not used those units before.'

'Not many have, sir. They're a new release for us too but seem to be very effective.'

'Yes, it looked that way. Did the laser rangefinder and electro-optic sights help a lot?'

'Oh! Yessir,' he replied enthusiastically. 'We can get about 90% of the first few rounds on target, whereas with the old MK19 and its open sights, it took several bursts to get on the target.'

'Good to hear that Terry, so I hope you shoot well tomorrow night. Anyway, I'd better go find the ladies before they get into trouble.'

He chuckled, 'I can say Sir, that they certainly had the wobbly boot on when I ran them out, so I've been keeping an eye on your boat since then, but all's been quiet.'

After I thanked him and said good night, I decided to go aboard and get my head down. Making sure the RIB was secured to a stern cleat, I had a pee off the stern, as one does, before heading for bed. All was quiet throughout the boat, although a couple of cabin lights were on as I made my way quietly down below, Jasper and Krazy greeting me as I passed through the saloon. One dim light was on in our cabin, but I wasn't expecting the second female head on the pillow beside Sandy, or maybe I should have been expecting it!

Sandy had shown on a couple of occasions in the past that when she connected with the right person, she was happy to fool around with another female, Tracy being the last one she'd had fun with. However, it was always light-hearted so I never felt left out. And Clare was certainly a nice person. Built nicely too!

On this occasion they were both deeply asleep, the sheet only pulled up to their waists which made for a stirring sight, so I did what any real gentleman would do and cleaned my teeth, before getting undressed and climbing in beside Clare who was in the middle. She felt very nice and cuddly, but I was too tired and probably too drunk to do any fooling around of my own and promptly fell asleep.

I was disturbed a couple of times through the night by someone sliding out of bed to presumably go pee, but they returned each time so all was well.

The first faint light of the promise of dawn showed through the open hatch over the bed when I awoke at my usual time and feeling the pressure of a full bladder, I slid out of bed to relieve the problem. It was a toss-up whether to stay up or go back to a warm, comfortable bed but as no one else was stirring above; I forced myself to return to my bed with the two naked ladies in it, still managing to fall asleep.

I woke some time later to the sound of giggles and whispers before a firm and shapely female bum was pushed against my mid-section with predictable results. Those predictable results led in turn to the inevitable and the delightful feel of Clare, for that was who did the pushing in the first place. Things certainly worked out very well for both of us and having had a good rest extended the mutual pleasure considerably.

It's probably just as well that I never know when Sandy is going to be in one of these moods, so I've learned to take what's on offer and make the most of it. As was the case this time where I thought we should have at least a second round to make sure the first time wasn't just a very pleasant accident. With one thing leading to another, it was well past breakfast time before we were decent enough to get up, wash up and join the rest of the hung-over crew.

'I can see the bar had better stay closed tonight,' I said to Sandy as we took in the pathetic sight of five of the crew sprawled around the cockpit seats or laying on the daybed with eyes closed. Tracy was present for the first time in several days and although looking utterly wrung out, was also in a very happy mood.

The rest of the morning was devoted to doing absolutely nothing, although Paul and Barbara came over in the afternoon. Clare left since she had the Afternoon Watch starting at 12:00. With Paul and Barb also well rested, we went over the plans again and Dave and I told them of our slightly refined plan for our side of the operation.

Paul spoke up, 'One thing I wanted to ask was, what's the plan for afterwards when the raiding parties have been knocked out?'

'Good point and I should have talked this through earlier, but we need to hit the camp and see who's left. There will be non-combatant staff like cooks and admin types who are relatively harmless and

I'm not too worried if they bug out, but the two masterminds, Terry and Paula are supposed to be there and they must be collected, alive if possible, but if both failed to survive it'd be no great loss. I was thinking that after we check for computers and paperwork, we might torch the place, making it look like a fire drove everyone out.'

'Good idea. How about if we close the coast as soon as our RHIBs have done the job and been recovered. Then if you do the same coming up from the south, at least one boat will be there ASAP.'

That sounded good to me, 'That'll work, but there's one more thing, I don't want to leave *Firebird* out here and there'll be Tracy and Melissa staying aboard, so I'm having a rethink about boat and crew arrangements although it won't affect your deployment.'

I thought a bit more, mentally shuffling chess pieces around the Oceanic board.

CHAPTER 37

The others waited patiently as Sandy explained how it was when I drifted off into one of these mental planning missions, there was no value in trying to hurry things along.

'OK. Here's the new go. You know what you have to do and just need a start time, but Corrine will be supplying that today or tomorrow.'

Paul nodded, 'Yes. Understood.'

'Right. You don't need me here to hold your hand when I can update you via SatPhone, because both *Firebird* and *Seeker* will leave here tomorrow afternoon about 15:00 and head in for North Sandy Island which is about 12 miles offshore from the camp and 5 miles west of the track their RIBs should be taking to the platform.

We won't attempt to hit the guys heading for the platforms. They're all yours because we'll be waiting for the next lot heading south.'

He saw the possible flaw straight away. 'Are you sure you won't be too close to the coast?'

I nodded, 'They have to expect other boats to be in the area through the day, so a pair of pleasure boats are harmless. You're the one we don't want anybody seeing, even though the Admiral told me you routinely patrol down as far as Exmouth. We've not seen any boat patrols from the camp and certainly not 12 miles out, so I reckon we're safe at North Sandy Island. It also means we're in a good position to chase them and attack from behind which will be much easier for the gun crews. Don't forget, they can't outrun us.'

He was more comfortable after that was explained. 'That sounds better. I was concerned about the side-on attack, but a trailing position is much better, especially if you can keep well back and track them with that fancy digital radar. Even if you close to one kilometre, that's a good range for the MK47s and don't forget they've got IR sights as well as daylight EO ones.'

'Good point. I had forgotten that. So that would be a perfect position to attack from?'

'Yep. Clare could tell you more, but it's the plan I'd use. They won't be looking behind too much and you said they don't mount radar on the RIBs. A one-kilometre trailing position at night means you'll be invisible.'

'Great! That's our plan then, unless Mouse comes up with something different.'

Before they left to return to *Glenelg*, Paul took me aside and said, 'I wanted to thank you for taking Clare under your wing, so to speak. She's had some trouble mixing with the others on board, but this layover seems to have sparked her up dramatically. She's extremely good at her job, but it was just the loner bit that, as her CO, had me concerned for her.'

'I understand and I must say she, and Sandy in particular have been getting on really well, but she fits in wonderfully with our whole crew.'

'Thanks Harry. Let me know when you hear from Corrine.'

As he and Barb returned to *Glenelg* in their expensive water taxi, Sandy and I had a chuckle between us.

'It was a lovely night and morning,' she said, giving me a quick kiss. 'Thanks for being so understanding and letting me occasionally indulge my little eccentricities!'

'More than delighted, my dearest lady,' I smiled, 'don't forget that I indulged myself too!'

She giggled, 'How could I forget? Several times you greedy pig!'

'Always plenty left for you,' I reminded her.

She rolled her eyes, 'I remember, but hold yourself back. I've invited Clare back here after she's off-watch and is free. *Glenelg* is still in shore-leave mode so she'll be with us until noon tomorrow.'

I gave a lecherous grin, 'Oh dear, she'll be totally corrupted by then!'

Sandy smacked my arm. 'Just because she said how much she enjoyed this morning, don't let it go to your head…or anywhere else for that matter! She enjoyed last night as well and so did I!'

That was worth a good laugh and we decided to swim ashore and go for a run to sweat off the excesses of the night before, but just before we left, the SatPhone trilled a strange tone.

Picking it up I saw that it was a text message, so holding it out to Sandy, I asked, 'how come we can get text messages on this thing? I didn't think they could do that.'

She took the device and clicked a bunch of buttons. 'You've got an app called 'X-Gateway' on here. It's a data compression feature that allows emails and text messages as well as a bunch of other things. It's really neat.'

'Terrific!' I said. 'But who's it from and how do we open it?'

She clicked more buttons then said, 'It's from Corrine dopey. Who else? Here, have a read of this.'

'Hi all. I think this should get through to you via Harry's SatPhone. I'm sure it has the app to receive messages but anyway, here's hoping. I can't have a conversation, because even though I have one of the few single rooms, there are way too many people around with big ears. The assault launch is still set for Monday night and both targets are to be hit at midnight.

Due to the distance to the platforms, I've had to allow the RIBs to pre-position at a place called Pansy Island, between Trimouille island and North-West Island. The drop-off will be around 15:00 on Monday afternoon using the work barge. They'll stay on Pansy Island waiting for the launch from there at 22:50. To help your planning, I'll make sure that the NCOs will keep everyone laying low so they won't be going exploring either on foot or by boat. They don't have spare fuel for any buggarising around anyway.

I wanted to position them closer inshore but the troops are going to be really crook due to seasickness, so even if we were going all the way to the platforms, they'd be utterly useless. I realise the Pansy Island location might make it more difficult for you to intercept them, but for what it's worth, the launch time will be strictly adhered to.

The launch from the camp will be with the other two RIBs and the work barge. Myself and the three people who I intend to pull out, will be in the lead boat and I've positioned the other RIB and the work barge side-by-side, about 100-metres apart and 200-metres behind us which means there'll be an arrow formation. I'll have a small blue light down in the bottom boards which hopefully will show up if you can get Dragonfly overhead and I'm going to show a yellow light at the stern of our RIB, supposedly so the other two boats have something to follow. Otherwise, we're the RIB in front and will have a UHF CB on Channel 24.

Because the distance is only a little bit longer, the launch from the camp will also be at 22:50, but we will be maintaining a slightly higher speed due to calmer water closer inshore.

Be advised that Terry and Paula are staying in camp along with the deputy security dude Drew, four cooks and two admin types. There's a 25-foot fishing boat with a large outboard at the camp which was captured some time ago. I don't know where the owners are, although I could make a good guess!

I'm certain if Terry and Paula get the slightest hint of anything going wrong, they'll bail out and leave the others to walk overland to the highway. That's over 30 kilometres through what is effectively desert. Do try to nail the bastards if you can. Please.

I hope that I've covered everything, but if there's something you need to tell me, I'll have this thing turned on again 30-minutes from now. Mark.

My number will be on your screen. Good luck.

'Fuck!' was Sandy's contribution, so I had to settle for, 'time to re-plan!'

'OK. We need an immediate conference with Dave, Paul and Barb.'

While Sandy dug Dave out of his afternoon siesta, I went into the Nav station and called *Glenelg* on the Inter-ship UHF radio.

'*This is Glenelg. How may I help you Commander?*'

'Skipper, please. Urgent.'

'*Stand by one.*'...'Glenelg *actual.*'

'It's Harry. Can you guys get back immediately? We need to re-plan.'

'*Will do Harry. On our way.*'

Barbara must have been close for within a minute I saw them at the gangway platform with the RHIB taxi curving up in a shower of white spray to collect them. Another minute and they were climbing the stern steps, inquiring looks on their faces.

'Corrine?'

'Corrine,' I replied. 'Text message. Sandy's just printing it out to make it easier.'

Sandy was back by the time they were seated and passed a copy each, so I gave them a couple of minutes to read through it.

'Bugger!' was Paul's reaction. 'We'll have to rethink the whole thing.'

Barb just looked thoughtful, although I was sure her rapier mind was figuring all the permutations.

'Not necessarily,' I said with the benefit of having had the most time to consider the changes necessary to get us back on track. 'Probably the only difference for the *Seeker* team is that we won't have time to get *Dragonfly* back over us, but the way Corrine's set up the formation and the stern light, we can still do the stern chase routine and it should work out. It's your positioning that's different.'

'Yes,' Paul said thoughtfully, 'we'll have to work out how we can do this effectively.'

'I get the impression Harry has already thought it through,' Barb observed with a wry grin.

Paul looked surprised. 'Oh? Really? Well, let's hear it!'

'Just a suggestion, but Corrine is putting them on the little island for a reason. It's too small for them to escape and hide if they see you too soon and it still lets you position *Glenelg* in an intercept position out of sight to seaward of them.'

'How so?' he demanded. 'Unless we hang about in the open water and that's not a very good option.'

I smiled, hoping to defuse his agitation. 'The next island to the north-west is, oddly enough, North-West Island and about midway along the north-east side there's a little finger of a cape sticking out. If I were in your place, I'd be inclined to park *Glenelg* in the little bay behind that finger of cape on the north side and when the time comes for the attack squad to leave Pansy Island, you could up anchor and hold position with the engines and bow thrusters, ready to shoot and or drive straight out in chase.

Additionally, when it's fully dark, say around 21:00, I'd pre-deploy my two, armed RHIBs to a nearly land-locked little bay on the south west side of Trimouille Island that's only about 1.2 miles from Pansy Island. To avoid detection, I'd send them the long way around the west end of North-West island and outside a few of the other small islands in that western area, but because it's only a trip of six nautical miles, they can take it quietly. They'll need to be careful when navigating among the small islands, but they've got the best nav systems so it shouldn't be a problem.'

Paul had a frown on his face as he thought my suggested plan through, but Barbara was way ahead.

'It'll work, Paul. We'll have the UAV overhead telling us what's going on, and by positioning the RHIBs behind the bad guys, they get to do what Harry's going to do with the other force. Hit them right up the bum when they won't be looking, while we're waiting further ahead just off to the side of their course. There's no danger of friendly fire accidents so long as the RHIBs don't proceed too far into the crossfire zone. But *Dragonfly* can also help us avoid that.'

Paul was silent a bit longer, before his frown cleared. 'You're right and I should have seen it sooner. Must be getting old! Good plan Harry, thank you.'

I smiled at his praise, then suggested, 'Just one more thing. If the attack squads are going to be dropped off tomorrow afternoon, you can easily be ahead of them if you leave here by mid-morning. It's a 20-mile run if you loop up the west side of the archipelago and come down from the north to that little bay on North-West Island.'

Paul looked at Barbara. 'How about we cancel shore leave from 09:00 on and plan to anchor-up at 10:00? And cancel the beach breakfast tomorrow, but leave the BBQ and shore leave on for tonight.'

She nodded as she pulled a small notebook from a pocket, 'Yep. That'll work fine. I'll get a work detail to pack up the BBQ and other gear in the morning, but those who've been sleeping out can continue for tonight.'

She looked at Sandy, Dave and me. 'When we declare shore leave, a lot of the crew choose to sleep off the boat in a place like this. It's a novelty, it's safe and for the enlisted sailors, a chance to have some privacy. Things are a bit cramped at times on board.'

'Then in the morning, we just need to send the MK47 crews over here along with six boxes of 40 mm grenades. I can't think of anything else that has to be done. Do you guys have anything else to add to what we've talked about?'

'Apart from sending a message back to Corrine, there's nothing from me,' I offered.

The others shook their heads and with that, they thanked us and called for their taxi which was just 50 metres away waiting for the discussion to finish. They hadn't been gone long, when the RHIB came back with Clare in it. She was off-watch and in civvies, looking to my untrained eye to be wearing a tiny amount of make-up and with a faint blush to her cheeks, she looked slightly nervous. Sandy noticed and a small grin lingered around her lips as she winked at me. Cheeky bitch!

It occurred to me that as much as we enjoyed last night, it was mostly unplanned, but knowing it was going to be repeated, allowed one to experience the thrill of anticipation and that just added to the spice of the encounter.

I sat down at the Nav station, fired up the SatPhone and asked Sandy to guide me in composing a message for Corrine. What we ended up with was; 'Hi dear girl and thanks for your message. Our assistance package will be taking care of the offshore group close to their start point and the home team will be taking care of the inshore group. Your travelling formation is noted and will fit our plan, which will be to hit the other two from behind, leaving you in the clear. If you can, please lead the formation down the coast staying close inshore. We'll be in Seeker tucked in behind Thringa Island, which is about 9 miles from the camp. We'll pick you up on digital radar and hopefully no one will be looking astern, but we'll be staying back a way. Don't be too surprised when things start going bang in the night, but when they do, break off to the right and head seaward for two klicks. In case your passengers get second thoughts, stay there until we've cleaned up. You'd better show that blue light as you approach Seeker and make a call on UHF 24 as well to avoid getting shot.

In any case, I'll call you on UHF 24 when everything is clear. We're due to meet our new friends at the camp when both groups are dealt with, to see who's left and grab Terry and Paula.

That's about it. Keep your group inshore and if possible keep your speed at 25 knots.

Keep your head down and I'll be talking to you.'

We double-checked the message was sent, and then re-joined the crew.

After the big night last night, everyone was happy to eat in and go easy on the booze, so a couple of beers and wines went with the meal and to finish up, I made up some NQ teas which went down very easily. I was fairly heavy-handed as usual and three were enough to settle everyone down. It was no surprise when crew started drifting off to bed quite early. That made it easy for us to do the same, so once I'd done the boat checking rounds, I joined the ladies in our cabin. They were already well ahead of me when I arrived, having undressed and climbed into bed, so by the time I'd peed, had a wash and cleaned teeth, they were fooling around a bit with each other. They didn't stop when I climbed into bed so I moved well over to give them plenty of room, but they weren't being very active so they didn't need the room.

I found I enjoyed watching them, although they seemed to take such a long time to get anywhere that I drifted off to sleep. I was awakened by the feel of a warm, female body being pressed against me and, again, rose to the occasion rather quickly. That in turn led to the adoption of a more conventional position which was extremely enjoyable.

I thought there was no need to rush proceedings and Clare must have thought the same so the result was a long and highly enjoyable episode where Sandy fell asleep, leaving us to proceed at our own pace.

Tiredness finally caught up and we both slept. Sandy must have wanted some time with Clare, but before dawn had progressed beyond a faint greying of the eastern horizon, I managed to get her back again to resume where we'd left off, however time was running out and after one final and delightful encounter, I sent her aft to the shower before someone came looking for their Weapons Officer.

CHAPTER 38

GLENELG, SEEKER, FIREBIRD, MONDAY

Glenelg was a hive of activity when I ran Clare back at 08:00 after a quick breakfast, and shortly after, the taxi RHIB came alongside *Seeker* to deposit the two fire teams of four sailors including, and under the control of, Petty Officer Jane Glen. The other gunner I recognised was the boat driver from two nights ago, Leading Seaman Terry Boone. They brought with them cleaning and repair kits for the MK47s and a small overnight bag each, just in case, along with six boxes of 40 mm high explosive rounds for the launchers.

Dave got their gear stowed down below and let them get settled in since there was no point removing the covers and checking the launchers just yet.

Promptly at 09:00, *Glenelg's* anchor chain went vertical and the few ripples that grew at her bow turned into a feather of white foam as the anchor was hauled into stowed position and the power slowly fed to the two V-16, 6225 horsepower MTU diesels. Dave and I both sounded our brass air horns in salute, even though the sound was reminiscent of a pair of elderly sea lions trying to mate and the long grey warship returned it with a blast from her much deeper-toned horn that sounded like a real boat's horn! I made a mental note to try to get one of those!

We had decided to travel to North Sandy Island separately in case of a stray encounter with a boat associated with the EarthSquad mob. Amanda and Melissa, both travelling on *Seeker*, would launch the UAV before we got there to make a sweep of the area around North Sandy Island for any boat traffic. They would then send it to make a high-level pass over the camp to check the latest activity level.

Seeker would take the long way around the west side of Barrow and Boodie Islands, before tracking for North Sandy Island, while *Firebird* would track direct.

I called a briefing with all the crew, including the Navy gunners, to make sure everyone knew what was happening and what they were expected to do. Strangely enough, it was the first time in four days the whole crew was together, rather than scattered between boats and various places ashore.

'Shortly we'll be leaving for North Sandy Island which is eleven miles north-west of the camp and it will be our initial staging point. It's only a small sandy island, so we don't expect any traffic there. *Firebird* will stay there with Sandy, Tracy and Bree aboard as security. Sandy knows how to get *Firebird* underway on the engines in case we need the extra boat in a hurry for some reason. The attack group we'll be chasing will leave the camp at 22:50 and head southwest along the coast, but before then at 20:30, *Seeker* will head inshore further down the coast to an ambush position. It's another small island called Thringa Island and it's 9 miles from the camp, but is right on the coast, at about 200-metres out.'

'Questions so far?' There were none so I carried on.

'At Thringa Island, we'll park *Seeker* on the west or down-coast side and keep watch with the radar which gives a fine resolution image and will easily pick up the RIBs. Corrine will be making sure the three boats keep close in to the shore on the run down so we shouldn't miss them, but we'll have to be very careful since we won't have any coverage by the UAV.'

Petty Officer Jane Glen asked, 'Where will the UAV be, Sir? It would be a great help to have it overhead, I would think.'

'Yep, it certainly would be, but as the two attack groups are launching at the same time, but from different places, *Dragonfly* is covering the offshore group *Glenelg* has. Because we have the better close-range radar and the MK47s have IR sights, we'll have to make the most of that. The plan is; when we spot the three boats approaching on radar, we let them go past and when the range is out to around one kilometre, or at least well beyond visual, we come out from behind Thringa Island and swing in behind them. They should be cruising at 25 knots and it will be a straight, no-deflection shot at the two rear-most boats.

What you gunners really need to remember is you'll be firing at one RIB and the work-barge. They'll be travelling side-by-side a couple of hundred metres behind the lead RIB which will be showing a yellow rearward-facing stern light. The lead RIB is not to be targeted at all, only the other two.

Please be careful, the leader in the front RIB is a dear friend and part owner of *Seeker*. Dave will be very, very pissed off if someone shoots his partner!'

That drew a chuckle, necessary to dispel some pre-action nerves.

'If the arrow formation is as planned, I think the left MK47 should take out the left boat, whatever it is and the right one takes the right boat. Is that what you recommend, Jane?'

She nodded, a trim, competent young lady who looked as if she should still be at home with Mum and Dad and doing school homework, but maybe it was just my age.

'Yes Sir, that's the simple way. If the boats cross over, each launcher will have to stay in its own segment to avoid tangling with the other launcher. But hopefully with the laser ranging IR sights and the ballistic computer working for us, we should be able to score first burst hits to at least stop both targets.'

'Excellent, thanks Jane. If there aren't any more questions, we'll make ready to get underway. One last thing. In case we sight other traffic, you gunners might like to lose your camo uniforms so you don't spoil our image as that of a bunch of depraved, layabout drunken boat bums having a good time tearing up money and getting pissed!'

That drew another laugh, so I terminated the briefing and we split up into separate crews to get underway.

After separating from *Seeker*, I took *Firebird* out of the bay and was able to lay a direct course for North Sandy Island.

Unfortunately, the constant south wind meant we had to motor, but since there was plenty of time, I dialled up an economical 12 knots and let Tracy cope with keeping us pointing in the right direction.

Behind us, Dave took *Seeker* around the north end of Bridled Island so he could angle out to pass down the west side of Barrow Island. He also kept his speed down to something that passed for economical on a boat with nearly 10000 horsepower available.

We passed just one other yacht, a single-masted something about 36 feet in length with two couples aboard who waved cheerfully. They were headed for the Montebello Islands by the look of their course and I hoped for their sake they stayed away from North-West Island tonight. A big orange-coloured rig tender, apparently heading for Barrow Island, was the only other vessel we saw and I discounted both of them as being involved with the EarthCare mob.

The SatPhone stayed quiet, so I took it to mean that the prowling UAV hadn't spotted any boat traffic in the vicinity of our anchorage which might affect our movements.

It was a relaxed and comfortable run taking two and a half hours which meant that right on lunch-time, we pulled into the small anchorage on the east side of North Sandy Island. Being all of 750 metres long, it had little to recommend it as an exciting tourist destination, unless one was into the stark desert, bugger-all grows on it, type of landscape. There wasn't even any coral around it to dive on and the only asset from my point of view was a little hook of a sand-spit curling around to provide some swell protection from the south and west.

Seeker joined us 10 minutes later and we rafted up together, both boats hanging on *Firebird's* anchor, since it would only be there a few hours and the weather was typically winter-stable. I was amused to see the gunner crews had listened to my earlier request and taken their camo jackets off and draped them over the MK47s to disguise the tell-tale outline of the protruding barrel on each.

Jane had gone one step further and borrowed a pair of shorts from Melissa so she rather nicely fitted the boatie bum image and seemed to be enjoying our casual way of operating. I took her aside after lunch.

'Is everything right with the MK47s?'

'Oh, yes Sir. Even though they did very little work on the firing exercise, we've still serviced them, which mainly involves greasing and oiling the moving parts. We've also been through the boxes of rounds and re-seated each round in its link to keep the feed smooth. We find it helps with reliability to fire in short, three-round bursts. They won't let us down.'

'Excellent!' I nodded at her borrowed shorts and nicely filled Navy T-shirt. 'And I see you're getting into the spirit of our disguise.'

She laughed. 'Well, you did say! Melissa loaned me the shorts and has been telling me about the last operation you were involved in. It really sounds a lot more exciting than chasing illegal fishermen.'

I nodded ruefully, 'Yes, it was. But it's not like that very often. We only get called for special, covert operations like this one.'

'If you don't mind my asking sir, what is so special about this operation which needs to be kept so secret. Our Skipper has been telling all the crew they can't ever talk about this operation when it's over.'

'I'm glad he said that. Apart from the political aspect where the Western Australian Government would be severely embarrassed if it were known they gave two million dollars to an eco-terrorist organisation and helped them establish a base right in the middle of the largest gas and oil field in Australia. Additionally, that organisation seems to be funded largely by Union Super Funds channelled via a small, but very vocal political party which has very substantial financial backing.'

Her big, brown eyes widened at that news. 'Wow! I can see why it's classed as 'Secret'! That's dynamite, but thanks for telling me sir. I find it helps to know why we're shooting at somebody.'

'I meant to ask you earlier, but have you and your team been given specific firing orders for this part of the operation?'

'Only that we are to follow your orders implicitly, Commander.

You say; we do.'

I nodded, impressed by her bright-eyed enthusiasm. 'Now you know what the targets are, what's your take on how the shooting part will go down?'

She looked a bit puzzled by the question, so I clarified it a bit. 'Do you realise these bad guys are quite likely to shoot back?'

Her puzzled look cleared, 'Oh, yessir! I expected that. And the Skipper told me before we deployed, you had requested the targets be totally destroyed. Was that correct?'

'Yes, that's correct Jane, and if you and the other gunners can achieve that objective, the job will be done properly.'

'No problem sir. We have plenty of rounds, but we may need to close the targets to ensure a 100% kill rate.'

I was pleased she was prepared to do the job properly, but slightly appalled this pleasant young woman was both competent and happy to totally wipe out the bad guys.

'Excellent, Jane. The way it'll work, is you tell Dave where you want the boat placed, and he'll do it. We work as a team on stuff like this. Getting the job done quickly and efficiently is what counts.'

She grinned with pleasure, 'Thank you Commander. That'll make it a lot easier. But I don't suppose you know if the bad guys have any long guns?'

'Unfortunately, they do. But I'm reliably informed that the best marksmen amongst them won't be doing any shooting, so as far as I know, the standard of the ones who might get a few shots off shouldn't be very high.'

'That's a relief, sir. But we'll still be careful.'

'Good. Try for those first burst hits. That'll do the job.'

'Yessir. We'll do just that and thank you for giving me the extra information on the mission. It's greatly appreciated and I'll bring the gunners up to date.'

'Any excitement?' I asked Dave when he swung across to chat.

'Nah! Didn't see another boat, although *Dragonfly* showed the camp is very busy, but nothing unusual showed up apart from what looked like some dudes loading jerry cans onto the fishing boat with the big outboard. We'll need to keep an eye on it when we get *Dragonfly* back. It just might be Terry and Paula's bug-out machine.'

'Good call. You're probably right on that. Ask Amanda to pull *Dragonfly* off *Glenelg's* coverage the moment they report all targets are down and send it over to the camp at maximum speed.'

'Will do. Anything else for now?'

'Nope. Rest and relaxation if that's possible until 20:30.'

He grinned, 'Sounds good. I'm so looking forward to getting my girl back.'

'Yeah. Me too brother! She's copped the rough end of the pineapple this time.'

On *Seeker*, we'd set up Amanda and Melissa down in the galley saloon as the communication centre with *Glenelg*, so they'd be out of the way and have less background noise. We rigged the SatPhone with an external antenna and did the same with *Dragonfly's* Ground Control Station which was set up to feed the video signal to the big-screen TV monitor down there. They would pass situational awareness info from the UAV to *Glenelg* and call the movements of all the combatants. Sandy, Tracy and Bree on *Firebird* would listen in and pass any news affecting our operations, but I had doubts anybody would visit this remote blob of sand in the middle of the night.

Still, when we took Jasper and Krazy ashore for a run and play, we could see Jasper was missing all his new friends from *Glenelg*.

The afternoon seemed to drag as we thought over the plans for things we'd missed or where a problem might pop up. As an afterthought, we even checked over and laid out the medical kits. More than once, I talked the plans over with Jane and Sandy, and Sandy was as impressed as I was with Jane's down-to-earth common sense. However, nothing new was added to the planning and we had an early tea as the sun sank in a blaze of golden glory which was hopefully a good omen, with a series of horizontal cloud layers adding to the stunning colourful display and helping to paint the sea orange long after the last tiny arc of the sun's orb had disappeared from sight.

Even though Sandy, Tracy and Bree recognised the need for them to remain behind looking after *Firebird* and monitoring the radios, they were still unhappy about being left out of the action.

'And don't you dare give me any of that shit about, 'They also serve who only stand and wait!' or I'll shove it up your bum sideways!' Sandy stated in her delightfully direct style when I dared to go over what they were supposed to do. 'And you're even taking Jasper!'

I'd debated having Jasper along, but in the end, I decided to bring him just in case; especially as I thought the risk to the girls was almost non-existent.

I was just deciding to keep my mouth shut after that verbal serve, when Dave called out from *Seeker*, 'Harry! Come and take a look at this.'

I scrambled over the rails and into the saloon where Dave was peering at the radar screen where a sharply defined red blip was tracking across the screen from left to right. It took me a few moments to check the scale, which showed that it was nearly 5 miles away to our north, travelling at 25 knots and tracking north to south.

'I reckon that's the work-barge returning to camp after dropping the offshore squad on Pansy Island. So now we know that their plan is coming alive.'

I nodded, 'Yep. Concur with that and they were too far off to see us.'

'Amanda, would you mind letting *Glenelg* know the work-barge has returned to base presumably after dropping the two RIBs at Pansy Island and we're taking it to mean their plan is being followed.'

'Roger Harry. Will do.'

Before we deployed *Seeker* to Thringa Island, we needed to dig out the small arms we had and check them over.

Amanda, Melissa, Alf and Charlie elected to have their Service Glock .40 strapped on and the various hidey-holes on *Firebird* yielded two shotguns, a mini-Uzi submachine gun and my Grizzly .44 magnum pistol. I wanted to leave *Firebird's* crew with Sandy's Glock and a shotgun, but we'd take the rest.

Similar concealed lockers on *Seeker* produced another shotgun, two .357 magnum pistols and an H&K MP5-SD6 submachine gun. The automatic weapons were very nice but because they were only firing standard 9mm Parabellum ammo, they were close-range only. Cleaning and checking the weapons of choice burned up a few hours until it was time for a late, light dinner which was only picked at as tensions were on the rise.

Finally 20:30 came around and it was time to move to the ambush point.

To be as stealthy as possible, Dave decided to just use the turbine for the run in to Thringa Island, so with it whistling quietly in the background like a boiling tea kettle and a froth of white water under the stern board as the direct-drive water-jet ran in neutral, we loaded everybody except Sandy, Tracy and Bree who sadly waved goodbye. I had Amanda bring *Dragonfly* down for a quick refuel to ensure it had maximum endurance for the night and after re-launch, she put it back into orbit around the camp until it was time to send it out to North-West Island. We worked out the flight time to the Islands would be around 40 minutes at best speed, so to be in place before the attack squad launched at 22:50, it would have to depart the camp by 22:00 at the latest and probably should leave a bit earlier to be sure.

I was hoping the attack on the raiders by *Glenelg's* RHIBs wouldn't take long which would release the UAV to head back our way sooner, but that was just being hopeful.

After the UAV re-launch, Dave took the speed up to 30 knots, which only used a fraction of the 5600-horsepower available from the surprisingly compact unit that squatted like an extra generator at the back of the engine room and was dwarfed by the pair of massive MAN V-12 diesel main engines. Emitting a droning whistle which at that low power setting wasn't anywhere near as loud as the bass thunder of the big diesels, we tracked around the north side of the little pile of sand and headed for the western side of Great Sandy Island, which in reality wasn't really all that great, being simply a long, skinny finger of sand 1800 metres long by 170 metres wide and offering the visual appeal of a bar of soap!

From there we made a straight run in to little Thringa Island which lay very close to shore in murky shallow water that looked like just the sort of home a monster crocodile would love, even though there were very few this far south. It was just twenty-five minutes after leaving North Sandy Island that we parked up on the south side of the island held by an anchor on a very short length of chain so it'd be quick to retrieve.

I called a final brief with the crew. 'It's 21:00 folks, so the bad guys will be launching in one hour and fifty minutes at 22:50. Gunners, are you set?'

'All good to go, Commander,' Jane replied quietly, 'our stand is secure, the mounts double-checked and ammo feed boxes in place. We've fastened bags to the breech outlet of the launchers to catch the empty cases and links, and if these become full, they can be emptied quickly into the bin underneath. IR sights and laser range finders have been tested.'

'Thanks Jane, good job. The attack plan for you hasn't changed. Has anybody else got something to add?'

No answer was the stern reply, so we broke up and went back to monitoring the SatPhone and the radar for the first sign of movement from the north.

CHAPTER 39

Twenty-two fifty came and went without any signs of life from the north, but then logic said, '*Why would it? Even if they were exactly on time, which would be a miracle, there was some land in the way of the radar beam so it couldn't view the camp directly.*'

Ten minutes later however, three blips appeared on the radar screen at the six-mile range marker and the radar course plotter drew a track that would pass three hundred metres out from our little island ambush point. Dave already had both diesels rumbling and the turbine spooled up, the anchor raised and was holding position with the docking joystick so our bow was pointing out to sea to present the lowest profile.

As the three blips came abeam of us, I could just make out the white of their wash as they swept past at 25-knots. Dave, who was an action movie freak, just had to say the classic word, 'Showtime!' as he smoothly pushed the diesel throttles forward and we swept out from hiding to fall in behind the trio at about 700 metres, leaving the turbine idling in reserve. I could only pick up the trace of the three raider boats by the wake they left behind, the boats themselves totally invisible in the gloom which meant they couldn't see us either and Corrine had said they didn't have night vision goggles.

However, the sights on the MK47 grenade launchers did have IR vision.

I called up to Jane, 'Are you guys seeing the targets?'

She laughed, 'Crystal clear sir. Do you want us to shoot now or close in a bit more? They aren't looking back with NVGs and we'll be invisible to the naked eye.'

I thought a moment, then replied, 'OK. If you're comfortable, we'll close in a bit more, but don't take chances and overdo it. We don't want to spook them into splitting up. You call it to Dave directly. You're weapons free except for the lead boat.'

'Weapons free. Spare the lead boat. Roger that sir. Skipper, turn 5° left and increase speed 5 knots, please.'

'Roger,' was Dave's reply as he gently moved the wheel and tweaked the throttles just a fraction.

'Steady Skipper, if you can come a fraction back to the right, that'd be spot on. Good. Hold it there, stand by for firing and to cut the throttles.'

Moments later, there was the familiar loud coughing banging sound from both MK47s as they fired together. The first burst was only short and must have been tracer rounds since I could see bright green dots of light streak out into the darkness ahead of us before a second burst followed the first before they had even reached the target.

Suddenly there were a series of bright flashes to the left and right of our bow, followed by a big explosion from the right-hand target.

'Throttle cut, now, now, now!' sang out Jane, Dave responding immediately as another longer burst spat out in a deadly green stream from each launcher, angled further to the left and right than the first ones. Both targets were now easily visible as they were both on fire, the right-hand one revealed as the work-barge sending up a column of fire a hundred feet high. I was looking at it when I saw the first few tiny red eyes winking and instantly knew what that meant.

'Incoming!' I yelled up at the exposed gunners above the roofline, but they took no notice until one of them yelled out and slipped awkwardly down off the firing platform and fell to the cabin sole, clutching at his shoulder.

'Ah, fuck it' I cursed. 'Melissa! First aid quickly. Wound dressing on the shoulder.'

The red eyes were still winking and I heard a bullet zing off a mounting as the loader cried out and dropped down as well, swiping at her face.

'Dave. Power on, but not too much and turn toward the work-barge.' I climbed up the platform and poked my head up behind the launcher. I could see there was a belt of rounds still attached to the breech of the gun and everything looked intact. Jane had her gun banging away with short bursts at the other RIB which looked to be sinking fast, so I grabbed the handles, pointed it in the right direction and squeezed off a short burst. Three green dots arced away from the stubby barrel in seemingly slow motion, before falling just short of the flaming work-barge. A slight lift of the barrel and another brief squeeze of the trigger sent more pretty green dots flying barge-wards, but this time they impacted with a series of vicious yellow flashes.

'Great shooting Commander,' Jane called over the din. 'Pour it on. There's plenty of ammo!'

So I did, holding the trigger down longer and hosing a steady stream of green dots that started at the gun barrel and connected with the flaming wreck of the work-barge. That was until a final red eye winked at me and I felt the unpleasantly familiar thump against my left shoulder, which went instantly numb. The blow swung me painfully around but I kept hold of the gun handle with my right hand and pulled back into position, my left arm hanging numb and useless by my side.

'Sir! Sir! Are you OK?' Jane was yelling, while still firing at the RIB.

With a feeling of detachment and unreality, I braced myself before replying, 'Give me a moment, thanks Jane, while I have a quick word with the person who just shot me!' Apparently, with a savage grin on my face, I squeezed the trigger hard and sent another stream of green dots of death arcing toward the hapless target, feeling no remorse whatsoever as I calmly walked the shells back and forth over the wreckage and the crew floundering in the water, until the box of rounds was empty and the bolt locked open.

Jane had stopped firing and looked at me with deep concern, 'Sir. You've been hit in the left shoulder. You need to get below and get treated immediately. We'll take care of what's left, although there isn't much.'

I didn't really take in much of what she said as I felt hands guiding me to the floor.

Dimly, I heard Melissa say, 'Shit, Harry. What the hell have you done! Sandy's going to go spare.'

As she poked and probed at my wound before cleaning then bandaging it, I felt a great deal more pain, which in my experience, meant that she must have been doing the job in a very professional manner.

'Through and through, Harry!' I dimly heard her say, 'even missed the bones! You'll be fine.' I think I must have passed out at that point in the proceedings, since I floated up out of a sea of pain to hear the rattle of the H&H MP5 and the faster buzz-saw sound of the mini-Uzi getting rid of its extended magazine of thirty 9mm rounds in about two seconds flat!

Then there was a tickling and snuffling around my face as Jasper got in on the act. I reached up with my good, right hand and stroked his soft fur, but then he mewled softly and I felt him take my left shoulder in his jaws and squeeze lightly. I started to protest, but as he continued to hold me with a light pressure, the pain slowly ebbed until there was nothing left but a faint residual ache. He kept up the clamping pressure and I felt his warm saliva soaking the bandage and running down my arm.

'Easy boy, you're making a mess of my bandage Melissa just put on.'

His answer to that mild protest was to huff at me quite loudly, so I shut up and let him do what he wanted. After all, I just wanted the pain to stop and he'd pretty well done that.

Finally, he let go, but not before he'd growled softly at Melissa who was trying to tie another dressing over the first. In the background I vaguely heard Dave cursing and swearing at the raider force before Jasper's jaws were replaced by another set of hands feeling around my shoulder. That made it start to hurt again and

I said so, only to be told by a familiar voice, 'Don't be such a pussy, Harry. You've had worse than that and still carried me a couple of hundred metres!'

I opened my eyes to see Corrine standing over me dressed in combat uniform, hands on hips and a grin on her face.

'Hiya Mouse! Welcome home.'

'Jeeze Harry, I leave you alone for a few days and look what happens. My boat sprouts guns and you get shot! You can really be a goose sometimes!'

'Sorry about that. I was hoping to welcome you home in style.'

'Yeah. You need to do something about that style...it sucks! But seriously, how do you feel?'

'Better now you're here and okay, but I still feel a bit woozy, although whatever Jasper did has worked miracles. Nearly all the pain is gone!'

'Brilliant. I've always said he's a clever pussy, but this is a new trick.'

The clever pussy in question had laid himself down beside me and was purring so loudly I could feel my chest vibrating and it was strangely soothing.

The upper deck seemed to be full of people, including three strangers in desert camo's who I presumed were Corrine's rescuee's. I was still lying on the floor, next to the gunner who was also shot and had a bandage wrapped around his shoulder and with his loader who'd copped a spray of bullet fragments across her face. It turned out the gunner was Terry the boat driver I'd met on the beach and he'd only suffered a grazing across his upper arm. His loader had been sprayed with hot bullet fragments, but they'd missed her eyes, so she was hurting, but otherwise OK.

Petty Officer Jane was crouched beside her charges making sure they were OK.

Corrine came back up with her little medical kit and quickly prepared an injection of something for them which was very potent because within a few minutes, they were both sitting up and discussing what had happened quite lucidly.

I felt much brighter and without sitting up because Jasper had one huge paw across my chest preventing such independent movement, called out, 'Local Sitrep, Dave?'

'Two boats sunk without trace,' he reported briefly, 'and unfortunately, it seems there were no survivors from either boat. Three persons injured here, one relatively minor, one minor and walking and one hardly affected.'

I nodded which was not a good idea, Jasper's magic notwithstanding. 'Good work everybody. Job done as required. Now a Sitrep from the offshore team, Amanda?'

'All good as well,' she reported, 'no injuries and a 100% no-survivors outcome with two boats sunk. The only bad news is that *Glenelg* reported one of the RIBs managed to get a very brief radio message off before they were silenced. We're not sure what was said, but the UAV is inbound to the camp at full speed and is due on station in 10 minutes.'

'Thanks Amanda; Dave?'

'Here Harry.'

'Oh. Sorry mate, I didn't see you. Can we get going at best possible speed for the camp right now?'

'On it, Harry, but what about Corrine's RIB?'

'Fuck! I forgot about that. Get Alf to jump in it and follow at best speed. It's got a full GPS nav system and it's not far.'

'Consider it done.'

Shortly after, I felt the boat accelerate sharply as the diesels bellowed and the rising howl of the turbine as it spooled up. Close inshore the sea state was only 2, but at 75 knots, it was enough to make for a soft, swooping ride that wasn't uncomfortable and once again I mentally praised the designers of this marvellous boat although the wind of our passage created a minor cyclone on the open sundeck but at least laying down I was out of the direct blast.

It was only a few minutes at speed to get close to the camp, so when I felt Dave throttle back, I persuaded Jasper to let me up and shakily made it to my feet. My big cat jammed himself against my legs to help hold me steady. Dave was at the offset helm station staring intently at the radar screen repeater and grinned when he saw me on my feet.

'Good man Harry. But you need to have a look at this.'

I lurched over to him, my legs freeing up by the minute as the general aches and pains subsided and I thought that I should have a long talk with my cat before either of us became too much older.

I peered over Dave's shoulder at the radar screen and asked, 'What am I looking at?'

He pointed with his finger at a moving red outline that was crawling up the coast, staying close inshore. 'This looks like it started from the camp, because there's nothing else down this way until you get to Onslow, so it must be that rotten fishing boat with Terry and Paula aboard.'

I was having some trouble seeing so I asked Dave, 'How far has it gone?'

'About 17 miles and it's doing 35 knots.'

'How certain are we that it originated from here?' I asked.

'Ninety-eight percent' was Dave's answer. 'There's always a remote chance it belongs to some innocent fisherman, but I doubt it.'

'Yeah and pink pigs might fly!' I grumped, looking for the inter-com handset that connected with Amanda and Melissa down in the main saloon where they were manning the control and communication centre.

'Amanda, where's the UAV right now?'

'Three minutes out. Do you have a task?'

'Yep. Divert it please, to head north to pick up on a boat that left the camp not long ago. It's the 25-foot half-cabin fishing boat doing 35 knots and is about 17 miles up at the moment. We need close-up eyeballs on it ASAP to see who's aboard.'

'Roger that. On it.'

I put the handset down and looked at Dave. 'At a chasing speed differential of 45 knots, it's still going to take the UAV twenty-odd minutes to catch up. We'll take the punt it's Terry and Paula, but I need to ask Corrine to go into the camp and see who or what's left.'

Melissa had put my left arm in a sling which made things a lot more comfortable, so I was able to make my way down to the saloon without too much trouble where I found Corrine and her rescuee's; one of whom was a giant of a man whose head barely cleared the cabin ceiling. I was introduced to Sergeant Julie Hegarty, Lieutenant Brian Towson and the huge Corporal Alex Chetty.

'Welcome aboard all and I'll be speaking with you shortly, but I must talk with the Major here for a moment, it you don't mind.'

To be honest, I didn't give a stuff if they did mind, but I was being respectful of Corrine's choice of personnel to rescue, particularly the giant Corporal Chetty, clearly of South African origin with the charming accent of that country.

I took her inside to the forward part of the saloon where things were quieter and less populated.

'What's up Big Dog?' she asked.

'It looks like Terry and Paula have bugged out in that fishing boat like you suggested they might. Amanda's got the UAV chasing it, but if it is, it can't do anything except see where they go, so we need to chase them in *Seeker*. But I also need you to go back into the camp and see if anyone is left and what paperwork can be salvaged which shouldn't get into the hands of the press. In case of trouble, take Alf and Charlie with the submachine guns.'

She nodded understanding, 'I grabbed a fair bit of stuff before I left. It's in a large duffle bag in the RIB tied up astern again, but there will be more. I'll get the two boys, but Corporal Chetty will probably insist on going as well. Since I promoted him instead of killing him, he's been very attached and protective of me. Quite bizarre! Oh, almost forgot to tell you that we hung onto our issued H&K MP5-SD6 subbies. As well as the usual issue of Glock 17s and a 19 for me. We also grabbed two Browning M2HB-QCB heavy machine guns, several cases of .50 cal ammo for them and there's a box of F1 hand grenades.'

'Bloody hell Mouse, great grab; especially the two Brownings. That'll boost the armoury stock on board but where the hell are we going to put it all? Anyway we'll worry about that later. The Corporal sounds like a good story for the debrief, but for now, get moving. We've got two very bad guys to catch!'

It was the work of a few minutes for Alf and Charlie to load up with extra magazines for the mini-Uzi and the H&K MP5 and with the huge bulk of the enigmatic Corporal Chetty acting very solicitous around Corrine, they boarded the RIB and roared off toward the camp which was nearly abeam. As soon as they were clear, I called up to Dave to come down before we made the speed run north toward Karratha.

All three engines were still idling quietly, so the crew aboard were warned to sit or hold on as Dave seated himself at the inside helm and steadily opened the throttles. He ran the two diesels up to 85% power and when the speed stabilised at 50 knots, he fed fuel to the turbine, the noise level rising dramatically. It was comical to watch the faces of Lieutenant Howson and Sergeant Hegarty, as they'd not been exposed to a boat of this size and speed before, while the speed built toward 75 knots. I hovered over the plot which showed *Dragonfly's* position, then compared it to the radar screen showing the fleeing fishing boat still well ahead of us.

Amanda caught my eye. 'What do you want *Dragonfly* to do when it catches up?'

'Throttle back, match speed, and do a target hold on the camera. Zoom in when you can and try to get a close up of faces. We need to be sure it's Terry and Paula on that thing.'

'Will do.'

Then it was just a case of waiting until the UAV caught up, which only took another five minutes. Even on the IR camera, the resolution was more than good enough to recognise Terry's handsome face and Paula, who was looking a bit ragged around the edges. Amanda had taken the UAV down much lower, but still well above visual detection. Both Terry and Paula glanced astern frequently looking for the first sign of pursuit and it looked like there was one other person on the boat with them, a tall, good-looking guy in his mid-thirties who had to be the deputy security dude, Drew.

No weapons were in evidence, but handguns could be worn.

Amanda was running the numbers on closing rates and relative speeds and had bad news. Pointing at the chart, she explained, 'We aren't going to catch them before Karratha, I'm afraid. If they head straight into this bay beside the oddly named East Intercourse Island and run up to where this long causeway joins the land, they can be at the airport in ten minutes if they call a taxi. Even if Dave tries to go a bit faster, which may not be a good idea, we still won't quite make it.'

'Bugger it! OK, but we'll still keep pushing on in case they hit something or run out of fuel or something stupid like that. And while I think of it, will you contact *Glenelg*, update them on our situation and suggest that they RV with us back at the camp. They should be able to find good water well inshore of Cowle Island. We'll be back as soon as we can and have a joint de-brief.'

'Roger that Harry. Will do.'

I moved over and updated Dave over the thunder of the engines and he just nodded philosophically.

'So be it. We'll give our best shot though.'

I patted him on the back and let him concentrate on the job of keeping 90 tonnes of boat doing 75 knots from hitting something harder than water.

CHAPTER 40

MONDAY NIGHT, TERRY & PAULA

The fishing boat roared on with the big outboard running flat-out and the boat bounding from swell to swell, landing with a teeth-jarring thump each time. Drew, the deputy security chief was doing the driving since Terry and Paula knew stuff-all about boats and how to operate them.

For the tenth time, Paula leant over and yelled in Terry's ear, 'Do we have to keep on like this? I'm either going to be sick or break a tooth. That is, if the fucking boat doesn't break up first!'

'Yes, we do! Something went horribly wrong that got the bloody Navy involved. It could have been an accidental encounter, but I don't know, therefore we bug out and run as fast as we can in case someone is following us right now.'

'But there's been no hint of a problem and the training of the troops has gone really well. We're so lucky we had Corrine to orga-nise things. What a tough little bitch!'

'Yeah, terrific!' grumped Terry, still upset he'd failed to attract Corrine into his bed and naturally blaming her poor taste in men. 'I suppose she was OK.'

Paula patted his arm, 'She was better than OK, my dear man, she was brilliant! I know you're upset you didn't get into her pants, but you've had your pick of most of the lovely young things there, especially the very athletic Janine, but you had to let that moronic Colonel fuck her. Bad move dearest, bad move!'

Terry waved her logic aside. 'Have you called for a taxi and alerted the pilots yet?'

'Yes dear, of course. Pilots are waiting with the international flight plan filed. They say the aircraft can make it easily without refuelling. What do you think about this part of the operation? Was it compromised as well or are we just running away from ghosts?'

He shrugged. 'I truly don't know. But I've a healthy respect for coppers and jail and I don't want to get too close to either. So we bail out and check back by phone when we're out of the country. That's safe.'

Paula looked at him in a new light. 'You're not very brave, are you my dear?'

Terry found some steel in his backbone for once, and growled quietly over the engine noise, 'If you mean I'm not going to stick my neck out if the wheels are falling off this wagon, the answer is no, I'm not brave. But I'm not stupid either. If this thing has come unglued, it's because of insider information leaks and can only be someone of the executive group. In which case we hole up for a while then take a look at maybe doing it again. The money supply is still there.'

'The supply might be still there, Sweetheart, but I wanted the actual stuff in our bank account.'

He smiled grimly at the sexual goddess who was being a money-grubbing tart. 'Don't worry too much about that. I know how much you want money, so don't you think I would have made arrangements to keep at least some of it flowing our way. And that's on top of what we've siphoned off already. The last time I looked there was the best part of $10M in our account, both to sign of course! And it is being added to by the day.'

Paula almost purred, knowing such an amount of cash money was going to have a lot more effect and value in Indonesia. She was looking forward to being in their beautiful, traditional Balinese house, perched on the dizzying heights of the rim of an old volcano overlooking Lake Batur in the north of the country. Apart from being high enough to escape the crushing humidity of the lowlands, it was well away from the tacky tourist traps and bars that so entranced the hordes of visitors delivered every day like sheep waiting to be fleeced of their money. Conveyed in an endless procession of jet airliners, those same aircraft returned home full of sunburnt bodies who kept telling each other what a wonderful time they'd had spending too much money on too much booze. What wasn't mentioned was the number of visitors who went home hooked on the freely available drugs which were cheap and everywhere, despite the Government's harsh stand against drug use.

At least the hordes infesting Kuta and Denpassar didn't affect the rest of the beautiful country with its gentle, kindly people.

Paula dragged her thoughts back as Terry leaned close to her ear. 'What about your boyfriend here? I don't know why you dragged him along, since apart from driving this boat, he's outlived his usefulness as far as I'm concerned. You should have killed him like you did the cooks and admin types at the camp before we left.'

She smiled, but there was no warmth in it. 'Don't worry. I've learned enough to drive this thing and there's a navigational display which shows me where to go, so our deputy security head is surplus to requirements. Any time now.'

Like the evil temptress lusting for more power that she was, Paula carefully edged to the back of the boat, then returned to the steering position where she spoke up into Drew's ear. 'There's something wrong with the motor. I can hear a funny noise and see something's coming loose on the side of the motor.'

He looked alarmed, 'Bugger! I'll go have a look if you can take the wheel and keep us straight like I showed you.'

'Yes, my dear boy, I can do that. But please hurry. That thing looks like it's about to fall off any moment!'

She took over the wheel as Drew made his way back and peered around. Paula nodded at Terry who grabbed the safety rail tightly. Waiting until Drew was leaning far out over the stern to inspect the outboard leg; she quickly twisted the wheel hard one way, then hard back the other way. There was a scrabble and a cry as Drew was pitched over the stern and that was the last they heard of him. Paula's only regret was that she wasn't able to snuff his life force out with her bare hands; for her twisted mind, that provided the ultimate rush which was far better than the best orgasm sex could ever produce!

Terry was acutely aware of her nasty little addiction and thought, while it was a pity it took a human life to give the demented bitch satisfaction, so long as it was someone else's life and not his.

With Paula at the wheel, they roared on toward Karratha and the waiting jet.

Paula had finally got the hang of what she saw on the chart plotter and what she could see over the bow and managed to dodge a few islands, before making a wide, sweeping turn into the bay bordered by the three-kilometre long causeway and the strangely-named East Intercourse Island. She found the contrast in colours between the white of the salt stockpiles on the right side, while the island on the left was a deep red-brown from being covered in huge heaps of iron-ore waiting to be loaded.

With the shore in sight, she pulled the throttle back and slowed the boat too much, so she shoved it forward again, accelerating with a great lurch; nearly tipping Terry over the stern like the late and un-lamented Drew.

Finally she had a visual on where the inshore part of the causeway met the land, so she aimed for that. When just a hundred metres off the shore, she pulled the throttle back again, letting the boat run up on the sand flats near the causeway end. They grabbed their bags and as they were scrambling over the side to splash messily across to the rocky wall of the causeway, Terry looked back and cried, 'There's a big boat coming into the bay and it's really moving!'

Paula took a quick glance then gasped, 'Keep going unless you want to wait to have a chat with them, but you'll have to excuse me for not stopping.'

The rocks were quite easy to climb and seconds later, they were trotting towards a taxi waiting just 50-metres away. Tossing their bags in the back, Paula glanced briefly over her shoulder to see the big boat coming to a stop a few metres out from where the fishing boat was grounded.

'Go, go!' She urged Terry into the taxi and to the cabbie she gasped, 'To the airport as quick as you can!' To reinforce the point, she tossed a $50 note over the seat back as she slammed the door.

The cabbie shrugged, 'Sure thing, lady, but rushing won't help because there's no aircraft in or out for another three hours.'

'We have a charter waiting,' she said, 'and they are expecting us!'

'Oh. OK then. I guess I'd better earn that fifty. But I don't suppose you know the bloke who owns the big boat that just pulled up beside yours? He seems to be waving to you.'

'Nope. No idea,' she snapped. 'No friend of ours.'

'Oh, I see. But you shouldn't just leave your boat there like that. The tide will be coming in soon.'

'Look mate! I don't give a fuck about the blokes on the big boat, what happens to the little boat or anything other than getting to the fucking airport and getting out of this shithole!'

'Oh! So, you don't want the boat out there then?'

'What? ...Oh, don't bother, you can have the fuckin' thing, but drop us at the airport first, right?'

'Yes ma'am. Airport first, then boat. Thank you.'

'You're welcome. Now find where the charter jets hang out.'

'Oh, you should've said. They'll be over there.'

'I did say, you bloody idiot! Just drop us off where we can get on that plane.'

He pulled up beside a locked gate and yelled until a head popped out of the cockpit door, then a uniformed fellow with three gold bars on his shirt trotted over. He requested identification from Paula first, then opened the gate and took the bags from them, making no comment about the sand caking their wet shoes and jean's from the knee down.

A Customs officer in a sleep-rumpled shirt wandered down the air-stairs and asked for their passports, pulling a self-inking stamp from his pocket. He stamped them, made a note of the names and numbers in a small notebook, sketched a salute and wished them a good flight. As soon as he'd wandered off, the First Officer showed them into the cabin where a pretty flight attendant stood waiting, a professional greeter smile glued to her face. She also ignored the mess they were making of the thick gold carpet as she showed them to their seats and offered tea or coffee with breakfast once airborne.

A slim girl with four gold bars on her shoulders came back from the cockpit and introduced herself as the Captain and asked if there were any changes to the Flight Plan.

Paula shook her head, 'Nope. Just get us to Bandar Udara International ASAP. There's supposed to be a helicopter waiting to take us up country. Maybe you could check on that when we get going.'

'Yes ma'am. I'll do that. In the meantime, Cheryl will look after you and make sure you enjoy the flight.'

'I'll enjoy it heaps more when we get off the fucking ground!'

'Yes Ma'am. I'll just go and do that, shall I?'

Minutes later, the sleek Cessna Citation 650 was rolling toward the duty runway, no traffic on the ground or air to delay the issue of take-off and airways clearance to its cruise height of 39,000 feet.

CHAPTER 41

'Lost 'em Harry, I'm afraid,' Dave lamented. 'There's no more taxis waiting.'

I looked around, 'No you're right, but while we're here, we might as well have a look over the boat in case they left something which might tell us where they've gone.'

Dave shrugged, 'OK. *Seeker* will be all right here for a few minutes, but we'd better use the mooring ladder off the bow. This big bugger draws a tad more than the old AB68 did.'

I didn't want everybody traipsing around the sandflats with a 3-metre tide heading in, so just Dave and I climbed down the aluminium boarding ladder from the bow, splashing into a foot of water in our bare feet. The fishing boat had been driven aground at a low speed, but the motor was still in the down position and the ignition on, so by force of habit, I tilted the big Suzuki and turned it off. I also dug the anchor out of the shallow well up for'rard and walked it out 50-metres so the fool thing wouldn't drift away.

We were scratching around in the cabin when there was an indignant yell from the bow and a skinny little guy puffed around to the stern where he could peer over the side at us.

'What are you doing in my boat?' he demanded.

'Fuck off, mate,' Dave advised him. 'It's not your boat so don't come the raw prawn with us.'

'But the lady said I could have it!' was the indignant reply.

Curiosity aroused I asked, 'What lady and when?'

'The lady I took to the airport. She and some bloke wanted to go to the Executive jet park. I watched them get on a white jet that was waiting for them. She said they were leaving and didn't want the boat so I could have it! So I'm claiming it!'

I looked at Dave. 'We haven't found anything here, but the Tower will know where they're at least Flight Planned to.'

'Good thinking. You up to going and having a chat with that shoulder wound?'

I thought a few moments, the little taxi driver getting more agitated by the moment.

'Yeah, I'll be OK, but I might take Melissa with me.'

I included the taxi driver in the conversation, 'Here's the deal, Sport. You want this boat, right?'

He nodded, 'It's mine! My passenger gave it to me.'

'Ah, for Christ's sake, shut up about that. We know it wasn't hers to give in the first place, but since the original owners aren't around any more to argue the toss, you can have it. But...as the tides coming in fast, my mate here is going to tow it around to the Dampier Yacht Club jetty. As payment for us looking after your new boat, you're going to take a lady and myself to the airport and wait while I make some enquiries, then you take us to the Yacht Club. We go away and you do what you like with your new boat.

How's that for a deal?'

He shook his head violently. 'I don't know you. I won't see my boat again if this man takes it!'

I was getting a bit pissed off with this wombat so I leant over and awkwardly grabbed a handful of his shirt with my good hand.

'Listen, dickhead! We've had a very, very bad night. Either you take my very generous offer or I'll have several of the coppers on board that big boat charge you with impeding a Commonwealth investigation and slap the cuffs on you immediately. In which case we will take this pissant boat and give it to the first illegal immigrant we see so he can use it to go get the rest of his rellos from Indonesia! How do you like **that** deal?'

His eyes went wide and he said, 'My cab is just over there sir. I'll be waiting for you when you're ready.'

I smiled and patted him on the back. 'Good dog! Very wise

choice. Now fuck off over there and let us finish what we were doing.'

'Yessir. Here I go, fucking off as instructed! Yessir! Thank you, Sir.'

I shook my head. 'Bugger me! I can't figure some people. Anyway, there's nothing here we can salvage, so we'd better get the hell outa here. That bloody tide is coming in fast!'

While I splashed back through knee-deep water to *Seeker*, Dave retrieved the anchor and found a mooring rope that he tied to the bow bollard and followed me, towing the 25-footer behind him. Back at *Seeker*, we passed the rope back to the stern and I had Melissa come down and join me in the water. Luckily, she was wearing shorts, but she still complained.

'What's the go, Harry?' she asked as we waded to shore. 'You shouldn't be running around with that shoulder like it is. You have been shot, remember?'

'Yeah yeah. I remember, Mum! Anyway, we're going to the airport in that taxi. He's the driver who took Paula and Terry to get on a chartered jet. I want to talk to the dudes in the Tower to find out where they Flight Planned to.'

'Oh great. I'm so glad I've dressed for the occasion. They'll be really happy to tell all their secrets to a pair of sand-covered, barefooted beach bums!'

I grinned at her as we climbed the stone causeway wall, 'Sarcasm becomes you sometimes, dear girl, but don't despair. Uncle Harry has his all-purpose, handy-dandy, get-out-of-jail-free card tucked in his pocket.'

She just stared as if I'd gone mad, so I chuckled as we padded gingerly across the gravel-covered road to the waiting taxi.

'Airport, boss?'

'Yep, but to the Control Tower, please.'

'No problem. I know how to get to it. I often do pick-ups and drop-offs there. Always in a hurry those blokes.'

It was only a few minute's drive before we were threading our way in between two surprisingly large and open parking lots, then further down to Rowell St, a short left, right zig and there we were in the small car park outside the compact Tower.

'We won't be very long,' I said. 'Just talk amongst yourself for a little while and don't pick up any more passengers!'

He gave me a look that suggested I'd been out in the sun too long, even though the first hint of light was barely in the eastern sky.

Melissa leant over and said quietly, 'Don't mind him. He's been shot in the shoulder and he's still in shock. Shooting people does that at times.'

The cabbie gave her the same look and locked his doors as we walked away chuckling.

Naturally, there was key card access only to the Tower, although fortunately there was a handset intercom that I buzzed vigorously.

'Steady on, old chum!' came a disembodied voice from a wall-mounted speaker with a camera lens above it. 'We heard you the first time. And who might you be and what's your business?'

'My name is Commander Stevens and I need to see the departure logs for the last couple of hours.'

'Hmmm! I don't think we're allowed to do that, old chum! Can't have just any Tom, Dick or Harry wandering in here looking at confidential stuff. No sir. Sorry.'

'Strangely enough my name is Harry Stevens and I have credentials to show your shift supervisor.'

'Credentials? Really? How exciting! But it's been a quiet morning so far. Why don't you hold them up to the camera, nice and close and I'll have a Bo-Peep at them.'

I just love condescending pricks, especially Pommy ones.

'Stop being an arse-hole and send your supervisor down here now to check my credentials or I start making a fuss!'

'Oh, threats now? Excellent! That means I can call the Commonwealth coppers to come and cart you away. Unless you care to leave in the next five seconds?'

I sighed theatrically, 'Oh dear. Call them if you must, but please do it quickly. I'm getting very tired and my arm hurts.'

There was a short silence. 'You want me to call the coppers?'

'Unless you're going to let me in, then yes, call them, but stop fucking around and actually do it. I told you I was tired and I need to check those logs.'

'OK. I'm calling them now. They're just along in the terminal.'

'Terrific. I'll just sit here until they get here. Have them wake me up.'

I slid down the wall, feeling genuinely bone-deep weary.

'Are you OK Harry?' Melissa asked anxiously. 'You look like shit!'

I gave a tired laugh, 'Thanks girl. I feel like shit. Whatever Jasper did to my shoulder is starting to wear off.'

I'll give the coppers credit for being on the ball, since within a couple of minutes, a golf cart came whirring busily along the service road from the terminal and pulled up a few metres away, depositing two burly coppers in Commonwealth uniform instead of the khaki of the Western Australian Police.

'Good morning Sir, good morning Miss. Having a few problems are we?'

I dragged myself slowly up the wall, my tiredness mistaken by the coppers for drunkenness, particularly when they saw that we were both in shorts and T-shirts and had bare, sandy feet.

'Tell you what, Sir. There's a taxi right there. If you and the young lady get in it and go, we won't press charges. How about that for a good idea?'

I'd had just about enough of being patronised and condescended to for one morning, so with a row of smugly-smiling heads lining the canted-out windows of the Control Tower several metres over our heads, I slowly reached into the back pocket of my shorts.

The second, much younger copper must have been nervous, for he whipped his gun out and levelled it at my midriff.

'Whoa! Steady on sunshine. I'm getting some ID for your partner here.'

They hadn't checked Melissa or me for weapons, so I knew she had her Glock shoved in the waistband of her shorts at the back under her loose shirt.

'Hold your hands up Sir,' the young one with the gun said, testosterone taking over from common sense, as he approached me from behind and poked me in the back with his Glock. Bad mistake!

My military training took over and frustration at these fools who all wanted to be smart-arses blanked out common sense for a moment.

I could see Melissa start to open her mouth to say, 'Don't!' but my reactions were still pretty quick as I spun right, my right arm slashing down to impact the coppers arm, knocking his pistol out of his hand and sending it clattering across the hardtop where Melissa trapped it easily with her foot and casually picked it up, holding it low by her side pointing at the ground in best non-threatening fashion.

The young copper howled in pain, grabbing at his arm; forgetting about his pistol which is a major blunder in any armed confrontation. His senior partner took everything in and held his hands out from his side.

'Easy up, there Sir. There's no need to get excited, because I'm sure this is all a misunderstanding we can clear up without anybody getting hurt.'

Adrenalin was pumping, so I wasn't able to calm down too quickly, but training and reason helped stop me from kicking the fool in the nuts, so I took a deep breath and addressed the senior man who I noticed was a sergeant.

'Before this idiot pulled his weapon Sergeant, I was slowly extracting a card I wanted you to see. I'm going to repeat the movement and it'd be really good if both you and your trigger-happy companion here refrained from waving more guns around. You may care to notice that my companion is holding your officer's weapon, although her finger is well clear of the trigger.'

They both shot a horrified glance at Melissa standing with a grim look on her face and the errant weapon in her hand.

'Oh shit! Sorry Sir. Please proceed with the papers you were going to show me.'

'Step around beside your Sergeant, you fool,' I said to the young, dis-armed officer, with a snarl to my voice, 'I don't trust you behind me, even if you are incompetent!'

He started to open his mouth to protest, but I cut him off. 'Don't even think about saying anything, you idiot. You're in enough trouble as it is. Don't make it worse.'

So he didn't and I peacefully extracted a plastic card from a secure pocket in my shorts and handed it to the sergeant.

'I was going to show this to the shift supervisor in the tower,' I said, gesturing to the still-crowded windows above us, 'but you just might figure it out quicker than he would have.'

The Sergeant took the card gingerly as if it might bite him, as well it might after this clusterfuck, and he started to read. Seconds later, his face sagged and he sort of shuffled to attention.

'I don't know where to start to apologise, Commander, for all that's happened. Constable James here will be disciplined for his unjustified actions. How can I assist with your mission?'

The constable, still nursing his arm, stiffened at the use of my rank.

'Go sit in the buggy, Constable,' the sergeant said, 'while I sort out your mess.'

The crestfallen man did so, refusing to look at Melissa or myself.

'OK, Sergeant, what you can do is get me in that bloody tower so I can check the departure logs. That was all I was trying to do when some smart arse called you over.'

'No problem, sir,' he said, before speaking into the intercom handset. While we waited for the door to be unlocked, Melissa wordlessly handed him the constable's gun, fresh scratches from its journey across the parking lot proof of his stupidity.

Behind us the door opened.

'Are you the Shift Supervisor?' I asked without ceremony.

'Yes, I am. And you say your name is Commander Stevens?'

I waved the Sergeant forward without saying anything and let him stammer out an explanation.

'Commander Stevens is with the Commonwealth Police and has a card with authorisation from the Prime Minister himself which allows him unlimited access to any State or Commonwealth facility and to request and receive assistance from all State and Commonwealth employees up to Cabinet level.'

'Thank you, Sergeant. Hopefully I can take it from here, if there are no further issues you wish explained, Mr Supervisor?'

'No sir. No problem at all. And my apologies for the problem with the other gentleman. He did not follow procedure.'

'Seems like there's been too much of that today,' I muttered, 'however, can we get on with my enquiry now please? Time is wasting.'

'Certainly sir. Please follow me.'

A minute later, with Melissa standing beside me, I was presented with the departure logs which showed the Cessna Citation 650 departing for Bali with three crew and two passengers 90 minutes earlier. It even recorded that a Customs check had been made and the passengers were cleared.

'Where is the aircraft now,' I asked, causing a hurried consult of the departure times and position reports.

Throats were cleared and feet shuffled as the supervisor turned to us, 'The aircraft is in the late stages of its descent into Bandar Udara International Airport at Bali. It'll be on the ground within ten to 15 minutes at best guess. I'm sorry, Commander. I gather that the passengers were of interest?'

I laid a withering glare on the tower crew and motioned the supervisor to the back area. 'For your ears only Supervisor, there were two home-grown terrorists on board that plane. Less fucking around by people playing ego games may have led to the aircraft being turned back to Australia, but that's ancient history now. Despite my unconventional approach and appearance, you may care to review your security system and procedures, but I thank you for what you have belatedly done. We'll find our own way out. Good day, Sir.'

Five minutes later, we were back in the taxi and on our way to the Yacht Club, the cabbie finally keen to move quickly with the promise of a new boat once he was rid of his pushy passengers.

'Thanks for the back-up,' I said to Melissa, 'you did a good job. What a clusterfuck that was! One thing after another.'

She grinned, 'I liked that move you put on the constable. I've never seen a disarm happen so quickly.'

I laughed with her, 'Yeah. I nearly broke the dickhead's arm. But he should have known better or at least been taught never to approach a suspect so closely.'

'Isn't it risky with a gun pressed to your back and their finger on the trigger?'

'Not if the gun is touching your back. Then you know exactly where it is and that's the secret. The other thing you must remember about that disarm, is you can always twist and sweep an arm down faster than the guy holding it can react and pull the trigger. They often will fire a shot, but you'll have knocked the gun aside before it happens. Always be careful in a crowded environment as to where that shot might go!

The thing works because of reaction time and the slight relaxation of alert level when a gun is pressed close. The person with the gun thinks they have the advantage, but if you do it right, it's the other way around.'

'I'll remember that, thanks.'

'Anyway, I hate to think what the Area Commander's going to say when he hears. I'll stay out of it though. They've got enough dramas to sort out.'

TUESDAY MORNING, KARRATHA TO ONSLOW

There was a lot more turning up and down red dusty streets lined with tired-looking, red-tinged palm trees; the scene making me long for the clean, natural environment at sea, but finally the cabbie pulled into the parking lot of the public boat ramps right beside the Yacht Club.

I was happy to see *Seeker* nosed in alongside a finger jetty beside one of the boat ramps, being glared at by a steady stream of fishermen launching their tinnies and resenting the space taken up by the massive bulk of 100 feet of Italian speed machine.

The cabbie was even happier to see his precious new 25-foot half-cabin tied up to a nearby dock.

'Are we all done, boss,' he asked politely.

'All done my friend. Although if I may offer a piece of advice, go and change the registration into your name today. It might help you keep the thing.'

He looked puzzled by that, but shrugged and went to fetch it, while Melissa and I climbed aboard to a huge welcome from Jasper who promptly nosed me toward the nearest settee. While Dave fired up the big diesels and Melissa laughed, Jasper planted both huge front paws on my chest and pushed me down flat. He then proceeded to repeat the treatment he'd earlier given my shoulder by taking it in his powerful jaws and squeezing gently. I had to admit the exertions of the past couple of hours, including the disarming of the dickhead young copper, had taken a heavy toll and the wound was hurting.

Julie and Brian wandered over to watch and were slightly horrified to see my beautiful cat apparently chewing my shoulder off.

Melissa managed to dissuade them from intervening and Jasper got on with saturating the bandage with fresh saliva or whatever it was that flowed so copiously from his mouth. Jasper's treatment took 15-minutes and at the end of it, the pain was gone and I could move my arm almost without restriction. I was also glad I had asked Julie to make a short video of the unorthodox procedure that definitely wouldn't get written up in the 'Lancet' medical journal. It would be added to the video of 'Jasper and the Crocodile' to show Barbara, who'd probably wet her pants when she viewed them.

With Corrine in the camp, Amanda had left *Dragonfly* orbiting overhead in case there were any other surprises, but all had remained quiet, so with 90 minutes of fuel remaining, she directed it to home in on our position and asked Dave to come to idle until it was retrieved.

Brian, Julie and Alex were fascinated to watch the UAV's progress on the GCS and more so when the aircraft appeared like a ghost from the early morning sky and landed smoothly, without assistance, on the foredeck.

When Melissa and our new friends, Julie and Brian had pulled mooring ropes back aboard, Dave carefully reversed the big boat away from the finger jetty, but *Seeker's* sheer size in such a small area caused chaos amongst the flock of tinnies and stirred up some of the more aggro natures.

'Get that fucking great lump out of here!' and 'this area is for trailer boats not aircraft carriers, so fuck off!' were some of the more complimentary comments thrown at us, so after the sixth such piece of abuse, Dave grinned at me and called, 'It's Showtime again!'

'Oh no, Dave. This is not a good idea!'

'What's going on?' Melissa wanted to know.

'Just hold onto something,' I advised her and the others. 'This'll be interesting!'

Despite the abuse being hurled from left and right, Dave had been doing the right thing by slowly and carefully easing *Seeker* out of the little bay, but with the stern now clear of the finger jetty, he wound the wheel fully over and gave the diesel throttles a healthy shove forward. The better part of 4000 horsepower suddenly erupted from the two water-jet nozzles in the form of two horizontal columns of white water, each a half-metre in diameter, that behaved like two giant fire hoses.

With the wheel hard over, *Seeker* swept the small harbour like a home-owner hosing down the front path, except it wasn't leaves being blown around, but small fishing boats and real live fishermen. The twin blasts overturned boats, dumping male and female indiscriminately into the water and even blasting up the launching ramp where they blew two boats right off their trailers and filled the tow vehicles with water.

It was a good thing that the noise prevented us hearing the language directed at *Seeker*.

Cackling with glee like a schoolboy, Dave allowed the huge boat to do two full 360° spins in its own length, blasting everything in sight, before he pulled the throttles back and we rumbled sedately out of the scene of utter chaos. By now all the crew were laughing, appreciating the joke after all the unwarranted abuse.

Once clear of the 6-knot, no-wash zone, Dave opened the throttles again and let the big boat sweep majestically around East Intercourse Island before setting course at 50 knots for the Earth-Squad camp, 60-nautical miles away.

While Melissa and I had been playing silly buggers with the Air Traffic Controllers, Amanda had been in contact with *Glenelg* and Corrine.

'*Glenelg* is inbound the camp as requested and should be there just ahead of us. She'll try to anchor as close in as possible. Corrine sounded a bit funny and said to tell you that 'there's no one alive' in the camp.'

I felt my stomach turn over, 'Ah, shit! That's not good.'

'What does she mean, Harry?'

'It's an Afghanistan thing,' I replied. 'The bad dudes, or more especially their women, loved to kill everyone and anyone even suspected of being in contact with the Allied forces. It didn't matter if they were men, women or children; they were tortured first, then savagely killed. If that's what's happened here, we can't let Terry and Paula, particularly Paula, get away free. Anyway, we'll soon find out what's happened.'

When we finally slid inside of Cowle Island, *Glenelg* was already anchored about 500 metres off shore, but Dave took the 100-foot powerboat into the inlet beside the camp site, relying on the shallow draft the water-jet drives allowed. We took the RIB into the tiny creek leading to the camp wharf and tied up beside Corrine's RIB. It didn't look as though Paul or Barbara had come ashore yet, which might be a good thing if things were as bad as I expected.

Corrine met Dave and me at the wharf, a troubled look on her face.

'That bad huh Mouse?' I asked.

She nodded, 'That bad! It's got to be Paula's work. I can't see Terry having the balls to do stuff like this.'

'OK. We'd better have a look first, then decide what to do after that.'

It was just as well Corrine had prepared us for the sight of the burnt and mangled bodies of what must have been three cooks, two of them female, and three admin types.

While barely recognisable as human, the torture hadn't killed them, but the marks around the neck of each and the length of 5 mm lashing rope still tightly twisted around each victim's throat screamed 'Paula' loud and clear.

I dug the little UHF radio out of my pocket and called *Glenelg*.

'*Glenelg. How may I help you Commander?*'

'Skipper please.'

'*Roger, stand by one.*'

...'*Go ahead Harry.*'

'I'm in the camp and I think you and Barbara should come over. Just you two for now, and maybe two medics as well, but tell them there's no rush!'

'*Roger that. We'll be there in five.*'

'Do you have any body-bags in your store?' I asked Corrine.

'Yeah. There should be a few. I'll go and get six.'

We waited outside the hut where the massacre had taken place and Corrine was back just as a grim-faced Paul and Barbara came trotting up from the wharf with two medics following.

'We'll have the de-brief later,' I said, 'but you need to see this now before we bag and bury them.'

I opened the door to the one large room that had been a combination admin and communications room. The smell of death in the guise of blood, vomit and voided bowels, assaulted the senses like a smack in the face with a lump of four by two. The bodies lay in various positions around the room, with the common factor being that they'd all died fighting and in agony.

Paul took one look and whispered, 'Dear God! How could anyone do this to another person?'

'Very easily if you happen to be Paula,' I remarked.

'How can you be sure it's her?'

Corrine answered. 'Because strangulation is her trademark. After she's built up her excitement level to nearly orgasm point by torture, she gets her rocks off by watching them die one at a time. She probably had trouble walking out of here after six in a row! If you look at the way the cords are arranged, you'll find she stood in front of each one so she could get the full impact as they died.

This should remove any doubt that she's a seriously twisted individual and will stop at nothing to get what she wants. She cannot be allowed to go free, nor should she simply be captured and put on trial. Extermination is the only answer for vermin like this. She represents pure evil!'

'Well said, Mouse,' I commented.

Nodding at the medics, one of whom had already been outside to throw up, I said to Paul, 'Perhaps if your medics would bag them after we've taken some photos, then you could supply a detail to bury them. Neither of us is equipped to store them and the same rules of secrecy still apply, in that there can never be an enquiry into this whole mess.'

Paul was still shaken, but Barbara moved quickly and used the radio to request a suitably equipped burial detail to come ashore immediately. Corrine found a compact camera in one of the drawers in the office section and took a series of photos of each corpse from every angle.

When she was done making happy snaps, we helped the medics to bag the bodies before the burial detail arrived.

'Don't worry about cleaning up any mess,' I said, acknowledging their grateful looks, 'we're going to torch this place so hot there'll be no trace of anything left!'

'Aye Commander. Great idea! Nobody needs to see what happened here!' One of the medics said, her face still white.

We left the chamber of horrors and let the fresh sea air wash some of the stink of death and corruption away.

'Were there any papers which would give us any more insight into where they've gone?' I asked Corrine.

'No, 'fraid not. But I need to call Roger and Jill to tell them to bail out now and I'll ask them if they know if there was a bolt-hole on Bali.'

'Good idea, but won't you have to watch out for that nasty security creep listening in?'

'Yeah, I'll take some precautions, but I've a feeling that he's got the word and will have bugged out already.'

I smiled, "OK. I'll leave it up to you.'

SEEKER...TUESDAY

While the burial party did their job, we cleared everybody else out of the camp and retired to *Seeker*. I introduced Brian, Julie and Alex to Paul and Barbara, before I called *Firebird* on the SatPhone.

'Great to hear from you, Big Dog,' Sandy said. 'Is everything alright?'

I hesitated just for a second, but that was enough for Sandy to jump in with, 'How badly are you hurt?'

'Just a through and through in the shoulder,' I replied. 'Jasper has already done something mystical and my arm is working pretty well. One of the MK47 gunners got hit and a loader was sprayed in the face with a shattered bullet but they're both OK. Other than that, everything went well except that Terry and Paula got away in a chartered jet to Bali.

Paula left some of her handiwork behind, and I'll brief you on that soon. The main reason for the call was to ask you to bring *Firebird* over to the camp. *Glenelg* is here and we're about to have a debrief with Paul and Barbara. I'll tell you about it when you get here. Corrine extracted three new friends so don't be too surprised. They seem like pretty good people.

You'll see Dave's anchored *Seeker* in the inlet beside the camp, but there'll be plenty of room to raft up beside him. You know what to do. I've got faith! It's only 11 miles, so just motor in at 14 knots; it'll take about 45 minutes.'

'Thanks Harry, I'll give **you** faith when I see you. How dare you go and get yourself shot? Silly old fart!'

'Thanks, dear. See you soon.'

After that was sorted, we retreated to the upper sun deck for the debrief with Paul and Barbara.

'We really had no problems,' Paul said, 'things went very much as you suggested and having your UAV overhead was bloody marvellous. Amanda told us every time the situation changed, so we were able to counter every move they made and really, they didn't have a chance. It was just like having a God's eye view of the battleground. It made it so much easier and safer for our guys; we can't thank you enough. No injuries and 100% wipe-out of the bad guys!'

'That's great,' I replied, 'but did any of your people have issues with the 'no prisoners' directive?'

'Not at all. And hopefully you don't mind, but I've dropped a subtle hint that if the medics were to tell their mates what they saw in that hut, I wouldn't consider that a breach of security. I figured the story might go a long way to laying to rest any conscience issues!'

I chuckled at the idea of Paul issuing subtle hints, but agreed wholeheartedly with his reasoning and action.

'So, there was no trace left and there were no other boats that might have stumbled across the action. We did see a small yacht heading your way yesterday afternoon.'

'No trace left and no sign of any witnesses...radar clear, eyeballs clear and UAV clear.'

'That's great Paul. You've done better than we have. We let the principal bad guys get away!'

I proceeded to bring them up to date on what had happened at our end, managing to raise a few laughs along the way, particularly my description of Dave chucking doughnuts in a 100-foot $12M power boat and swamping half of Karratha's amateur fishing fleet.

With our side of the story told, I said to Paul, 'That's where we're at and really, once your guys have finished up ashore, I'll ask for your help in burning this place to fine ash, then I'm going to release you to normal duties.'

He nodded understanding. 'Fair call Harry. Our patrol duration has timed out, so we'll be heading straight back to our Darwin base to hand the boat over to the next crew, while we all take leave for three weeks. But before we go, we'll happily pour some fire on this place, and that'll help relieve some frustrations. But there's a lot of my crew who'd like to see the principals get what they deserve before we can call this mission successfully wrapped up.'

'They will get what they deserve, but I just don't know when it will happen. But it will happen, even if we have to go it alone without official support.'

'Bloody hell, Harry. That'd really suck, but I know what you're saying. A foreign country and all that shit! It'd have to be a small strike, way under the official radar.'

'Yeah, I'm working on that.'

'Good. I can't do anything officially, but if there's anything else I can do, unofficially, you've got my number.'

'Thanks Paul and you too Barb. Your support has been fantastic and I'll be telling the Admiral.'

'Anyway, how about we let the guys and girls play with fire. They love shooting and blowing stuff up, so this should be fun.'

After a round of handshakes and hugs from Barbara, they returned to *Glenelg*. Soon after, we heard the warning hooters sound and the forward gun mount with the 25mm Bushmaster cannon started banging away, methodically chewing the camp to pieces. The 25mm machine guns joined in, as did the MK47s which had done us such good service overnight.

Within seconds, the camp was ablaze with tents flashing into brief fiery life before turning into ash. The demountable huts were made of stronger stuff, but were no match for 25m high explosive and incendiary rounds and 40mm grenades, so after less than five minutes of noisy mayhem, the whole place was a raging inferno and still Paul didn't call a halt. The gunners had a marvellous time destroying everything over 25mm high.

Finally, the firing stopped as the gunners assessed how the destruction had proceeded and were rightly proud of their efforts. I had offered the surviving EarthSquad RIB to Paul, but he had nowhere to put it and couldn't have accounted for it anyway, so with very few regrets, it was shot to ribbons and let sink.

Soon after, *Glenelg* raised anchor and sounded a long blast on her horn as she slowly eased out of the confined waters to return to head north. We responded as best we could, but it was the usual weak imitation.

Sandy, Tracy and Brianna had arrived by then and I suffered the expected barrage of abuse from Sandy for getting in harm's way, but it was still great to see them again after all that had happened.

By mutual accord, everyone wanted to get away from that place with the stench of violent death hanging around, so we un-tied

Firebird, Seeker up-anchored and together we headed back to North Sandy Island. There were closer places to park, but it felt strangely comforting to drop the picks in a place which was at least partly familiar. There was a party of sorts that afternoon, although things weren't quite the same without the Navy around and our crew were greatly subdued.

<h1 style="text-align:center">CHAPTER 43</h1>

Before I drank too much, I called the Admiral.

'I thought I might hear from you, Commander,' he said with a chuckle. 'Your name has been crossing my desk virtually on the hour, every hour, for the last two days!'

'My apologies for that, Admiral, but we have been rather busy and we needed to get things done. It seemed nobody else shared our desire to get the work done quickly; there were a few minor conflicts.'

'I love your concept of 'minor conflict' Commander and I can't wait to hear your version of the incident at Karratha's Air Traffic Control Tower! I believe that story will bounce round the traps for years.'

I gave a dry chuckle. 'In hindsight, it was very amusing, but perhaps not so at the time. The gunshot had knocked me around more than I thought.'

'I haven't heard about any gunshot, Commander! Serious?'

'Shoulder sir, through and through and treated. Two of Commander Davy's people were slightly injured, one Gunner grazed lightly across the shoulder and one Loader with minor bullet shrapnel damage across her face, but she's all OK and they're both back on duty.

I'm pleased to advise that as of 12:00 today, I've released Commander Davy and *Glenelg* from their temporary detached duty to return to normal patrol. I understand Commander Davy intended to return to Darwin as his patrol period has expired, but you should hear from him shortly with a full report.

Naturally, this call will constitute my report for now, although

I'd like to deliver a more complete verbal report to you in person if that's ever possible. There are elements to this operation which are very disturbing and may have wider ramifications which I believe you should be aware of.'

'That's starting to sound suspiciously political, Commander. You're not about to feed me a line of bullshit, are you?'

'No Sir! I don't work that way! What I am saying is the potential for a huge shitstorm to come out of this is very high and neither you nor Commander Davy deserve to cop any of it. I might add that Commander Davy and his crew performed way above expectations and are a credit to you and the Navy.'

There was silence for a minute, then the gravelly voice returned. 'Speaking frankly Commander, in this job I try to stay out of the gutter where politics seem to live, but having lofty ideals doesn't always insulate me from the crap, so I appreciate what you're trying to say. If the situation is potentially that explosive, it would seem I could benefit from a face-to-face. Are you able to make yourself available near an airport this evening?'

The request surprised me for a moment. 'Ah...yes sir. The closest to us is Onslow and we could be there within the hour. The next closest is Karratha or there's Exmouth a bit further again. I suppose that it depends how you'll be travelling.'

He chuckled, 'One advantage of being in my position is being able to call on any transportation available. I can get a Challenger 604 from the RAAF that should do the job, so I'm just putting in my schedule to see what'll work.'

There was a lengthy pause before he came back on. 'OK Commander. Can you meet me at the Executive Aircraft Terminal at Onslow Airport at 08:00 tomorrow for the purpose of a full debrief on this operation?'

'Yessir, that won't be a problem. I'll have some material which will assist your understanding of this mess.'

'Very well Commander, I'll be seeing you then.'

Dave, Corrine and Sandy looked at me inquiringly as I

disconnected the SatPhone.

'Sorry Dave. Another run to Onslow to keep an appointment with Fleet Commander Australia, Admiral Stallman at 08:00 tomorrow at Onslow Airport.'

That raised their eyebrows. 'High politics indeed, Harry.' Dave commented.

I grinned, 'That's what us movers and shakers do, young fella.'

'Smart arse! OK. If we shove off at 06:00, the run should take an hour; so that gives you time to get a taxi out to the airport. We've burned a bit of juice, so I'll take the opportunity to refuel again. I guess I'd better let my new best friend in Onslow know that his favourite customer is back. Should I ask him to organise a taxi as well?'

'Yeah. That'd be great, thanks Dave. Now, while there's just the four of us together, we need to work out what we're going to do with the four rescue persons. I want to talk to them shortly but we have to work out a few things first.'

Corrine spoke up, 'I've got an idea I wanted to run past you guys that might have some bearing on the subject, so I'd better lay it out before we get to anything else.

Regarding the newcomers, Brian and Julie are a couple from the UK and were only with EarthCare because it paid well. They don't have a home in Australia, so at the moment, they're not rushing off anywhere.

Alex Chetty was also a mercenary and has had a massive change of heart and allegiance, but seems much happier and more settled since I made him Corporal and gave him some responsibility. He worked well with Julie when she was Sergeant and has become very protective of me.'

She patted Dave's hand. 'It's OK dear, he doesn't seem to be lusting after my body. He's just protective because he likes me. I did promise not to kill him if he behaved!

He has no home either since he can't go back to South Africa because of some sort of trouble. I think he'd like to stay here and he has a lot of promise. Despite appearances, he's very intelligent and previously just covered that up with the dumb-brute image to fit in with his little peer group. Brianna is also homeless, but I know very little about her. You guys probably know a lot more since you were the ones who grabbed her and locked her up.'

'Is this the big idea, or is there something else?' Dave asked with a cheeky grin.

'Watch it, boyo,' she responded, 'any more cheek and it's no nookie for you!"

"Oops, sorry Boss!"

'OK. The idea is that because it looks like we're almost finished up here, apart from Harry briefing the Chief of the Navy tomorrow, I have a little side trip in mind that we might like to make.'

'Does this still have something to do with our rescuees?' Dave asked.

"Yes, it does. When I was first at EarthCare, I got into a bit of trouble with one of the security heavies who liked beating up little girls. Paula took care of him permanently, so he's no longer around. My arm was badly bruised and Paula took me to the Medical Centre where I met a very nice doctor, Roger Jacobs and his girlfriend and Theatre Nurse, Jill Zellman.

They sort of guessed I wasn't quite who I appeared to be, but helped me anyway because they knew things weren't right with the whole EarthCare setup. They were just waiting for the right time to bail out before they got whacked by Paula. Roger treated my arm with a strange, green paste which had amazing properties. It was a very powerful painkiller, an incredibly effective aphrodisiac and healed my bruises very quickly.

They trusted me because I wasn't like the rest of the EarthCare mob and under the influence of this marvellous goop, I virtually admitted I was undercover, although I didn't say who sent me. Roger told me this incredible story about how he and Jill were sailing through the Indonesian islands when they came across a woman who'd escaped from a very bizarre situation involving a loopy ex-Russian, a strange half-caste man who was extremely well built and this island where the locals made this paste.

They used to just make enough of the stuff for their own use, but under the direction of the Russian, who'd set himself up as King, they made extra and a limited amount was sent to wealthy customers in Hong-Kong and Shanghai. It was marketed as a potent aphrodisiac, which it most certainly is, and they sold all they could produce at very high prices.

This mad Russian spent a lot of the money on the locals, improving their quality of life, but he's had to keep a low profile due to some trouble he's been in. That meant he had difficulty exporting more product, so this is the proposition Roger and Jill put to me.'

We were listening carefully as the whole thing sounded really weird, but the little worm of an idea was wriggling around in the deep, dark recesses of my mind, as Corrine continued.

'Roger and Jill were trying to save enough money to buy or charter a boat to go back to this island. There's no way to get there without one, so when I said that I had one, they opened up a bit more about their plans. The deal we ended up making is if we take them back to the island, they want to propose a deal to the mad Russian where they will be the distributors of the product, take a reasonable percentage off the top and return the rest of the income to the Russian.

Roger is certain the therapeutic qualities alone will make it a lucrative deal, quite apart from the aphrodisiac effect and the Asian market for that.

Our part would be to take them there and back safely with as much of the product as they have or we can carry. I can vouch for how effective the stuff is and a little bit goes a very long way!

We get a percentage of the income like Roger and Jill, and the rest goes back to the Russian and the villagers.

So I thought that as we have to take the boats back to the Gold Coast anyway, we could make a little bit of a detour on the way. Roger and Jill could fly over to meet us in Broome for example, where we would fuel to capacity and head for the islands. So far, they've kept it secret just where this island is, so we need them.'

Dave was deep in thought, while I was too, but on a different subject, and asked, 'How does all this affect our new crew?'

She smiled, 'The only ones here who don't have work to go to are Harry, Dave and myself. Sandy, you said the other day that you have a stack of rec leave owing, so you're okay for now, but Amanda, Melissa, Tracy, Alf and Charlie will all have to go back to work from what they've said and sooner rather than later. They may not even be able to make the trip back around to the Coast, but need fly out of Onslow or Karratha.

Therefore, I suggest we invite our newcomers, Brian, Julie, Bree and Alex to stay with us as crew, even just on a temporary basis. They all seem amiable enough and at least I've seen them working together and know they get along. Even our resident giant, Alex! What do you all think?'

We all took a few moments to consider her words and I thought I'd hold back my other thoughts for the moment as they'd piggy-back quite neatly onto Corrine's suggestion, although I did comment, 'So the plan is to help the people who helped you, see some different scenery and maybe make a few dollars along the way.'

'That's about it, Harry. Plus, it might help the new crew as well, since they've just lost their job and probably didn't get paid for what they've already done.'

Dave made the dry comment of the day when he said, 'A cynic might say that they're lucky they didn't lose their lives instead of just their jobs.'

'Behave, Dave!' Corrine cautioned. 'Right now, we're going to need them!'

'Yes dear, I'll be good.'

We were all in favour of Corrine's idea of a diversion to go find the mysterious island of green paste and also to sign on the new crew if they wanted to, so I said I'd talk to them and lay out the proposition.

Corrine jumped on the SatPhone to try to get in touch with Roger and Jill, while I rounded up the new guys and took them up to the sundeck on *Seeker*, which was big enough to hold a dance, complete with a six-piece band. When they were all settled with drinks in hand, I said, 'I haven't had much of a chance to talk to you all yet, apart from Bree who's been with us for a little while now, so I want to ask you what you want to do now that EarthCare is pretty well wrapped up.

I might add, unfortunately, the principals are out of the country and won't be returning since they're wanted for murder and intentions to perform terrorist acts against Australia.'

'Excuse me, Harry, but what murders?' Bree asked.

'Oh sorry... it's been a very busy morning. We found six bodies in one of the huts, but there was no identification with them, although we believe they were part of the new intake and were cooks and admin personnel and had been killed by Paula.'

Even though she wouldn't have known them, Bree still looked very upset. 'Is that why the camp was shot up and burned?'

'Partly that,' I acknowledged, 'and also because no trace of this operation can be allowed to hit the media. I'm going to ask all of you to understand the mess which would result if it got out that the Western Australian Government had allowed, and part-funded, an Eco-Terrorism organisation to set up camp in the middle of the biggest oil and gas fields in the country.

We also have some evidence that a major source of funding for EarthCare and EarthSquad came from a Tree-Huggers political party and from Trade Union Superannuation Funds.'

Brian Towson spoke up, 'I imagine it would have a rather disastrous effect on Australian politics!'

I laughed grimly, 'Yeah. That's exactly what it would do. Therefore, I ask you all to just keep quiet, especially because you've been involved. I can say, officially, if you go with the flow and say nothing, you will not be held accountable for the minor part you did play in this nasty mess. In other words, you've got a 'get-out-of-jail-free' card, if you stay quiet! Is everyone happy with that?'

Four hands were immediately raised, so I smiled at them. 'Excellent! In that case, there's no need to refer to the events of the past few days and weeks again, so I'll move on. My next question is a personal one and you don't have to answer immediately.

These two boats are normally based on the Gold Coast and since this operation is now over, we would normally be returning there, starting out tomorrow. Most of the crew are serving Queensland Police Officers and have to return to their normal duties. They can't spare the time to help crew these boats back to the Gold Coast and will probably have to fly out tomorrow, so I'm asking if the four of you are willing to sign on in their place. We'll still be one person short, but we should be able to work around that.

I have to say that this is a non-paying job, at least for now, but we will feed you.

Have a think about it, but if you want to leave, you can fly out with the others tomorrow from Onslow.'

Alex Chetty raised his hand almost immediately and spoke in his deep rumble of a voice, 'I would like to stay with you and Major Johns, please Commander. I have no other home to go to and Major Johns has been very kind to me.'

I nodded, 'Very well Alex and welcome aboard. I'll get Dave to assign you a cabin for tonight, although that may change tomorrow.'

He smiled; a move that transformed his normally grim expression, 'Thank you Commander. My needs are simple and I will do whatever is required to be of assistance. I am very familiar with boats as well, both sail and power.'

'Thanks Alex, that's even better news.'

I was about to break up the gathering when Bree stuck her hand up, looking a little anxious. 'I'll sign on too, please Harry. Like Alex, I don't have anywhere else to go and no home or money either. I don't even have any clothes or other possessions, except for my passport and wallet I had on me the other night so it's like a clean start at life. I don't have much boat experience, but I like cooking and worked as a sous-chef in a restaurant, for a while, but I'll do whatever I have to as well. I know now you'll treat me fairly.'

'Thanks Bree and welcome to you too. We'll set you up with clothes and anything else you need, just let Sandy know. You can stay where you are for tonight and we'll sort everyone out tomorrow.'

She laughed, 'That's OK Harry. I don't mind where I am. I've become used to it.'

'OK. But we'll see how things shake down tomorrow. Dave may be able to improve things for you.'

While these discussions had been going on, Brian and Julie had their heads together murmuring quietly. With both Alex and Bree on board as crew, Brian spoke up, 'We do have a home, even if it is on the other side of the world, so we'll go back there, but thanks for the offer, Commander.'

'Thanks guys and I wish you the best of luck.'

They left the group and wandered down below to find a bed for the night and to ask Sandy to book them a flight out in the morning, along with our old crew.

I looked at the two left, 'Now that you've signed on, I can tell you that on our way back around to the Gold Coast, we're making a bit of a diversion up into the Indonesian Archipelago. We'll be going to an island where the locals make a special paste from the bushes growing there. It has several very desirable and interesting properties which make it quite valuable. We will be joined on the way by two more people from EarthCare HQ, the medical team of Roger and Jill who know where this place is.'

They both said, 'I know them, they're nice people,' so I felt happier we'd solved a few potential problems. Both boats were crowded that night, but everyone had a bed and Sandy worked the phone making airline bookings for our original five crew plus the two rescuees.

CHAPTER 44

WEDNESDAY, AFTERMATH

Promptly at 06:00 the next morning, as *Seeker's* anchor came rattling up on its rollers, most of the crew were on deck since we were leaving *Firebird* behind with Corrine, Bree, Alex and Jasper. I'd managed to persuade Jasper to stay on *Firebird* but he wasn't happy that Sandy and I were going. Interestingly, Jasper had taken to Alex like a long-lost friend and the big man, after being wary at first, loved playing with both him and little Krazy.

We decided Sandy would come with me to see the Admiral, leaving the seven for the flight out go to the main airport terminal, while we went to the VIP terminal. Dave would look after *Seeker* and the refuelling.

The run went according to plan and we pulled up at the refuelling wharf at 07:15 to be greeted by the same cheerful and helpful young guy that served us last time.

He looked strangely at the seven getting off with their bags, but he'd done the right thing and organised a taxi for us. It didn't take the driver long to whistle up a second cab and we were all soon headed for the airport, four kilometres south of town. We'd said our goodbyes on board *Seeker*, so after dropping Brian and Jill at the main terminal, together with the others, Sandy and I went straight to the VIP Terminal, where a sleek Challenger 604 Executive jet in RAAF colours was just taxying in.

We waited until it parked, the engines dying with a fading whine and then a pretty young lady in Air Force blues lowered the Air-Stairs and came down to meet us.

'Commander Stevens? The Admiral is waiting inside and we have breakfast ready if you'd like some. We'll be leaving the air-conditioning on so it's more comfortable.'

We thanked her and boarded the aircraft which was way too big for one man, but both Sandy and I appreciated the full standing headroom and the generous conference table and armchairs toward the rear. Rear Admiral Stallman, the current Navy Fleet Command Australia, to use his full title, was only middle-aged, looked to be in very good condition and was of medium height, projecting a powerful, authoritative presence like an aura. Despite his indoor job, he still had the tanned and lined skin of a deep-water sailor and he graciously stood to welcome us, showing that he was dressed very casually in jeans, a polo shirt and joggers. He gave Sandy several appreciative looks and gave me several carefully assessing looks. I quickly got the impression that trying to bullshit this man would be a big mistake.

A very attractive young lady assistant he just introduced as Hilary, whose sole job apparently was to listen and take notes, accompanied him. She didn't sit with us, instead taking a window seat opposite the conference table which had a small foldout leaf table for her notebook. She ate, however with an appetite every bit as good as Sandy's.

'Let's talk as we eat, Commander. I hope you're both hungry. The RAAF has been very generous with the catering on this trip. No soggy sandwiches this time around!'

The RAAF Sergeant flight attendant had plates loaded with all sorts of good things and as she served us with a smile, I realised that I was hungrier than I thought. Sandy always had a good appetite and ate with relish.

'OK Commander, how about you tell me what's been happening these last few days. I have a report from Commander Davy, but he was trained to write reports in the style of, 'How to cover your own arse in times of crisis and controversy'. Therefore, I want to hear what really went on and why you needed one of my boats, if you please.'

He knew the reason for the operation, so I started with the setup of the camp, the training of troops in Queensland and the reinforcements Corrine had brought in.

He was a very good listener and only interrupted occasionally to clarify a point. 'That girl of yours did one hell of a job,' he observed at one point. 'Taking out that thug with her bare hands was brilliant'

He sympathised when I covered the escape of Terry and Paula to Bali, although he had a good belly laugh at my telling of the Control Tower story. He was interested, but made a non-committal sound when I said I was keen to extract the two fugitives from Indonesian soil.

'That might be a tough one, Commander. We can't do anything officially, of course, but I'll have a think about what might happen to fall off the back of a truck. Commander Davy was extremely complementary of the way you planned and ran the operation. He suggested you would want to try to grab these fugitives so I guess he got to know you quite well.'

I smiled at the recollection, 'Yessir. We all got to know each other. Being under fire tends to do that.'

'Yes. I can appreciate that you know all about that.'

I finished my recital by a brief description of the bodies we'd found and Sandy produced a folder with the extremely graphic photos of the mutilated and strangled persons.

Finally, something shattered his reserve and he swore loudly without apology as he flicked through them.

'These are dynamite, Commander. You'd better be very careful.'

'We will be sir, and we have some excellent personal security. I might add that there are only two copies of those photos and that's one!'

'I'm sure you realise no word of this Eco-Terrorist attempt must ever be released to the press or anybody else for that matter.'

'Ahead of you there, sir. The camp has been razed, all papers destroyed and the persons on the raids eliminated. The only witnesses were those who had already defected to us and I've reminded them, that despite their initial involvement, no charges would be laid provided they keep quiet. In my opinion, they will behave properly and I'm keeping two of them as crew for the time being as five Police Officers in my original crew have had to return to their normal jobs.'

'OK. That sounds like you've got things in hand. Good work both of you. Needless to say, you've done your country a great service and I'll be speaking with both your superior officers about appropriate commendations!'

I waved that away. 'I'm not chasing that sir, although it would help the Inspector with her career if she were to get a few more ticks on her record. My real concern is to find where these animals have gone to ground and do something about them.'

He looked carefully at me for a few moments, and then turned to Hilary. 'OK, my dear, you can take a break and go and chat up the pilots for a few minutes. I'll wave when you can come back.'

She gave him a small grin, closed her note pad and walked to the front of the cabin where she sat with the flight attendant.

'OK. Nothing official on this one Commander, but I can say there are a number of people higher up the food chain than me, who want exactly the same thing and recognise that diplomacy isn't going to do the job without all the details coming out. I dare to say they will be very pleased you feel this way and even happier if these two were to meet with terminal accidents, but you need to come up with a plausible reason to be sniffing around up there. The Indonesians are quite paranoid about being spied on!'

'Already done that, sir.' I briefly explained about the planned trip to look for the island where the paste was made.

His eyes sparkled. 'Bloody hell, Commander, I like the sound of that. What a perfect cover your two boats make! And an excellent excuse to be drifting around up there! Damn! I'd love to join you on this little jaunt! But I know I can't, so I'll content myself by helping as much as I can. Is there anything you need that I can reasonably supply?'

Not being noted for knocking back freebies, I thought rapidly, a plan taking shape as Sandy informed the Admiral that when I got the 'thousand-yard stare' going, plans were being hatched!

He had a chuckle over that, and waited patiently for my return to the here and now.

'I'm currently short of crew, sir, and I recall Commander Davy was headed back to Darwin to hand the boat over to the next crew. Any chance of borrowing four warm bodies for a few weeks?'

He laughed again. 'They'll be going on leave for a week, then training until their next boat comes available in rotation. I guess I could assign four crew to special duties for the duration. Can you make a guess how long you might be on the two tasks?'

'Best guess would be about three weeks sir, but it could extend a bit longer if we run into any aggro.'

He thought a few moments. 'That should still work. Paul won't be happy, but we have plenty of crew waiting to join the boats so he'll make do. I presume you know who you want?'

I looked at Sandy who nodded in silent agreement. 'We do sir, but I have another request my choice of personnel may help justify.'

He raised his expressive, bushy eyebrows questioningly, so I went on. 'When Corrine left the camp to head off on the raid, she took what weapons she could and among them were two .50 cal Browning machine guns. We have some ammunition for them, but if you could let us have some more, that would help.'

He nodded, 'Yep, I can do that. Anything else?'

I chuckled and said facetiously, 'One of those terribly effective MK47s we used on the extremists would be very nice, but that'd be going too far.'

He considered my words. 'Not entirely out of the question Commander, under the circumstances, so long as trained Navy persons were to be in charge of operating it. But how would you conceal it and the Browning's if searched?'

'It breaks down very easily, sir and if the various bits were scattered around, they'd surely pass inspection. It'll be the same with the Brownings. The ammo will have to go into some hidden lockers I've had built into *Firebird* and there are other lockers on *Seeker*. They can't be found unless the whole boat is literally pulled apart.'

He went into thought mode again then smiled. 'It's all a bit bizarre Commander, but I like what you've done and as I mentioned, there's a lot of unofficial pressure to resolve this mess without publicity. That can be arranged, I trust?'

'Yessir. We have the resources to do the job as required. Any assistance will make it easier and be gratefully appreciated.'

He nodded then called for'rard. 'Hilary. Bring your pad, phone and an area chart from the Captain, please my dear. We have some organising to do.'

She broke off chatting with the Flight Sergeant, ducked into the cockpit, and then came back to us, looking most attractive in her tight jeans and a red shirt that looked to be a size too small.

'Yes, Boss?'

'Would you get Paul Davy on *Glenelg* for me, please. We're going to help these people chase some bad guys.'

'Oh, you mean Terry Williams and Paula Henderson. Now that would be worthwhile. The PM will be very happy. He called during the flight but you were asleep, so I handled it.'

'Bloody hell girl, you should have woken me. What if it was important?'

She smiled sweetly. 'Then I would have woken you of course!'

He grumped a bit more about bossy female daughters, then handed the chart to Sandy and me, while Hilary looked up numbers and made the connection.

'...Fleet Command Australia for Commander Davy, please.'

'...Commander Davy, standby for Fleet Command actual.'

She passed the SatPhone over to the Admiral.

'Good morning Commander, this is Admiral Stallman, may I have your current position?'

'...48 nautical miles NE of Port Hedland? Excellent. I've just been briefed on the doings of the last few days by Commander Stevens and I must commend you and your crew on a job very well done. This situation has attracted the attention of Australia's highest authority and he's well pleased with the way it has gone.'

'...Yes, that's the one. He wanted me to pass on a 'good job' message to you personally. However, as you are well aware, there are still two loose ends who my caller and several other well-placed persons would very much like to see wrapped up without any fuss.'

'...Yes, I've been talking to him and in fact I'm with him now.'

'...It's not much of a problem when one has good relations with the RAAF, Commander and they have some very nice VIP jets.'

'...There was no time to waste and there still isn't, so I need to ask you to do something for me. I've decided we should assist Commander Stevens as much as we can without being too obvious, so firstly, I'd like you to change course to head for a small bay on the east side of a very small point of land called Cape Keraudren. It's 70-odd miles north of Port Hedland and on the coast just out from Pardoo Station. Looks a very pretty spot with white sandy beaches. You should be almost abeam of it right now.'

'...You found it? Excellent. Please proceed there, anchor in the bay and wait for Commander Stevens to get there. Unfortunately, that won't be until probably this time tomorrow so the crew could have shore leave if you so choose. That was the good news!'

'...Yes. The bad news is that I'm re-assigning four of your crew on temporary special duty to Commander Stevens for a period of approximately four weeks. That will probably take them up to the date of your next boat assignment, but to ease their pain, you can tell them that they can regard this as a four-week paid holiday, cruising the Indonesian Islands on a couple of luxury boats, living the life normally only enjoyed by the rich and degenerate!'

'...No, I'm sorry Commander. If I can't go, you can't either.'

'...No, that wouldn't work either as much as we'd both like it. But getting back to business, I'd also like you to supply Commander Stevens with some hardware.'

'...What? Have you become psychic now? Oh, yes. I see. Good

guess. Well, if you could package up one MK47 and say four boxes of rounds, I'd be obliged. But wait, there's more! Commander Stevens has managed to lay his hands on two Browning M2HB-QCB .50 cal machine guns.'

'...No, don't ask. He has some rounds for them, but would like some more and I've agreed, if you wouldn't mind adding a few boxes to the stack.'

'...Yes, I was just coming to that. The Commander has given me a list.'

'...What do you mean, all! They can't be serious, besides, there isn't room.'

'...Yes, just joking, but I am impressed they're so keen. Anyway, this list says...'

'...Commander, you're either psychic or you've been talking to Commander Stevens before I got here. They're the top names on the list. Are you happy to release them and more importantly, are they volunteering?'

'...Yes, I suppose it was a silly question. So, you'll have them ready to transfer, along with the hardware when Commander Stevens arrives tomorrow?'

'...Excellent! You can write the .50 cal rounds off to practice, but please remind your Petty Officer she is personally responsible for the MK47.'

'...No, I haven't asked about that yet, but I'll do so shortly. Maybe we can make time for a demonstration.'

'...Very well Commander. Well done yet again and good sailing back to Darwin. I'll be in touch again soon.'

CHAPTER 45

WEDNESDAY, ONSLOW TO PORT HEDLAND

The Admiral passed the SatPhone back to Hilary who disengaged the thing.

'Well, that's all arranged and I do hope you'll try not to start a fight with the Indonesians. We're really trying hard to be friends with them at the moment.'

I grinned, 'I guess it does look like a lot of firepower, but we are going into the heart of pirate territory so I'd like us to have the best protection possible. And as for hiding the weapons, we carry lots of cash just for the purpose of greasing palms!'

'By the way,' he said, 'that pushy Commander has reminded me to ask you about this fantastic UAV you've been playing with. He keeps on saying the Navy must buy 20 or 30 at least. I guess I'd better have a look at the thing. That is if you've got it with you?'

'As a matter of fact, we do. We normally keep it on *Seeker* because it has a big, clear foredeck for take-off and landing, although we have flown it off *Firebird* many times. If you can spare the time, we can show you now.'

He gave a big, beaming smile of eager anticipation. 'Commander, we'll make time. Hilary, grab our gear and let's go see a UAV.'

He hustled forward to the aircraft Skipper. 'We should be back in an hour or so, if that's alright?'

The Captain looked at her watch, 'Well, sir. We either have to be on our way in just over an hour from now, or we have to stay the night because we'll be out of hours. Sorry to be a pain, sir.'

He waved her apology aside. 'No apology needed, Captain. Crew fatigue rules are essential. Just a moment while I talk to my colleague.'

He popped out of the cockpit like a spring toy. 'How long would it take to sail to Port Hedland?'

I quickly reviewed the Captain's chart, did some clumsy mathematics in my head and came up with about 17 hours from departure.

He did some quick figuring of his own, before announcing, 'The aircrew are running low on hours, so either we go very soon or they get a motel for the night. I do need to see this UAV, so how about you take Hilary and me for a boat ride to where your catamaran is parked, and then we all head for Port Hedland. This aircraft can pick us up in the morning if you can drop us off, before heading for the RV with Commander Davy. How's that for a plan?'

I couldn't help laughing. 'I really like that one, sir. It will work out just fine. If we mess around with the UAV at North Sandy Island for a while, then the run to Port Hedland will take the rest of the day and all night. We could land you early morning tomorrow at Port Hedland.'

He beamed again. 'Perfect Commander! I don't tell too many people, but I'm actually a sailing nut, so I'm really keen to see how your cat goes. It looks like a good sailing breeze picking up.'

'It'll be a pleasure to have you both aboard, sir. Do you have any overnight things with you, or do we need to buy something here before we leave?'

He shook his head. 'No, all good thanks. Hilary is always prepared for the unexpected, so we have two or three days supply of socks, jocks and toothpaste always with us. But I'll just tell the Captain our new plan.'

Hilary smiled indulgently as she dug a couple of overnight bags out from the next row of seats back, tucked several phones and her notebook into a pocket and pronounced herself ready.

The Admiral ducked back into the cockpit to give the crew the option of staying in Onslow for the night or flying to Port Hedland now and camping there for the night. They decided to stay in Onslow and set about bedding the aircraft down and cancelling their Flight Plan for the day.

We left them to it and with plenty of time, walked to the main terminal to find a taxi.

On the way, a very big loose end suddenly popped into my head.

'Admiral, we're heading for Indonesia, but we have no clearance certificates for the boats or visas for the crew. Also, I think it would be best if our new Defence Force personnel had diplomatic passports so they can fly home with the MK47 if necessary, without upsetting either Security or aircrew. Are you able to help with that at very short notice?'

He shrugged and promptly looked at Hilary, 'Well, my dear, can we?'

She thought a moment. 'We have good contacts with the Indonesian Consulate both in Darwin and in Canberra. I can call the PM's office and get my friend Charlie to organise the diplomatic passports. They won't be a problem for Service personnel. Can you get me the details on both of the boats, four photos of each and the current market value of each? I can get details of the Navy personnel from our files and have them sent to Charlie.'

'Brilliant. I'll call Corrine and have her email the boat and crew stuff to *Seeker* and since we're going there now, I'll call Dave and have him put *Seeker's* papers together. You can use the comms on board.'

She nodded, 'That'll do. The Indonesians have a new Visa system that's a lot faster and simpler than the old one, and they're used to us requesting on short notice, so they usually process them quickly. Will a 30-day stay be enough? That's the easiest one to get.'

'Plenty! If we're not done by then, we'll be in trouble anyway.'

Dave had *Seeker* fuelled and ready to go, so after introductions were made, it didn't take long to show the Admiral and Hilary around and for the Admiral to get excited again. 'Commander Davy worked out that *Seeker* was just 30% the weight of the *Glenelg* with 86% of the horsepower. We took him for a ride and he loved it!'

'I don't wonder,' the Admiral mused, peering at two gleaming white, hulking V-16 diesels in the immaculate engine room. He marvelled at the comparatively small mass of the 5600-horsepower turbine occupying the centre engine mounting where a third diesel should have been. 'We should have specified something like this for the current *'Armidale'* class patrol boats,' he confided. 'Having a sprint ability would be very useful. We might do it better next time around!'

Before we left, I had Dave dig out the necessary documents on *Seeker* and give them to Hilary, while I called Corrine and had her do the same for *Firebird*. It took a bit more ringing around to get everyone's passport details, including that of the crew from *Glenelg* but finally it was all in Hilary's hands so we sat her at the table with her phone book and the SatPhone.

Once underway, Dave stayed close inshore among the litter of small islands that hugged the coast all the way up to Karratha, to avoid the swell that was being pushed up by a strengthening south wind. With the Admiral happily ensconced in the second helm chair, Dave gave the big MTU diesels their head. The MTU diesels on the patrol boat may have had more horsepower, but there wasn't the surge of acceleration and the rising howl for the Italian-designed exhaust system which was meant to raise the hairs on arms.

Certainly, the Admiral was affected the same as the rest of us, even Hillary giving a yell of delight.

With the speed steady on 50 knots, Dave eased the little chrome lever of the turbine throttle open until its shriek rose over the thunder of the diesels and 90 tonnes of Italian design genius shot forward with the speed climbing toward, then stabilising at 80 knots. At that speed, we just skipped straight over the small inshore swells, with the Admiral grinning like a kid and Hilary looking extremely excited, whilst standing between the helm chairs.

It was less than 40 miles along the coast, which took 30 minutes, before Dave reduced speed a little to 60 knots on diesels only as we angled out toward North Sandy Island, taking the increased swell on the port quarter. Even so, the superior hull design together with the gyro-stabiliser kept the boat within 5° of level at all times. The final eight miles took just minutes and soon we were rafting up against *Firebird.*

Dave didn't bother anchoring, although the stiff breeze against the bigger boat pulled both boats at an unusual angle to the single anchor chain.

Even though I'd pre-warned the Admiral about Jasper, both he and Hilary were slightly shocked at his size and menacing appearance, although as usual, Jasper won them over by doing his 'I'm just a big pussycat' routine. Hilary in particular was entranced by him and got down to his level immediately to cuddle and play with him, although she did comment on the size and whiteness of his fangs.

I refrained from telling her about the bad guys he'd ripped apart with those gleaming pearly whites!

Before Sandy dug out *Dragonfly*, we ate the stack of tasty toasted sandwiches that Bree had prepared for lunch, and she gave the Admiral a run-down on the stats. When we saw Hilary frantically making notes I dug out a printed sheet with all pertinent data already listed for the MKII version and passed it over.

Sandy then rigged the beast, letting the Admiral look at each part, reminding him that even in MKII form, it was still a hand-built prototype and not yet re-designed for production. Nevertheless, he was very impressed with the detail and the degree of miniaturisation in evidence, especially with the cameras and the satellite link.

Once fuelled and inspected, she placed it on the helipad moulded into the bow cabin top, fired up the Ground Control Station and input a Flight Plan with the Admiral and Hilary watching every move. They were equally attentive as the oddly shaped, tandem-wing UAV fired up, lifted off and departed on planned track. Sandy had set a low 1000-foot cruise height as there was no need for stealth and directed it in over the EarthCare camp to show what had been the cause of so much mayhem.

It was interesting to see that among the charred and blackened remains, absolutely nothing was left standing, although the stoutly constructed short wharf was untouched. Sandy zoomed in for some close-up shots and even used the IR camera that showed a few warm spots, but nothing else of interest. As a demonstration of the stabilised zoom on the cameras, Sandy took it up to 4000 feet and made a few orbits before hitting the 'Return to Home' button.

Six minutes later, the mottled blue-grey form of *Dragonfly* dropped into circuit overhead, the engine a muted purr as it was almost idling on the long descent. With Sandy sitting back from the GCS, not touching any control, the UAV came to a steady hover, moved sideways and gently touched down on the pad. One minute of idle and the engine shut down as the Admiral said. 'That's very impressive, Inspector. Now I understand Commander Davy's enthusiasm for the thing. And you said it has eight hours endurance?'

'Yes sir, although that's with about 70% of the flight at loiter speed and power. A sustained full speed, 80 knots dash would reduce it to about six hours, but that is still a radius of 240 nautical miles.'

He nodded. 'Well, based on that short demonstration, I'll be recommending the Navy conducts a more thorough evaluation test of the unit, pending an order, that is if the designer is willing.'

'Thank you, sir. I'm sure he will be. This is the MKII version and so far, it has performed faultlessly for us, so I'm sure he's ready to have the Navy evaluate it. He'll be quite happy to incorporate any mods you might need if you proceed to the ordering stage.'

'Is he ready to go into limited production?' he asked. 'Because I can't think of any changes that we'd require, apart from maybe changing the radio frequencies to purely Navy ones, but that should be relatively simple.'

Sandy nodded, 'I can confirm that, sir. As a comms specialist, it would take a couple of hours to re-configure the comms package, as long as you didn't need a different radio. Everything is digital.'

When Hilary finished scribbling notes and the Admiral had asked a few more questions, I checked the time with the sun sinking inexorably into the western sea, and suggested *Dragonfly* be packed away and we get going for Port Hedland.

While Sandy did that, I checked *Firebird* over and fired up the generator, intending to sail out of the open anchorage. At the last minute, I had a thought and hopped across to see Corrine. 'I almost forgot. Can you call your friends, Roger and Jill and tell them to bail out of EarthCare immediately and head over here?'

'Already did that. They grabbed all their gear and went to a motel somewhere back toward the Gold Coast. They were concerned about being chased by EarthCare security dudes and were going to stay there until they heard from us with regarding what was going on.'

'OK, that's good. We need them to get over to Broome as soon as they can. We're going to do the Indonesian island run as well as try to take out Terry and Paula. Do you think they still want to move on the green gel deal?'

'Hell yeah! They'll jump at it. There's nothing else to do and they were very nervous about being anywhere near the fallout from the EarthCare collapse. Apparently when they left, the place was in chaos. The guards didn't know whether to lock the gates or not, but they got out without trouble.'

'Good to hear. OK, get them moving. They need to book flights immediately to either Perth or Darwin, then to Broome. Whatever one is the quickest! We'll be there early Friday morning if all goes well, so it'd be good if they made it by then.'

'I've already checked flights and Qantas do a direct flight, Sydney to Broome that leaves around 11:15 and gets to Broome at 14:35 local time so I've booked them seats Coolangatta to Sydney early tomorrow morning, then Sydney to Broome. They will be in Broome tomorrow, Thursday afternoon, so I'll call them and tell them to stay where they are tonight.'

'Great work, Mouse! Make sure they can make those connections. I really don't feel like fucking around too much more with passengers and travel arrangements!'

'Yeah, I know Harry. I'd like to be on our way again without all these distractions but it won't be long now.'

'Do we have a rough ETA for our arrival in Port Hedland?' the Admiral asked. 'I know it's difficult to be too precise, but if I can give the RAAF crew a time that'd be helpful.'

I thought a moment, 'The breeze is dropping, so we'll be back to our 14-knot cruise speed on one engine, so we should be there around 06:00. If they were on the ground by 06:00, you won't be too far away.'

'Thanks Harry. I'll get Hilary to give them a call.'

That reminded me to tell Hilary that Roger and Jill were going to be on an aircraft out of Sydney at 11:15 tomorrow morning, so they could bring the Navy Diplomatic passports.

She beamed, 'Great idea, Harry. I'm sure Charlie can get a package to the airport in time for them to collect it. I'll get on the phone right away!'

That was a good cue for us to get moving as well so I signalled Dave to drop his lines and move out so I could haul anchor. I had Sandy show the Admiral and Hilary their quarters and explain the boat systems. They both said they were delighted with the accommodations and loved the boat and in Hilary's case the two cats, Jasper and Krazy.

'As a sailing sailor,' the Admiral stated, re-joining me in the cockpit as the anchor chain rattled in and the huge mainsail unfurled out of the boom and climbed the mast, shedding wrinkles on the way, 'I'm very keen to see how this arrangement all works. You seem to have it set up differently to others I've seen.'

'That's because I often sail single-handed and I wanted reliable systems which would let me do everything from the cockpit in safety if a blow were to hit suddenly.'

He approved. 'Very good thinking. Too many yachts seem to be set up with very labour-intensive systems and not enough crew to work them safely in bad weather.'

When the anchor was stowed and generator shut down, I hauled up the inner staysail and sheeted it to the upwind side which forced the bow off the wind, the big main flapping noisily as I'd let the sheets fly loose. With the bows falling nicely off the wind and pointing away from the dry land, I sheeted the main in slowly, feeling the big cat accelerate smoothly under the pressure of the stiff breeze.

As the speed increased quietly, I dialled up a course on the autopilot to clear the mass of islands off Dampier and Karratha and trimmed the two sails. With 14 knots showing, and the apparent wind coming in from the starboard beam, I then unfurled the huge screecher mounted on the forestay. It was a vast spread of purple and yellow fabric that filled the forward view almost completely and the effect on *Firebird* was to haul it smartly from 14 knots to well over 20 in just a minute.

With all sheets secured, the Admiral asked with childlike excitement shining in his eyes, 'Can you turn the autopilot off and let me steer, please Harry? I'd really love to feel a cat at speed. I sail a lot on a friend's boat, but it's a monohull and doesn't have the sheer speed and flat stance of this.'

I smiled at his boyish enthusiasm. 'Sure thing! The course is on the autopilot-heading bug in front of you so just maintain that. Remember Dave will be idling along off our windward quarter, but he's letting us set the pace.'

While the Admiral prepared to do his steering stint, Hilary told me the boat clearances and crew visas would be processed on an urgent basis and would all be handled through the Marina Del Ray at Port Gili Gede on the island of Lombok within 24-hours.

'The clearance system is so much simpler now,' she enthused, 'it's all done online and for a fee, the Marina handled everything. I hope you don't mind me spending your money?'

I laughed, 'Dear lady. Thanks for arranging it. With everything going on, I'd quite forgotten, which might have been a bit embarrassing.'

'Not really, Harry. The Marina people say that even if you just turned up, so long as you can pay, they'll still arrange everything on the spot. It's very impressive. Charlie will have the passports waiting at the check-in desk at Sydney Airport. Your friend's names have been red-flagged, so there's no chance they'll miss either the package or their flight. They're now VIPs!'

The Admiral took the wheel, standing for a while as he got the feel for things and expressed delight at how well the boat tracked at speed. As the evening closed in, the girls served dinner when we altered course slightly to the right as we passed Legendre Island and laid a course direct for Port Hedland. As the evening breeze was quite cool, even though it had lost a lot of the strength it'd had through the day, we ate inside. The Admiral was prised off the wheel only with threats from Hilary, with George the autopilot taking over while we ate.

The Admiral insisted on standing a watch, so I let Sandy and Hilary take the watch through to midnight, then he and I would do the rest including the approach to Port Hedland, which could get busy at times with iron-ore carriers moving in and out of port.

I had no trouble sleeping until Sandy woke me to say all was well with no problems and as usual, there was a hot, sweet mug of tea waiting in the galley for me. Hilary had stirred the Admiral and he soon appeared, getting stuck straight into the mug of coffee that was waiting for him. With one engine purring away boosting our sailing speed up to around the 14-knot mark, there wasn't much to do apart from monitor the radar, check the course and have a look around topsides for any chafe on lines or sails.

Seeker maintained a steady position off one stern quarter or the other and the chart plotter was happy to tell me that we'd be just off Port Hedland at 06:47. I checked the chart and the Port directions, noting that most wharves were used by commercial traffic 24/7, so I decided to drop our passengers off at a public boat ramp in the outer harbour, right on the edge of town.

Apart from dodging a few iron-ore carriers, it was an uneventful landfall and after waking Sandy and Hilary in plenty of time to wash up and get ready, it was just on 07:00 when I gently nosed one of *Firebird's* bows in against a narrow walkway between the two launching ramps to allow our passengers to hop off with dry feet. Conveniently, there was a Dome cafe directly opposite the boat ramp, with enticing breakfast smells drifting across the road.

'Keep me updated, please Harry,' the Admiral called over the stream of abuse from the flock of small boats being launched and the thought crossed my mind that they sounded like the same mob that had abused Dave at Karratha.

Hilary brought up a distant rear as she was already on the phone to the RAAF crew, telling them where their passengers were and how long they would be.

Sandy was keen to duck across the road to get a few bacon & egg rolls for breakfast, so she grabbed some money and followed the Admiral off the bow and over to the cafe, her normal boat rig of very brief stretch-towelling shorts and a small bikini top, while not really suitable for a public venue, proved sufficiently distracting for the vocally abusive fishermen. That distraction allowed me to back *Firebird* out of the way of the launch ramp and I found just enough room off to one side to park against some mangroves.

I held position on the engines for the ten minutes it took, and then nosed in to the finger walkway again to pick up my lovely lady and our breakfast. We chewed happily on this unexpected treat as I dodged the flock of tinnies, motored up the short channel then hoisted sail to head out to where *Seeker* was bobbing in gyro-stabilised comfort well clear of the shipping lanes. I nosed up alongside and Sandy tossed a bag of B & E rolls across, to the delight of the crew.

Five minutes later, we were clear of the harbour shipping lanes and on our way to an RV with *Glenelg* at the bottom end of the amazing white sand of the Eighty-Mile beach.

<h1 style="text-align:center">CHAPTER 46</h1>

With the southerly breeze kicking in again, we tracked north-east until we rounded Larrey, then Poissonier Points, before bending the course east then east south east to head for the charming little bay with the amazing white sand that marked the very lower limit of Eighty-Mile Beach. Five hours after the last of the lovely fresh B & E rolls had been consumed, we closed in on the small peninsula that had several campsites on both sides overlooking crystal-clear water and pristine, glaring-white sand beaches.

Rounding the last point, we spotted the familiar shape of the low grey warship laying at anchor, while the haze of brown smoke drifting from the two exhaust outlets on the rear of the main mast showed that her engines were idling and she was ready for departure.

I commented to Sandy, 'Looks like there won't be any hospitality visit today. Maybe Paul is a bit pissed.'

THURSDAY, *GLENELG* RV...MIDDAY

'You'd better call on the UHF and see what the go is. I'll take us in at slow speed.'

I handed over control and called on the UHF radio from the Nav station inside.

'*Glenelg*, this is *Firebird*. How copy?'

'*Good morning, Firebird. Good to see you again. Please raft up to us, your port side to our starboard to facilitate transfer of cargo and personnel.*'

'*Firebird* copy.'

I went out to take control, throwing the switch on the autopilot that allows a remote controller to operate engines and rudder via a Bluetooth® link from anywhere on deck.

I said to Sandy with a wry chuckle, 'you're right. I think he's pissed.'

Accompanied by Jasper and Krazy Catten (being not a kitten and not quite an adult cat), we went forward, the remote controller on a lanyard around my neck, and hung several large ball fenders over our left side. Then with all sails tightly furled, I edged us in toward the towering grey steel cliff of *Glenelg's* hull.

At least the stern deck was only slightly above our deck, as I nudged us carefully alongside where a large collection of uniformed crew waited with mooring lines that were tossed to Sandy and me and quickly secured.

There seemed to be a lot of interest in the fact that I was using a remote-control device to manoeuvre the boat, although my attention was on the tall, lean figure of the boat's Skipper, Paul Davy wearing his camo-pattern work uniform. As I shutdown the engines remotely, I pre-empted him and called out, 'Please come aboard, Skipper.'

He grinned and stepped through the gate in the safety railing and jumped lightly down onto our deck.

I was pleased and relieved to see a broad smile on his face as we shook hands and Sandy copped a kiss on the cheek as well, drawing a few cheers from the assembled group of onlookers.

'Good to see you two again even if you are going to pinch half my crew and supplies. I loved that manoeuvring with the remote, Harry. Very neat! There are a lot of times I'd love to have one of those. Ah well, one day. Now to business. That must have been some talk you had with the Admiral!'

We sat in the cockpit, where Sandy had laid out tea for all, although behind him, I saw several sailors calling to Jasper and the cheeky pussy jumped over onto *Glenelg* to greet his friends. I tried to ignore the very incongruous sight of Jasper capering around the grey steel decks chased by two petty officers.

I smiled at him, 'Yeah. It was. As you know, he wanted to come as well, but his daughter, Hilary, talked him out of it.'

Paul's eyebrows rose. 'What's he doing with his daughter out here?'

'She's his personal secretary, seems to do all the actual work and damn near runs the Fleet from what we could gather. She goes everywhere with him and handles most communications as well. She apparently was chatting with the PM on the way over while the Admiral was asleep.'

'Bloody hell! What's the PM doing involved with this?'

'It would seem that he's very keen to see a quiet and very permanent resolution to this mess without the Indonesians or the Aussie press catching even the slightest sniff of trouble. That's how high profile the wrap-up to the operation has become.'

'Shit! That almost changes things.'

Sandy and I gave him an enquiring look so he went on, 'Everything the Admiral and you asked for is ready to go and I'm very happy you asked. However, I didn't want to part with my Weapons Officer, Claire, since we only have 6 officers in total, but I decided to let you have the same four who crewed the MK47s on *Seeker*. I think you got on well with Petty Officer Jane Glen. She's very good value and is in line for promotion to Lieutenant. Do you think they will be right for the job?'

I looked at Sandy before replying, 'I'm sure they will be, Paul. I'm sorry to have to bludge any crew off you at all, but my crew had to go. Although in hindsight, we think it was a bit of an administrative cockup, but too late to fix quickly. Your four crewies seemed to me to be very switched on and competent, so yeah, I reckon they'll fit in just fine.'

He puffed his cheeks out in relief. 'I know you wanted Clare and she was busting to be part of it, but I think these four will do the right thing. Now I have all the other stuff you wanted, plus I had the cooks toss in as much of the bread-making doings as they could spare and there's some other stuff to keep you going, seeing as you're heading into Indonesian waters. Be careful what you eat and drink over there. All our supplies will be replaced as a matter of course, so you might as well have them.

The ammo we're writing off to practice, but we'll need the MK47 back if at all possible, so look after it. Jane will probably sleep with the bloody thing anyway!'

'That'll be fine, thanks Paul. The Admiral was going to rat the *Broome* for all the goodies, but as you were heading back to base, he thought you would be the least affected. We'll try to look after the boys and girls for you'.

He grinned, 'I know you will Harry. Just don't let the buggers have too much of a good time getting carted around the islands on this luxury cruise!'

I laughed, as he waved to a work detail of sailors and they started handing down boxes of gear to others who'd jumped down on to my decks. 'Just stack it all in the cockpit for now' I said to a Petty Officer who seemed to be in charge of the detail.

'Aye sir. No problem,' he said with a grin. 'Are you sure you don't want more crew. We could use the practice.'

Paul grinned. 'That's enough Simmonds. I think Commander Stevens has what he needs. You can't all go.'

'Yessir.'

They finished stacking an imposing number of cartons and boxes, far more than I'd requested, so I presumed Paul was doing his bit to help the mission.

The work detail had just left when my new crew, still dressed in their camo-pattern work uniform, kitbags at their feet, stood lined up at the gate in *Glenelg's* rail and asked permission to come aboard. I stood and formally gave permission.

There were the four as promised, Petty Officer Jane Glen, a slim, dark-haired young lady of medium height with bright, inquisitive eyes who shook hands with a big grin.

'Great to see you again, Sir and I'm very glad to be included in this operation.'

'Good to see you too, Jane. It should be very interesting.'

'Thank you, Sir.'

Next was Terry Boone, the tall, fit gunner who'd suffered a bullet graze to his shoulder, but appeared to be fully functional. I'd spoken to him several times and was impressed by his obvious intelligence.

Gillian Smith was a tall, lean, blonde with a freckled face and flashing green eyes, while the last was Richard Jackson, a short, red-haired, very muscular young guy with a pleasant, open face and a cheerful manner.

He shook hands readily and said, 'Thanks for including me too, sir. None of us will let you down.'

'I'm sure you won't, Leading Seaman, but I have a couple of things to say to you all while your Skipper is still here.'

I had their attention as I sat on the edge of the daybed, Krazy Catten clawing her way up my shirt to perch, purring loudly, in her favourite position on my shoulder.

'To put it simply, this part of the operation is to locate and eliminate the two principals who conceived and put into place the organisation which we all helped tear apart. They were going to dismantle the Australian Oil and Gas industry in the belief they were saving the earth from itself. You helped show them they were wrong, but the two who escaped cannot be allowed to try again or to even to spread their warped messages to anybody else. Especially since Indonesia has a minority of anti-Western fanatics who would be only too happy to help them. Our task is to stop them without upsetting the Indonesian Government.'

They nodded understanding and even looked excited.

'The second thing is that we are very much undercover and that means you have to fit in with, and be part of, our cover for the duration. There can be no communications out to family or friends for the duration, regardless of the circumstances. None, zero, zilch, zip it! Is that very clear?'

I was gratified to see four positive nods and hear four voices say, 'Yessir!'

I nodded back. 'Good! Now the important bit is our cover. The role you have to get into as quickly as possible is that we are a bunch of wealthy, rather degenerate layabouts, who have the money and the means to bum around in luxurious boats looking for good dive spots. There is another actual mission on this trip and that is to go look for an island which produces a green ointment that has a whole bunch of good healing effects on humans. We have two people to pick up in Broome who know where this place is, but that won't be until after we've fixed the main problem first.

The other important thing about our cover is that there must not be any formal behaviour on board. It must be first names only at all times, regardless of our real rank and position. That means I'm Harry, my lovely lady here is Sandy and the other boat has Dave, Corrine, Bree and Alex. Joining us in Broome will be Roger, a doctor and Jill, a theatre nurse. I might add that Alex and Bree are ex-military.

You must wear casual clothing at all times as appropriate to the circumstances. No uniforms at all. If you don't have enough civvie gear, we'll get it in Broome. You're going to have three days before we hit Bali to learn your role.'

'The last thing is to allocate where you'll camp. The MK47 will be remaining on this boat so Jane, since you're in charge of the thing, you get the port forward cabin and Richard, you'll have the port aft cabin here. You two get to share a bathroom, but if anyone gets caught short, there's another toilet and shower starboard aft.

Terry and Gillian, you guys get the luxury suites on *Seeker*. That means a twin cabin each with ensuite!'

'Another thought for Terry and Gillian; do you two know how to operate the Browning M2 .50 cal?'

They both nodded. 'Sure, s... ah Harry.' Terry replied. 'We're all qualified on it.'

I smiled. 'That's good because there are two of them over on *Seeker*. You'll find Corrine is quite expert on the heavy great lump, especially in sniper mode. As I am, for what it's worth.'

Jane stuck her hand up, 'Ahh, Harry. Where can we mount the MK47 where it'll be secure?'

'We've got three days to come up with something, but I doubt we'll be using it to attack something from behind again, so perhaps it should go somewhere aft around the cockpit perimeter here. Have a think about it.'

She nodded, so I wrapped the briefing.

'Thanks for your support and help, Paul. I won't delay you any longer.'

We stood and shook hands, as he did with his four ex-crew persons. 'Do the Service proud!' were his final words before he climbed over the rail, flashed me a salute and headed for the bridge at a fast walk.

I made sure I spotted two large black ears and a long tail before I fired up the engines and asked the new crew to go release the lines tying us to the grey warship. They responded with alacrity and there were many rude comments tossed back and forth as I let the breeze drift us clear of *Glenelg*. A quick blast of her impressive horn, a boil of white water at her stern and she accelerated smartly out of the pretty little bay leaving us to move the short distance to raft up against *Seeker* who'd anchored nearby.

CHAPTER 47

Straight after we'd rafted up, Corrine came across, introduced herself to the crew who were still in camo gear and said to me, 'I just took a call from Roger. He and Jill are safely in a motel in Broome for the night. They had no trouble making the flights, have a package from the PM's office and saw no other signs of any goons from EarthCare. If we give them a call in the morning, they'll meet us wherever suits.'

'OK, thanks for that. Another loose end tied up thank goodness. But let's get all this stuff sorted and stowed then you, Dave, Sandy and me need to do some forward planning.'

She grinned at my general concern. 'De-stress, Harry. It's all coming together and we've got good people aboard. All we have to do is tell them what's going on and what they have to do. They'll do the job, no problem.'

I nodded ruefully, 'Yeah. You're right Mouse. It's that faith thing you keep going on about, you reckon I don't have enough of!'

That earned me a smack across the arm, but I probably deserved it.

The sorting out of gear, transferring it to where it belonged and allocating bunks to the new crew took the next couple of hours, but everyone worked well and was happy.

With Bree, assisted by Jane and a very helpful Alex sorting out the galley and food stocks on both boats, I checked with Dave and Corrine where to put people and they agreed that Jane and Richard should stay on *Firebird* with a cabin each, while Bree and Alex were actually happy to stay in the forward crew cabins for now, although Corrine reported with a giggle, they both were showing a bit of an interest in each other.

'If they decide to hook up properly, we could move them into the twin cabin Terry's in and put him in one of the vacant crew cabins,' she observed, 'and that'd leave us with a spare twin bunk crew cabin just in case.'

I smiled fondly at her. 'What a good housemistress you are, but a good idea all the same. Maybe if you think they really will get to play nookie, you might suggest to Terry he shouldn't settle in too much just yet!'

She laughed, but I knew she'd do just that. We checked the munitions stocks and were delighted that Paul had seen fit to supply six boxes of .50 calibre ammo, so in addition to the three Corrine had snagged from the camp, we could wreak some serious damage on anything that challenged us.

The boxed-up MK47 had five boxes of linked rounds for it, and with 32 rounds per box, we had 160 rounds to blow stuff up. Given the high probably of first strike success using the laser sights with a ballistic computer, I was sure that these were enough for Jane and her team. I left the issue of where to mount it to them, although Dave commented that the mounts on *Seeker* were still in place and could be shifted elsewhere.

While the crew seemed to be getting on happily with the unloading of all sorts of goodies Paul had seen fit to toss our way, including a heap of frozen steaks, chops and mixed vegetables, I raised the point that Broome was a very inhospitable place for boats.

'There's a huge tide range that's regularly up 8.5 to 9 metres and there's no marina. Refuelling is only at the commercial jetty and isn't designed for pleasure boats. I suggest we don't bother refuelling here and do it in Bali. I've got enough and you guys should also.'

Dave nodded, 'Yeah. We're fat for fuel and there's 1000 litres spare if you need it.'

'OK. That's settled. The next problem is finding a place to load Roger and Jill and their gear without getting everyone wet. There are only a couple of boat ramps and both are exposed to the open ocean on the south side!'

'Bloody hell!' Dave exclaimed. 'Doesn't the Council want boating activity?'

I shook my head, 'It certainly doesn't seem like it. However, what I suggest is this. The southerlies have set up a bit of a swell, so the north side of the peninsula is quite protected. High tide is at 10:25 and will be a 7.5 metre range, so we don't want to mess around too long in shallow water. There's a beach access track out near the end of a road called Gantheaume Point Road. A taxi driver should know it.

I'll take *Firebird* in before high tide and nose up onto the beach. If Roger and Jill are waiting, I can put the bow-boarding ladder over and get them up that way. The tide will still be making so I won't get stuck so long as they are ready.'

The others all nodded and Dave said. 'Sounds like a good plan, mate. I can't see why it won't work, so long as we get there before high tide.'

'That's the thing, but we should be OK for that. It's a 13-hour trip at 14-knot average, although I should be able to beat that if the breeze holds. But even if it doesn't, we'll motor-sail. It's 16:45 now, so if stuff isn't stowed properly yet, we can finish up on the way. I suggest we get the right crew on each boat and get going now.'

That plan met with agreement, so we shuffled the last bit of gear to the correct boat and made sure we had the right crew. We untied and moved out, leaving Dave to up anchor and follow when ready.

There was stuff scattered everywhere so I tried to ignore the mess and just looked after the boat, while Sandy, Richard -- who preferred to be called Rick, and Jane sorted everything out. By dinnertime, they had everything ship-shape and we decided to open the bar for a while to welcome our new crew.

With the breeze still blowing quite hard, we were making 15 to 16 knots under sail alone which was peaceful and efficient, so I was able to set the autopilot and join them for sundowners around the saloon table.

I set watches with Sandy and Rick for the first until midnight, then Jane and me until dawn when I hoped we'd be close to Broome. Jane and Rick were in a very buoyant mood, regarded the whole operation as a holiday and were determined to make the most of it. Their mood helped to lift Sandy and me as well, since we were feeling the stress and strain of what had been a very active and stressful operation. There'd been only a few chances to relax, which probably accounted for the occasional excesses that occurred when we did.

It was something Corrine and I were unfortunately all too familiar with from our Middle East time, as was everyone who worked in a very high stress environment. Accumulated adrenaline took time to disperse and often resulted in heavy-duty play when away from the action!

This however, was a restful opportunity to get to know two highly trained and intelligent young individuals who were keen to do a rather dirty job, to the best of their ability. We told a few war stories, which they soaked up with relish and wanted to hear more. They both loved Jasper and Krazy, even though they'd already met Jasper briefly on the job. Both pussies made the most of fresh playmates and provided their usual delightful distractions.

As normal at sea, the bar closed early and Jane and I retired (separately) to get some sleep before the midnight call. Luckily, both she and Rick were used to the watch system and the broken sleep/wake cycles which went with it

Finally awake at midnight, I half-listened as Sandy made her hand-over report of 'nothing happening except the wind dropped a bit', then wandered out to find a steaming mug of tea and a plate of toast, courtesy of my new watch-mate. The bright and cheery greeting of, 'Good morning, Harry', was almost too much for my bleary brain, but I did appreciate her enthusiasm, along with the tea and toast!

Both she and Rick had taken my earlier briefing to heart and appeared in standard plain clothes, but I thought I'd check, 'Do you and Rick have plenty of civvies? Because if there's anything else you need, Broome will be the last opportunity and even then, Roger or Jill will have to get it for you. We won't have a chance to go ashore for shopping.'

She gave her lovely smile, looking disturbingly attractive, even at this unholy hour, in tight shorts and a nicely bulged T-shirt. 'All good thanks. I don't know about Rick, but we have all our kit with us and that includes several sets of casual gear. We're heading up into the tropics, so we won't need much.'

I was happy with that, so I checked the chart plotter and the paper chart and saw Sandy had marked the midnight position as usual and we had 75 miles to run to Broome. There was no point in arriving before dawn, so I was content to let the speed decrease with the usual early morning dropping of the wind. To make sure, I furled the big screecher and that slowed progress so much that I decided to call *Seeker* and unsurprisingly, found Dave on watch so I passed on my thoughts as our speed settled around 10 knots.

I did some rough reckoning and thought we should be off Broome at 07:00 and the chart plotter more or less agreed. I told Dave I'd call Roger at 06:00 to get them moving for a 07:30 beach pick-up. The remainder of our watch was quiet with only a couple of radar hits to seaward that could have been iron-ore carriers, gas tankers or rig attendant boats. At 06:00 I fired up the SatPhone to call Roger and was pleased he answered almost immediately.

'Hello?'

'Good morning Roger, this is your early morning wake-up call. It's Harry Stevens on *Firebird*.'

I could hear the relief in his voice when he said, '*Oh, Harry. Great to hear from you. Where are you?*'

'About an hour out and all's well here. How about you, ready to go?'

'*Yes please. We're OK. Just nervous, I guess. We keep waiting for something to go massively wrong!*'

I laughed, 'I know the feeling. Things keep getting more

complicated with this gig, but this should be the home stretch. At least we'll be on our way to Indonesia.'

He sighed. '*Yes, that will be good. Strangely enough, I feel the urge to leave Australia for a while.*'

I laughed again, 'Hang in there, brother. The cavalry is arriving! Now I have some instructions for you, but first, do you have everything you need with you?'

'*Yes, we do. After we got in yesterday, there was plenty of time to go shopping, so we got lots of stuff we thought we all could use. Plus, I've got my full medical kit as well.*'

'That's really good because this place is very unfriendly to small boat owners like us. I won't bore you with details, but the best way to get you aboard is off the beach on the northwest side of the peninsula. We are also being messed around with the huge tides, so here is the deal. Naturally, you'll need a taxi, and he's to take you out toward Gantheaume Point on the road of that name. About two-thirds of the way out to the Point, there's a dirt track on the right that provides access to the beach. It's very well defined and it's the only beach access track on the Point road.

The driver may not take you all the way down it since it looks pretty rough, but do what you can. OK so far?'

'*Yes. All good, keep going.*'

'OK. By 07:30 be on the beach with your gear ready to go. I'll bring my catamaran in on the rising tide and run the bows up on the beach. I'll put a boarding ladder over the bows and you'll be able to get up it. We can't hang around, since the tide will be coming in quite fast so be prepared for that. We'll transfer you to Corrine's boat once we're off the beach. Will you be alright with that?'

'*Oh yes. We'll be just fine with that, thank you Harry. We'll see you on the beach at 07:30 sharp.*'

He repeated the directions to be sure and we disconnected. I radioed Dave the information and sent Jane to wake Sandy and Rick. Fifteen minutes later, I was chomping into a lovely bacon, egg and cheese toasted sanger, a fresh mug of steaming tea at my elbow and the unlovely, unrelenting and rugged landscape surrounding Broome slowly sliding past to my right. The low sun angle hid much of the detail of the desolate scrub, but for eyes that longed to see verdant green vegetation, it was just more of what we'd been seeing for weeks.

We needed to slow a bit more to make the RV on time, so we idled along, Broome slowly rearing out of the sea haze. At 07:20, we were rounding the final point, the arrangement with Dave being that he would hold station not far off the beach ready to head in if I had trouble.

I'd briefed my crew on the plan and they had the aluminium bow-boarding ladder ready, as running the bows up on a sandy beach is the best and simplest way to access the beach without getting wet feet. Using the chart plotter to orient myself, I spotted the access track cutting through the scrub and headed in just as a taxi turned onto the track from the sealed point road. Running in, I grounded the bows onto sand in clear, shallow water, leaving both engines idling in drive to hold us firmly pinned as the tide rose alarmingly quickly so that we were slowly edging further up the beach.

Fortunately, there were only small waves lapping the shore that didn't bump us too hard against the bottom.

Five minutes later saw Roger and Jill and their collection of bags on the foredeck, looking around while the crew pulled the ladder back aboard and secured it. I had time to welcome them before engaging reverse and with a decent squirt of power, we slid smoothly off the beach to the amusement of a few campers and some locals. I moved out to nestle up against *Seeker* so we could transfer Roger, Jill and baggage.

We'd just touched against the big, blue hull when Dave appeared above me and called out, 'Why don't we anchor here for a while. There's bugger-all swell and plenty of water and we need to have a round table session in comfort rather than in the middle of the ocean.'

I looked around and shrugged, 'Suits me. Good idea. There's not quite so much of a rush now.'

So Dave dropped his massive Aussie anchor while I shut down engines and the crew secured mooring lines.

'Tea's up!' came the call from *Seeker* and we all traipsed across.

There wasn't time to get to know Roger and Jill as we clustered around the big saloon table with tea, coffee and bickies, but they were a very pleasant couple. Roger was a good-looking man, tall and slim with a shock of thick, dark and very unruly hair. Jill was short and blonde, but trim and curvy with the look of a gym-junkie and a bubbly personality. The descriptive name of Pocket-Rocket sprang to mind for some reason.

We had a general planning session about our entry port, and what we'd declare for our subsequent movements.

'I think we should stick with the dive sites touring idea,' I said. 'Both boats have scuba gear; some of us have Open Water Certificates and there's plenty of snorkel gear for the non-scuba ones. That'll let us go most anywhere since there are hundreds of superb dive sites scattered throughout the islands. It will also account for us not having a fixed itinerary.'

Roger spoke up. 'That's good, Harry. A lot of Aussies come up to Indonesia by boat to do just that, but we have to make sure we have all the right papers for the boats and crew. Officials in some of the more remote islands can get very difficult!'

I smiled, 'Can I presume that some palm-greasing always goes over well?'

'Oh yes. Of course, so long as you have enough, although most officials will be happy with $20 or $30 tops.'

I smiled, 'We have quite a few thousand in Aussie and American dollars just in case we have trouble. Hopefully, that'll be enough.'

'Oh yes. It certainly will be.'

We talked over a few more things, but then I asked the one question we really needed to know which was how to track the fugitives. I felt a bit of a dill when it turned out to be as simple as asking Roger and Jill if they knew if Terry and Paula had a house in the highlands of Bali.

'Oh goodness me, yes,' Jill said with a funny grin. 'I've seen photos of it and it's a beautiful place built with local timber that used to be either a small hotel or an annex to a larger one. It's perched right on the rim of an old volcano in the north of Bali and they meant to use it as a retreat to reward senior EarthCare staff and others that took Paula's and Terry's fancy!'

'I don't suppose you know where it is?' I asked, trying hard not to sound too anxious.

She was no dummy and the tone of my voice alerted her that things weren't quite normal.

'Is there something we should know about, Harry?'

I thought a moment, but it was Sandy, as usual who spoke with the voice of reason.

'Tell them, big dog. They need to know and it'll be better sooner rather than later.'

So, I explained about finding the room at the camp with the six bodies and what had been done to them. 'That's definitely Paula's work,' Roger chipped in, 'I've had to clean up or repair the result of her excesses on far too many occasions. She is pure Evil with a capital 'E'!'

He looked intently at me for a moment, 'Hang about! This trip isn't just to go looking for green paste, is it? We were wondering why a Rear-Admiral is flown across the country by the RAAF in a very expensive Executive jet, and then suddenly there are two private yachts heading for Indonesian waters with a very mixed crew, most of whom are combat-trained and ... '

Jill jumped in and finished his thoughts off, 'You're going to find Terry and Paula. Are you planning to bring them back to Australia?'

I smiled grimly, 'Good guesses and the answer is...'Yes and No'.'

She looked solemn. 'As in 'Yes', we're going to find them and 'No', we're not going to try to get them back to Australia?'

'Yep. That about sums it up. But we are still going to find the island for you. Corrine promised you a boat and we always deliver on promises.'

She made a huffing sound remarkably like my cat, 'Oh, c'mon Harry. We want to find the island, but it's far more important to nail that evil bitch and dopey fuckwit Terry. She leads him everywhere by his dick! She's only got to wave her panties at him and he turns into a puddle of semen! So she's the main one who's got to be nailed! How can we help?'

'Sold! You're in. Where's their place?'

'It's perched on the edge of the cliffs overlooking the guts of an old volcano. There's a big lake in the old crater called Lake Batur and where they are is close to a hotel, the very aptly named Volcania Kintamani. The house looks like it might have been an annex to the hotel at some stage, because it's supported on pilings and hangs way out over a very steep drop. The view, from what you could see in the photos, is stunning, but I'm not sure I'd trust the timber pilings holding it up. They look a bit too weak to me.'

I got the 'thousand-yard stare' going as an idea formed quite quickly, so I worked on it for a few moments, then came back to earth with an evil grin on my face.

'People! I think I have the start of a cunning plan'.

Harry Stevens, the Middle-Eastern war hero from Hitch-Hikers, the first book in the *Firebird* series, thought that having dinner at the pub and chatting up the waitress was a safe and pleasant way to pass an evening, but circumstances conspire to dump the delivery of a new super-drug as well as a large bag of bikie gang cash in his lap. Assumptions are made, confusions are leapt to, shots are fired, people are dead and Harry finds himself in the middle of a bikie gang war with both sides looking to take him out. And that's not to dinner!

Being on the hit lists of all the Outlaw Motorcycle Clubs in SE Queensland, Harry is forced to run for his life, but not before stocking up on lovely girls, rum and a few select close friends. Harry's mystical giant cat, Jasper once again proves that he's more than worth any two humans in a fight.

Harry, the floating trouble magnet, discovers that being shot in Afghanistan was nothing like being the focus of attention of all the OMC's in South East Queensland. His inventiveness gets the workout of a lifetime as he tries to stay one jump ahead of the bad guys as they form strange alliances to find him.

"This is Book 2 in the Firebird Series, and *Backpackers* leads us on another adventure with a maritime background. All the drama and action we have come to expect from Ian, we are left with just one question… when can we expect book three?"
—Alison Lewis, author of "Missing"

Praise for *Hitchhikers* (Book 1 of the Firebird Series)

"The hero, Harry, when asked what he has been doing lately, answers
"Boats, bad guys, bullets and old friends." What he fails to add is — beautiful women, sex, a bad-ass black cat, and Bond type cunning to overcome the bad guys. Piqued your interest? This is a great fast paced fread and I am looking forward to the next phase of Harry's life as promised by the author.
—Judith Flitcroft, Author of *Walk Back in Time*.

ALSO BY THE AUTHOR
IN THE FIREBIRD SERIES

Harry Stevens, a Middle Eastern war hero, thought that recovering in Eden with his huge and mystical cat, Jasper, after his catamaran is bashed around by a storm, would be a delightful break from his sailing voyage around Australia. However, the finger of fate in the very pleasant form of an abused, runaway wife and her two lively, wilful and beautiful teenage daughters lands Harry in more trouble than he could ever imagine.

Harry's hopes for a quiet time in this beautiful and peaceful town are shattered as he learns that the psychotic, vengeful husband is pulling out all stops in an effort to locate, not just his wife, but even more so the girls for his own, much darker purposes. Suddenly on the run, Harry is forced to fall back on his natural inventiveness and SAS training to combat an increasingly resourceful foe who shows that there is truly no limit to human lust, greed, depravity and treachery.

Barely staying one step ahead of his pursuers, Harry forms some most unlikely alliances to try to defeat his many opponents with their limitless resources.

"It is always a pleasure to read a new and entertaining series from a first-time Australian author. This novel will take you on one hell of a ride where the goodies are okay and the baddies are really BAD."
—John Morrow's *Pick of the Week*

"The hero, Harry, when asked what he has been doing lately, answers "Boats, bad guys, bullets and old friends." What he fails to add is — beautiful women, sex, a bad-ass black cat, and Bond type cunning to overcome the bad guys. Piqued your interest? This is a great fast paced read and I am looking forward to the next phase of Harry's life as promised by the author.
—Judith Flitcroft, Author of *Walk Back in Time*.